If Today Be Sweet

Also by Thrity Umrigar

fiction

THE SPACE BETWEEN US

BOMBAY TIME

nonfiction

FIRST DARLING OF THE MORNING

IF TODAY BE SWEET

THRITY UMRIGAR

HARPER PERENNIAL

NEW YORK • LONDON • TORONTO • SYDNEY • NEW DELHI • AUCKLAND

HARPER PERENNIAL

This book is a work of fiction. The characters, incidents, and dialogue are drawn from the author's imagination and are not to be construed as real. Any resemblance to actual events or persons, living or dead, is entirely coincidental.

A hardcover edition of this book was published in 2007 by William Morrow, an imprint of HarperCollins Publishers.

FIRST HARPER PERENNIAL EDITION PUBLISHED 2008.

Designed by Susan Yang

The Library of Congress has catalogued the hardcover edition as follows:

Umrigar, Thrity N.
If today be sweet : a novel / Thrity Umrigar. — 1st ed.
p. cm.
ISBN: 978-0-06-124023-2
ISBN-10: 0-06-124023-0
1. Bereavement—Fiction. I. Title

PS3261.M75I35 2007
813'.6—dc22 2006052992

ISBN 978-0-06-124024-9 (pbk.)

08 09 10 11 12 DT/RRD 10 9 8 7 6 5 4 3 2 1

Insights,
Interviews
& More . . .

*

About the author

About the book

Read on

Meet Thrity Umrigar

Noshir Umrigar

THE FIRST WRITING I ever did was the anonymous poems I wrote to my parents when I was angry at them and fuming over some perceived injustice. I must've been five or six years old then. I'd wait until the coast was clear and then dart into their bedroom and stick these anonymous poems on the door of the teakwood wardrobe my dad had built. To my amazement, and despite my best attempts at concealment, my parents always figured out the identity of the author. I thought they were geniuses. To my chagrin, the poems seemed to amuse them rather than convince them of the errors of their ways.

Looking back, it seems to me that my reasons for writing have not changed since those early days. Now, like then, I write for two reasons: one, to express my deepest feelings about something, and two, to protest some outrage or injustice.

By the time I was seven, I knew I wanted to be a writer. But I didn't have the guts to say out loud—or even to myself—that I wanted to write books. A brown-skinned kid in Bombay wanting to be a writer? I may as well have said I wanted to be a Broadway actress. Then someone told me that people who wrote for newspapers such as *The Times of India* (whose stately stone building with the printing press at street level I loved driving by) were called journalists. So that's what I went around saying I wanted to be when I grew up. It seemed safer than saying I wanted to be a writer. And indeed, a journalist is what I grew up to be.

I worked as a daily reporter for seventeen years. And as I wasn't writing literature, I tried to infuse my newspaper articles with as much literary flavor as I could get away with. I gravitated toward magazine-style stories—stories about human beings, not sources; stories with complexity, with shades of gray; stories that challenged the conventional wisdom. The same themes that I later explored in fiction—how power twists and corrupts human relationships, ▸

> "I worked as a daily reporter for seventeen years [and] tried to infuse my newspaper articles with as much literary flavor as I could get away with."

Meet Thrity Umrigar ***(continued)***

the gap between the haves and the have-nots, the transformative power of love—I tried to explore within the confines of daily journalism.

At times, I succeeded. My two favorite stories were both long-term projects that took topical issues and put a human face on them. The first story was about a single mother on welfare raising two children. I wanted to understand the nagging, demeaning aspect of poverty—how it takes all the spontaneity out of life, how it makes you agonize over the smallest decisions—and then explain this to my readers. For this, I needed to witness poverty, and the choices it forces people to make, up close. I moved in with the woman's family for a week and told their story in journal form, day by day, as it unfolded.

The second story was about a young couple who had given birth to a perilously premature baby. Technology now makes such births possible, but many moral, ethical, economic, and medical issues remain unresolved. But what fascinated me most was the grace with which this couple faced the challenges before them. Watching them come close to their breaking point and then, somehow, rise to the occasion again, sustained only by their love for each other and their belief in their baby, was an awe-inspiring experience for me. I reported that story for four months, from the moment of the baby's birth to that incredible day, four months later, when he left the hospital.

So you see why the leap from journalism to fiction doesn't seem all that huge. What matters most to me is the human heart that beats at the center of all great stories. When I look back on my writing life, I see that the vehicles may be different—poems, short stories, newspaper articles, novels—but the passengers remain the same. The passengers are always grappling with the darkness and trying to find the light; they are often inchoate and inarticulate but fumbling toward greater human communication; and they are almost always held together by that shaft of grace that we call love.

“When I look back on my writing life, I see that the vehicles may be different—poems, short stories, newspaper articles, novels—but the passengers remain the same. The passengers are always grappling with the darkness and trying to find the light.”

If Today Be Sweet: Themes and Inspiration

IT IS THE MOST ENDURING and beloved of all the Parsi legends: Fleeing religious persecution in their homeland of Iran, a small group of Zoroastrians land on the shores of Sanjan, India, seeking political refuge. The local Hindu ruler eyes the foreigners warily, loathe to grant them entry. Unable to speak a common language, he takes an empty glass and fills it to the brim with milk. The symbolism is clear: the land is full and cannot accommodate newcomers. But the Zoroastrian head priest is a smart man. He stirs sugar into the milk, careful not to spill a drop. His message is clear, also: if you let us in, not only will we not displace or disrupt your culture, we will sweeten it with our presence.

Thus, the Zoroastrians—or the Parsis, as they came to be called—find a home in India and, true to their word, become a model community, their contributions enhancing the culture of their new homeland.

This story, drilled into the head of every Parsi child, was part of my subconscious and became especially poignant after I came to the United States as an immigrant. For years,

“For years, I had an ongoing fantasy that I was too embarrassed to share with friends . . .”

I had an ongoing fantasy that I was too embarrassed to share with friends: that somehow, someday I would do something large, grand—rescue a child from a burning house, maybe—to justify America's faith in me, to thank America for taking a chance on me, to pay back a country that had taken in a confused, lost twenty-one-year-old and shaped her into an adult. I wonder how many countless immigrants harbor some variation of such a fantasy in their minds.

But along with hopes and fantasies, immigrants also carry something else: they carry a hole in their heart. Along with the promise of a new country, there is the wound of giving up the comfort of the old; along with the excitement, the optimism, the belief, there is doubt and loss and mourning. The old saying is true—in order to gain something, you have to give something up. But this giving up is costly and hard, and it extracts a price.

And in all the political debates about immigration that have been raging across this country, amid all the easy, glib rhetoric about America being a nation of immigrants, this loss, this toll, this terrible giving up, often goes unmentioned. The popular media focuses on what is gained: freedom, liberty, material wealth, opportunity, independence, the ability to recreate ▸

If Today Be Sweet:* Themes and Inspirations *(continued)

yourself. But here's what is lost: identity, language, family, lovers, friends, pets, routines, hobbies, the names of streets you grew up on, the rhythms of your old neighborhood, your favorite family foods, the color of the sky at dusk. Sometimes, even your name.

In *If Today Be Sweet*, I wanted to tell the story of Tehmina Sethna, a woman who, because of circumstances she has no control over, is being asked to undergo the traumas of immigration. In middle age, she is being asked to give up everything that she once knew and called her own—home, country, neighbors, friends. Her son has gone through a similar process many years earlier, but even he cannot help her. It is a journey she has to travel alone.

But while faced with the larger choice of whether to stay in America, Tehmina is confronted with another, more urgent choice: whether to live in America as a stranger or as a citizen. Citizenship implies connection, participation, joining in. Destiny beckons in the form of two young, troubled children next door. It is the plight of these two boys that forces Tehmina to choose. To decide whether she will forever straddle the fence and live in a no-man's-land. Or whether she will jump into the fullness of her new life in America.

Tehmina jumps. And in doing so, she fulfills the long-ago promise of her forebearers, to sweeten the life of the people in her new country with her presence. The irony is that she expands the fabric of community in suburban America by stubbornly holding on to her own Indianness.

But Tehmina's jump also lands her on the front page of the local newspaper and into celebrity culture. She is now a local hero as America accepts her with open arms. The novel's other theme is a tongue-in-cheek look at how the media shapes our culture. As an outsider, Tehmina has a lot to learn about how fortunes can turn on a dime in America.

If Today Be Sweet is about many things: it is a novel that celebrates family and community and critiques the sterility of suburban life and the tinsel of celebrity culture. But if it is about any one thing, it is about movement—about moving forward. And about the importance of getting off the fence. Of making a choice, taking a stand.

Tehmina learns this lesson in the end. America teaches it to her.

"The irony is that [Tehmina] expands the fabric of community in suburban America by stubbornly holding on to her own Indianness."

Read on

Excerpt
The Space Between Us

Poignant, evocative, and unforgettable, The Space Between Us *(William Morrow, 2006) is an intimate portrait of a distant yet familiar world. Set in modern-day India, it is the story of two compelling and achingly real women: Sera Dubash, an upper-middle-class Parsi housewife whose opulent surroundings hide the shame and disappointment of her abusive marriage, and Bhima, a stoic illiterate*

hardened by a life of despair and loss, who has worked in the Dubash household for more than twenty years. A powerful and perceptive literary masterwork, this national bestseller demonstrates how the lives of the rich and poor are intrinsically connected yet vastly removed from each other, and how the strong bonds of womanhood are eternally opposed by the divisions of class and culture.

Here follows an excerpt from chapter 9. . . .

SHE ALMOST GROANED in frustration when Bhima stopped for a second to make more of the mixture. Now Bhima was gently turning her on her stomach and undoing the back buttons of her dress. "Poor Serabai," she was murmuring. "So many burdens this poor body is carrying. So much unhappiness. Give it up to the devil, give it up, don't carry this around." While her hands circled Sera's smooth back—plucking at the stringy muscles, pounding on the painful spots, her fingers moving up and down the vertebrae as though they were piano keys, Bhima kept talking to her in words and languages Sera barely understood. As her body relaxed under Bhima's wise hands, ▸

Sera felt herself receding, moving backward in time, so that for a moment she was a young bride sitting astride her new husband's lap as he rocked her back and forth in a sexual rhythm, and then in the next moment, she was a young child on her mother's knee, being rocked to sleep after a hot, restless night, and then she was older and younger than even that—she was a small fish floating around in a warm world of darkness and fluids, a being as formless and translucent and liquidy as her bones felt right now. And still Bhima was talking to her, her words flying out of her mouth as fast as sparrows at dusk, her tongue working as fast as her hands were, so everything was a blur of words and rhythm; of speech and motion. And Sera was fading now, caught in the undertow of an ancient, primal memory, drowning in a pool of sensation and feeling, old hurts and fresh wounds being exorcised from her body, leaving her feeling as bright and new as the day she was born. Paradoxically, as the hurt left her body, she began to weep, as if now that pain had stopped occupying her body, there was at last room for tears. The tears streamed down her face and were caught by the pillow, but if Bhima noticed the heaving of her back, she did not comment on it. Bhima appeared to be in a trance herself; the strange murmurings continued over Sera's soundless weeping, a fact that Sera was grateful for.

The last thing she remembered before she fell asleep was the smell of the oil in the room. It reminded Sera of the smell of her grandmother's apartment, and the thought of her grandmother, a stout, gruff woman with a large, pillowlike bosom, to which she would press her granddaughter's head, made Sera smile.

When she woke up a few hours later, the bruises on her arm had shrunk. If they had originally looked like the map of the world, now they were down to the size of the map of Brazil. Any other time she would've been surprised, but after the dreamy strangeness of the massage from Bhima, anything seemed possible. She rose from the bed, slid her feet into her rubber slippers, and walked into the kitchen. Suddenly, she felt unaccountably shy in front of the woman who was leaning over the sink, scrubbing dishes with the same ▸

intensity with which she had rubbed her back a few hours ago. She wanted to thank Bhima for her kindness, wanted to explain to her how hot and wonderful life felt when it trickled back into one's veins, wanted to tell her about how cold her heart had felt after this last encounter with Feroz and how Bhima had warmed it again, as if she had held her cold, gray heart between her brown hands and rubbed it until the blood came rushing back into it. But a net of shyness fell over Sera as Bhima looked up from the dishes and at her. She had long accepted that Bhima was the only person who knew that Feroz's fists occasionally flew like black vultures over the desert of her body, that Bhima knew more about the strangeness of her marriage than any friend or family member. But now, Sera felt as if Bhima had an eyeglass to her soul, that she had somehow penetrated her body deeper than Feroz ever had. "Better?" Bhima asked, unsmilingly.

In reply, Sera raised her arm so that Bhima could see the receding marks on her skin. The older woman nodded briskly. "By tomorrow morning, there will be no signs of . . . no signs, at all."

Sera felt her face flush at what

Bhima had not said. No signs of Feroz's brutality, that was what Bhima had wanted to say. Mortification made Sera turn her head away, so she didn't notice that Bhima had abandoned the kitchen sink and taken a few steps toward her, drying her hands on her sari as she walked. "Serabai," she said softly, "You are much wiser than I am, an educated woman while I am illiterate. But, bai, listen to me—do not tolerate what he is doing to you. Tell somebody. Tell your father—he will march in here and break his nose. You are trying to cover up your shame, bai, I know, but it is not your shame. It is Feroz seth's shame, not yours."

Sera's eyes welled with tears. She felt exposed under the X-ray vision of Bhima's eyes, but the relief of another human being acknowledging out loud what Feroz was doing to her was immense. "Does—does Gopal never beat you?"

Bhima snorted. "Beat me? Arre, if that fool touched me once, I would do some jaado on him and turn his hands into pillars of wood." Then, seeing Sera's shocked face, she smiled. "No, bai. With God's grace, my Gopal is not like the other men's. He would sooner cut his hands off than hurt me."

Forthcoming in November 2008

First Darling of the Morning

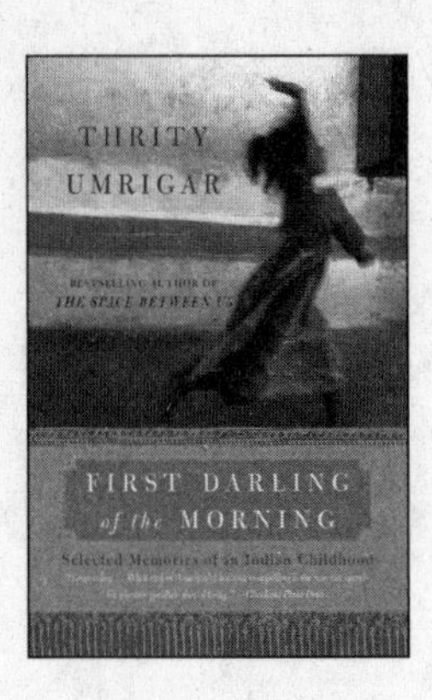

Two coming-of-age stories collide in this sensitive, beautifully written memoir: the story of a small child and the story of a nation. From her earliest memories of life in a middle-class Parsi household to her eventual departure for the United States at age twenty-one, Thrity Umrigar traces the full arc of her Bombay childhood and adolescence. Emotionally charged scenes take an unflinching look at family issues once considered unspeakable—including intimate secrets, controversial political beliefs, and the consequences of strict parental discipline. Politicians, pop stars, and other public figures also appear in Umrigar's story, offering a fascinating glimpse at the secular, liberal climate of Bombay in the 1960s and '70s.

Punishments and tempered hopes, struggles and small successes, all weave together in this evocative, unforgettable memoir. Lyrical but guileless, *First Darling of the Morning* is at once a compelling personal story and a beautiful homage to a lost time and place.

This one belongs

to

Eust and Homai

Ah, fill the Cup:—what boots it to repeat

How Time is slipping underneath our Feet:

Unborn Tomorrow and dead Yesterday,

Why fret about them if Today be Sweet!

—Omar Khayyám

PROLOGUE

Already, I am not here. It is happening. Already she cannot sense my presence in the room, cannot feel the final kiss that I place on her forehead. This is how it should be. And I am not sad, I am not diminished by this. Rather, I am proud. I have done my part. After all, it was my push, my prodding, that finally got her off the fence. All the months of fussing and fretting, of torment and worry, are now behind her. I can see it in her face, the relief of resolution. It is in her walk, in her posture, in the angle of her head. Once again, she is the woman I loved, the woman whom I married. She has always looked deceptively fragile and God knows she is sensitive as a sparrow, but inside, inside, she is tough as nails. That's what I've always been in love with—that strength, that inner compass that has steered her through so many storms. After all, she took care of my cranky old mother until the day she died, didn't she? And if she could have survived dealing with mamma, why, she could survive anything. That's what I kept telling myself during the first awful months. That my wife was a survivor. That she would find her way in the world without me.

Still, I cannot tell a lie: It is good being here. I miss them all—my dearest wife, my son, my daughter-in-law, and my precious little grandson. Even all the others gathered here to usher in the new year. If I could figure out how to do it, I'd have one of them pour me a good, stiff Scotch. And pop one of my wife's kebabs into my mouth. But this is not my place. I do not belong here anymore. The new year is not mine to celebrate, to bring in. And just when the loneliness seems unbearable, I look at my son's face. At his eyes. They are searching the room. Even while he's putting a lamb kebab into his mouth, even while he's sipping his wine, whispering in his wife's ear, slapping his best friend on his back, while he's doing all these things, he is searching the room. He is looking for me. He is missing me. I have to turn away from the grief I see on that beloved face. I long to run my fingers across that face one more time. What is it about these humans—and here I ask myself, am I still human?—that injects this string of sadness during the happiest of occasions? And so, despite my best intentions, I find myself interfering one more time. Slowly, gently, I turn my son's chin until his eyes come to rest upon his son. My grandson. Seven years old and as beautiful as the world itself. I see the fog of incomprehension and grief lift from my son's eyes. They become clear and focused again as they rest on what he has created. And he sees what I see—he sees some outline of my visage in his son's face. Even though I am—was—an ugly, wrinkled son of a bitch, he sees something of me in my grandson's unblemished, unlined face. I see it, too. Not only that, I see my father's face—the pointed nose, the alert eyes—in the boy's face. Isn't that something? My old man from Udwada, dead for twenty years, playing peekaboo from behind the face of a sandy-haired, light-skinned boy in America. And then I have to wonder—how dead can I really be, as long as my son and grandson exist? I wish I had thought of saying that to my wife earlier today. It would have cheered her up, given her something to hold on to.

But this is just vanity. The nonsensical thoughts of a self-indulgent dead man. The fact is my beloved doesn't need me to point any such profundities to her anymore. She is the architect of her own life. An hour from now, she will approach my—our—her—son and tell him her decision. He will be surprised, shocked even, but he will accept it. And soon, he will be proud of her, proud of her independence, of her determination, of her sheer instinct for survival. He will learn, as I did, to see past her tiny, 115-pound body and notice instead the iron will, the strong moral compass, the roaring heart of a giant.

I am—I was—Rustom Sethna and I was married to a woman who was a fool. A woman who so adored me, who so relied on my strength that she forgot to measure her own worth, who never knew she carried the world, my world, in the palm of her hand.

But this is not my story. I am done here. This is now her tale. It is she who will carry it forward, take it into the new year.

I have done my part to help shape her story. And for that, I am proud. But it was she who crafted the final chapter and there was no ghostwriter—pardon the pun, I am, after all, a Parsi gentleman and bad puns are mother's milk to us—to help her with that.

Yes, there was a time when my beloved sat dithering, unable to make up her mind, and yes, I grew impatient and gave her the bloody push that made her get off the damn fence. But the free fall, the blind drop, the beautiful flight into her new future, why, that was all her own.

CHAPTER ONE

Tehmina "Tammy" Sethna sat on a lawn chair next to her daughter-in-law, Susan, and basked in the warmth of the hot sun that she had brought with her all the way from Bombay.

It was a week before Christmas and Ohio was enjoying a virtual heat wave. The two women sat in a companionable silence on their front lawn, Tehmina wearing a navy blue sweater over her batik-print shalwar-khameez. Her gray hair was held down with two bobby pins, so that the slight, lazy breeze that ran its fingers through the grass on the front lawn could not do much to ruffle it. There was not a lick of snow anywhere.

"Seventy degrees," Susan said, for the fifth time. "December in Cleveland and it's seventy degrees. This is unfrig—unbelievable."

Tehmina beamed. "I told you," she said.

Susan pushed her sunglasses down her nose and peered at her mother-in-law. "Well, you've made a believer out of me," she said lightly. "Importing all this sunshine from India. Heck, Mom, if this trend continues, there's no way we'll let you go back to India. The mayor of Rosemont Heights will pass a proclamation or something, forbidding you from ever leaving."

Something inside Tehmina melted and turned to honey at Susan's words. She looked at the younger woman at her left. The sunshine had massaged and lifted Susan's mouth, which usually curved downward, into a smile. Susan's hands—Tehmina still remembered the first time she'd seen those hands and marveled at how large and masculine and raw American women's hands were—Susan's hands were resting limply by her side, unclenched, relaxed. The harried look that she wore most of the time, that made Tehmina jumpy and nervous around Susan, that look was replaced by contentment and happiness.

Tehmina remembered how Susan had been during her past visits to the United States—relaxed, fun-filled, happy. Something was different this time around, something was missing, and Tehmina knew exactly what—who—was missing. Her dearly departed Rustom was not with her this time. Rustom with his big laugh and boundless confidence; Rustom who could step foot anywhere—in a new restaurant, a new apartment, even a new country—and make himself and the people around him feel at home right away. Rustom who could make his white, blond daughter-in-law giggle and blush as if she was a schoolgirl again. Rustom, who could make his serious, earnest son, Sorab, burst with pride over his old man.

Tehmina pulled on her lower lip with her thumb and index finger. Unlike me, she thought. My presence only burdens Susan and Sorab now. Not like the old days. So many times Rustom and she had visited the children in America and always it had been a good time.

The light shifted in the trees across the street and it reminded Tehmina of something. An incident from last year. "You know what we're doing?" Rustom had bellowed at all of them from the pool at the hotel in San Diego. "We're making memories, for the future.

Something happy for you kids to think of, when we oldies are no longer around."

Sorab had immediately thrown one arm around his father's neck. The two men were standing knee-deep in the water, while Tehmina and Susan lay poolside in lounge chairs. Little Cavas, whom everybody called Cookie, had been napping next to Susan. Tehmina looked at the blue water and at her husband and son. Water glistened off their brown faces and chests. She noticed idly that Rustom's belly was firmer than his son's. Too many years of this pork-beef diet for Sorab, she thought. I need to remind him again about his cholesterol.

"What're you talking about, when you're no longer around?" Sorab said, tightening his grip and bringing down Rustom's head so that it rested on his son's shoulder. "The way you're going, Dad, you'll outlive all of us."

Rustom shook his way out of his son's grip. "When it's your time, it's your time." He grinned. "'The moving finger writes, and having writ moves on,'" he added, swimming away from Sorab.

Sorab groaned. "You and your Omar Khayyám," he said. He turned to Susan. "I swear, my dad has an Omar Khayyám poem for every occasion."

Tehmina now shifted in her chair to look at Susan. "Remember our trip to California last year?" she said. "Remember what my husband said in the pool? About the moving finger writes and then moves on? Do you think he had a—a feeling or a sense—about his death?"

Susan stared straight ahead. Even behind her dark glasses, Tehmina could feel her daughter-in-law stiffen. The suddenly cold silence buzzed around them. When Susan spoke, her voice was tight as a ponytail. "Mom, you remember what Sorab told you? About how you're not to keep thinking about the past? What's the point of thinking about—the sad stuff—if it just brings you down?"

Tehmina started to reply. She wanted to say: When you have known Sorab and loved him for as long as I'd known my husband, then you will know what it's like to miss someone so badly it's like your own organs betray you. Your heart, your skin, your brain, all turn into traitors. All the things you thought belonged to you, you realize you shared with the other person. How to explain to you, Susan, what the death of a husband feels like? Such a shock it is, like experiencing your first Ohio winter, with that bitter wind slapping you on your numb face."

She also wanted to say: That's what's wrong with you Americans, deekra, you all think too much of laughter and play, as if life was a Walt Disney movie. Something a child would make up. Whereas in India, life is a Bollywood melodrama—full of loss and sadness. And so everyone rejects Bollywood for Disney. Even my Sorab was seduced by your Disney life—all this pursuit of happiness and pursuit of money and pursuit of this and that. But this year, I've learned a new lesson. Maybe the Indian way is better after all. See how much money you spend on therapists and grief counselors and all? Even my own son keeps telling me to take that capsule—what is it called?—Prosaic or something. That's because your periods of mourning don't last as long as they need to. Why talk to a therapist who you have to pay to listen to you, when you can talk to a grandparent or an aunt or uncle? Sort of like visiting a prostitute, isn't it, having to pay someone to listen to you?

Into the brittle silence, Susan laughed, a sound so tight it snapped like a rubber band. "Come on, Mom. Cheer up. It's too beautiful a day to waste moping around."

Tehmina felt her face twist with anger. To cover it up, she forced her mouth into a yawn. "You're right. But all this sunshine is making me sleepy. I think I'll go inside for a few minutes."

"Mom." Susan's red hand touched Tehmina's. "I'm sorry. I'm an idiot. Sorry. I know Pappa's death is hard on you. It's just that . . .

well, it's been hard on Sorab, too. And seeing you down makes him feel so sad that, well, it upsets me."

Tehmina took Susan's hand in hers and held it to her cheek. "I know, my darling. I know. And I promise to try harder. It's just that my Rustom was such a pillar of strength that I feel as if something inside me has collapsed this past year."

The two women stared at each other, both blinking back their tears. The afternoon sky suddenly felt cold and wintry and Tehmina gave a shiver. Noticing this, Susan pushed herself off the lawn chair. "You're cold," she said. "Listen, why don't you go inside for a bit? I'll wait for Cookie when he gets off the school bus. And then we can all have some mint tea and snacks. After all, it's not every day that I can be home on my son's last day of school."

Tehmina's face lit up at the thought of her grandson being home soon. She eased her body out of the green-and-white lawn chair. "Good thing we got all the shopping done this morning," she said. "The little one will be glad to find you at home, instead of just his old grandma." The two of them had spent the morning at the mall. Susan had taken the day off just to do some Christmas shopping.

"It feels great to be home in the middle of the week. Seems like any more there's never time to do all the things that . . ."

The slamming of a car door and the squeal of brakes from next door ate up the rest of Susan's words. Tara Jones backed her car out of the adjacent driveway and pulled onto the street. Her window was rolled down, and from where they were standing, the two women could see the red blotches on Tara's skin and the brown hair, uncombed as always.

Susan shuddered. "That woman," she muttered as Tara stepped on the gas and peeled away without so much as a wave. "I can't wait for Antonio to sell his house in the spring so that she has to get out. God knows she's only been here for a few months and already it feels like we've been putting up with her loud music and her yelling at the kids for years."

"The music I can tolerate," Tehmina replied, thinking of the music blaring from loudspeakers on the streets of Bombay during every Hindu festival. "What I can't stand is how mean she is to her children. Such sweet boys, they are. I wish Antonio would do something about that."

Susan gave a snort. "Antonio. Let's not talk about Antonio. Ever since he and Marita moved to the country, he acts as if he has nothing to do with this house. As if it's not still in his name. As if this Tara is some stranger who broke into his house, instead of Marita's half sister. He acts as if he has no control over the situation."

Tehmina had been home the day Antonio, an amiable, gregarious man in his seventies, had stopped by to see Sorab. For years, Antonio had owned a popular Italian neighborhood restaurant where the Sethnas had been regulars because it was one of the few family-owned restaurants in Rosemont Heights, a town that was dominated by chains like Applebee's and Cracker Barrel. In fact, it was during a meal there that Sorab had casually mentioned that he was looking for a new house and Antonio had recommended that they look at the house next door to his in Evergreen Estates.

When Tehmina had brought tea and cookies on a tray into the living room, the two men were sitting across from each other, their knees almost touching. Sorab had the pained look he got on his face anytime he had to broach a difficult subject.

"So how's the new house, Tony?" Sorab started.

"Terrific, terrific," Antonio said, leaning back in his chair. "Got five acres of land around the house, see deer every morning. The missus loves it." He accepted the cup of tea from Tehmina with a smile. "You folks must come out and visit us soon," he said. "Especially while Tammy is still in town. Be good for young Cookie also, to run around the place. Get rid of some of that energy, huh?"

"We'd love to," Tehmina said graciously, handing Antonio his cup of tea.

Sorab cleared his throat. "Um, so when will you put the house up for sale, Tony?" he asked. "Not good to let a house sit empty over the winter."

"Exactly. That being the whole reason I agreed to let Marita's half sister move in there for a few months, long enough for her to get back on her feet, I hope. After she got evicted from her last place, she and those kids got no place to go. Not good, a young woman and two small children, alone in the world. Seems there was a boyfriend but don't ask—" Antonio rolled his eyes. "With the young people, who can tell? What do they say? Easy come, easy go."

Sorab glanced at his mother. "Yes, well. It's just that … they don't exactly fit into this neighborhood, you know what I'm saying, Tony?"

Antonio stared at Sorab for a second and then guffawed. Mother and son exchanged looks of puzzlement while Antonio laughed and laughed until his eyes leaked water. "What's so funny?" Sorab started to ask, but Antonio just shook his head, helpless with laughter.

"Don't fit into this … sorry, sorry," Antonio said finally, wiping the tears from his eyes. "It's just … God, man, what a diplomat you are, Sorab." He leaned toward Sorab, and put his hand on his knee. "You know me, right? Zero tolerance for bullshit. So I'll tell you the truth. Listen, you and I both know what this woman is. There's a word for it—white trash." Seeing Tehmina wince, he nodded respectfully in her direction. "Pardon me, Tammy, dear. But I'm talking to Sorab here, man-to-man."

He fixed his gray eyes back onto Sorab's embarrassed face. "So here's the deal. I promised Marita I'd let her freeloader sister live here until the house sells. Help her get back on her feet. As you know, moving to the country was my idea. Marita didn't want to leave the old neighborhood. Serves me right, marrying a woman almost fifteen years younger than me. Anyways, she was sure she'd be bored to tears in the countryside. Says she'll move only one one condition. And so I agree to let Tara stay here, just to keep my missus happy. A compromise, you can say."

"But, Antonio," Sorab interrupted. "Tara can be so difficult. Rap music playing till late at night and *loud*. And my God—the way she yells at her children . . ." He shuddered.

"Spoiled brats, that's what they are." Antonio nodded, as if in sympathy. "And listen, you have my permission to tell her to keep her music down." Then the line of his usually humorous mouth grew tighter. "Sorry, Sorab. But I have to think of my home life. And anyway, I can't turn a single mother and her children out on the streets, can I? Besides, look, this is only for a few more months. Hopefully, I can unload that house as soon as the weather breaks."

Now Tehmina wondered how much of the conversation with Antonio Sorab had repeated to Susan. "Antonio said he'll sell the house in the spring," she said cautiously.

"Well, then I can't wait for spring to arrive," Susan snapped. Then, gazing at the miraculously blue December sky, she smiled. "I can't wait for spring to arrive," she repeated. "Although, today, it feels like it's already here."

Tehmina carried the memory of that smile indoors with her as she took two slices of daar-ni-pori out of the fridge and turned on the oven to heat them. Thank God Susan had a sweet tooth, just like the family she'd married into, she thought. They would eat the warmed pastry along with the tea.

When Cookie burst into the kitchen fifteen minutes later, it seemed to Tehmina as if the day got even brighter than before. "Mummy's home, Mummy's home, Mummy's home," the boy yelled. "And Granna, too," he added as he hurled himself at Tehmina's belly for his afternoon hug. "Yeeeaah. Let's call Dad and ask him to come home, too."

Tehmina felt a gust of love so strong, for a minute she thought a window was open. Such a boy this is, she thought to herself, as warm and affectionate as a young puppy. "You are the best hugger in the world," she whispered as she kissed the top of Cavas's head. In response, the boy squeezed even harder, until Tehmina pretended to gasp for breath. "Where's your mummy?" she asked, and then, "Go upstairs and change your clothes and then come straight down, okay?"

"Okay." Cavas grinned. "Wait for me right here."

Tehmina left the kitchen to look for Susan. She frowned. The front door was still open.

She found Susan in the driveway with the two Jones boys.

Susan turned toward her before she could say hello to Jerome and Joshua. "This is incredible," she said to Tehmina, as if the two boys were not present. "Seems their mother is not home and the boys are locked out of their own house. We're hoping she gets back soon."

Tehmina glanced at the two boys. Jerome was seven, Cavas's age, while Joshua was five. Both boys had sharp, birdlike faces, with brown eyes and thin noses. Right now, both noses were running and Josh was trying to get rid of the snot by inhaling it and simultaneously wiping his nose on the back of his hand. The boys' white faces also had streaks of black, as if they'd spent the afternoon cleaning chimneys. Gazing at their necks, she saw lines of gritty black and her fingers itched at the thought of putting those boys in hot water and scrubbing the grit off those necks.

Funny, Tehmina thought to herself, how poor white children always look so much dirtier than poor children in India. Either the dirt didn't show as much against brown skin or what she'd always heard about cleanliness being next to godliness in Hindu culture was true. She remembered how, when her car drove past the slums in Bombay, she often saw groups of slum women returning to their homes, carrying large copper pots of water on their heads. From the same pot of water they probably cooked, washed their dishes, and bathed their children. So why was it that here in America, where everyone had running water and everything, there were still children who looked like Jerome and Joshua?

Tehmina's indignation gave way to pity. "I'm making Cavas an afternoon snack," she said to Susan. "Maybe these boys are hungry, too."

Susan shot Tehmina a disbelieving look. How could you do this to me? the look seemed to say, but Tehmina looked away. Just then, Josh spoke up. "I'm so hungry, I could eat a house," he said loudly.

Jerome slapped his brother on the shoulder. "No you're not," he said. "Besides, Mamma will be home soon." And as if to convince the two adults eyeing them, Jerome added, "Joshy is always hungry. My mom says he must have worms or something."

This time, Tehmina stared directly at her daughter-in-law, silently willing her to do the right thing. Susan stared back at the older woman and then lowered her eyes. "Tell you what," she said to the two boys. "Why don't you come in and have some hot chocolate while we wait for your mommy? What'd you say, Jerome?"

They all waited in silence while Jerome looked intently at Susan for a minute. "You're pretty," he said suddenly, as if that had been the question before him. "Okay, let's go."

"Thanks a lot, Mom," Susan muttered silently as the boys rushed in ahead of the two women. But Tehmina could hear the smile in her voice. I must remember this the next time Susan is upset with me, Tehmina said to herself. When faced with a question, answer it with a compliment.

The boys sat at the kitchen bar, waiting for their hot chocolate. "I like the pretty pictures you have on your walls," Josh declared. "We got no pictures in our house."

Jerome hissed at his younger brother. "We do, too," he said. "I'm gonna tell Mom you told a big fat lie. You have a picture of Jesus in the Garden right above your bed."

"That don't count," Josh replied. "I mean, pictures of lakes and birds and flowers and stuff."

Just then Cavas walked into the kitchen, wearing his blue jeans and clutching his Calvin and Hobbes book. "Hi, Jerome; hi, Joshy," he said, as if finding the two boys in his home was the most common thing in the world.

"Come sit down, Cavas," Tehmina said, pointing to the bar stool beside the kitchen counter. "Your hot chocolate will be ready in a minute."

The two boys giggled and poked each other in the ribs. "Cow ass," Jerome repeated. "She called you cow ass."

"Granna," Cavas said through gritted teeth, his eyes filling with tears of embarrassment. "Stoppit, please." He turned to his visitors. "My real name is Cookie."

The two boys giggled even more. "If you're a Cookie, I'm gonna eat you," Josh said, lunging at Cavas.

"What kind of a cookie are you?" Jerome added. "Chocolate chip? A sugar cookie?"

Josh licked his lips. "I *love* sugar cookies," he said. "Yummy, yummy, yummy."

"Okay, boys, that's enough." Susan's voice landed like a whip. "This is just a family nickname for Cavas, you understand? You know, like your mommy calling you sugar pie or honey."

"My mommy says my nickname is Trouble," Josh announced proudly.

Tehmina suddenly felt something thin and metallic and sharp pierce her heart. Trouble. What kind of mother nicknames her son Trouble? She went to the fridge and pulled out two mutton cutlets left over from last night's dinner. Sorab had asked her to save the cutlets for him to eat again tonight, but she knew he would understand. Ignoring Susan's inquiring gaze, she warmed the cutlets in the microwave and then placed them on two of the chappatis that she had baked just this morning.

"Here," she said. "Eat."

Jerome looked at the cutlet on the plate in front of him and made a face. "Eww," he said. "What's *that*?"

"It's a mutton cutlet. It's good. You'll like it. Taste it."

"A cutlet? What's *that*? And what's *mutton*?"

"It's a hamburger," Susan said. "Take a bite. If you don't like it, you don't have to eat it." She shook her head slightly so that only Tehmina caught the motion.

"I love McDonald's hamburgers," Josh said. "When I'm older, I'm gonna work at McDonald's and eat three Big Macs a day."

"Take a bite, beta," Tehmina coaxed, rolling up the cutlet in the chappati and holding it up to Josh's mouth. This boy was breaking her heart each time he opened his mouth.

The boy bit into the sandwich. "It's good," he said, and took a second bite before he had swallowed the first.

"Easy now, easy," Susan said. "I don't want any puking in my kitchen."

For some reason, all three boys thought this was hilarious. "No puking in the kitchen," Jerome said as he proceeded to wolf down his sandwich. "I don't want no puke in my kitchen."

Tehmina leaned against the refrigerator, smiling at the boys. Nothing gave her as much satisfaction as feeding people. It was as if feeding others fed her own appetite. Rustom always used to say, "Two things you should never refuse another human being—food and education." As always, her dear Rustom was right about this, also. Tehmina sighed.

Hearing her sigh, Cavas turned to his grandmother. "Granna," he said. "Where's your tea?"

Tehmina gave a short laugh. "Oh dear," she said. "In all this hustle-bustle I forgot to make any tea."

"Hustle-bustle," Jerome repeated, giggling to himself. "Hustle-bustle. Piggy-wiggy. Wig-wam."

Cavas shook his head at Jerome. "You're silly," he declared. He turned his head to face Tehmina. "Granna," he called. "I want you to drink your tea out of the mug I got you for your birthday."

Tehmina and Susan exchanged an amused look. This was Cavas's way of apologizing to his grandmother for his earlier outburst. Tehmina's heart rattled with pride and pleasure. She wanted to go up to Cookie and kiss him on his sweet head, but she didn't know if that would embarrass him even more in front of his friends. Instead, she contented herself by pulling out the coffee mug that read #1 GRANDMA.

She and Susan had barely sat down with their tea when they heard the distinctive rat-a-tat of the muffler on Tara's car. Tehmina saw Susan's eyes narrow. "Well, sounds like your mother's home," she said to the boys.

"I don't want to go home," Josh said. "I want to stay here."

Tehmina wanted to slit open her belly, hide Josh in there and keep him where he'd be safe and warm forever. Never again would anybody ever call the boy Trouble. Never again would that Tara yell and scream at this child. But Susan had other ideas. "No can do, soldier," she said, getting to her feet. "Your mom's gonna be worried when she sees you're not in the yard. Come on, I'll walk you over."

"I'll come, too," Tehmina said. She had never before taken a good look at the woman next door, never noticed anything past the blotchy skin and the unkempt hair. Now she wanted to look deep into the eyes of a woman who could take two precious gifts from God and refer to them as Trouble. She wanted to know what she would see in the eyes of such a woman.

"There you are," Tara called as she saw all of them cross their front yard and head toward her driveway. She slapped Jerome lightly on his head as he approached her. "You little brat," she said. "I'm gone for two minutes and you're up to God knows what mischief. How many times have I told you not to go into people's homes?"

Susan spoke up. "In fairness to Jerome, he refused our invitation at first," she said. "He only came when we insisted that he not wait for you outdoors. After all, even a sunny day like this would get cold for a child."

Tara stared at a spot beyond Susan's shoulders. "I wasn't gone that long," she mumbled. She nodded toward her car. "With that junky car, they know I never go too far."

"As a matter of fact, the children were at our house for probably over a half hour," Susan said evenly. "That's too long to leave two young children alone."

Tara narrowed her eyes. "Look, lady, I don't need anybody monitoring my comings and goings. I'm thankful and all that, but next time just let my kids wait . . ."

Susan's lips had almost disappeared and her voice was quiet and steady. "I hope there won't be a next time, Tara," she said. "The fact is, it's against the law to—"

Tara snorted. "Hey, I know damn well what the law says. I don't need nobody to teach me the law. I've lived in this country my whole life, so believe me, I know what's what and . . ."

Tehmina felt Susan stiffen by her side. "What did you mean by that remark?" she asked, and her voice had December frost in it. "What does living in this country or not living in this country your whole life have to do with following the law?"

"Hey, hey, don't lose it, lady. I didn't mean nothing by that remark. I mean, I wasn't even thinking of you being married to a foreigner—that's your business, not mine." She looked at Tehmina and nodded. "I got nothing against Indian people or Chinese people or black people. I . . . I just don't like to be talked down to, that's all."

Beside his mother, Josh started whimpering. "Mommy, I'm cold," he sniffed. "Come on, Mommy, let's go in."

Susan turned on her heels and took Tehmina by the elbow and Cavas by his hand. "Yes, it's time for us to go in. We've lost enough of our afternoon to all this."

"Hey, lady, look, no hard feelings," Tara yelled after them. "Thanks for watching my boys for me." Tehmina wanted to turn back to respond, but Susan's grip on her elbow tightened.

"Just keep walking, Mom," she muttered through clenched teeth.

Back in the kitchen, their tea had grown cold. "So much for a nice, peaceful day off." Susan sighed. "Just wasted an hour of my day." She turned to her son. "Go upstairs and read for a little while, baby. Then we want to go out and do some more Christmas shopping before Daddy gets home, okay?"

Tehmina wanted to ask Susan about whether she believed that Tara had meant to disparage Sorab; she wanted to thank her for leaping to her husband's defense. She wanted to know more about this kind of casual racism, how common it was and whether it made Susan vulnerable, being married to a brown man. And if Susan felt it and had experienced it, surely it meant that Sorab—Sorab, despite his pressed clothes, his groomed fingernails, his American accent, his gold watch, his good job, his many degrees—surely her Sorab experienced it, too. Tehmina's stomach clenched at the thought of some ignorant fool like Tara spewing poison that could affect even a hair on her son's precious head.

"That woman is a junglee," she said to Susan. "Why God gives people like Tara such sweet children, I'll never know."

Susan shrugged. "Just goes to show. Any fool can have a child. The sad part is, those boys are going to grow up to be wild. You can already see the aggression in the older one. I don't want them to be around our Cavas anymore." She turned to face her mother-in-law. "You have a good heart, Mom. I really appreciate that, but I want you to listen to me—I don't ever want to have those boys over again. I hope you can respect my decision."

Tehmina's face clouded over. Before she could reply, Susan spoke again. "I'm sorry, Mom," she said. "But I *really* need to ask this of you."

"Sure," she mumbled, but her mind was somewhere else. Because Tehmina had heard what Susan was too polite to say—when you're in my house, you follow my orders. For a moment, she thought longingly of her large apartment in Bombay, an apartment that was sitting empty while she decided where she wanted to spend the rest of her life, in which country she wanted to live out her days. India or America. In her wildest dreams she had not imagined that she would have to make the same choice that Sorab had made years earlier. But then, in her wildest dreams she had not imagined that Rustom would drop dead of a heart attack and leave her to live out her life without him.

As Susan turned away with a satisfied smile, Tehmina thought: You think you know me, my daughter-in-law, but you don't. For instance, I bet you don't know that I'm a space traveler. But I am. And I do. In my mind, I travel through time and space in ways you cannot even dream of—from Ohio to Bombay to Ohio again; from the land of the living to the land of the dead, where my Rustom resides; from my wallpapered bedroom in this house, to my painted bedroom in Bombay, of which I know every inch—where the embroidered handkerchiefs are kept in the bottom drawer of the chest of drawers; what books are on the bedside table; the color of the frame that holds the painted picture of Lord Zoroaster that Rustom got me for my fiftieth birthday.

Yes, I may be older than you, Susan, and my knees may creak when I get up in the morning, but I can run faster and fly higher than you will ever know.

CHAPTER TWO

Eva Metzembaum honked four times before Tehmina eased out of the front door and waved to her.

"Good God, Tammy," Eva said as Tammy got into the car. "What's the matter with you? Moving as slow as a snail this morning. I was afraid I was going to have to leave the car and come get you." Eva glanced at the bulge of her stomach under her red dress, as wide as a ledge upon which she could lean her elbow. "Not that a little exercise would kill me," she added.

Tammy smiled. She loved this about Eva, how she could make fun of the world in one breath and then turn her humor on herself, like the flash of a knife. In India, Tammy would have been embarrassed to be seen in public with a woman as large as a small yacht. But here in America, Eva Metzembaum had become the only person to whom Tammy could confide just about anything.

They had first met five years ago during one of Tehmina's visits, when Eva had approached her at the neighborhood block party, said hello, and then asked, "Do you play bridge? Cards? Anything?"

Tammy shook her head. "No, I'm sorry, no. I mean, years ago, I used to play cards. But that was so long ago I'm sure I don't remember a thing."

"Nonsense. Like riding a bike. You never forget. Tell you what. A bunch of us girls get together Tuesday afternoons to play. Why don't you join us this week?"

Instinctively, Tehmina looked around to find her husband or her son. She was not sure how to respond to this large, round woman with the bright red lipstick, who towered over her like a Ferris wheel. "I . . . I'm not sure what our plans are for next Tuesday, Mrs. . . . ?"

"Mrs. Metzembaum. But don't even try getting your tongue around that name, darlin'. You just call me Eva."

"And I'm Tehmina. Though most people call me Tammy."

"Oh, I know who you are. Know your son, too. Who I simply adore, let me tell you. Such a sweetheart. Just the other day I'm coming home from Costco's weighed down by boxes and bags, wondering how I'm ever going to get them into the house. My Sol—that's my husband, Solomon—is right in the garage, tinkering with his vintage Chevy, but you think *he's* going to help his wife unload the car? Forget it." Eva made a dismissive sound and then stared at Tehmina blankly. "Now why am I telling you all this? What was my point?"

"You were mentioning knowing my son . . ." Tehmina said.

Eva grinned. She had enormous teeth. "That's right. I tell you, ever since menopause, my memory isn't what it used to be. Either that or it's the gin and tonics my Sol makes for me each evening. You like gin and tonic, Tammy? Whaddya mean, you've never had one? Why, I'd rather give up oxygen before I'd give up my gin and tonics. Tell you what, dear. When you come to our cards club next week, I'll have my Sol prepare a pitcher or two for all the girls."

This woman goes from one topic to another the way the sun goes in and out of the clouds, Tehmina thought. "So you know my

Sorab?" she asked cautiously, wanting to steer the conversation back to her son.

"Sorab?" Eva pronounced it Sowrab. "Oh sure. He's a mensch, I tell you. We live in that gray house down there, see?" Eva pointed to a large, modern house that, to Tehmina's untrained eye, looked like every other house in the housing development. "And your Sorab and his little boy are taking an evening walk and he sees me struggling with the boxes. And next thing you know, he's helping me haul my groceries in. Even your little grandson—it was so cute, Tammy—he takes a huge box that's twice his size and staggers up my driveway with it." Eva looked around her where the neighbors were gathered around the smoking barbecue grills. She lowered her voice. "Can you see any of these others being that helpful? No, they'd just keep walking, pretending to look the other way." She beamed at Tehmina. "I asked your Sorab, you sure you aren't a Jew? And he laughed and said he was just being neighborly, that's all. A proper gentleman, your boy."

Tehmina was embarrassed and proud all at once. She decided she liked this big, good-natured woman very much. Anyone who was a fan of Sorab was a friend of hers.

Rustom strolled up right then, holding a paper plate laden with food. "Darling, aren't you going to eat?" he asked. "Shall I bring you a plate?"

"Not yet," Tehmina said. She turned back to face Eva. "This is my husband, Rustom," she said. "Rustom, this is Eva."

Tehmina watched with fascination the flesh jiggling on Eva's sleeveless arms as she vigorously shook hands with Rustom. "My hubby is around here somewhere," Eva said. She waved her hand dismissively. "Not that you'll see him. He's probably hiding under the hood of a car, somewhere. Well, if you see a short little guy with grease spots on his hands, that's my Solomon. Working on cars, that's his passion."

Tehmina smiled uneasily, not sure of how to respond to Eva's description of her husband. But Rustom appeared unfazed. "Does your husband do this for a living?"

"Oh heavens, no. He used to own a small dealership, but he's retired now. So he spends his time tinkering with his 1941 Chevy. Swear to God, he'd marry this car if it was legal. Suits me fine, though. Keeps him from getting underfoot, I always say." Eva shot Tehmina a confidential look. "You know how it is, Tammy. Men are happy with objects—their cars, their lawn mowers, their boats. Whereas we women, we need—*people.*"

Rustom raised his eyebrows. Bowing slightly before Eva, he drawled, "Well, excuse me, ladies. I can see you have a lot to talk about. As for me, I'm going to answer the call of my—hammers and cars."

Tehmina flushed, ready to explain her husband's dry sense of humor to this warm, large woman. But to her relief, she saw that Eva was guffawing with laughter, shaking her head at Rustom's receding back. "He's a devil, that one is," she said, all of her multiple chins dancing to the sound of her laughter. "I can tell. Bet he keeps you on your toes, Tammy."

Now, remembering that old conversation, Tehmina felt a rush of affection for her friend. Thank God Eva needed people. With Rustom gone, Tehmina more than ever needed to be around someone who loved people. Although she hated herself for thinking any ungenerous thoughts about Sorab and Susan, sometimes Tehmina felt as if both children had become so busy with their jobs and houses and cars that they had become slaves of their possessions. Tehmina remembered the old science-fiction cartoons they used to show before the feature film in Bombay when she was a kid. Many of them starred robots carrying out the wishes of their masters. But here in America, it seemed as if the opposite had happened—the humans had become the robots, carrying out the wishes of their mechanized gadgets.

But then, what do you know? she chastised herself. When is the last time you got your Bombay apartment painted? Here, the children paint two rooms each summer. And look how Sorab maintains their cars—waxes them, cleans them, vacuums them. You are a ghaati from Bombay—who are you to judge them?

But then a memory rose like sour milk inside Tehmina. A buffet at their house two weeks ago. Twelve guests and Tehmina had spent the whole day in the kitchen, making shrimp curry rice and sali boti. Maybe her hands shook because she was tired or maybe it was because she had had two glasses of wine, but for whatever reason, a few morsels of rice fell from her plate onto the living-room carpet as she sat on the couch with the plate perched on her lap. And Susan had gotten up immediately—Tehmina noticed her daughter-in-law's lips thin and tight with disapproval—and brought out the portable vacuum cleaner. To Tehmina's mortification, Susan had proceeded to vacuum the carpet around Tehmina's feet. She had sat there, rooted to the couch with shame, not knowing where to place her feet, whether to get up or remain seated.

Sorab had finally caught her discomfort. "Hey, Suse, that's enough," he'd said lightly. "I know that obsessive-compulsive disorder is going crazy today, but control yourself, hon."

Susan's clenched retort was drowned out by Percy Soonawalla's bark of laughter. Percy was an old childhood friend of Sorab's who had virtually grown up in the Sethna household and was now a successful immigration lawyer. "Arree, bossie, that's what's wrong with these interracial marriages, yaar," he said, glancing at his fourth wife, Julie. "All these American women have the OCD gene. Whereas their good-for-nothing husbands from India have the bindaas gene." He turned to his wife. "You know what *bindaas* means, honey? It means . . . devil-may-care, carefree . . . the way most Parsi men are."

Eva Metzembaum glanced at Tehmina as she put her tan Buick in reverse and slowly backed out of the driveway. "Oi, Tammy, had something bad to eat for breakfast this morning, did you? Why such a sourpuss face?"

Tehmina shook her head. "No, sorry. Just thinking, that's all."

"Well, if thinking makes your face ugly as a dried prune, better not to think, I say. Better to have a completely vacant mind, which is what my Sol says I have, anyway."

Tehmina grinned. Eva had a way of always cheering her up. "How is Solomon?" she asked.

"Solomon? Oh, he's fine. The old guy just keeps ticking away. Now that it's too cold to work outdoors on his precious car, he's moping around the house, reading his automotive magazines and getting in my hair. But come summer he won't even know if I exist. I think a hundred years from now, when I've been reincarnated as a hamster or something—you Indian people believe in reincarnation, right?—they'll find Solomon with his head still under the hood of his precious car."

"You know, Eva, a few years ago you would have shocked me. But now I know you too well. One day without Solomon and you'd be lost."

"Oh, I don't dispute that," Eva said. "Sol's all right." She smiled slyly. "The face of a beaver, maybe, but a good man."

"Tsshh. What crazy things you say." Tehmina laughed.

"Well, girlie? Ready for the farmers' market? And then maybe if we have time we can stop at Target? What time is Cookie getting home from school?"

Tehmina's face fell. "School's out," she said. "But Susan didn't want to leave him at home with me even during Christmas week. So she's enrolled him in some special enrichment class."

"Oi. Enrichment class," Eva said, clucking her tongue. "In my day, the only thing that was enriched was rice. But these parents today—not enough for them to raise happy and healthy children. No, the kid must dance like Fred Astaire and do math like Einstein." She placed her heavy, wrinkled hand over Tehmina's, covering it like a bowl. "It's not just you and your daughter-in-law, Tammy. Same nonsense going on everywhere. Nobody thinks grandparents know enough to teach their grandkids anything. You take my son, David, and his wife in Florida. They treat their son as if he's the Messiah."

"But that's something I don't understand, Eva," Tehmina replied. "Why are the children in America so isolated? Look at our housing complex, for example. All these new and big houses but no sidewalks. How can they design these houses to the last degree—the high ceilings, the fancy bathtubs, and all that—and then forget to install sidewalks? I tell you, in Bombay even the poorest neighborhoods have sidewalks—and the fact that they are all broken and cracked and everybody spills out on the roads to walk is another story."

"Oh, I hear you, Tammy, I hear you," Eva said. "Why, in my time, we children lived on the streets. Winter or summer, that's where our life was, playing outdoors. Now take my grandson. Plays so many computer games, I tell him he'll have stubs instead of thumbs by the time he's fifteen. And if you ask him to go for a walk with you, he looks at you like you've asked him to rob a bank. Indignant."

It felt so good to be able to talk to someone like this and not be misunderstood. Susan and Sorab both got this pained, defensive expression on their faces if she said anything that they thought was critical of America. "And it's so funny," Tehmina continued. "Every house with young children here at Evergreen Estates has its own identical play set in the backyard—you know, the swing set, the slide, and all the rest of it. So why don't all these parents get together and just buy one or two such sets and put it in a common compound? Then all these children can play with each other. I mean, my Cavas has a few other friends in the complex. But there are so many kids he never even sees. I don't think he's ever played with the kids next door."

Eva sighed dramatically. "If only you and I ran the world, Tammy. We'd take care of all the young uns, wouldn't we? Me and my siblings, we were poor as New Jersey dirt, but I tell you—we had each other and we were happy. Not one kid in our old neighborhood we weren't friends with. And if we did something wrong, God help us. Every woman on the street thought it was her God-given right to correct us. And if that meant a whack or two, well, no use complaining to your parents. They'd just say that you probably deserved it."

Tehmina smiled dreamily. "New Jersey sounds just like Bombay," she said. She debated whether to recount to Eva the altercation with Tara a couple of days ago. But just then Eva asked, "So what do you think, honey? Shall we try to go to Target after the farmers' market?"

Tehmina didn't have to think. "I'd love to," she said. "Who knows? This may be my only chance to do some Christmas shopping for the children while they're away."

Eva braked for a squirrel who darted across the street. "Christmas," she said. "What's the point of a holiday that just stresses people so? Tell me, have you ever seen a happy Christian on Christmas Day? The only cheerful ones are those religious nuts, and they're so loony they don't know any better than to be happy all the time. The rest of them, they're running to their therapists the day after, and for what? So that they can lose their minds all over again in time for next December."

"In India, when I was a schoolgirl, we used to long to experience a real white Christmas." Tehmina smiled. "You know, we'd see Christmas cards with lights and trees and snow. None of us had ever seen snow. We even put up a small tree at my school each year. But you know what we'd use to imitate snow? Cotton wool."

Eva snorted. "Yah, even here you have young Jewish kids running around wanting to be Jesus Christ and Mother Mary. Brainwashing is what it is, if you ask me." Eva sighed. "Wish I could go someplace to get away from these mad Christians for a week. They spot a Jew from a mile away and they want to convert."

Tehmina laughed. "Eva, you're all talk. Why, you must have more Christian friends than anyone I know."

"Did I ever say I didn't? I got nothing against Christians. No, what I'm against is the hoopla that surrounds the holiday. I mean, you been inside a store recently? All those people foaming at the mouth as they run around buying up stuff. Do any of these people look happy? Are any of them thinking of Christ? No, I'll tell you what they're thinking of—they're thinking of PlayStations and plasma TVs and surround-sound systems. That's a religion?"

"I know. I know, Eva. I think of the same thing. Susan and Sorab, they both work so hard. I mean, I see my son come home some nights and my heart just throbs with fear. I wonder, doesn't Susan see how tired, how exhausted he looks? Doesn't she care? And then I notice the same look on her face. And I ask myself, for what are they working so hard? Why can't they buy a smaller house, with a smaller yard and all? Why does Sorab have to work such long hours?"

"Because he got on the treadmill." They entered the parking lot for the market and Eva cruised around slowly, trying to find a parking spot. "You know what a treadmill is, right? Okay, well, ever tried jumping off one of those things when it's still moving? Very hard to do. No, the way to do it is to hit stop before you can step off. And in this country, nobody ever wants to hit that button."

Tehmina turned to Eva. "Eva, that's my biggest fear. As you know, the children want me to stay here. Sorab, especially, is worried that with Rustom gone, there's nobody in Bombay to care for me. We are a small family—not many cousins or uncles. And I well remember how lonely I was in the months after Rustom's death." She paused, willing herself to not remember the difficult days that had followed her husband's funeral. "And yet . . . Bombay is my home. Here, I am afraid that I will always be a stranger, that I will never get used to all these ways."

Eva eased into a space and put her car into park. But she didn't turn off the engine. Instead, she eyed Tehmina assessingly. "Tammy," she said at last. "You're like family to me. So may I speak to you from the heart, the way I would to my sister Rose? What I want to say to you is, my God, Tammy, don't be a fool. Your son and his wife want you here, so stay. And how can you call yourself a stranger here? A stranger is someone who comes to America, clicks a few pictures of the Statue of Liberty, rides the trolley in San Francisco, and then returns home thinking they know America—that's a stranger. Whereas you and your late husband have been here so many times you know the price of milk at the grocery store. And if you lived here, I would teach you to drive. Your son can buy you your own car, so as you can be independent."

"Eva, it's not that. It's just that . . . in Bombay I am in my house, living my life. Two days a week I volunteer at Shanti Center, a home for orphaned children. I help my elderly neighbor with her grocery shopping once or twice a week. Every few weeks I meet up with my old friends. We've stayed in touch for over forty years, you know." She leaned over and looked intently into Eva's blue eyes. "See, there, in Bombay, I feel like a person—a person whose life has meaning, whose life follows a path. Here, despite all of Sorab's efforts, I can't help but feel like an ornament, a decoration. Sort of like a package that someone has dropped off at his door. I think—what I'm saying, Eva, is—I don't feel needed here. Apart from the occasional worry, the children will be perfectly happy without me here."

Eva sighed. "It's funny, life is so funny," she said almost under her breath.

"What?"

"Oh, nothing. I was just thinking . . . if my David and his wife were to ask us to move closer to them, I would fit my whole house into a suitcase and move the next day. But they are so busy raising their little pampered son—private school, music lessons, day camp for the gifted—who has the time or energy to spend with their parents? You're lucky, Tammy, that your son wants you to stay close to him."

Tehmina swallowed. "I know. Believe me, I know. Ten times a day I tell myself I'm an ungrateful old woman. It's because of Sorab that I can't decide what to do. Part of me wants to stay here and help—you know, help relieve my children's burdens as much as I can. I want to cook for my Sorab, be home when Cookie gets home from school. Eva," Tehmina cried. "This is not a decision that I expected to make at my age. It was hard enough that my only child left us when he was twenty-one. I didn't think that someday I would also have to follow him to a new country."

Eva's lower lip trembled. "Oh, honey. It's okay. Oh, my dear Tammy, this is so hard, I know. You know, they call us Jews a wandering people. We're used to living like birds, I suppose, going from place to place. But you . . . most people have only one place they call home. I understand, honey, I swear I do. This is a big decision to make."

"And Rustom's not here to help me make it. That's the strange part. I find myself looking for Rustom to decide for me. And then I remember—he's the whole reason I'm faced with this decision in the first place."

"It becomes like skin, another's life," Eva murmured. "If you're married for a long time, the other becomes as familiar as skin."

Tehmina nodded gratefully. "That's what I can't explain to anyone. Susan, Sorab, they all expect me to ... why, just this week Susan snapped at me because I mentioned my husband's name."

Eva clicked her tongue. "What can you expect, Tammy? Your daughter-in-law, nothing against her, but she's a goy. These white people—they're good at making the buses run on time. Everything else, anything that needs a ticking heart, forget it."

"But *you're* white," Tehmina protested.

"Yes, but not white like Susan. Not like my daughter-in-law. I'm more like you, Tammy. I know the world is made of blood and pus and sweat and shit. And I'm not afraid of that. People like your daughter-in-law, they think the world is sugar and spice. And the strange thing is, that for people like them, that's the face the world wears."

Thinking of Susan's sallow, tired face when she got home from work, Tehmina felt a moment's unease at Eva's description of her daughter-in-law. Surely what Eva was saying was not true. Surely Susan had suffered, surely she had seen the dark side of the world, also. She shook her head and turned her attention back to the woman sitting beside her. "Eva," she said. "I have a favor to ask, something I've wanted to ask for a long time."

Eva looked surprised. "You want to go somewhere else?" she said.

"No. No, not like that. I wanted to ask—can you call me Tehmina instead of Tammy? After all, that's my real name."

Eva grew still. Then she put her arm around Tehmina. "Sorry," she said. "We Americans are so arrogant. We can't get our tongues around somebody's name, so we expect them to change their names for us. Happened to so many of my ancestors, too. And here I am ..." She shook her head. "Anyway, it will be my honor to call you by your real name, Tehmina. And I'll make sure the ladies in our card club do so, too."

"I don't care what they call me," Tehmina said. "I just . . . it's you that I wanted to use my name, that's all."

Eva pushed her bulk out of the car. "I'm flattered. It's settled. Tehmina, it is. Now come on. Let's go buy some fruits and veggies before they get all picked over."

Tehmina loved being at the farmers' market. She felt comfortable and human, here. The dirty, stagnant water on the floor, the shouts of the brown-skinned, sweaty vendors competing for customers to sample their wares, even the smell of rotting fruit and fresh fish, all felt familiar to her. Shopping at the farmers' market was like shopping in Bombay—noisy, crowded, buzzing with activity. Touching the fruit and vegetables, occasionally haggling with the vendors, tasting their offered samples of cut fruit, all made her feel human, like the market was rooted in a section of the world she still recognized and lived in. What a contrast it was to the antiseptic, air-conditioned, clean, brightly lit supermarket where the children shopped for their groceries. A place where tomatoes and zucchini came wrapped in plastic trays and where people looked at you funny if you touched a piece of fruit and held it up to your nose. Not that smelling the fruit made any difference—none of the fruits and vegetables in the grocery stores of America had any scent or flavor to them, anyway. It was as if the country was so enthralled with size and color—the bananas and the peaches and the apples were all bigger than anything Tehmina had ever seen in Bombay—that it had forgotten that fruit was more than decoration. To bite into an American apple or an orange was to taste disappointment. Nothing burst with flavor, nothing tasted as sweet or as tangy the way fruits did in Bombay. Even the roses of America had no perfume to them, a fact that Tehmina still couldn't quite accept.

Now, winding her way down the market's narrow aisles, she felt giddy with excitement and a strange, deep satisfaction. She felt as if she had rejoined the human race, that she was engaged in an activity that connected her with the rest of the world. From the markets of Istanbul to the bazaars of Bombay, this is what women did—they held and touched the food they were later to cook, they spoke and argued and joked with the men and women selling them that food. Unlike at the grocery stores, no sheet of plastic protected the fruits and vegetables until they themselves tasted of plastic; no clean-shaven man in a spotless, white coat looked at her with silent distaste if she touched an object and then put it back. The grocery stores looked like they were built for a race of perfect beings; the farmers' market was built to human scale, a place for ordinary, fallible human beings.

There was another thing both Tehmina and Eva enjoyed about coming here. "Look at that one," Eva was now saying, nudging Tehmina. "I think I see her every time I'm here." They both smiled at the sight of a short, old, dark-skinned woman walking around in a white fur coat, looking as imperial as any queen, inspecting the bell peppers and the carrots as if they were her royal subjects. Right next to her shuffled a ragged-looking man, his eyeglasses held together with tape and holes in his dirty winter coat. That was the amazing thing about the market—it was a pageantry of humanity, as if a kind of democracy was sprouting between the garlic and the bok choy. Tehmina thought again of the grocery store where Sorab and Susan shopped. How dull, how uniform the people who shopped there looked, much like the houses in their development. Everybody in the supermarket looked healthy and clean and well scrubbed, with none of the individuality and the colorful eccentricities that the shoppers at the market wore on their interesting, multicolored faces.

Tehmina loved leaving the anemic suburban streets of Rosemont Heights and coming into Cleveland. Why couldn't the children have bought a house in downtown Cleveland instead? she now lamented, although she knew the answer. Sorab had told her last month, the night after Thanksgiving when they had gone to Public Square to witness the ceremonial lighting of the Christmas tree. Despite the frigid night air, Tehmina had been warm that night. Perhaps she was warmed by the hot cider and the hot chocolate that Sorab bought for all of them as they shivered through the interminably long speeches by the city leaders, waiting for the moment when Public Square would erupt in a burst of red and green lights. But it was more than that, Tehmina knew. What had warmed her soul was the crowd of ten thousand people, all huddled together, all leaning slightly toward one another, a mass of bodies seeking warmth and closeness and refuge in one another. And what a crowd it had been. Cheerful, boisterous, good-natured. They cheered lustily for the high school bands and the local DJ who was emceeing the show; they booed lustily each time a new politician took the stage. The crowd was made up of people of every race and color, every class background, so that men in fine wool coats were exchanging pleasantries with the homeless men who spent their days hanging out at Public Square, men whose shoes had holes in them. There were ten thousand of them there for the tree-lighting ceremony, but to Tehmina it had seemed as if they were one. One mass, one organism, moving together in time to the music, inhaling the frigid air together, exhaling clouds of frozen breath together. It was wonderful. It was exhilarating. And it made Tehmina feel totally different from what she felt like in Rosemont Heights. In this crowd, it was easy to disappear, to leave behind her own body and become as vacant, as limitless, as expansive as the sky. A part of a whole. Whereas in Rosemont Heights, she was self-conscious of her body, felt the weight of her head as it balanced on her neck, the heaviness of her hands as they hung by her sides, the tingling pressure of her brown skin. She knew that there was another biracial couple living in Evergreen Estates. And that a Chinese-American doctor lived the next street over. But other than that, the housing colony felt uniformly similar. No men with holes in their shoes and whiskey on their breath lived in Evergreen Estates. And even if they did, nobody would laugh and talk to them the way the well-dressed men were doing right now.

She turned to Sorab, careful to modulate her voice so that he could hear her over the music but that Susan could not. "Do people live in downtown Cleveland?" she asked.

"Some people do, these days," he yelled into her ear, over the music. "Mostly young singles, though. Not too many families."

"Why not?" she asked, hoping he didn't hear the wistfulness in her voice. "It's such a beautiful place."

Sorab made a face. "The schools are terrible, Mamma. There's no way we'd send Cookie to Cleveland schools." Then, following her gaze as she looked at the point where Terminal Tower touched the sky, "The buildings are beautiful, I'll grant you that. But you should see this place most days after the office crowd leaves. It's a ghost town. No one here except the winos. It's no place to raise a family."

Despite herself, the words escaped her lips. "It reminds me of South Bombay. Of some of the old, majestic buildings, like the Elphinston College building and VT station. And doesn't Terminal Tower remind you of the old Bombay University tower?"

Sorab shrugged his shoulders. "Not really. I mean, it's a different kind of architecture." Then his face softened. "If I'd known this would make you sentimental about Bombay, we'd have stayed home tonight." He smiled. "This was meant to cheer you up."

"Oh, I'm happy to be here. Very happy." She took his gloved hand in hers and squeezed it hard. "How can I not be happy when my son is with me?"

Now Tehmina sighed heavily, and although Eva had seemed distracted by the sign that said LIMES, 10 FOR $1, she noticed. "What's wrong, Tamm—Tehmina? Why're you wheezing like an old train?"

"Oh, I was just thinking." She turned toward Eva, her face moist with the mist of memory. "I wish you'd come visit me in Bombay. There's—we have this market called Crawford Market? I wish you could see that. Oh my God, you should see the fruits there, Eva. Just the mangoes alone . . . and then we have a fruit called custard apple and another called chikoo. A chikoo almost looks like a kiwi fruit, you know. But it's sweet as sugar from the inside."

Eva clucked her tongue. "You always get sentimental when we come to the farmers' market," she said. "But I knew coming here would cheer you up. Nothing like home, eh, Tammy?"

Tehmina was about to answer when she felt someone push her gently on her side. She moved away slightly, but the second nudge was accompanied by a familiar voice. "Hey, hey, lady," the young voice said, and Tehmina looked down and saw it was one of the boys from next door. It was the younger one, looking up at her with a wide grin on his face. Tehmina noticed his long eyelashes and big brown eyes.

"Well, hello," she said heartily, hoping he would not notice that she had forgotten his name. "How are you? And how's your brother?"

"I'm fine," a soft voice said shyly behind her, and as she swung around in the direction of the second voice, she remembered both their names. Jerome and Josh. Of course.

"I knew it was you soon's I saw you," Josh said, looking so pleased with himself that Tehmina had to fight the urge to bend down and plant a kiss on his head. "I'm the one who saw you first, not Jerome." He looked around. "Is Cookie here?"

"I'm very pleased you said hello," Tehmina replied. "And no, Cookie is—he's at a class."

"But school's out." Jerome looked puzzled.

"I know. But Cookie goes to a—special class." Tehmina looked at Eva for help. "This is my friend Eva. And these are my two friends,

Joshy and Jerome. They live . . . in the house next door to us." She and Eva exchanged quick looks. Eva had known Antonio, though Tehmina wasn't sure if she'd ever met Tara or the boys.

Both boys were suddenly shy, mumbling their hellos. Eva looked around. "Who are you with?" she asked. "Where's your mamma?"

Jerome eyed Eva suspiciously, but Joshy answered her. "She's gone to the inner market to buy hot dogs." He lowered his voice. "Jerome's scared of going in there because that's where they sell the dead animals and stuff."

"I'm not scared," Jerome replied immediately. "I just stayed here to protect you."

"Uh-uh. You are, too. Mamma said you're a big fat scaredy-cat."

Jerome looked ready to punch his little brother and Tehmina knew it was time to step in. "I hate going into the inner market, also," she said. "I'm so afraid of it. That's why I always bring my friend Eva with me."

Jerome eyed Eva's bulk and nodded. "That's 'cause she's older than you," he said solemnly.

Tehmina turned to Eva to see if she was offended, but Eva was hiding her laughter behind her handkerchief. Only the jiggling of her arms gave her away. "That's right," she said. "I'm at least four hundred years old."

Both boys giggled. "Naw, you're not," Jerome said. "You're funny," he added.

"Well, how old do you think I am?"

Jerome stared at her for the longest moment. "You're at least thirty-eight," he said finally.

Both Tehmina and Eva burst out laughing. "A regular charmer this one is." Eva turned to Tehmina. "Children and flowers," she said. "How can anyone doubt God exists as long as there's children and flowers?"

Joshy tugged at the side of Tehmina's tunic. "I'm hungry," he said urgently.

Jerome smacked his brother on his back. "You're always hungry," he said contemptuously. "My mom says he has a tapeworm or something. She says he's a little beggar, always asking for food."

Tehmina thought of the million different games she had devised to make Sorab eat his dinner when he was a young boy, how she had felt as if her belly got full with every bite her beloved son ate. She couldn't imagine a mother begrudging her little boy his food. "Did you eat breakfast today?" she asked cautiously, wanting and not wanting to know.

"I had a cupcake," Josh replied. "But that was ages ago."

"Would you like a banana?" Eva asked, reaching into her blue plastic bag.

Josh made a face. "Bananas are slimy," he said. "You got some candy?"

"Not good to have so much sugar so early in the morning, sonny," Tehmina began, but she noticed the boys were not listening. She followed the line of Josh's vision and saw that he had spotted his mother approaching them. The boy's face lit up. "Mommy," he cried.

Something died in Tehmina when she saw the bitter hostility on Tara's face. The woman's eyes looked mean as she approached them, and despite the red blotches, her face seemed gray under the smoke of her cigarette. I really don't like this woman, Tehmina thought with surprise. It was so rare that she took a dislike to someone. Still, for the boys' sake, she forced her face into a pleasant smile. "Hello, Tara," she said.

Tara looked at her as if she had caught Tehmina in the act of kidnapping her children. "Hi," she mumbled, and then immediately turned her attention to Jerome. "I told you boys to stand near the side door," she said, smacking his finger out of his mouth. "What're you doing, walking around and talking to—people." She flung a contemptuous look at Tehmina.

Tehmina could feel her face flush at the obvious insult. "The children were just being polite," she said, hearing the frostiness in her own voice. "They recognized me and just came up to say hello."

Tara looked at the older woman insolently, letting her glance fall slowly from the top of Tehmina's head to her feet and then looking her straight in the face. Tehmina fought the urge to squirm under Tara's dismissive gaze. "Oh yeah?" she said indifferently. "Well, they're not allowed to talk to strangers."

Beside her, Tehmina heard Eva emit something that sounded suspiciously like a growl. But before any of the adults could say anything, an impatient Joshy interrupted them. "Mommy, I'm hungry," he said urgently. "Can we go to Mickey D's?"

Tara reacted as if the boy had asked for a thousand-dollar check. "I just spent three bucks on your goddamn hot dogs," she said as she grabbed Josh by his arm, pulled him toward her, and began to move away. "You brats think that money grows on trees. If your good-for-nothing father paid his child support, maybe I could afford to . . ." The rest of her words were swallowed up as Tara walked away, pulling Josh with her. Jerome flung a hasty but forlorn look at Tehmina and then followed behind them.

"Whew," Eva said. "What was *that*? That woman is a—you know, the word that rhymes with *witch*."

Tehmina nodded. "She's a nasty woman," she said, and was surprised at the fact that her voice was shaking with emotion. "She doesn't deserve those two sweet boys. Earlier this week, she left them alone for a half hour after they came home from school. The last day of school it was, if I remember correctly. Susan and I—we took them in. Susan wasn't happy about it, let me tell you. She doesn't want to have anything to do with that Tara. Sometimes we even hear her late at night, yelling and screaming at those children."

"Poor things," Eva said, shaking her head. "You know, you all should complain about that woman to the housing association or something. About disturbing the peace. Was that Antonio soft in the head that he rented his home to such an awful woman, anyhow?"

"He didn't. That is, Tara is his wife's half sister. He's just letting her stay there through the winter until he sells the house next spring. At least, that's what he says."

"Ach, family," Eva said, fanning herself with a brown paper bag. Tehmina noticed that even though it was cold at the market, Eva was perspiring. In contrast to the thick coat and neck scarf that Tehmina had on, Eva only had on a wool sweater. The next minute, Eva pulled her large, man-size handkerchief out of her pocket and mopped her flushed face dry. "What's with this heat?" she said. "Solomon says I look like grilled salmon. And this, in December, in Ohio."

How could Eva possibly be hot? Tehmina thought. That one warm day they'd had earlier this week was gone. She noticed that all the vendors were wearing knit caps over their ears and gloves with the fingers cut off. But before she could say anything, Eva continued: "Didn't I suffer enough with my in-laws, not to mention my own parents, God bless their souls? And even now, think I have a minute's peace, with seven brothers and sisters? Anything goes wrong in their lives and they're on the phone with me quick as a flea on a dog. And now even their children have taken to calling their auntie Eva, minute they need something." She grinned. "Okay. Enough of my kvetching. You know what my poor mother used to say? This wicked world was here yesterday and will be here tomorrow. No use shedding tears over it."

They resumed their shopping, Tehmina going from stall to stall inquiring whether they had any red pumpkin, which she needed for her dhansak daal. But the mostly Greek and Italian and Mexican vendors looked at her blankly and she decided to wait until the children took her to the Indian store. Instead, she bought some Japanese eggplant, okra, squash, bell peppers, and a dozen tangerines and bunches of fresh-looking cilantro and grapes. Maybe she could spare the children a trip to the grocery store later this week.

"Tehmina," Eva gasped finally. "You better slow down, darling. You buy any more and we'll have to call a cab to take the stuff to the car. And you want to leave us some time for going to Target, yah?"

The sun was out as they left the old stone building of the farmers' market and made their way to Eva's car. Maybe it was the sunlight in Tehmina's eyes that made them fill with water. But as she helped Eva unload the grocery bags into the trunk, Tehmina recognized what she was feeling. It was happiness. For the first time in months, she felt truly free and happy.

Still, something was nagging at her. Concentrating on that black spot within her, she recognized what was troubling her: it was the earlier run-in with Tara, a solitary dark cloud in a perfect, blue sky.

CHAPTER THREE

Women.

Sorab Sethna felt like he was drowning in women. His new boss, Grace Butler, was only the latest female who seemed put on earth to make his life torturous. Take earlier today, for instance. Grace had ordered him into her office to discuss his long-standing plans to take a vacation the week after Christmas. Never mind the fact that he had put in for the time off almost a year ago. Never mind the fact that he had taken that same week off for the last eight years. And that all his colleagues and former bosses knew this and had never begrudged him this. After all, Sorab almost never used up all his accumulated vacation time. His last annual evaluation had been as glowing as the one before that. In fact, Sorab usually thought of the phrase *glowing evaluation* as one word, stitched together by the uniform praise he garnered from his superiors. Let the other executives spend their hours looking over their shoulder and fretting about who was catching up on them. Let them spend their evenings crafting the exact words with which they would ask their bosses for a raise. Sorab had never asked for a raise in his life; in fact, every time he switched jobs he never so much as asked his new salary, knowing that it would be more generous than his last. And despite being the golden boy at every agency he had worked at, Sorab had also escaped the ulcer-inducing backstabbing and scheming and plotting that had felled so many others. He expected nothing but fairness and good treatment from others, and somehow, miraculously, he got it. When Sorab was a young boy at Cathedral school in Bombay, his father, Rustom, used to tell him, "Never begrudge another man his success, sonny. Remember, all of us live out our own destinies. All our lives run on a parallel path—someone else's success neither pulls us down, nor does his failure boost us up. You just focus on your own report cards and your own work." Sorab had taken his father's message to heart, first at Cathedral and then in college in America and now in the corporate world. He still remembered his horror when he had first heard about the Tonya Harding–Nancy Kerrigan Olympic scandal. His first thought had been, Why didn't Tonya simply work harder and beat Nancy fair and square?

Hard work triumphed over all else. Sorab knew this to be as true as the fact that he was Rustom Sethna's only son. Canfield and Associates, where Sorab was now a vice president, hired executives fresh out of prestigious business schools. They were young, and square-jawed and aggressive. Above all, they were single, which meant they could put in the kind of hours that Sorab couldn't. But still he wasn't concerned. With no false modesty, he knew that brain cell for brain cell, idea for idea, he could stack up against any of them. On numerous occasions, Sorab had left men fifteen years younger than him sitting openmouthed and slack-jawed in staff meetings.

At least that had been the state of Sorab's tenure at Canfield until Grace Butler had taken over from the kindly Malcolm Duvall, six months ago. Now Sorab often found himself sitting in his office doodling and thinking dark thoughts about Grace Butler instead of focusing on the report in front of him. The way she had cut him short during one of his presentations and said, "Well, that's fine and dandy, Sorab, but that's *so* twentieth century. What do you have that, y'know, would make the hair at the back of my neck crackle and pop?"

That's how she spoke, in clichés. Who else except bubble-gum-popping airheads on sitcoms actually spoke like that? Fabtastic. That was another of Grace Butler's favorite words. Now all the junior executives were going around saying words like *fabtastic* and *wondersonic*. What, during Malcolm Duvall's reign, was merely good was now *imfuckingpossibly brilliant*. What used to be great was now *the mother of all cool*.

And what she had pulled during the executive meeting today was beyond loathsome. Sorab had mentioned that he was going to be off the last week of December and Grace had turned to him with an expression that said that Sorab had just confessed to a series of bank robberies across the United States. "But that's impossible." Grace gasped. "Oh my God, that's like one of our most important weeks. There's no way a senior executive can be off then. Besides, I'm planning on taking some time off around the holidays, myself."

Sorab looked around the conference room, unsure of what to do. Did Grace really want to discuss his vacation schedule during a staff meeting? But before he could reply, Grace bailed him out. "I'll see you in my office immediately following the meeting, okay?" she said. "We need to resolve this." Was it his imagination or did Gerry Frazier, the new guy who Grace had hired from the Weatherhead School of Management, flash a sympathetic smile at Grace?

He was seething by the time he got to Grace's office. But he managed to keep his face blank. "Nice flowers," he said, nodding toward the large bouquet of yellow roses on Grace's desk.

"Thanks," Grace said. "They're from Bryan. We had a bit of a spat last night. Guess it's his way of saying sorry." Bryan was

Grace's boyfriend, and although Sorab had never met him, he felt an instinctive twinge of sympathy for the unknown Bryan every time Grace mentioned his name.

Not now, though. Stupid fool, Sorab thought. Should've quit while he was ahead.

Grace opened her mouth and Sorab knew he had to preempt what he guessed was coming—personal disclosures about Grace and Bryan's relationship, which would then segue into a discourse on the unpredictable, exasperating ways of men, a subject that seemed to endlessly inspire Grace. She was this unnerving blend of frostiness and familiarity. Sorab was often amazed at how a woman who ran the agency with such stealth, who kept her cards so close to her chest, also talked about her personal life with her colleagues as if she was talking to her therapist. Not for the first time, Sorab thought with longing about the patrician, formal Malcolm Duvall—tight-lipped Malcolm with his British accent, his clear delineations between the public and the personal, his steady, sober demeanor. How could Malcolm have picked this flinty, flighty blond woman in her too-short skirts, as his successor? Although it was Joe Canfield, who had founded the agency and now was chairman of the board, who had made the final decision, Sorab knew Joe would have never picked Grace without Malcolm's blessings. Was even good old Malcolm ultimately not immune to the lure of style over substance? And was he, Sorab, such a third-world bumpkin, so hopelessly old-fashioned, so unforgivably *desi*, so utterly—oh my God, so utterly *twentieth century*—that Joe had chosen Grace over him?

"Bryan's a nice guy," Grace was saying. "But sometimes, God, I just—"

"Grace." Sorab's voice was louder than he'd thought. "I must say, I didn't appreciate—that is, I wish you'd waited to discuss my vacation plans until we were—"

"Oh good grief, Sorab, stop being so damn *sensitive*. You're forever thinking I'm gunning for you. See, it's stuff like this that makes me wonder if you're really ready to take over the department when Kurt retires."

Sorab stared at the woman sitting before him. "I don't see what this has to do with my running the department," he said at last. "My only point was that—"

"Yeah, well, my only point is that I don't think you should've planned your vacation without checking with me. Bryan wants to take me on a skiing trip for a few days and I can't believe you—"

"Grace," Sorab said carefully. "I'd put in for my vacation almost a year ago. That's the way we've always done it here at Canfield. The sign-up sheet goes around in January and—"

"Well, see, here's another example of that old-boys-club thinking. Always harkening back to the way it was. That's what I'm trying to do here, Sorab, shake things up. All you good ol' boys have been complacent for too damn long. And I may as well tell you right now—things are going to be different around here."

Old boys club? Does she even see me or the color of my skin? Sorab thought. Is she lumping me with all those middle-aged white men who have worked here forever? Does she think I wear green plaid pants and go golfing every weekend? But then he was distracted by another, more pungent thought. "What exactly are you saying, Grace?" he asked, draining his voice of any emotion. "What's going to be different?"

He noticed at once that she avoided making eye contact with him. Instead, she glanced at the wall clock behind Sorab. "Look, I really don't want to get into all this now. It's way after six and I *reeeally* need to get out of here. But seeing how we've stumbled upon the subject ... I guess I may as well be frank, Sorab—I'm getting cold feet at the thought of you taking over the department once Kurt leaves next year. You, I don't know, you seem distracted of late, and I just get the feeling . . . That is, I'm just not convinced that you're ready for the job."

Inexplicably, mortifyingly, Sorab felt an urge to cry. He sat rigid in the brown leather chair, stiff with embarrassment at how his body seemed ready to betray him, to capitulate before Grace's shaming, untruthful words. But the fact was, in his entire professional career, nobody had ever told Sorab that he was unfit for a job. All his bosses had thought of him as the wonder boy, the go-to guy for problem solving. The last time a superior had expressed disappointment in Sorab had been in third grade, when Principal Francis D'Mello had tsk-tsked at the young boy sitting before him and asked him what devil had driven him to participate in a water-balloon fight. Even that, the mildest of reprimands, had been too much for Sorab to handle and he had steered clear of the wilder boys in his class after that incident. Now he felt a combination of emotions—outrage at Grace's accusations, revulsion at her duplicitousness, and—worst of all—a desperate, schoolboyish desire to placate her, to make her see the error of her ways.

He cleared his throat. "I don't quite know what to say," he began, and could see from the slight narrowing of her eyes that she had heard the treacherous quiver in his voice. "I guess . . . I guess I just didn't see this coming, Grace. And frankly, I'm not quite sure what you're referring to when you say—"

Grace jumped up from her seat. "God, I'm sorry but I really have to run. Bryan has tickets to the orchestra for tonight. I've heard the guest conductor is fantabulous." She glanced at Sorab. "Look, I'm not saying that I've decided anything. But I just wanted you to know that I'm keeping all my options open. Several people have mentioned Gerry's name to me and there are other worthy candidates as well."

Gerry? Gerry Frazier? Had he heard right? That cocky, arrogant, know-nothing, schmoozing, glad-handing new guy with eyes as vacant as the sky? Gerry looked like Dan Quayle with a tan and muscles. Hell, just the other day Sorab had heard Bill Dixon snap, "Good God, Gerry. If you'd spend more time in the office than at the gym, maybe you'd learn something." Gerry had only flashed his usual smile, the one that made all the secretaries swoon. The thought of Gerry running the department was as preposterous as Paris Hilton running the Pentagon.

Grace zipped up her tan leather briefcase. "Well, gotta go. Tell you what, let's do lunch later this week. And let me know what you decide about your vacation."

Back in his office, Sorab locked the door and did something he'd never done before—kicked the trash can. The wrapper from the chicken sandwich he'd had for lunch rolled out onto the floor. The Coke can oozed a trickle of leftover liquid. Sorab reached for his briefcase. He was to meet Susan for dinner at Tropez tonight and now he'd have to drive like a maniac to get there on time. All because he had to sit in that schizophrenic bimbo's office and listen to her do what she did best—nothing. The B-word rose like a flame in Sorab's mind, but he threw some sand on it and doused it. He hated ugly words directed toward women. And thinking of women made him think of the dark, thin face of Juanita, the middle-aged Hispanic woman who cleaned the office every evening. He could not leave this mess on the floor for Juanita to clean up. Bending down, he picked up the sandwich wrapper and then the Coke can from where it had rolled under his desk and threw both into the trash can.

In the car, he wondered whether to call Susan to tell her he was running late. Eyeing his watch, he figured he could get there on time if he drove fast and hit mostly green lights. Instead, he reached for the cell phone and dialed his best friend Percy Soonawalla's number at the law firm. After the encounter with Grace, he needed a simple, uncomplicated, agendaless conversation with another male.

"Michelle?" he said into the phone. "Hi, it's Sorab. Is Percy still there?"

A moment later, Percy's familiar, comforting voice came on the other end. "Hey there, bossie. Kem che? You still at work? Want to meet for a quick drink?"

Sorab smiled. Good old Percy. They had been friends since third grade at Cathedral, and after Percy's mother's death, he'd practically lived with the Sethnas. Two years after Sorab had come to the U.S., Percy had followed. Now Percy was an immigration lawyer in the area's largest law firm. "Can't," he answered. "I'm meeting Susan for dinner."

"Ah, crappers. I've been craving a Scotch all bloody day."

Sorab sighed. "I know what you mean." He paused. "Remember that evening at Anil's when we were in ninth standard? Wish I could get pissing drunk like that again. Maybe it would help obliterate the memory of my latest encounter with my lovely boss."

"Why can't you?" came the prompt reply. "Arre yaar, that's why we came to America in the first place, right? To have the freedom to chase women and get loaded whenever we wanted to? After all, isn't that what the pursuit of happiness is all about—the right to down a few pegs of Scotch, to look up the skirts of our long-legged, blond American sisters, to eat enough meat and eggs to raise our cholesterol to new and uncharted heights? Heck, they don't call it the Promised Land for nothing.

"I'm telling you, Sorab, you should learn to enjoy your Constitution-enshrined rights," Percy continued. "That's why you're going to end up with an ulcer, bossie, from lack of fun. If I were you, I'd ditch Susan tonight and go out drinking with me."

And that's probably why you're on your fourth wife, Sorab thought. He still couldn't believe it sometimes—how Percy, who was no Gary Cooper, went through women the way other men went through dinner. And the weird part was, each time he married a new women, Percy's happiness was so immense and infectious that he managed to convince all his friends—not to mention himself—that this time he had found the real deal, his soul mate, his true love. And then, within a year or two, he would be moaning about alimony and divorce settlements. "You know what your problem is, bossie?" Sorab had once said to him. "You have the Elizabeth Taylor syndrome—you don't seem to understand that you can sleep with someone and not marry them."

Percy had shrugged. "Guilty as charged. Guess I'm a hopeless romantic."

Now he heard Percy suck his breath on the other end. "Chal ne, gadhera," Percy said. "You're going drinking with me or not?"

"I can't," Sorab said. "Susan's waiting for me at Tropez. Speaking of which, I'll have to hang up as soon as I get there, okay? Thanks to my inconsiderate boss, I'm running late. And Susan hates to wait alone in restaurants."

"Can't say I blame her," Percy said. "So what happened with the she-devil today?"

"The usual bullshit. Acted all surprised that I'm taking the week after Christmas off. When even the cleaning lady knows that I do this every year. And to make matters worse, she said . . ." But the thought of telling his old friend about Grace's threat to refuse him the promotion was too shameful for Sorab. After all, they were Cathedral boys and Cathedral boys were always successful. The Indians that he and Percy socialized with—doctors, lawyers, engineers, businessmen—had all come to America and built their fortunes. Many of them were married to American women; many of their children attended Yale and Stanford; most of them had large homes in the suburbs. Sorab had long let it be known among this circle that he soon expected to head his department, and someday, the company. Until a blond-haired bimbo with Bryan on her brain had decided to bust his balls. Shit. Now he was sounding like Percy, making alliterations.

"Hey. You still there?" Percy's voice came crisp and urgent on the phone.

Sorab exhaled. "Yup, I'm here. You know, bossie, I think you have the right idea—working for yourself, getting divorced when things don't work out, and trying your luck again."

Percy had heard something in his voice, as he'd known he would. "What's the matter, Sorab? Everything not okay at home?"

"Oh no, I mean, everything is reasonably fine. It's just that, Susan and I . . . that is, it's hard, you know, having Mamma with us for so long. I mean, it's the first time she's been here by herself since Daddy's death. And, I don't know, it's just not as much fun as when he was around. And Susan keeps asking me what Mamma's plans are, whether she's going to settle here permanently or not, and I don't know the answer myself. It's like every time I try to pin Mamma down, it's like trying to spear a fish, you know? She just wriggles and moves out of my grasp. So, you know, well, sometimes it causes friction between me and Susan."

Sorab could hear Percy frowning on the phone, as he did when he was concentrating on something. "Yeah, I've been meaning to ask you about this myself. Just was waiting for the holidays to get over. If she's going to stay, I need to file papers soon asking for an extension at least, depending on what she decides. You know what the damn INS is like—the continents will rejoin before we get an answer from them. She really must decide soon, Sorab."

"I know. I know. But to be honest with you, bossie, I don't know what it is—whether Mamma is depressed or something. Or maybe she was just used to Daddy making all the major decisions. But she seems paralyzed. One day, I get the feeling that she could live here, even be happy here. But the next minute she'll say something about her beloved Bombay and how she's looking forward to her bridge parties when she returns in February and then I don't know what to think. It's driving Susan crazy, also."

"Women," Percy said. "Women. Just goes to show, at any age they're still the same—indecisive, unpredictable, irresolute. And isn't it funny how everyone always misses Bombay as long as they're not living there? But listen. I'll talk to her, okay? You guys are coming to Homi and Perin's party this week, correct? I assume you're bringing Mamma to the party? Good. I'll try to say something to her then. As her lawyer, I need to know."

"That would be great. Maybe she'll be less evasive with you."

"Maybe I should have a talk with demon woman, also. Tell her to treat my best friend with more respect."

Sorab snorted. "Respect? That woman wouldn't know how to spell the word."

"Too bad you can't divorce your boss. I think they should start a whole new category of people you can divorce—bosses, teachers, immigration officials, parents, children, pets, landlords, Tom DeLay, Donald Trump, Wal-Mart greeters. After all, why should the joy of divorce be restricted to spouses?"

Sorab grinned. "I feel a new lawsuit coming on."

"Yeah, a class-action suit, representing ninety percent of all Americans."

Sorab pulled into the circular driveway of Tropez and parked his car in front of the black sign that said VALET PARKING. "You know something? You have the same idiotic sense of humor that you did in high school. Remember how you used to drive poor Mr. Singh nuts with your limericks and puns?" He handed his car keys to a young man in a tan shirt.

"Hey, you just made a pun yourself. Singh and nuts, get it? *Singh* means 'peanut' and you said—"

"I get it, I get it," Sorab groaned. "Ae, listen, I'm at the restaurant. I'll call you later, okay?"

"Go. Have a good time with your lovely wife. And tell her about my standing invitation—if she gets sick of you, she can always marry me instead. I'm sure Julie won't mind me taking another wife. I mean if the Muslims and the Mormons can—"

"I'll tell her," Sorab interrupted. He cast an eye around the restaurant for Amy, the dark-haired girl who usually seated him. "And hey, Percy—thanks for everything. As usual."

"No mention. Us guys have to stick together against these wicked women with their wily ways. Listen, don't worry. I'll talk to Tehmina mamma. We'll get things sorted out, okay?"

As he hung up, Sorab's eyes fell on Susan at a table near the window. As usual, she had brought a book to read while waiting for him. On their first official date, he had been stunned when Susan had shown up at the restaurant carrying a novel, and had misunderstood her reasons. Did you really think the date would be so boring you'd have to read? he'd asked her. But after all these years together, Sorab knew how shy Susan could be and how she hated waiting alone in a restaurant or in any public place. The book provided a welcome escape.

Susan looked up and spotted Sorab across the room. Shutting the book, she waved. Inexplicably, Sorab felt his throat tighten. Good old Susan. How solid, how substantial she felt after the brittle superficiality of Grace Butler. Susan would never use a word like *brilliantastic*. Susan was home, a harbor, a refuge from the gaudiness of the world.

As he crossed the restaurant to meet his wife, Sorab felt his body relax for the first time all day.

CHAPTER FOUR

"Hi, hon," Sorab said, bending down to kiss his wife on the cheek. "Sorry to keep you waiting. I was all ready to leave when Grace decided she had to talk to me just then."

Susan smiled. "It's okay. I figured you were running on Bombay time."

Was that a slam? Sorab gave his wife a closer look. These days, it was impossible to know what Susan was really thinking. That old closeness, where he could read Susan's thoughts and complete her sentences for her, seemed elusive now. And suddenly he felt the loss of that intimacy acutely, as strongly as he still felt the loss of his father, eight months after Rustom's death.

"Oh, for Christ's sake, Sorab. It was a *joke*. I told you it was okay. Stop being so damn sensitive."

This was not the way he had envisioned this evening going. The whole point of the dinner with Susan had been to spend some alone time together, away from his mother's benign but obtrusive presence. But two minutes into it, and already he was on the defensive, feeling much the same way as he did at home these days. Shit, he thought. Might as well have stayed home and saved myself fifty bucks. Cheaper to be miserable at home. He remembered his earlier encounter with Grace Butler and had the same feeling of the conversation galloping away from him. How did women do this? he wondered. How did they make a man feel guilty about taking a much-deserved vacation? How did they make a man who was about to shell out good money for dinner feel like a piece of shit for arriving five minutes late? He looked around for a waiter, unwilling to let Susan see how much her words had upset him.

"Hon," Susan said, cupping his hand in hers. "Listen, I'm . . ."

But just then the waiter, a new guy whom Sorab didn't recognize, came over to take their drink order. "Margarita, on the rocks," Sorab said. "With salt."

"Make that two," Susan added. Her hand still covered Sorab's.

She turned to him as soon as the waiter left. "Listen, let's just start again, okay? I feel like we got off on the wrong foot."

He made a conscious effort to shake off the gloom that hovered around him. "Okay." He smiled. "So picture me entering the restaurant, okay? And here's me bending down to kiss you. And I'm saying, 'Sorry, hon. Traffic was a bitch this evening.'"

"And I say, 'God, Sorab, you look drop-dead gorgeous tonight. Say, how about if we skip dinner and you know, um?'"

"Your place or mine?" he said, happy to play along.

Susan's eyes were green and golden in this light. "I'm afraid it will have to be my place. Your place has a little boy and his elderly grandmother and a goldfish."

His voice was husky. "And what will we do at your place?"

Susan licked her lips. "Anything you want. Anything. Satisfaction guaranteed."

Despite Susan's playfully exaggerated slutty impression, Sorab felt a slight stirring in his groin. "Darling," he said. "I'm beginning to think that skipping dinner is a great idea."

They were laughing as the waiter set down their drinks and took their meal order.

"Boy, this place knows how to make margaritas." Susan sighed. She took a long, hard gulp. "You know, I kinda wish I did have a place of my own—just a getaway place when Cookie and—and everything else—gets too much to handle."

He had heard what she hadn't said. "Mamma was being difficult today?" he asked quietly, dreading the answer.

"No, not really. I mean, she was gone shopping most of the day with Eva Metzembaum. Turns out they went to the farmers' market. God knows why. She came home loaded with fruits and vegetables. As luck would have it, I went grocery shopping after work today. So now we have bushels of tangerines and about five hundred pounds of okra at home."

Despite Susan's valiant attempt to keep her tone light, Sorab heard the frustration in her voice. He felt a moment's irritation at his mother. Why on earth did she have to go to the market on her own? She was forever telling Sorab that Cookie didn't eat enough fruits and vegetables. Was this her way of rubbing it in? His mother could be passive-aggressive, he knew that. All bloody Parsi women were.

To Susan he said, "She was probably just trying to be helpful. You know how much she wants to pull her own weight within the family."

Susan sighed heavily. "I know. Sorab, I know. It's just that—why can't she help in ways that are useful? I mean, the things I expect her to do—like clean the bathtub after a shower or vacuum on occasion, those things she won't do. Do you know that I have to rinse out the tub every day before I can take a shower? And I've told her so many times, 'Mamma, if you want to help, please take over the vacuuming.' But she waits until I finally bring out the machine. And then she insists on pulling it away from me."

Sorab felt the familiar rush of heat in the back of his neck that he felt each time Susan said something critical of Tehmina. He heard the frustration in his wife's voice, but behind his eyes there was another, older image—of his mother bent over the kitchen counter chopping onions, her face flushed from the steam from the pressure cooker and the sting of the onions. Do you realize that my mother spent—wasted—her entire youth cooking and taking care of five other people? he wanted to say to Susan. Dad and myself, my grandparents, and later, Percy. And that's not counting all the street urchins and stray dogs that she fed. Surely she has earned the right to relax in her own son's home? As for not rinsing out the tub each time, my mother lives in an apartment that has not seen a fresh coat of paint in twenty years. It's not meanness, Susan, it's just that the thought doesn't even occur to her. And I'm too embarrassed to tell her to do it. Besides, I hate the thought of my mother, with her bad hip and all, bending over that tub, looking for every telltale gray hair. I don't want her to feel like she is a guest in our home. I want her to believe this is her home.

"What?" Susan said. "You think I'm being a bitch?"

Not for the first time, Sorab marveled and bristled at his wife's perceptiveness. Even as Susan became more shrouded in mystery to him, she could still read him like a book.

"No, not a bitch. Not that at all. It's just that . . ."

It's just that . . . there are some things, some thoughts so elusive that they wiggle like fish out of the web of words. Some differences were so great that they were beyond language, beyond explanation. How envious Susan had been when he had first told her that his mother had always had servants. That the fisherwoman and the newspaper boy and the baker and the butcher all made their morning rounds to the house, delivering their wares. How easy, how luxurious Susan had imagined his mother's life to be. And yet that's not how he remembered her life, at all. What he remembered of his childhood was a blur of ringing doorbells and raised voices and his mother's tired, flushed face and the complaints of neighbors and the haggling with the vendors and the arguments with the servants and the chain of unexpected visitors and demanding relatives who dropped in without calling first. And somehow, like the conductor of a mad orchestra, his mother had to manage it all—had to tame the crashing protests of the cymbals, hush the under-the-breath rumblings of the percussion, console the aggrieved wail of the violin. He had never asked and his mother had never said, but Sorab knew that Tehmina would have willingly traded in the servants and the vendors who came to her door for a dishwasher that didn't complain, a vacuum cleaner that didn't ask for a raise, a supermarket where the prices were fixed, a clothes dryer that didn't talk back, a food processor that chopped onions without leaving a trail of tears in its wake.

He looked at Susan, trying so hard to understand him, and he felt the gap between them as enormous as the distance between Bombay and Ohio. How to explain to his wife the rift that opened up in his heart each time there was a conflict between the two women he loved most in the world? How to describe to her his first few years in America, when he had felt that rootlessness that only immigrants feel, so that he felt as if his head was touching the skies of America while his feet were rooted in Bombay, as if he was straddling two continents. He had looked forward to his dreams in those days, because in his dreams he could look out of his apartment window and there would be his father's old Ambassador parked on the snowy street. Or Mamma was cooking him fish curry rice in the tiny kitchen of his Ohio apartment. In his dreams, his fingertips still touched his old life. Sorab wanted to tell Susan about how, for years, he had longed for his life to be seamless, how he yearned to have all his loved ones under the same roof. And how, after his mother and father began to visit him in Ohio, he had finally felt whole, complete, seamless.

"What're you thinking, honey?"

Sorab shook his head briskly. "Nothing. I mean, that is, well, I am just sorry that things are not smooth between you and Mamma this time, you know?"

Susan's lips disappeared in a thin line. Had she always worn this icy expression of displeasure? Sorab wondered. Or was it simply more frequent and noticeable these days?

"I'm sorry, too," Susan said. "I—I just don't know what's gotten into her during this visit. She's just so—I don't know—obstinate or something this time. Like I try to help, but she just doesn't seem as free and outgoing as she has in the past."

"Or maybe she's just hurting," Sorab snapped. His voice was hard but he didn't care. "Did you ever think of that? After all, the woman's just lost her husband of almost forty years."

Susan stared at Sorab openmouthed. Her eyes glittered with tears. "That's so not fair. That's a real low blow, Sorab. You think I'm not aware of the loss that she's suffered? Hell, you think it's been easy living with you the last eight months, the way you've been moping around? Oh, I know you try to hide it, honey, but I know you miss your father. And here's a news flash—I miss Rustom daddy, too."

"Susan," Sorab started. "I'm sorry."

"You-all ready to order?" It was the new waiter, and for a moment Sorab hated his guts. Bloody interrupting idiot.

"Go ahead," he said to Susan. "What would you like?"

He turned to his wife as soon as the waiter had left. "Honey, listen to me. I know things are rough now. I . . . I honestly don't know what to do to make anything easier on anybody. It's just such a hard time. You know, I wish Mamma would decide what she wants to do, once and for all. It's the bloody uncertainty that's killing me."

"Speaking of which," Susan interrupted. "If she does decide to settle in America, we're going to have Rosalee come to clean every week, instead of our usual every two weeks, okay? This is the one thing I'm going to insist on, Sorab. I don't care if—"

"I thought we'd already decided we'd do that," he said, hearing the coldness in his voice. "Why are you bringing that up again, Susan?"

"Because I know you think I'm being too nitpicky about the house. I know you don't get it, my need for a clean bathroom and a neat house."

"Susan, please stop treating me like I'm some third-world bumpkin. What do you think, I don't appreciate a clean bathroom? It's just that other things—like peace at home, f'instance—matter as much to me. You don't know how you come across with Mamma at times—like you're some white-skinned princess ordering her underlings around."

"Listen to you. Just fucking listen to yourself." Susan's voice was loud but he resisted the urge to ask her to lower the volume, knowing it would only infuriate her more. "We were talking about the house and suddenly you've brought race and global politics into it. Honey, I married you knowing you were a—how'd you put it?—a third-world bumpkin, okay? And what the color of your skin has to do with my not wanting hair in my damn bathtub when I take a shower, I don't know." Susan was choking on her words now, using the cloth napkin to wipe away the hot tears hovering below her eyes.

"Dammit. This is the last thing I want to do tonight, get into a fight with you. All I was trying to tell you is . . ." He stared at her dumbly, miserably, not sure of how to salvage the evening. "Maybe asking Mamma to live with us is not a good idea," he mumbled finally. "Maybe she needs to go back home at the end of her six months."

"So that she can be lonely in that big flat all alone? And so that you can go crazy with worry each time she has a cold or something?

Or are you planning on rushing back each time something's wrong there? Remember how you almost went out of your mind during the Bombay riots? And that was when your dad was still alive." Susan's voice softened. "Sorab, I love your mother, you know that. At least, you *should* know that after all these years. We'll . . . we'll manage something, okay? If she decides to live in the U.S. we'll make it work, I promise. Part of the problem is, with the holidays and all, we're all so stressed out. Let's just get through the next few weeks."

Sorab sighed heavily. "That's the other thing. Grace called me in her office today and acted all shocked that I'm taking the week after Christmas off. Asked me to reconsider my plans."

Susan's eyes blazed. "She asked you what?"

He felt a spurt of gratitude for Susan, for how instinctively she leaped to his defense. That's the advantage of being married, he thought. There's someone always on your team when you're battling the world. "Yeah, she wants me to consider not taking the week off. Seems as if she has a ski trip planned the week after Christmas."

"I'll tell you what you should reconsider. You should reconsider whether you want to keep working for your asshole boss. The woman's making your life miserable, Sorab. Maybe it's time to look for a new job."

His earlier gratitude turned into irritation. "Good jobs don't grow on trees, hon," he said. "Just the stock options in this job alone are—"

"Fuck the stock options." Susan's voice was loud enough that the elderly couple sitting at the table to their right turned to look at them. The older man shot a look at Sorab that was equal parts sympathy and bemusement. "Goddammit, Sorab, who are you turning into? God, I remember a time when you would've handled ten Grace Butlers with the flick of your wrist. I mean, you've never even had to hunt for a job, hon. Just spread the word that you're looking and they'll come to you. What the hell do you care about some piddly-assed stock options?"

"They're not piddly-assed," he mumbled automatically. "And I'm not as young as I once was, Susan. And we now have Cookie to think of."

"I *am* thinking of Cookie. And what Cookie deserves is a father who is happy at his job, who carries himself with his head held high. That's what Cookie needs, not a goddamn college fund. And as for not being as young, what are you? A hundred and four? Fifty-four? You're thirty-eight years old, for Christ's sake. Your father went mountain climbing in Argentina when he was in his fifties."

"My father was a king," Sorab said. "I'm not in his league, I'm afraid."

"Bullshit. You're every bit the man your father was. I know it and let me tell you something—your father knew it, too. He was so proud of you. Do you know what he once told me? That you were the most honorable man he knew."

Sorab stared at the mural on the wall behind Susan, not daring to speak. God damn these tears. He could feel Susan's eyes on him as he struggled to pull himself together. "Thank you," he said at last. "I . . . thank you for telling me."

Susan nodded. "He was proud of you, you know that." She waited until his lower lip had stopped trembling. "Hon, listen. I know you're under a lot of pressure. But don't let Grace or anyone make you doubt yourself." She smiled. "Remember, I had a hundred and one suitors and I chose you. Doesn't that tell you how terrific you are?"

They were on familiar ground now. "And of course, they were attracted to your extreme modesty and humility." He grinned.

"And my outrageous good looks. Let's not forget the good looks."

He looked her in the eye. "Darling, I never forget the good looks." He let his eyes fall suggestively on her breasts.

Susan burst out laughing. "Stop, you creep. You're embarrassing me."

Sorab signaled to the waiter for two more margaritas. Turning to her, he said, "I'd like to embarrass you good and proper. In bed, tonight."

She groaned. "God deliver us from the Parsis and their awful sense of humor."

"Sweetheart, there are some things that I never joke about." He was smiling deeply.

"That's the other thing. If Mamma decides to stay with us, I definitely want us to move into a bigger house. Let's look for one with a mother-in-law suite, okay? It's hard to, you know, make love, knowing she's in the next room."

"Honey, my mother has forgotten what sex feels like, much less what it sounds like. If she ever hears us, she probably thinks we're using the weight machine, or something."

"Don't kid yourself. Your father was a passionate, red-blooded man. And I've seen pictures of your mom in her youth. She was quite a looker. I'm sure they had a great sex life."

Sorab shuddered. "Stop it. I don't want to go there. Some things are too awful to contemplate."

"Chickenshit." Susan laughed. "Why is it that everyone has such a hard time imagining their parents in bed?"

"Well, can you? Can you see your mom and dad, you know, doing it?"

"Only after I've had two margaritas," Susan said, taking another sip.

Sorab tossed back his head and laughed, so that for a moment he looked ten years younger. This is what I love about Susan, he thought—the sharpness, the wit, the humor. He reached over and squeezed her hand. "I love you. You know that?"

She squeezed back. "I do know that. Though sometimes I wonder if you know how much I love you."

They were smiling at each other when the waiter came to clear their plates. Shoo, Sorab thought. Vamoose. Disappear. Instead, the waiter asked, "Dessert?"

"An order of fried coconut ice cream," Sorab said. "Two spoons." That was the other great thing about being married. Some things, some traditions, you just knew.

"Suse," Sorab said. "I'll talk to Mamma, okay? About deciding what her plans are? Though, actually, I spoke to Percy today and he said he'd talk to her also, at Homi's party. So you don't worry about it. I know you have enough on your plate, just getting through Christmas."

"Last Christmas Rustom daddy was still alive," Susan said softly. "It all feels wrong this year."

Sorab leaned back in his chair. "I know. I also don't know what to do about . . . I keep wondering if I should give Mamma a present from Dad this year or whether that will only make things worse. He bought her something each Christmas, you know? God knows how the tradition started, given that we're Parsis and all. But you know what Dad was like—any excuse to have a party or give a gift."

"Let me think about it. If I come across something that I think she'll like, I'll pick it up for her, okay?"

"Thanks. I haven't even bought her something from me, yet. I know we have the shawl from both of us. But I want to get her a small something from me. You know how sentimental she is. Maybe I'll just pick up a photo frame and put in a picture of the four of us."

"That's part of the problem. If she's going back to India in February, I don't want to buy her heavy things. If she's staying, it doesn't matter."

"I know. Percy's going to impress all this on her when he talks to her."

They ate their ice cream in a companionable silence. "Well, as much as I'd like to sit here all night, I guess we should get back to that little boy of ours," Susan said finally. "I hope he didn't give Mom a hard time about going to bed."

"I'm so friggin' stuffed that if they'd just grease the floor, I could slide out of here." He got up to help Susan with her dark blue coat.

"Next year, you're going back to watching your cholesterol," Susan said as they stepped out into the frosty December night. The unseasonably warm day they'd had earlier in the week already felt like a distant memory.

"Next year," Sorab repeated as he opened Susan's car door for her. "Hard to imagine a whole year has gone by." He thought of his father's death, how he had been in a plane six hours after getting the news of Rustom's heart attack, the mad drive from the airport to Breach Candy Hospital. Rustom was still alive when he got there, as if he'd used every ounce of his formidable willpower to stay alive to see his only son one last time. "Take care of Tehmina," the old man had whispered.

"You don't have to tell me that, Daddy. You know I will. Now, rest quietly," Sorab replied. It was their last conversation.

"Hon." Susan rolled down her car window and looked up to where Sorab was standing. "Next year will be better, I promise. Just . . . just trust me, okay? Everything will work out fine."

He waited until she pulled her car out of its space before walking toward his own vehicle. Good old Susan, he thought. Good old American optimism. That's why he'd come to this country, to bask in the warm glow of its can-do spirit, its optimism, its blithe shrugging off of the past and history. And for a long time it had infected him, so that he had felt golden, untouchable, transcendent. But his father's death had made him realize that fate was stronger than faith, that even America could not protect him from life's tricks and detours. And now, for the first time, under Grace Butler's tinsel presence, even the American Dream was beginning to lose its sheen, to look a bit tarnished. All of America was now beginning to feel like a reality show, a Hollywood production. It was no longer enough, it seemed, for its citizens to be Joe Blow or Sorab Sethna. Now everybody had to be Tina Brown or Tom Cruise or Steve Jobs. Everything was cutting edge. Everyone needed an extreme makeover. Everything was now available 24/7; everybody was wired and Bluetoothed; everyone was an American Idol. It was no longer enough to live your life; now you had to be a Survivor.

Sorab stood in the large parking lot, watching the flecks of snow dance in the golden halo of the streetlights. The cold wind whipping his face felt punishing but liberating. Maybe it will be a white Christmas, after all, he thought. Earlier this week, he'd had his doubts. And maybe next year *would* be better, as Susan had promised. Nobody else had made him that promise—not the politicians, not the newspaper writers, not the nihilistic rock and rollers, not the pretty, jaded Hollywood stars. Not even his mother, steeped in that brew of pessimism, fatalism, and superstition that made up the Indian character, could ever make him that bold a promise. Only Susan could—and had—made him that promise.

So Sorab got in his car and made his way home to that promise.

CHAPTER FIVE

This boy is as slippery as an open bottle of olive oil, Tehmina thought. And I'm too old to run after him like this.

"Cavas," she panted. "Stop this nataak, please. It's way past your bedtime. Your mummy-daddy will make mincemeat out of me when they get home and find that you're not asleep."

Cavas danced a jig just out of Tehmina's reach. "My name is not Cavas," he sang. "It's Cookie. And don't use Gujarati words when you talk to me. I'm an American boy and I only understand English."

"Arre wah. Your daddy is an Indian, so you are half-Indian, also. Never forget that, deekra."

The grin on Cavas's face turned into a frown. "No, I'm not," he said, stomping his foot. "Indians are old and they speak funny. Mommy says I'm an all-American boy."

Too late Tehmina saw that the line of conversation was inciting her grandson. She needed to calm him down before the boy threw a full-blown tantrum. "Listen, Cavas—I mean, Cookie," she said in her most appeasing voice. "If you come to bed in the next two minutes, you know what I'll do? I'll let you eat a Cadbury's éclair. Would you like that?"

Cookie gazed at her thoughtfully. "Will you also read me a story?"

"Of course. What about the Akbar and Birbal book I got you last year?"

"No. That's a boring book. I want you to read *Even Steven.*"

He's just a seven-year-old boy, Tehmina told herself. Remember what Sorab said the other day—he's just going through a stage where he has to pretend to hate everything that isn't the norm. "He's just trying to fit in with his friends, Mamma," Sorab had said. "Kids at this age are very conscious about fitting in. So don't take it personally, achcha?"

And yet, Tehmina had to admit that Cavas's disdain for everything Indian felt like a rejection of her. Just last year, when his grandfather was still alive, Cavas seemed enthralled by Rustom's stories about Akbar the King and his wily minister, Birbal. He even listened intently when Rustom told him who Omar Khayyám was. But then, everything is different this year, she reminded herself. Why should poor Cavas be immune to the changes that have entered all our lives since Rustom's death?

Tehmina pulled herself together. "One, two, three," she counted. "If you're not in bed by the time I count seven, no chocolate for you."

"Okay, okay," Cavas squealed as he tore across the room and jumped under the covers. "Now, where's my chocolate?"

As Tehmina dug into the pocket of her dress for the small treat, she felt a hot rush of guilt. Susan, she knew, would be shocked if she found out that Tehmina was bribing her son into bed with a piece of candy. Especially after he'd brushed his teeth.

She went into the bathroom and got a glass of water. "Now gargle properly after you finish your treat," she said. She hoped that Cavas knew better than to mention the chocolate to his parents. She wanted to tell him to let this be their little secret, but her pride stopped her.

"Are you going to read to me?" Cavas asked from under the covers. But he was yawning even as he asked and Tehmina knew he would not last till the end of the story.

She hated herself for asking but despite herself, she said, "Don't you like the Akbar and Birbal storybook anymore? Last year, you loved that book."

"I only like it when Rustom nana reads it to me," Cavas said, and Tehmina's heart wobbled at his words.

"He was a good reader, eh, deekra?" she said, caressing the boy's hair. "Your nana really loved you. He picked out that book special-special for you."

"Granna," Cavas said. "How come Nana can't read to me anymore?"

Tehmina stared at her grandson, unsure of what to say. Sorab had rushed to Bombay immediately after Rustom had had his heart attack, leaving Cavas and Susan at home. What had Susan told him to explain his father's abrupt departure? What had Sorab explained to the boy after his return? "Nana's in heaven," she said at last. "He now reads to the angels, instead of to you. But every night when you say your prayers and get into bed, he looks down and kisses you good night."

Cavas nodded. "I know. Dad says Nana is keeping watch on our house when we're asleep. One time, during a thunderstorm I was scared and stuff, but Dad said the thunder was only Nana laughing at a joke that God told."

Tehmina smiled. "Your grandpa had a laugh like thunder," she said. "Anu, our neighbor in Bombay, always used to say that Rustom could raise the dead with his big laugh."

The boy scrunched his face. "Why do you always talk about

Bombay? Here we're trying so hard to make you feel at home, Granna, but you just keep talking about Bombay and stuff."

Tehmina stared at her grandson in horror. For a minute, it had seemed as if the boy was channeling his mother. Cavas's voice had that same starched, tight-lipped quality that Susan's did whenever she was frustrated with her mother-in-law. Also the same self-righteous outrage and put-out feeling.

The boy was simply parroting his mother's words, Tehmina knew. But suddenly all the things she couldn't say to her daughter-in-law, all the hot shame and unease that Susan's suffering presence elicited in her, she now directed toward the boy. "Because Bombay's my home, you understand?" she said, not trying to keep the fierceness out of her voice. "Just like this is your home. I've spent all my life there. And while others may only see a dirty, filthy city where the buses break down and the electricity doesn't work, the true Bombayite sees past all that, sees the city's big, generous heart. And that's what most people can't see."

Cavas's lower lip was trembling. "Then go back to your stinkin' city," he yelled. "See if I care. And," he added deliberately, "I won't miss you at all. I'll just go visit with Grandma Olsen instead."

Watching Cavas's outraged, teary face, watching his tiny, heaving chest, Tehmina felt her own chest fill with love and remorse. The boy is caught up in my indecision, she realized. Children need stability and the poor boy doesn't know where I'll be two months from now. Why do adults think children are oblivious to the family dramas that are enacted in their presence?

"Cavas—I mean, Cookie," she said. "Just because I love Bombay doesn't mean I don't love you. In fact, I love you so very much that I can—" She stopped, unsure of how to proceed, of whether to let the little boy lying beside her see the raw, jagged edges of her own heart. It had been so long since she had raised Sorab that she had forgotten how to act before a young child. And Cookie was so much more mercurial, so much more outspoken and emotional than Sorab had ever been. Her son had been a good, proper Indian boy, whereas her grandson was so—what was the word?—so *American*. Yes, that was the best word to describe Cavas. She never felt as excruciatingly, painfully Indian as she did when she was around Cavas. Rustom, on the other hand, had simply taken his grandson on his own terms. How effortlessly Rustom had adapted to life in America—mowing the lawn with Cavas trailing along, planting a vegetable garden alongside Susan, going grocery shopping with Tehmina and casually filling the cart with products from the overflowing shelves as if he'd done that his whole life. Why, Rustom even drove in America—a source of great pride to his son. Drove on the right side of the road despite the fact that he'd driven on the "wrong" side (as Susan would say) all his years in India. And to Tehmina's utter amazement, Rustom never so much as veered into the wrong lane.

She felt Cavas's eyes on her and realized with a start that the boy was waiting for her to finish her sentence. "I love you so much that you are part of my own liver," immediately realizing from Cavas's disgusted expression that translating the sentiment from Gujarati to English was a mistake.

"Ewww," the boy squealed. "That's gross, Granna."

She bent and nuzzled him with her chin. "I love you so much that I can give you a million, billion kisses and still give you a few more."

"That's nothing," Cavas said promptly. "Dad gives me a zillion, trillion kisses every night." A cagey look came upon his face. "You know what you can do for me to show your love?"

"What?" Tehmina asked, knowing she was walking into a trap. She felt helpless in her love for this little boy with his red lips and long, dark eyelashes.

"You can lie down with me until I fall asleep." He smiled his most guileless smile. "And," he added, cupping his mouth to her ear, "if you do that, I'll even let you call me Cavas."

How well she knew that seductive look. It seemed like a week ago when Sorab had smiled the same smile—the time she smelled a whiff of cigarette smoke on him when he came home from school, and knew immediately that he had been smoking, the time he had begged her to let him attend an overnight picnic with his college friends, admitting upon her prodding that there would be girls present, the time Rustom had driven by Flora Fountain and had almost run off the road when he'd spotted his only son taking part in a student protest against Bombay University. Rustom had come home and paced the balcony until he had spotted his son's slender figure enter the apartment building at seven that evening. "How was your day, sonny?" he had asked casually, though Tehmina had heard the dangerous edge in his voice. "How was college?"

"Oh, fine," Sorab said with a yawn. "Just the usual stuff. But I'm tired today."

"Never knew accounting and marketing could be so exhausting," Rustom replied, and this time, there was no mistaking his tone.

Sorab looked up sharply. "I—well, you know how hard—"

"What I do know is that I cannot drive through Fountain without seeing my only child acting like a common mawali on the streets of Bombay," Rustom said quietly, ignoring the pacifying look Tehmina threw his way. "What I also know is that my son lies to his parents."

Instead of getting flustered or defensive, Sorab threw his father a shy smile. "That's exactly why I didn't say anything, Daddy. I knew you wouldn't approve."

Despite his anger, Sorab's lack of guile seemed to disarm his father. "So, you're admitting that you were on the streets instead of in college?" he said. Tehmina could hear the anger leaking out of his voice.

"Sure. But ask me why I was there, Daddy." Without giving them a chance to reply, Sorab continued. "We were protesting Bombay University's decision to rewrite the college curriculum. They want the whole country to be a fundamentalist Hindu nation—and they're rewriting the history books to glorify the Hindu majority. They're saying, if Pakistan can be an Islamic country, why can't India be a Hindustan? Can you imagine, Dad? These people don't believe in secularism—and they're brainwashing us with all their false mumbo jumbo. It's like the Muslims and the Parsis and the Catholics simply don't exist."

"Yah, without us Parsis to build it, their Bombay would still be a bunch of islands floating around in the sea," Rustom growled. Tehmina marveled at how effortlessly her son had managed to defuse his father's anger. As if he had sensed her relief, Rustom scowled at his son. "But that's no excuse to interrupt your education with all this nonsense," he said. "Best to leave all this agitation and protest to the professional troublemakers."

Sorab looked his father straight in the eye. "But, Daddy," he said, "fighting for what you believe is part of my education, too. You are the one who taught me that."

Remembering that incident, Tehmina felt a pang of remorse. What had happened to that quietly resolute boy? What had happened to his clear-eyed way of seeing the world? She had thought that going to America would broaden Sorab's horizons, would make him stand on the shoulders of his parents and see farther than they ever had. But instead, the opposite had happened. In some strange way, Sorab seemed to have shrunk and his world had narrowed. He seemed personally happier, yes, but—but maybe that was the whole problem. Living in this housing complex, where the layouts of many of the homes were identical and even the cars and the play swings in the backyards all looked the same, Sorab had traded a dull contentment for the intense passion of his boyhood. Tehmina didn't get it—how could a boy who had grown up on the crowded, tumultuous streets of Bombay, who had jostled with the noisy crowds to catch a train to college, who had eaten pani puri and drunk sugarcane juice from roadside booths, who had witnessed the whole carnival of human experience—the millionaires, the lepers, the jewelry stores, the slum colonies—how could such a boy encase himself in a timid, clean, antiseptic world that was free from germs, bacteria, passion, human misery? Where even the straws were wrapped in plastic and people at gyms sprayed their seats each time they rose from a machine, as if human sweat was more dangerous than the chemicals they sprayed. (She knew, she had visited the gym in their housing colony.) And how did he expect his sixty-six-year-old mother to live in that world?

The worst part was, there was no reaching Sorab. He had disappeared, like a snail in a shell. Over dinner the day of the run-in with Tara, for instance, she had tried to tell her son about how their neighbor had left the two boys alone at home, how she and Susan had taken them in. If Susan hadn't been present, she might have confided in Sorab the fact that Susan had made it clear that she didn't want any more interactions with the family next door, and how it broke Tehmina's heart to think of those poor boys in that home. She may have even broached the subject of gathering up some of the books and toys Cookie had outgrown and presenting them to Josh and Jerome. But as it was, Sorab had listened for a few moments, nodded his head, rolled his eyes, and said, "Some people should never be parents in the first place. I'll be real glad when that woman moves out of Antonio's home."

Tehmina suddenly thought of Percy, Sorab's best friend, whom she and Rustom had virtually raised after Percy's mother had died when he was a boy. Sorab and all the others in their group teased Percy for his multiple marriages and Tehmina herself was shocked and saddened by how often the boy traded wives. But one thing about Percy, she now thought. America has not changed him the way it has the others. She had heard the outrage in Percy's voice when he had described an immigration case where a political refugee had run up against the cold heartlessness of the government. She had heard him discuss passionately the injustices that his clients faced as a result of laws put in place after the horror of 9/11. Somehow, Percy's world seemed larger and more real than Sorab's narrowly defined world of home, family, and office.

She had offended her own sense of maternal loyalty with this last thought. That's not fair, she argued with herself. It's Percy's job that forces him to have to deal with the outside world. Whereas my Sorab—working for a large advertising and consulting agency—his job is by definition limited to the concerns of his clients. Why should he worry about immigration and such? And it's not as if he's not generous. Tehmina knew that Sorab had written a check for $500 when the tsunami hit. And when she was in Bombay, Sorab was forever telling her to let him know if there were any deserving cases that needed help. Four years ago, he and Susan and the other local Parsis had arranged for Dina Madan's infant daughter to come to the Cleveland Clinic for the heart surgery that had saved her life. Dina had even brought little Malika to Rustom's funeral and had the child shake hands with Sorab. "Here's the man who saved your life, deekra," she'd said to the little girl. "He is a great man, just as his daddy was."

"Granna, are you going to lie down with me or not?" Cookie's plaintive voice brought her back into the present. She looked at the sweet face, so much like Sorab's despite the fair skin and light brown hair. If I had not met Rustom, you would not have been born, she marveled, and despite its banality, she felt her heart warm at the thought.

"You can call me Cavas, if you like," Cookie repeated. "But just for tonight." She forced herself to look sufficiently impressed by his magnanimous offer. "All right, Cavas," she said, getting under the covers with him. "I'll lie with you for a few minutes. But no talking, you hear? Good night."

They were silent for a second. Then Cookie said, "Did you know my mom when she was little?"

"No, Cookie, of course not. She lived here in America, whereas we—we lived in India."

The boy looked lost in thought for a minute. Then he shrugged. "I thought so."

"What made you think that?"

He shrugged again and Tehmina had to be satisfied with that. "Do you remember Bombay at all?" she asked. She knew that she was risking Cavas being fully awake again, but she couldn't help herself. Getting Cavas to acknowledge his love for India was like a pimple she kept prodding at with her fingernail. How foolish you are, she scolded herself. The boy was only three when he came to India. Of course he doesn't remember.

"I remember Grandpa," the boy replied. "He took me to his office one day. There was a big picture of me and Mom and Dad on his wall."

Tehmina blinked her tears away. That photograph now sat on top of her TV in her apartment in Bombay. She decided against telling Cookie that.

"Grandpa was *fun*," Cookie said. Tehmina knew immediately what the child was too kind to say—*and you're not*. Did she imagine the hint of accusation she heard in his voice?

She sighed. "Everybody loved Grandpa. I did, too. Still do."

Cavas must have heard something in her voice because he leaned over and kissed her on the cheek. "I love you, Granna," he said in that singsong voice he used when petting a puppy or talking to children younger than he was. "And you're so much nicer than that stupid old babysitter. Nighty night." He curled into a ball and pressed himself tight against Tehmina.

"Good night, little kitten," Tehmina whispered, kissing the top of his head. But it was *her* heart that was purring.

CHAPTER SIX

Snow.

It had been snowing all night long, with a quiet, ruthless efficiency. Dense cotton balls floated and landed upon the skeleton trees, bestowing upon them a jaw-dropping beauty. The beauty was so acute, so startling, that the motorists returning from last-minute trips to the malls, who slid and swerved off the road, were unsure whether to blame the wet, slick roads or the distracting magnificence of those snow-covered trees. Or perhaps it was the sight of the countless, dizzying pebbles of white, exploding like fireworks before their windshields, and making their eyes wide with dazzle and fatigue.

Sorab lay awake in bed, glad to be home. His head was a little woozy from the two margaritas he had consumed earlier in the evening. Susan's gentle snoring, which usually irritated him, filled him with a soft, mellow peace tonight, so that he felt as if her familiar breathing was a kind of prayer, a reward. I'm home with my family, he thought to himself, and as always, the words filled him with wonder.

In the golden light of the street lamp that cast a beam into their bedroom, Susan's hair shone like satin on the pillow. He looked at her familiar, thin face—the long, straight nose, the narrow lips, the high cheekbones, the arched eyebrows. Even after all these years, Susan's simple Midwestern beauty still affected him. He looked away from her to see flecks of snow, thick and white as dandruff, coming down outside his window. He shivered and the next second his thoughts went back to those shapeless, formless lines of the street people who lined the pavements of Bombay, sleeping on the hard sidewalks through all kinds of weather. Tugging on his down comforter so that it covered his ears—he had learned during his very first winter in Ohio that covering his ears was the key to staying warm in this hard, cold country—he thought of the faded, fraying cotton sheets that the homeless in Bombay used to cover their thin, shivering bodies. What a life he'd had. First, to be born middle class in India. That alone was like winning the friggin' lottery. And then, to have come to the U.S. To America, the place that had dominated his dreams since he was at least twelve years old. Of course, in those days America had meant what to him? Probably no more than Levi's jeans, Wrigley's chewing gum, Coca-Cola, Archie comic books, and rock and roll. Above all, rock and roll. It was the music that had seduced him, that had planted the seed in him, had led him out of his perfectly happy, complacent, normal life in Bombay, to seek a new challenge, a new horizon, a new home. Others may have seen America as the land of milk and honey. He saw it as the home of rock and roll. The boy whose father had worshipped classical music was ready to order Beethoven to roll over and tell Tchaikovsky the news.

He still remembered the look of hot envy on the faces of his college friends when he announced his admission at an American college. "Fuck, man," his friend Hanif had said. "America. Damn. That's better than—what?—than sleeping with Cindy Crawford."

And indeed it had been. Better than sleeping with Cindy Crawford, better than fucking Juliette Binoche, better than attending a U2 concert, better than a cup of hot cocoa in front of a roaring fire. He had always thought he was ambitious, a dreamer, but his life had turned out to be more audacious and grander than even his dreams.

And as if being allowed into America was not gift enough, there were all these other gifts. A son, as perfect and pure as the moon. A wife who was sometimes prickly, yes, who smiled less often than he would like, yes, but who loved him and was fierce and loyal in that love. A career that, until the appearance of Grace Butler, had soared like a rocket. A home that was beautiful and comfortable and, most important, large enough that he could offer to share it with his mother.

His mother. A thin needle of worry was making its way into the fabric of contentment that Sorab had been weaving for himself. Mamma really needs to make up her mind, he thought, remembering his conversation with Susan at the restaurant. This not knowing is too hard on Susan. Two months will fly by and there's so much we need to do if she's going to stay—start the immigration paperwork, look for a bigger house, decide what to do with the house in Bombay. Besides, God, it would just be nice to know whether we're going to have another member here come spring. Susan and I both need the time to make the mental adjustment, dammit. Cookie, too, probably. I need to prepare him for the separation if she's going back, but how can I if I don't know what she's thinking? Mamma is so damn secretive. Was she always like this? Or has Daddy's passing away changed her? How come I don't know the answer to that? I'll have to ask Susan what she thinks. If I can bear to ask Susan any question regarding Mamma, that is. What's up with her these days, anyhow? This thin-lipped, schoolmarmish look that she gets on her face? Has she always worn this look and I've just never seen it before? How come I don't know the answer to that? I'll have to ask Mamma.

He caught himself. You stupid son of a bitch; he laughed to himself. Trying to figure out the fairer sex. If you did, they'd give you the MacArthur genius grant. You're surrounded by secretive, manipulative women, isn't that a fact? If it's not your wife and mother, it's your lovely boss at work. Wait, make that your fantastical-fabulous-scrumptiously-divinely-delightful boss. Why settle for one adjective to describe her when you can use ten?

"Sorab, for crying out loud. What are you doing?" Susan asked sleepily.

"What?"

"Why are you tossing and turning in bed? Jesus, you're keeping me up, hon."

"Sorry. I thought you were asleep."

" 'Sokay. Go back to sleep."

He lay quiet and still for a few minutes. Then, "Hon? You still awake?"

"I am now." Susan's voice was between a sigh and a hiss.

"It's snowing. I mean, it's really, really beautiful. You wanna come stand at the window and look at it with me?"

Susan groaned. "Oh, for God's sake, Sorab, you can't be serious. I just finally got warm."

He sat in the dark, saying nothing. But he was listening, hard. What he was listening for, he wasn't sure. But he knew he'd know it if he heard it.

He was fighting back the disappointment that was forming at the back of his throat when Susan spoke. "Okay, come on. Just for a minute, okay? Jesus, I must be crazy." As Susan threw back her covers, he felt as if she'd thrown back the gloom that was beginning to descend on him. His step was light as his feet hit the cold wooden floor.

They stood at the window watching the languid fall of the snow. Sorab put his arm around Susan. "This is like old times," he said. "Remember, in college, how we used to wake up early and go to the river just to see the sunrise?"

Susan yawned. "Yes, dear. But that was like a hundred years ago, when we were young and pretty and—unemployed."

He smiled. "Those were the days, huh? Unemployment sounds pretty damn great these days."

Susan squeezed his hand. "Look at that maple tree in Ruby's yard. It's like a postcard. I'll bet you anything Mom will want to take a picture of it in the morning." She leaned into him. "You were right, hon," she murmured. "It really is a beautiful snowfall."

"Worth waking up for?"

"Ask me in the morning."

He kissed her head. "Well, seeing how you are wide awake and all, can I at least make it worth your while, darling?"

"And how do you propose to do that?"

"Allow me to demonstrate."

Snow is so different from rain, Tehmina thought. Rain in Bombay was like a heavy-footed, clumsy intruder, crashing and falling over the furniture, dropping the china, making its heavy, sweaty presence felt upon the hammered, beaten streets. But the snow here! Tehmina marveled at its stealth, its subterfuge, its light touch. Why, one could sleep through the night and not even know that it had snowed until morning.

Rain and snow. The perfect way to describe the difference between Bombay and America, Tehmina thought. One was loud, chaotic, tumultuous, and erratic. The other was calm, antiseptic, genteel, and polite. So ironic it is, she thought. In Bombay, where everything is dangerous, people live their lives bindaas, fearlessly, almost thoughtlessly. Here, where there is no reason to fear anything, these people are afraid of life itself. How can they survive like this, watching and weighing everything? From terrorism to germs to the flu, these people were frightened by everything. A whole country going into a panic because there was a shortage of the flu vaccine. And sealing their pain pill bottles in such a tamper-proof way that no adult with arthritis could ever open one of them. Even their drinking straws came wrapped in plastic. Whereas, in Bombay, dear God, we breathed the foulest air and ate food at roadside stalls where they washed the plates in water as brown as mud. And look at me—a robust, hale and hearty sixty-six years old. Old Dr. Mehta always used to say, "If there's ever a plague or global catastrophe, Tehmi, I swear those Americans will die like flies. They have no immunity against anything. And us Indians, with our iron constitutions, we will rule the world."

It was the same thing with seat belts. My God, how Sorab and Susan used to look at her when she'd refused to wear her seat belt during her first visit here. Like—like they were personally disappointed in her, the way you'd be in a relative who insisted on committing suicide before your very eyes.

Tehmina tossed in her bed, willing away the memory that was emerging. Last year, when they had vacationed in California, she and Susan had taken Cookie shopping while the two men stayed back at the hotel. Susan's hands were laden with gift bags and Tehmina was holding on to Cookie as they waited for the traffic signal to turn. They stood in a crowd of friendly, tanned, ice-cone-licking tourists, waiting on the sidewalk to cross the street. So much for land of the free, Tehmina thought to herself in amusement. Not a car in sight but still they all wait like sheep for the sign to tell them to Walk or Don't Walk. In Bombay, a thousand people would have crossed the street six times by now. Perhaps it was the thought that propelled her forward, but the next second an impatient Tehmina tugged at her grandson's hand and began to cross the street. Behind her, she heard Susan gasp, "Mom!" but it was too late to stop. By the time they got to the other side, she knew she had done something wrong. Something uncivilized. Something—well, something—Bombayish. Something Indian. Something uncouth.

Despite the hot California sun, Susan's face was pale as she crossed the street and faced her mother-in-law. Tehmina noticed that her lower lip was trembling. "Beta, I'm sorry," she began, but Susan didn't hear her. "I can't believe you did that, Mom," she began. "I can't believe you exposed your only grandchild to that kind of danger."

Danger? There had not been a car in sight. "Susan dear, the road was clear and—"

"That's not the point." Now Tehmina noticed with wonder that there were tears in Susan's eyes. "The point is, you're teaching my son unhealthy habits. What happens if he tries darting across the street when he's at school? After all, we're not with him twenty-four hours a day. And what if a car had suddenly appeared from somewhere? You know how these people drive here, anyway."

Tehmina felt a confusing array of emotions—outrage, shame, guilt, disbelief. People were watching them, their mouths puckered in disapproval. But disapproval of whom? Susan, for making a public scene over a trifle matter? Or at Tehmina, for being a stupid, dumb peasant who didn't know how to cross the street?

"I'm sorry," she repeated. "I . . . I—what to do, dear? You know, we are so used to crossing the street like this in Bombay that I wasn't even thinking. You know the last thing I would do is hurt Cookie."

At the mention of his name, Cookie began to cry. "Mom, stoppit," he said. "Stop yelling at Granna."

Susan pursed her lips. "Oh, shoot. Let's all just get out of this sun and go back to the hotel, shall we?" She looked down at her son and her face softened. "I'm not yelling at Granna, honey. It's just that

Mommy is upset because Granna scared her, okay? Tell you what. Let's go for a swim in the pool when we get back, all right?"

Susan tried to carry on a light conversation in the cab all the way home and Tehmina responded, happy to be distracted. Because otherwise the dark, heavy feeling of shame and sadness that was weighing on her would have to be acknowledged. It had been many years since someone had spoken to her, had scolded her, the way Susan had. And that, too, in public. There were no boundaries in this country, no divisions between the public and the private.

Late that night, when she and Rustom were lying in bed, she described the incident and her mortification to him. To her surprise, her voice cracked and her eyes were teary as she repeated Susan's chastising words. But she should've known better than to expect Rustom to side with her. So many times, she had noticed, Rustom stoutly spoke up for their daughter-in-law, even siding with her against his own son. It was Rustom's own way of putting the harmony and well-being of his son's family over all else, she knew. "Crazy old woman," he now said gruffly. "Of course Susan was upset. What do you think this is, your run-down, beaten-up Mumbai? These people are used to discipline and good manners. And there you come, Mrs. Ghaati Bombayite herself, breaking all the traffic rules and corrupting our Cookie on top of it. And you expect Susan to just stand there and take it? It's a good thing she didn't push you into two lanes of traffic."

"But that's the point. There was no traffic," she began heatedly, but then she saw the gleam in his eye and she began to laugh. "How come you side with everybody in the world except your own wife?" she asked.

Rustom put his arms around her. "Because you are the strongest person I know. Other people need defending. But you—you are a pillar of strength. You don't need my protection."

Wrong, Rustom, she now thought. Wrong, my darling. Look how

I am floundering without you. Look how I can't make the smallest decisions without you.

Tehmina got out of her bed and made her way barefoot to the small desk under the window. Opening the drawer, she groped around in the dark until her fingers found the cool metal of the small picture frame.

Her hand on the light switch above her bed, Tehmina hesitated. The last thing she wanted to do was have the light spill from her room and disturb the children as they tried to get some hard-earned sleep. She decided to turn on the small lamp by her side instead. Sitting up in bed, the down comforter wrapped around her so that only her cold hands stuck out, Tehmina opened the double picture frame. She had bought this frame from Akbarally's just before she left for America this time, knowing that she had to carry her Rustom close to her if she was to survive the long journey away from the land where her beloved husband had died to the land where her beloved son lived, worked, breathed. She had hesitated over which two pictures to carry with her—one of their wedding pictures? The picture of Rustom holding Sorab for the first time, a half hour after Sorab's birth? Rustom's passport picture in which he looked uncharacteristically serious and stern? In the end she had decided on a picture of a young Rustom in his twenties and a picture of him a few months before he died. How much time, how many lifetimes, had passed between those two pictures. In that flash of time between the two clicks, they had had a son, raised him on a diet of parental love and pride and worry, felt that same trinity of feelings—love, pride, worry—when he'd left for America, been saddened but not shocked when he'd announced that he was marrying an American woman, had accepted and come to love Susan once they'd spent some time with her, been delirious with joy at the birth of their grandson. In that same sliver of time, they had attended the funerals of their parents, lost some of their close friends to an assortment of illnesses, survived

Rustom's own scare with prostate cancer. (Till today, Tehmina believed that Rustom actually did have prostate cancer at the time of his test but that her most sincere and heartfelt prayers had altered the biopsy results.)

So much of her life had been lived with this man who now stared back at her from his glass prison. Holding the picture frame up to her face, she brushed her lips against Rustom's full, sensuous lips. It was hard to believe that someone as passionate, as hot-blooded and larger than life as Rustom could be confined to a small, cheap photo frame. It was hard to believe that all that gusto for life, all that grandeur, all that magnificence could be felled by a heart attack, that the bones and flesh of this man were now decomposing in the well at the Tower of Silence, no different from the flesh and bones of more mediocre, frightened men. What was the point, Tehmina thought, the point of all his hard work, his success, his passion, his hunger for life, the buzzing energy that coursed through his veins, the relentless ticking of his intelligent mind, what was the point if all that could be snatched away at the age of sixty-seven, as abruptly as someone stilling the hands of a clock? Not to mention the labor pains his mother must have experienced when she gave birth to him, and the sacrifices that his parents made to send him to good schools, the sitting up with him when he burned with a fever as a child, oh yes, all the love that they—and later, she, Tehmina—lavished on him, and the pains that she took once they were married to make him happy—to make him saffron rava for breakfast every Saturday morning, to learn to make dhansak that tasted just like his mother's, to make love to him even when she wasn't in the mood—was none of this powerful enough to keep him alive beyond sixty-seven? So much went into the making of a man—the amount of rice and sugar and lentils that had to be grown for him to consume, the number of chickens and goats and lambs that had to be slaughtered so he could have meat in his curry. And it was more than even this, really.

It went back to the beginning of the world, to the splitting of the continents, to the rise of a species who could walk upright, who had opposable thumbs, and it carried on, down to the invention of fire, to the making of the fist, to the throwing of the first stone. How many untold thousands had died trying to figure out which berries were poisonous and which weren't? Who was the first man or woman to discover that rice needed to be boiled for twenty minutes or that corn tasted better roasted? How many empires rose and fell, how many millions died, in the search of spices? And all this labor, all this knowledge, all this blood and sweat, all these tears, all this achievement, all this triumph, all the glories and all the miseries of human history, for what? So that a man—a man as grand as a mountain, as large as the ocean, as generous as a continent—so that such a man could die at sixty-seven?

Tehmina, Rustom said. Darling, forgive my saying so but you're going a little potty, my dear. A man as generous as a continent? Please, darling, I'm blushing at your verbosity.

Tehmina looked around the room. She had heard Rustom's voice as clear as if he was lying in bed beside her. But there was no one else there. I'm going mad, she thought to herself. No wonder the children have been worried about me.

But then she saw Rustom, sitting cross-legged and straight-backed in the corner of the room. When he saw that she had spotted him, he got to his feet in one swift motion, without the revealing grunt of middle age that accompanied every movement that Tehmina made. Even as it snowed outside, Tehmina noticed that Rustom was dressed as if they were going to a movie on a warm Bombay evening—dark pants and a pale blue half-sleeved shirt that revealed his strong, muscular forearms, brown and shiny as leather. Despite the faint light in the room, she saw the familiar thin scar that ran across Rustom's left arm and her fingers itched to caress it as she had a million times before. But then fear overtook Tehmina as her dead husband crossed the small guest room and stood in front of her. "Rustom," she whispered. "How? What? What are you doing here? Darling, you are—"

"Baap re, woman. You should see your face right now. You look like you've seen a ghost." Rustom grinned at his own joke.

Despite herself, Tehmina smiled reluctantly at the teasing affection she heard in her husband's voice. This was so much like Rustom, to rise from the dead and walk into her room halfway across the world and then to mock her for her astonishment. This is what she had loved and this is what she missed about him—the casual ease with which he occupied space wherever he was, the benign assumption that the world would give him his due and respond to him with friendliness and generosity. And some of this had rubbed off on her so that while he was alive it had been easy to delude herself that life was indeed hers for the taking, that the world was a house ready to be moved into and occupied. How effortless, how untroubled living had been when Rustom had been alive. Like riding in a Mercedes-Benz, Tehmina now thought, with tinted windows that kept the outside squalor at bay and shock absorbers that smoothened and muted all of life's bumps. And now, without Rustom at the wheel, she suddenly felt as if she was traveling in the old Ambassador her father used to own, with its rattling doors and the kind of shocks that made you feel every pothole at the base of your spine. Her fall from grace had been as quick and astounding as Rustom's heart attack.

But then again, here he was, in her room in Rosemont Heights, pushing her gently as he got under the covers with her. For a moment, Tehmina was sickened at the thought of sharing her bed with a dead man. But then she felt the warm heat of Rustom's body as it brushed against hers, smelled that stomach-dropping, familiar combination of Old Spice and sweat, felt the hair on Rustom's legs tickle the smoothness of her own, and her whole body seemed to sink deeper into the bed, as she felt herself give up a burden, a grief, that she had

had no memory of carrying. How stiffly she had been holding herself since the day she last saw her husband at the Tower of Silence, Tehmina now realized. She saw now what sorrow had done to her body, how it had made her heart feel as if it were a nylon bag that carried in it a thousand sharp pebbles, how a permanent nausea had wormed itself into her stomach, how depression had weighed down her tongue, sat on her eyelids, had conferred a kind of prickliness on her skin.

But all that was gone now as she touched Rustom's collarbone and felt the strap of his white sadra under her fingertips. How many of these muslin-cloth sadras she had stitched for him over the years. When they had first married she had insisted on ironing the thin undershirt for him until he at last put his foot down and told her that he had married her for love and companionship, and if he'd wanted someone to wash and iron his clothes, he would have married his dhobi instead. That, too, was part of Rustom's splendor—despite being always well dressed, he was the least vain of men. And his sense of fairness, his moral outrage at the inferior status of women, made him an object of good-natured ribbing from his male friends and Tehmina an object of whispered envy from their wives. How many times had one of those women pulled Tehmina aside at a party and expressed wonder at the sight of Rustom helping her in the kitchen. "What's the secret, Tehmina, yaar?" they would whisper to her. "How did you train him so well?"

"I had nothing to do with it," she would respond, trying to keep the pride drained out of her voice. "He came to me this way. My Rustom is the fairest person I know. He believes in equal rights for women."

But now, her fingering of the strap of his undergarment conjured up another, unwelcome memory. Of her well-groomed husband lying on a slab on the floor of the Tower of Silence, stripped of his usual clothes and dressed instead in a simple white sadra and pajamas. Even in death Rustom looked powerful, the muscles of his dark legs pushing against the thin cotton of the pajamas. But when the woeful-looking professional pallbearers came to lift Rustom's body to take it to its final journey to where the vultures were circling over the well, Tehmina had to admit that even Rustom could not beat death, that death had managed to turn the tanned, brown face to a kind of chalky gray, that it had opened and twisted Rustom's mouth into a grotesque O, that death's dark bolt of lightning was greater than the electric energy that had buzzed through Rustom's body. How pathetic, how small Rustom suddenly looked, how dirty and disheveled he seemed as the pallbearers lifted him up against her sobbing protests. For months later she had tried to blind herself to this final insult, had tried to forget how rigid with anger she had been when she realized that all the stony-faced pallbearers saw was a corpse, a lifeless body not much different—except perhaps a bit taller and heavier—than all the others they had carried. That they were completely immune to the uniqueness of Rustom—how his laugh seemed to encompass an entire octave, how he jiggled his leg or tapped his fingers impatiently if he ever had to wait in line, how he had a joke or an Omar Khayyám quote for every occasion, how he did a wonderful Charlie Chaplin imitation. But like death itself, like the vultures who hovered over the dreaded well, the pallbearers were indifferent to all this. And it was this indifference, the realization of this indifference, the acknowledgment that the world would continue to spin without Rustom in it, that had made Tehmina rigid with anger and pain. Until the rigidity had become a shell around her body, until it had become as natural as skin.

"Tehmina," Rustom was now whispering to her. "Tehmi, open your eyes. Listen to me. I have a message for you."

She opened her eyes and saw the heart-twistingly familiar brown eyes staring intently into hers. "Tehmina. Darling," Rustom said. "What I want to say to you is, be brave. Courage, janu. That's who

I'd fallen in love with in the first place, my brave, outspoken wife. Who is this mouselike woman in her place? This woman I don't recognize. So please, janu. Be happy. Life goes on, you know?"

"Can you stay?" she whispered. "Then I will be happy." But she saw the pained, distant look that came over his face and immediately regretted her words. "Will you at least come visit again?" she tried. "Come see me again?"

This time Rustom smiled, a smile so kind and loving and timeless, that Tehmina felt that all of history, all of the immensity of the universe, was in that smile. "Tehmina," he said. "Don't be ridiculous. What do you mean, come and visit you? How can I do that, when I'm always at your side?"

So this is what happiness feels like, Tehmina thought. She had forgotten the feeling but recognized it immediately, like the face of a schoolmate that one has not seen in thirty years. "Will you stay with me tonight?" she asked even as she snuggled her chin into the V of his chest.

"I told you. I'm here. Now go to sleep," he said as he stroked her hair.

And so, Tehmina slept.

CHAPTER SEVEN

She was awakened from a deep slumber by the ringing of the phone in Susan and Sorab's room next to hers. Her eyes flew open into the pitch dark and her heart began to race involuntarily—a phone call in the middle of the night usually spelled bad news, didn't it? Immediately, she reached for Rustom's warm body, but he was gone, scared away by the ringing of the phone, probably. The mattress felt cold, as if Rustom had left soon after she'd fallen asleep. Apprehension won over disappointment as she rolled over and turned on the light on her alarm clock. Four A.M. Who could be calling at four A.M.? Her thoughts flew immediately to Susan's eighty-year-old grandmother, a frail but feisty old woman with a voice that sounded like a pickup truck going down a gravel road. Old Ruthanne had always been short-statured, but her osteoporosis had almost bent her double. But what she lacked in size, she made up in personality. As bent over as she was, those twinkling eyes never missed a thing and that gravelly voice never wavered even when Ruthanne told jokes so bawdy they made the listener gasp at the incongruity of the speaker being a sweet old lady with a soft Oklahoma accent. That voice made you ignore her misshapen body and see the spirit contained within it. Truth be told, she was Tehmina's favorite member of Susan's family and Tehmina's heart was already beginning to ache at the thought of the old lady being dead. Now she wouldn't get a chance to give Ruthanne the blue sweater that she had knitted for her for Christmas. Involuntarily, she began to say an Ashem Vahu to pray for Ruthanne's soul.

Tehmina could hear Susan's muffled voice through the thin walls that separated her bedroom from theirs. She braced herself for the tears that would follow once Susan hung up. Susan adored Ruthanne, Tehmina knew. Often, she would ruefully admit that her grandmother was the only "colorful" member of her family, and then Tehmina never knew whether it was polite to agree or disagree. Certainly, Susan's father, Fred, a tall, ruddy-cheeked man, was nothing like his flamboyant mother, although he had been nothing but gracious to her and Rustom. In fact, it was Fred who had insisted that Rustom learn to play golf during their first visit to the States. A divorcé who lived in Texas, Fred was also deeply appreciative of Tehmina's cooking—though when he had first met them, he had boasted about being a staunch meat-and-potatoes man. "Wow, this sure beats Burger King, Tammy," Fred had said to her the first time he ate one of her meals, which Tehmina didn't think was much of a compliment. But Susan had beamed and marveled at the fact that her conservative, rigid father had even agreed to try something different from the burgers and pot roasts that he lived on.

Now Tehmina remembered the first time she had met Ruthanne. It was at Sorab and Susan's wedding reception. Ruthanne noticed the proud look with which Tehmina caressed her son every time he walked past her. "That boy of yours reminds me of my late husband," the old woman had said, sidling up to Tehmina. "A good, decent, solid man, your son. Good thing that granddaughter of mine had the sense to marry him."

Tehmina turned to Ruthanne with grateful eyes. One of her misgivings about Sorab having married a white American was whether he would be accepted into his bride's family. Although Tehmina was too young to remember too much about when the British ruled India, she had heard enough to believe that all white people considered themselves superior to nonwhites. And the thought of anybody considering her smart, handsome son less than perfect was enough to make her bristle. "Thank you," she said to Ruthanne. "My Sorab is ... I can assure you he will make a good husband to your Susan."

Ruthanne laughed a strangely irreverent laugh. "Aw, honey, I ain't worried about that," she said. "A boy that's built the way he is ... oh, he's already making my Susan very, very happy. I can tell from that Cheshire-cat smile she has on her face all the time now. Naw, that son of yours knows how to keep a girl satisfied, that's fo' sure."

Tehmina blushed, scarcely believing her ears. Luckily, Sorab came to her rescue. Grabbing Ruthanne's bent body from behind, he put his arms around the older woman. "Now, Grandma." He grinned. "You better mind your manners around my mom, here. None of your naughty jokes, you hear? And if I catch you flirting with my dad once again, why, we'll just have to cut off your beer."

Tehmina marveled at how effortlessly Sorab picked up the cadences of Ruthanne's speech, of how easily he teased his in-law. Sorab doesn't just belong to us anymore, she realized with a pang. He now belongs to this other family, also.

"It ain't the father I'm interested in," Ruthanne was saying. "It's the son."

And her laughter was so loud and wicked that even a slightly scandalized Tehmina felt compelled to join in.

By the time there was a tap on her bedroom door, Tehmina had already finished saying twelve Ashem Vahus for Ruthanne's recently departed soul. "Yes, dear?" she called back. "Come in. I'm awake."

A grim-faced Susan stood at the door, but what Tehmina noticed immediately and with some surprise was that Susan was not crying. "I'm so sorry, beta," she began, but Susan cut her off with a quizzical look.

"It's for you, Mom," she said. "It's Persis auntie, calling from Bombay. Guess she forgot what time it was over here." Tehmina could tell that Susan was fighting to keep the annoyance out of her voice.

"Persis?" she said, getting out of bed. "Calling at this time? Has she lost her mind?" And then, stricken by another thought, "Is she all right?"

"She's fine," Susan said tightly. "But it seems as though there's a situation with your apartment. But—well, she's waiting to tell you. You can take the call in our bedroom. Save you a trip downstairs." Now Tehmina could hear the sleepiness in Susan's voice.

She hurried behind Susan murmuring her apologies. That Persis was an idiot. Why had she ever entrusted her apartment key to her? And what was so urgent that it couldn't wait till morning? Entering the bedroom, she noticed immediately that the call had woken up Sorab also. To block out the overhead light, he had covered his head with a pillow, but still he was tossing and turning and muttering about inconsiderate callers. She made up her mind to get off the phone as quickly as she could.

"Persis?" she said, trying to keep her voice low. "Su che? It's four in the morning here, bhai."

"I'm so sorry, so sorry," the voice at the other end sobbed. "I . . . what to do, Tehmina, I was so shocked that I just didn't even think of the time difference and all that."

Now Tehmina felt a slight panic. "What is it?" she repeated. "Is . . . everybody all right?"

"Everybody is fine, fine," Persis said. "Except that shameless nephew of mine. I swear, when he wakes up, I'm going to skin him alive. Badmaash, betraying my trust like this."

Persis had called her in America at four in the morning to complain about her nephew? Was her neighbor mad? Was this early dementia, something that affected so many Parsi men and women?

"Persis," Tehmina said cautiously.

"No, no, Tehmi, don't be angry with me, please. Let me explain. See, my nephew Sharukh was visiting us from Pune. But what to do, Tehmi, my sister and her children were visiting the same week. And, Sharukh has had such troubles with the bottle, Tehmi, remember? Anyway, he promised me he is totally clean, swears he's not had one drink since the last three months. And my small flat is so crowded with all the company. So, like a bevakoof, I tell him he can stay at your apartment. I know it was wrong, I should've asked your permission, Tehmi. But I'm thinking, it's just for two nights, and after all, your apartment was empty and only two floors below us. That way, the whole family can be together, you know?"

Out of the corner of her eye, Tehmina could see Sorab rolling in bed, trying to find a comfortable position. He was muttering something about a hangover and a bad headache. "Persis," she whispered into the phone. "If you're calling about this, I don't have a problem with—"

Persis sounded even more distraught. "No, no, you don't understand. That ungrateful nephew of mine, he—oh my God, Tehmi, I am so ashamed—he stole your TV and your stereo. Must've done it in the middle of the night. Loaded it up in his car and sold it. Turns out he's still hitting the bottle. I went down this afternoon to let the servant in as usual, and you can imagine my shock. Immediately I noticed that something was not right. And like a roadside ruffian, there's Sharukh, passed out on the bed. I tell you, Tehmi, I shook him so hard, he would've woken up even if he was as dead as the Dead Sea. Confessed everything to me before falling asleep again. But he scared poor Hansu so that she refused to stay alone in the house with him there. So I had to let her go without cleaning your apartment today. Though of course, with these servants you never know—probably just did some acting-facting, to get out of having to work. As if my Sharukh could've done anything to her. Snoring loud as a freight train, he was."

Tehmina felt her head spinning. If only Persis would stop talking for a moment. This would teach her to entrust her apartment to someone as flighty as Persis. "So, what else is missing?" she asked, trying to focus Persis's attention on the theft.

Persis wailed so loudly Tehmina was afraid Sorab would hear it. "Oh, God, Tehmi, that's the whole problem. I don't know. I haven't even looked through the whole apartment yet. And that besharam nephew of mine is still sleeping, so I can't even ask him. Forgive me, Tehmi. I am so ashamed. My sister said we should call the police, but Sharukh is my dead brother's only child. How to call the police on him, Tehmi?"

Despite her irritation, Tehmina felt her heart soften. "Of course you can't call the police on your own flesh and blood," she said, and heard Persis's sigh of relief. "The stereo and TV were both old anyway. And there's nothing to forgive. I'm grateful to you for keeping an eye on the apartment for me and making sure it gets dusted and cleaned every day." She thought for a moment. "Listen, Persis. You still have Sorab's e-mail address, yes? Good. Tell you what. After you find out whatall Sharukh sto—that is, whatall is missing—just send me an e-mail. That way, you don't waste your money on another phone call. And now get some rest. Put all this out of your mind. Just—please—just make sure you take the key back from Sharukh."

As she hung up she wondered: What if the boy had made a spare key to her apartment? Should she write to Persis and have her change the lock to the flat? Lost in her thoughts, she turned absentmindedly toward her son. "Sorab," she said, "looks like Persis's nephew has stolen a few items from my flat. Do you think I need to change my front-door lock?"

Sorab let out a cry. Tossing off the pillow covering his head with a violent shake, pulling off the bedcovers, he sat up, a mad look on his sleepy face. "I don't give a rat's ass whether you change the locks or not," he hissed, his voice shaking with outrage and anger. "I'm tired of having to blow my nose each time someone sneezes in Bombay."

"I'm so sorry, beta," a startled Tehmina said, but Sorab went on as if he'd not heard her. "It's friggin' four in the morning. I have to be up in less than two hours. Every day I go to work like a fucking zombie. Is that woman crazy, to call in the middle of the night? I tell you, Mamma, I don't know how much more of this I can—"

"Sorab." It was Susan, and Tehmina heard the sharpness in her voice. "Shut up. Don't say anything you're going to regret in the morning."

The room fell silent. Sorab blinked rapidly several times and looked down at his hands, as if he was trying to recognize the man he had become. Susan was staring at her husband as if seeing him for the first time. And Tehmina, Tehmina stared at the floor, waiting for it to open up and swallow her whole. Sorab had never before spoken to her in this way. More than his words, it was his tone, the bitterness in his voice, that made her realize how much frustration her son had been bottling up. The tears welling in her eyes were not of self-pity but of remorse and self-recrimination and sympathy. Her heart bled for her son. For she had heard it as clearly as if he'd said it—Sorab was tired of living this half-life, living in the state of suspension that her indecisiveness was forcing upon them all. To him, the theft in Bombay was simply a symptom, a reminder of the fact that happenings in a city, in an apartment eight thousand miles away, could still cast a shadow over their lives here. And truth be told, hadn't her first instinct upon hearing Persis's news been to want to rush back to her apartment, to wash the sheets upon which the drunken Sharukh had lain, to take an inventory of her clothes, to make sure that the boy was too stupid to know the value of the Hussein that hung in the living room? Perhaps Sorab had read her treacherous thoughts—had known that at the slightest mention of the Bombay apartment, his mother had been willing to abandon him and his family and rush back to safeguard the apartment that Sorab, to Tehmina's eternal incomprehension, had left behind so utterly.

Sorab made a choking sound that awoke Tehmina from her reverie. "I'm sorry," she whispered. "I'm so—"

"No." Susan's voice rang out. "You have nothing to apologize for, Mom. It's this one here"—and she nudged Sorab hard on his back—"who needs to apologize."

Tehmina appreciated what Susan was trying to do, but she wished she wouldn't embarrass Sorab further. She knew her son well enough to know that he was already eaten up by remorse. And sure enough, Sorab looked at her with glistening eyes. "I don't even know what I'm saying, Mamma," he mumbled, looking exactly the way he had when he was seven. "I'm just so tired that the lack of sleep is making me nuts. But I'm truly sorry that I—"

"Please." Tehmina took a few steps toward Sorab and stroked his hair. "Please, my darling. I know how hard you work. You need your sleep. Nothing to apologize for. I should've known better than to trust that crazy Persis with the apartment."

"Well," Susan began, and Tehmina could see that she was readying for an argument, wanting to assure Tehmina that she hadn't done anything wrong. But as much as she appreciated Susan coming to her defense, she knew she didn't need defending against her own son.

"We all need to go back to bed," she interrupted, walking toward her own room. At the doorway, she glanced back. "I love you both. Good night," she said with a smile, hoping that Sorab would see that there was nothing to forgive.

She headed for the bathroom. May as well use the bathroom while everybody was still up. This winter cold made her pee so often, it was a running joke in the family. Sorab had taken to calling her B.B. for baby bladder.

Back in her room she climbed into bed. She could hear the children murmuring to each other in the other room and she wished she could urge Susan to stop chastising Sorab and let the poor boy go back to sleep. But in the solitude of her room, her instinctive resolution to forgive her son for his harsh words, to ignore the shocked hurt he had caused her, receded a bit. In its place, she felt a certain coldness, an icy feeling of disappointment and grief. Sorab had never spoken to her in this tone before. It was a measure of how much pressure he was under, how many burdens she had put on her son's head. And now a flood of emotions assailed her—guilt at adding to Sorab's problems, sadness at his impatient words that now stung at her like mosquitoes, shock at having her house violated by a drunken thief, revulsion at Sharukh dirtifying the clean sheets on her bed.

Her bed. The bed that she had shared with Rustom for most of their marriage. Closing her eyes, Tehmina remembered the beautiful, dark polish of the teakwood, the intricate carvings on the headboard. They had had so little money in the early years of their marriage when Rustom had made this extravagant purchase. How she had yelled at him then. And he had stood, grinning at her impudently, waiting for a break in the tongue-lashing she was giving him, to put his arms around her. "It's fine, it's okay, my darling," he had murmured. "The business is beginning to pick up, God willing. And I want the bed where all my children are going to be born to be grand as a king's throne."

"But, Rustom," she protested, worried about the money they had already borrowed from his parents.

"But, fut, nothing," he said firmly, holding his finger to her mouth. "Now come on, woman. Don't you want to try out this wonderful bed I've spent my hard-earned money on?"

Tehmina smiled at the memory, but her smile was tinged with something bitter. Rustom had always declared that he wanted at least five children. He himself had been an only child and he had sworn that he would never settle for just one child, that it was an unfair thing for parents to do, that children needed siblings. She, too, had been happy to oblige. But fate had decreed otherwise. What was that Omar Khayyám line? She thought for a moment and then it unfolded in her head. But instead of hearing it in her own voice, she heard it in Rustom's.

Love! Could thou and I with Fate conspire
To grasp this sorry Scheme of Things entire!
Would not we shatter it to bits—and then
Re-mold it nearer to the Heart's Desire!

She still didn't know what had gone wrong, why Rustom and she had been unable to have more children after Sorab was born. Even that birth had been a miracle, coming three years into their marriage. Every doctor they went to said there was nothing wrong with either one of them. For a while, Rustom's mother, Bikhumai, made Tehmina swallow a series of foul-tasting tonics and powders. Bikhumai took their inability to conceive more children as a personal insult, as a sign of God's displeasure with her. For a year, the woman gave up eating chocolate, as an offering to appease Ahura Mazda. Then she swore off ice cream, which everyone knew that she loved. But when she announced that she was renouncing bread until God saw fit to bless her son with another child, Rustom put his foot down. "All this nonsensical faras must stop immediately, Mamma," he roared one day when they were having Sunday dinner at his parents' home. "Bas, if we are meant to have more children, we will. In the meantime, just enjoy your grandson. What is it, is my Sorab not enough for you that you keep doing all this nataak-nakhra?"

Despite Rustom's severe tone, despite the fact that he had banged his fist on the dining table, something in his tone told Tehmina that this was mock anger, that her husband was playing out a role in a time-honored ritual.

And since she understood her exact role in that ritual, Bikhumai pretended to tremble under the fury of her son's anger and swore that she would resume eating all her favorite things, if only he would stop being angry with her. And then, continuing to play her part, she grew indignant and chided Rustom for accusing her of not loving her only grandson enough and swore that if even a hair on her beloved Sorab's head were to get bent, why, she would be beside herself with grief. After fifteen minutes of such protestations and declarations of undying love for Sorab, Bikhumai was finally exhausted into silence. Glancing her way, Rustom gave Tehmina a quick wink. The rest of the dinner proceeded happily and Tehmina never again had to endure her mother-in-law's home remedies.

Tehmina turned in her bed, which suddenly seemed narrow and bleak compared to that generous teak bed in which she and Rustom had slept every day of their married life. She remembered the feel of Rustom's strong arm around her as he cradled her every night, her back against his hard chest, his brown hairy leg wrapped around hers. Just like early tonight, when he had visited her in this bedroom. No matter how tired or restless she had been, leaning against Rustom's body never failed to bring her comfort, a feeling of homecoming, like a train entering a station. And that was what she missed most, she now realized, that feeling of protection. As long as Rustom was alive, he had stood like a wall between her and the world, protecting her from its demands and barbs and hurts. Even after Rustom had neutralized his mother's interference into the child-bearing problem, he had further insulated Tehmina from all gossip and conjecture. Ever so subtly Rustom would drop hints that made it sound as if the lack of another child stemmed from his inability to impregnate his wife. Just some whispered hints about how the doctor wanted to run more tests on him but he had refused. And if that wasn't enough to convince his listener, he would add that the whole thing had been so hard on poor Tehmina, but she had learned to hide her disappointment, God bless her. No other Parsi male whom Tehmina knew would've done that. No other. Tehmina knew of several men, who, despite a low sperm count, automatically blamed their wife's barren womb and with a straight face lapped up all the sympathy and pity that inevitably came their way.

He had been this protective of her from the day she'd met him at a party at Nilu Sukharwala's home. Tehmina had grown up in Calcutta, the only child of a doctor, but through a program at her school, she had started corresponding with Nilu, who lived in Bombay, since both girls were fifth graders. Now, for her twenty-fifth birthday, she had begged her father, Hoshang, to let her travel to Bombay to meet Nilu. Her pen pal had already visited her in Calcutta the previous year and had spun Tehmina's head with stories of Bandra, where the movie stars lived, and Juhu Beach, where Bollywood movies were shot on location, and Colaba, where one could shop for just about anything. What sealed the deal was a letter from Nilu's mother, promising Hoshang that they would take care of his daughter as if she were a member of the family. And Hoshang had finally given his consent, but even at the train station he looked nervous until he finally got hold of an elderly Gujarati couple traveling in the same compartment as Tehmina and made them promise to watch out for his daughter. Tehmina was embarrassed, but as soon as the train took off, the unexpected pleasure of freedom, of being away from home for the first time, overrode all other feelings.

It seemed to Tehmina that Nilu had invited all of Bombay to her party. It turned out that Nilu's parents were a lot more relaxed than Mrs. Sukharwala's note had indicated. They were attending a dinner party themselves, leaving the two girls at home with Nilu's older brother, whom everybody called Smits, and Geeta, the servant girl who helped them set out the food.

The noise, the heat, the music, the loud laughter and conversation, the gaiety of the crowd, the easy, casual way in which the boys and girls spoke to one another, were all intoxicating to Tehmina. I'm in Bombay, she kept saying to herself. These are all Bombayites. Everything she'd ever heard about Bombayites seemed true—these people were more mature, more sophisticated, more urbane than her crowd in Calcutta. Her birth city suddenly seemed drab and mellow to her, compared with the pungent, thrilling sharpness with which these people spoke and acted. Although she knew this was far-fetched, she kept glancing at the front door, expecting a film star to walk in at any minute.

So that she was the first to notice Rustom when he walked into the room a little after eight. She spotted a thin, tall man in a blue, half-sleeved shirt, his eyes darting around the room, searching for his host. She saw him run his hand through his thick, dark hair in a gesture she recognized as nervous uncertainty. She saw him smile apologetically at the woman he had bumped into as he made his way into the crowded room. She could tell that like her, he had not expected to find so many people at the party, that he was a little out of his element. Now he was turning his head, trying to locate either Nilu or Smits. He must've felt her eyes on him because he looked at her, raised his eyebrows a bit in greeting, and then quickly looked away. But the next second he was looking at her again, this time holding her glance, so that she felt compelled to walk over to where he was standing.

"Hi," she said, annoyed to hear the breathlessness in her voice. "I'm Tehmina. Are you looking for Smits or Nilu?"

"Aha. Tehmina. So you're the famous friend from Calcutta?"

She blushed. "Not so famous." Her voice trailed away as she found herself focusing on the small pimple at the left corner of his lips. It was the cutest pimple she'd ever seen.

The man cleared his throat. "Ahem. So, Tehmina. Tell me. How do you find Bombay?" Up close, he didn't seem as uncomfortable as he'd looked a moment ago.

"You take the train from Calcutta and get off at VT station."

He started. "Oh, no, what I meant was—" He caught the twinkle in her eye and broke into a wide grin. "I see. Well, I fell for that."

Tehmina suddenly felt like life would only be sweet and worth living if she could make this man smile again. "Sorry. I'm just being silly."

This time, the smile was slower, more calculating, and there was a gleam in his eye. "Well, hello, silly. Nice to meet you. I'm Rustom Sethna."

"And I'm—but I already told you. You know who I am." Get hold of yourself, Tehmina said to herself. You're acting like a fool.

Rakesh, one of Smits's friends, staggered up to her. "Ae, Tehmi, sure I still can't get you something to drink? Not even a Coke?" The boy had been making a pest of himself all evening long and she had tolerated him, but now Tehmina hated his intrusive, drunken presence. She wanted to shut her eyes and have Rakesh gone when she opened them again. Actually, she wanted every person in the room to have vanished when she opened her eyes. Everyone except this handsome, smiling man standing next to her.

She threw Rustom a glance that was equal parts apology and distress. And as if he had read her mind, Rustom took her by the elbow and led her away. "Hey, thanks for offering, yaar," he tossed back at Rakesh. "But I've already gotten my cousin's drink order."

"Your cousin? Oh, okay. Sorry, boss." Rakesh looked so despondent and confused that Tehmina had to bite down on her lip to stop from laughing out loud.

"Well, now that we're relatives, I may as well know your taste in drink." Rustom smiled as they walked a few feet away.

"I'll have whatever you're drinking," she said impulsively.

"Okay, good. Listen, I have to go find Smits for a minute to say hello. And then I'll be straight back with your glass. Where will you be?"

"I'll wait right here," Tehmina said. "Just like the Boy Who Stood on the Burning Deck." She knew she was being reckless, flirting so shamelessly with a stranger. But she didn't care. She would be back in Calcutta in a fortnight and she would never see this beautiful young man again. Her heart contracted at the thought.

"You know that story? My mom used to read it to me at least once a week when I was a boy. I loved that story."

"Me, too. Though I cried every time I read it."

There was something in Rustom's eyes that she couldn't quite figure out. "So you believe in that kind of loyalty and faithfulness?"

"Absolutely, yes."

"My friends used to think that boy was foolish." He was looking at her so hard, it made her feel translucent.

She shrugged, partly to hide her embarrassment. "I believe in keeping my word."

He smiled again, as if they had settled something. "Good. So stay here, okay? I'll be back in a jiffy."

Her knees were so weak she couldn't have moved even if she had wanted to. She watched as Rustom found Smits and both men hugged each other and Smits thumped Rustom on the back. She watched as Smits went off to find Nilu and noticed the look of deep pleasure with which Nilu greeted Rustom. Instinctively, Rustom turned around to find her and threw her a wink. She blushed and looked away. And then there he was a few minutes later, holding two beer glasses and making his way toward her.

"The food smells heavenly," he said.

"Hope so. Nilu and I were in the kitchen all day today."

"And what dishes did you make? I want to taste them all."

"We just cooked together. I made the pallov and the daar, though."

He groaned. "Oh God. That's my favorite. I'll tell you what, though. Bet your pallov-daar isn't as good as my mom's."

"What's the bet?"

"The bet is . . ." He thought for a minute. "Okay. The bet is if your cooking is as good as my mom's, I take you out to the Sea Lounge for tea. If it is not as good, you treat me to the Sea Lounge."

"What's the Sea Lounge?" she asked.

"The Sea Lounge? Oh yes, I forget you're not from Bombay. It's a restaurant at the Taj. They have the best grilled chicken sandwiches." Even she knew that the Taj was the best five-star hotel in Bombay.

The thought of seeing this man again made Tehmina forget any doubts about spending too much of the money her father had given her. She would just have to forgo some of her shopping.

"Okay. It's a bet. As long as Mrs. Sukharwala allows me to go out."

Rustom laughed. "Smits's mother? Don't worry about her. She's a very modern woman."

The easiness of his laugh bothered her. "My father . . . in Calcutta I don't usually go out with—that is, my father doesn't allow me to go out with—strangers."

Something flickered in his eyes again. "I understand that, Tehmina. Honest. I didn't mean to imply anything." He smiled. "But we're cousins, remember? So you're not going out with a stranger. And my intentions are honorable, I promise."

"Okay," she said. "Now come try the food."

In later years, they would try to remember who had won the bet. Rustom claimed that she had, whereas Tehmina recalled Rustom saying that her pallov-daar was good, exceptional even, but not as great as his mother's. In any case, they met at the Sea Lounge two days later and ordered a grilled chicken sandwich, a chicken roll, and two teas. "This is an amazing restaurant," Tehmina said as they sat near the large picture windows overlooking the Gateway of India.

"It's my favorite place to relax," Rustom said. "I love coming here after a day of work and just having a beer or something."

Tehmina realized how little she knew about this man in front of her. She had tried to pry information out of Smits, but Smits was only interested in talking about their high school days and all the pranks that he and Rustom had played on their teachers. And all that Nilu knew about Rustom was that he was one of the most eligible bachelors in town and bore a strong resemblance to the actor Shashi Kapoor and didn't Tehmina think so?

"What do you do for work?" she asked.

"I've just started my own business. I used to work for a builder. Now I have a small factory. I manufacture door hinges and knobs and other metal fittings."

"I see." It sounded dreadfully boring. Tehmina tried but failed to imagine this intense young man in front of her caring much about metal fittings. He looked like he should work in clay or wood, she thought, something that was fresh and warm and came from the earth and smelled good.

"God, Tehmi," Rustom said. "You have an amazing face—it's like it's made of glass. I feel I can read your thoughts and see every emotion behind your skin."

Strangely, she believed him. "What was I just thinking?"

"You were thinking of how utterly boring my job is."

She was flustered. "No, not really."

"Come on now, Tehmi." He laughed. "Tell the truth." He grew serious. "But listen, actually I love what I'm doing. And making parts for doors—I think it's the most important job a man can have."

She started to laugh but he raised a hand to stop her. "I'm not joking. Think about it. What would any civilization be without a door? Think of what a closed door can hide—tears, intimate relations, scandals, murders, mysteries, family secrets, national secrets. Countries spend millions trying to get behind each other's closed doors, no? So do lovers. Conversely, think of what an open door symbolizes—an invitation into someone's home, someone's heart, an entry into a kitchen, a dining room, a bank vault, even"—here his voice dropped a notch—"a bedroom. And what is it that makes it possible to have all those doors opening and shutting?" He paused, looking at her expectantly.

Tehmina felt dizzy under the spell of Rustom's words. "What?" she said stupidly.

"Hinges," he yelled triumphantly. "It's the humble hinge that lets one decide whether to lock the world out to let it in. See why what I do is so important?"

He went on like this for another ten minutes, his face flushed with excitement, the words tumbling out. Tehmina barely understood most of what he was saying but she didn't care. Mostly she enjoyed just looking at that sweet face, gazing upon it as if it was the face of a movie star in a magazine that she'd stare at for hours in bed.

Rustom cut himself off by slamming his right fist into his left palm. "Look at me," he said. "What a bloody idiot I am. I have a pretty girl in front of me and I'm putting her off to sleep by talking about my stupid job."

She didn't know whether to react to the compliment or assure him that she was interested. He saved her from deciding by signaling to the waiter for the check. "Come on," he said. "Let me show you the Gateway of India. It's a beautiful structure." He looked at her full in the face. "And there's a legend that says that if you stand under the arch and make a wish, it comes true." His voice fell to a whisper. "I know what I'm going to wish for. Do you?"

The day she left to go back to Calcutta, Rustom saw her off at the station. He even boarded the train to make sure she and her suitcase were properly situated. Much to her amusement, he searched the compartment until he found a couple he liked and asked them to take care of Tehmina, much as her father had done. She promised to write the first letter and started it minutes after the train had left the station. He promised to write back and to come see her in Calcutta very soon.

Two months after her return home, Rustom knocked on their door one evening. Tehmina had known he was coming but had been too scared and embarrassed to say anything to her parents. A curious Hoshang let in the nervous young man who said he had just come in from Bombay on a very urgent matter. After Tehmina's mother had fussed around him and made him a cup of tea, Rustom got to the purpose of his visit. He had come to ask for Tehmina's hand in marriage.

Hoshang Vakil refused the proposal on the spot. He would never agree to marry off his only child without meeting her prospective in-laws. You should've brought your mummy-daddy along to make the proposal, deekra, he admonished a chastised Rustom. After all, a marriage is between families, not just between the couple, is it not?

It took another month before the two families could meet. Four months after that meeting, the wedding was held in Calcutta. There was a second reception in Bombay. Because of the two receptions, Rustom and Tehmina always celebrated their wedding anniversary twice.

After the wedding, they moved into a small second-floor flat in a building in Nana Chowk. Their first major, extravagant purchase was the bed that Rustom had delivered one afternoon. It was on that bed that Sorab was conceived.

On Sorab's twenty-first birthday, they took their son to the Sea Lounge. They had long ago given up their small Nana Chowk apartment for a spacious three-bedroom flat in Colaba from where it was an easy walk to the Taj.

Over high tea at the Sea Lounge, they argued over who had won the bet that had led to their second meeting. If Sorab looked totally uninterested, they didn't care. "Hey, all I want to know is, who paid for the tea," the bored birthday boy finally asked.

In this, their memories were in agreement. "She did." Rustom grinned with great satisfaction. "Anyway, it doesn't matter who won, yaar. Your mummy was so lattoo-fattoo about me that she would've bought me the Qutub Minar, if I'd asked."

Tehmina fell into a restless sleep. In her dream, Persis was sitting across from her at the Sea Lounge, sipping on a cup of tea. Glancing out of the large picture windows of the restaurant, Tehmina saw the blue-gray waters of the Arabian Sea. The warm afternoon sun danced upon the water, along with hundreds of anchored boats. It was a sight Tehmina had seen a dozen times before. But now there was a new object on the water and the incongruity of it made Tehmina sit up with such a jolt that she spilled some of the tea on her arm. For, sailing among the boats, bobbing on the water, was a bed. A large, ornate teakwood bed. Tehmina turned to Persis but found to her terror that she could not speak. She turned her head again toward the large glass windows and saw that Persis was gazing at the same spot in the distance as she was. But her companion did not seem to have noticed anything strange. Instead, Persis was talking about house keys and telephone bills and other incongruous subjects. And then Tehmina noticed another strange thing—Persis was speaking in Rustom's voice. Or rather, Persis's high voice was tinged with some texture of Rustom's baritone. Like raw cashews rolled and roasted in salt. Tehmina wanted to speak, wanted to point out to Persis the bizarre things that were occurring around them, but she had lost her ability to speak. This is what it must be like to be blind, she thought, and immediately chastised herself for the inaccuracy of her analogy.

Rustom, Tehmina called as she looked around desperately. Where are you? What is my bed—our bed—doing floating on the water? As if in answer, a particularly savage wave rose up and the beautiful dark object disappeared from view. And despite the fact that Tehmina had only had a few minutes to get used to the incongruity of her marital bed floating on the Arabian Sea, she now felt something akin to nostalgia for the sight, felt a hole in her heart the size of the hole in the water created by her drowning bed. She'd never been this alone in her life.

The sound of her own whimpering woke Tehmina up. Persis and the Sea Lounge receded from view as her eyes adjusted to and acknowledged the cold Ohio dark. But the feeling of desolation, of loss, of being utterly alone, remained, as did the terrifying memory of her loss of speech, of being unable to communicate the enormity of her feelings to any living person. She felt the dampness on her cheek and realized that it was the hotness of her tears that she'd earlier felt on her arm, not the spilled tea she'd feared in her dream.

And then she climbed deeper into herself, walked into the dark bylanes of her heart, and picked up the sharpest pebble. Sorab. Yelling at her. Using foul language. The vein bulging on his forehead.

His voice bitter and scary in its frustration. Her son. Raising his voice at her. It wasn't herself she felt sorry for. Not really. No, she was sorry for him because she knew her boy, knew he would suffer from remorse and guilt and shame, would beat himself up for his reckless words, would be unable to forgive himself. Knew that his words would stick like a bitter pill in his throat. Whereas for her, forgiving her children came as easily as swallowing butter. Effortless. Gliding. And yet ... Forgiving, yes. But forgetting—ah, that was a different matter. The memory of Persis's frightened voice on the phone. And then Sorab's sleep-torn, hysterical one. Followed by Susan's shocked, indignant tone. And then the soft, chastising murmurings that followed her from their room into hers. She prayed that Sorab wouldn't apologize to her in the morning. Because she wouldn't be able to say what she wanted to. Because what she'd want to say was: Beta, does a painful gallbladder apologize to the rest of the body for a bad night? Does the heart apologize for a malfunction? You are my heart and my gallbladder and the rest of my body. You are me. So how can one part of myself apologize to the rest of me?

Home, she thought, and the solitary word singed like a fire. I need to be home.

But where home was, she was no longer sure.

CHAPTER EIGHT

Hey, hey, Cookie. Yo, wait up for me."

They were about to get into Sorab's car when Josh came flying down the driveway toward them. Although it was cold outside, the boy had no jacket on and a green glob of snot hung from his nose, Tehmina noticed. Despite her affection for the boy, she instinctively pulled her grandson toward her so that he would not come in contact with the grinning boy who stood before them. God knows what germs Josh was carrying. And children passed germs and viruses between them as casually and generously as a Hindu distributing sweets on Diwali. No point in Cavas getting too close to their neighbor.

But Josh seemed oblivious to the way in which Tehmina had positioned herself between the two boys. "Hi, Cookie." He giggled, poking Cavas in the arm with his index finger. "How you doin'? My mommy says you're a brownie, not a cookie. Just like your dad."

Behind her, Tehmina heard Susan gasp. But before any of the adults could react, Cavas spoke up. Flexing his muscles and striking his favorite he-man pose, he said, "I told you, I'm the Cookie Monster. If you're not careful, I'll gobble you up."

Both boys found this incredibly funny. "Gobble you up," Josh repeated, spluttering with laughter. "Not if I gobble you up first."

Sorab leaned out of the car. "Okay, you crazy boys, we have to go." He turned toward Cavas. "All right, soldier. In the car."

"Hey, where you going? Can I come, too?"

Cavas immediately turned toward Sorab with the pleading look all of them had come to fear and dread. "Yeah, Daddy. Can Joshy come with us?"

Susan cleared her throat. "I'm afraid that's not possible, boys," she said. "This is a family outing—you know, we're going to the mall to do some Christmas shopping. And I'm sure your mom has other plans."

Josh looked crestfallen. "My mommy said all I'm getting for Christmas this year is a lump of coal." But then his face lit up. "But Mommy's not even home. It's just Ernie watching us. And he won't care if I'm out with you."

"Who—who's Ernie?"

In response, Josh went tearing down his driveway. At his front door, he turned around. "Wait for me. I'll be right back." Inside the house, they could hear him yelling. "Ernie, Ernie," he shouted. "Can I go to the mall with Cookie?"

Susan turned to face the two other adults. "How on earth did we get roped into this?" she said. "Come on, let's just get in the car and go."

But a second later a tall, burly man in a white undershirt and jeans was walking toward them, with Josh tugging at his forearm. Tehmina noticed that both his arms were covered with large tattoos. His salt-and-pepper hair was tied back in a ponytail and his gray eyes were sleepy and insolent. "Yeah?" he said to them, as if picking up midway through a conversation.

There was a short silence. Then Sorab got out of the car. "I'm afraid there's been some misunderstanding," he said in the prim, formal tone he slipped into whenever faced with an awkward situation. "We simply mentioned to Josh here that we were going to the mall and, er—it seems like, well, Josh wanted to—"

"I wanna go with them, I wanna go with them," Josh screamed, jumping up and down.

Ernie thumped Josh's back hard enough that the boy stumbled a bit. "Well, you're not. So quit your whining this instant. And get back in the house. Wait till your mommy finds out that you were almost getting into a car with—strangers." And somehow the way his lips curled when he said "strangers" felt like an indictment.

"Where *is* their mother?" And from the frost in Susan's tone, Tehmina could tell that she had picked up on the insult also.

Ernie looked at her evenly. "That, lady, is none of your damn business."

"Listen, buddy," Sorab said. "Watch how you speak to my wife."

Ernie's hands were still in the pockets of his jeans, but somehow he managed to flex his biceps in a way that was subtly intimidating. "And you people stop poking your noses into our business. And don't ever try to lure them kids here into your fancy Saab again."

Tehmina saw her son's face flush red. But before he could say a word, Susan grabbed hold of her husband's arm. "Come on, hon," she muttered. "It's not worth engaging with people like this. Come on, let's just get in the car and go."

Ernie smiled, revealing a gold front tooth. "That's right. Just get in your pretty little car and drive away." He looked down at Josh, who was looking tearfully from one adult to another. "And you. If you know what's good for you, get inside the friggin' house now. Now."

They rode part of the way in a shocked, disbelieving silence. "I don't like that man," Cookie finally said. "He's mean. He looks like Scar in *The Lion King*."

"That's right, darling," Susan replied. "He *is* mean. Just promise me you'll never speak to him, okay?"

"Promise." Cookie was silent for a second and then, "But I really, really like Joshy."

Susan sighed. "I know, hon. We all do. But we can't be friends with him, okay, baby? You can be nice to him on the school bus but no playdates or anything, understand, munchkin?"

And Tehmina heard what Susan did not say—Yeah, we like Joshy. But we can't save the world. She turned her gaze to get a better look at her son's profile, silently willing him to say something, something kind and generous and honorable. But Sorab was silent. He's changed, Tehmina thought, and her eyes inexplicably stung with tears. This country has changed him. There was a time when my Sorab would have never stood by and watched a little child being abused by that brute of a man. But he's ... duller now. Not that sharp young man from Bombay who saw injustice on every street corner.

Tehmina remembered an incident from many years ago. It was the only time she had ever heard Sorab openly challenge his father. During the 1992 Hindu-Muslim riots that inflamed Bombay, Sorab was almost beside himself with worry. He phoned every day from America to make sure his parents were okay. Several times, he threatened to swoop into Bombay and take them back with him. Realizing how worried his son was, Rustom made Tehmina swear to not tell their son that they had a Muslim family living in their apartment. Tehmina herself had been upset when Rustom had come home one evening and told her that he had just run into Ismail Husseni, the architect who lived on the ground floor of the adjacent building and who was petrified at the thought of the Hindu mobs breaking into his home. "I told him he and Mrs. Husseni should move in with us until all this blows off," Rustom said casually. "They'll be coming over in a few hours. The poor people have not left their flat in a week. I told them to stay for as long as they need to. They can sleep in the guest bedroom, right, darling? And oh, Tehmi. Ismail wants us to keep their jewelry for him. So empty out the safe, would you, so that they have room for their stuff?"

"Rustom, are you mad?" an aghast Tehmina said. "With servants and the dhobi and others coming through here, you think we can keep this a secret, that we have a Muslim family staying here?"

"Who said it has to be a secret?" Rustom's chin jutted out slightly, a sure sign that he had made up his mind.

"Janu. I know you mean well. But surely the Husseni have some other relatives? So many Muslims have already left Bombay. You are putting us at risk, janu. And—it's not even like we know them that well."

Rustom looked angry. "And how do you think they can get out of town, with Hindu mobs prowling the streets looking for Muslims to kill? And bloody hell, why should they leave Bombay, anyway? This is their home."

As always, she gave in. And her doubts and recriminations were silenced when she saw the gratitude in the eyes of the Husseni when they rang the doorbell a few hours later. Ismail Husseni had always been a large, gregarious man. Now he seemed diminished, as if fear had eaten away at him. Tehmina was horrified by the change in the man and that horror steeled her against the dark mutterings of the Hindu servants and the Parsi neighbors, who complained that the Sethnas were poking their noses in matters that didn't concern them.

Two days later, when the Sethnas stepped out of the building to go to the nearby fire temple, Krishna, the homeless man who lived across the street, slid up to them. "Salaam, Rustom seth," he said. "Something important I have to tell you."

For no apparent reason, Tehmina's stomach muscles suddenly twisted. But Rustom's voice was steady. "What is it?" he said dismissively.

"People are talking, seth. Saying ugly things about you. Rumor is you have a family of beef-eaters living with you. The Hindu brothers are angry, seth. They say they will burn down any apartment that harbors those Muslim dogs." Krishna squinted at them and in the evening light there was a strange, ecstatic look on his face.

A bellow emitted from deep within Rustom. "Listen, you traitorous bastard," he roared. "You tell your goonda friends that if they have the balls, to come and talk to me directly. I'll break their scrawny necks with my bare hands, I will. Saala, chootia, everybody's a hero under the cover of the night. But if their pricks still work, tell them to try talking to me in broad daylight. Then we'll see who the real warriors are. One more thing: In my house, I will have any guest that I want, understand?"

An ingratiating smile fell across Krishna's face. "Rustom seth, calm down, calm down. Lower your voice, please. Why for all unnecessarily you're getting so excited. I was just saying that—"

"I know exactly what you were saying, you fucker. You eat my family's food, you wash your bloody arsehole each morning with the water my wife heats up for you, and this is how you repay us? You tell your Sena friends if they harm one member of my household who's under my protection, they'll have my wrath to deal with. The bloody police commissioner and I played together in our diapers when we were infants, understand, chootia? My connections go all the way to Delhi. You eunuchs find some other family to bully."

"Rustom seth, please. Calm down." This time, Krishna's distress seemed real. "Tehmibai, please. Take your husband away. All will be fine, bai, I promise. You trust your Krishna. I'll take care of everything."

As they walked away, Tehmina squeezed her husband's hand,

hoping he could sense her pride in him. Much to her surprise she saw that his shoulders were shaking and that Rustom was trying his best to suppress his laughter. "Did you see the look on Krishna's face when I made up that cock-and-bull story about knowing the police commissioner? Shit, the fellow is at least ten years younger than I am. Hope nobody checks."

Much later, after the riots had ended and the Hussenis were back in their apartment, she had told Sorab the story. She had wanted to brag about Rustom's bravery, but to her dismay, Sorab was furious. "Has he lost his mind, Mummy? Why all this herogiri? Why does he have to be the only one to always stick his neck out?" Even over the phone wires she could hear the indignation in her son's voice. "Let me talk to Dad, immediately."

It was the first time Tehmina had ever heard father and son exchange words. Unable to hear the disappointment in Rustom's voice, unable to face up to the stunned looks he kept flashing at her, she had left the room and busied herself in the kitchen. Later, she heard Rustom hang up the phone and head to their bedroom. She knew she should go comfort him, but something made her hesitate. Fifteen minutes later, Rustom came into the kitchen and leaned on the kitchen counter. "Well, I guess you heard our son's reaction," he said, and Tehmina could hear him struggling to strike a light tone. "Guess he thinks his old man is crazy."

She took a step toward him. "He's scared, Rustom, that's all. Him being so far away, he worries about us, janu."

Rustom shook his head. "I suppose. Still, he's changed. Sorab has changed."

Now, almost against her will, Rustom's words came back to her. She caught Sorab glancing at her in the rearview mirror and for a guilty second she thought her son had read her uncharitable thoughts.

Susan's voice broke her reverie. "Well," her daughter-in-law was saying. "This is supposed to be our family outing. Let's not let some petty people spoil our evening, okay?" Tehmina heard the brittleness in the short laugh that followed that sentence. But she also heard something else—a pleading, a hesitant coaxing, a wistfulness in Susan's voice, and she responded to that.

"Silly people everywhere. The world over," she said. "My God, the stories I could tell you about some of our neighbors in Bombay. Did I ever tell you about Dina Master, the old lady who lived upstairs from us when I was a young girl in Calcutta? No? Well, she was a terror. Mean as anything. Used to call the neighborhood children to her apartment and then frighten us with her tall-tall stories. She had a big jute bag that she kept in her living room and she told us that it was filled with rats and snakes and whatall and that if we misbehaved or disobeyed our parents, she would put us in that dark sack along with the rodents."

"Good Lord." Susan gasped. "That's abuse. Why, this country, you could call Children's Services on that woman in a heartbeat."

"The worst part was, our parents all knew this. In fact, they probably even encouraged her. It was a kind of discipline, you see, to make sure we didn't get bad report cards and all. And the funny part is, I believed that mean old woman for years and years. I was so afraid of that gunny bag, I can't tell you."

"Oh, Mamma." Sorab laughed, and even from the backseat, Tehmina sensed that he was rolling his eyes at her. "You were always so gullible. Good thing you married someone as worldly and smart as Dad—that's probably the only thing that saved you. The way your parents had you spoiled I don't think—"

"Spoiled? You think allowing your child to be terrorized by a crazy old woman is spoiled?" Susan was indignant. "That's not my definition of *spoiled*."

Sorab flashed his mother a quick look in the rearview mirror and Tehmina caught that look. She knew exactly what her son was saying to her—that some things simply didn't translate. For Susan, the old lady's treatment of the young children who lived around her was abusive, something serious enough to report to the police. Whereas the truth was more complicated, more subtle than that. Yes, she had been afraid of Dina Master, but even as a child, she knew somewhere deep within her that her parents would die before putting her in harm's way. There was that blind trust, that confidence in their devotion and love for her. She had responded to the neighbor as she would to a wicked witch in a scary novel—she was frightened but she was not traumatized. She wondered if poor Josh felt that same kind of security she had known as a kid, if he had experienced that safe, smug feeling that came from knowing you were unconditionally loved. Somehow, she doubted it.

"Here's something I've never told you children before," Tehmina now said. "Do you know that until I got married my mamma used to spoon-feed me? I was a very fussy eater, you see, and so Mamma would coax me to eat. Even to the extent of feeding me herself."

Sorab snorted. "Hah. How's *that* for being spoiled?"

Susan shook her head. "That's weird," she said. "You Parsis are just weird." And mother and son exchanged a grin in the rearview mirror.

Susan turned in her seat. "How come you didn't raise your son like that? How come you taught Sorab how to cook and clean and do all the things none of his Indian male friends would dream of doing?"

"That was his father's doing," came the immediate reply. "I'm afraid I can't take any of the credit for that. That's how my Rustom was raised, you know, and he insisted that his son be able to look after himself. Possibly the only fights we ever had were about this issue."

"Well, then I wish you'd won those fights." Sorab laughed. "Would've made my life a lot easier."

Susan punched her husband's arm affectionately. "Oh no you don't."

They were silent for a moment as the car flew smoothly down the freeway. Tehmina spoke into the dark. "I saw him last night. I mean . . . I dreamed of him last night."

Even in the dark, even with the stereo on, she sensed the sudden tension in the car. She immediately noticed that Sorab didn't ask her to go on, didn't ask her to describe the dream. It is as if Rustom has been banned from our lives, she thought. Each time I mention his name, it's as if I've broken some social rule, as if I'm smoking a cigarette in a nonsmoking restaurant. Does everything in this country have an expiration date? she wondered. Even grief and mourning?

She had thought that Cookie had dozed off, but now he shifted beside her. "I want to buy a Christmas present for Grandpa," he announced. "To put under the tree."

Sorab cleared his throat. "Grandpa's in heaven, sonny," he said, as if he was explaining this to his son for the first time. "He can't receive presents."

"Well, maybe he'll come down the chimney with Santa," Cookie replied. "I can write to Santa and tell him to bring Grandpa."

There was a brief pause and then Susan said, "That's a great idea. But let's buy him something small so that it can fit in the chimney, okay?" She half turned toward Tehmina. "What do you think, Mom? Think Rustom pappa would like some candy?"

Tehmina blinked back the tears that formed in her eyes at hearing Rustom's name on Susan's lips. "That . . . that would be lovely. Rustom always had a sweet tooth. We all do."

"And I want to buy something for Joshy," Cookie said. He was on a roll now.

Tehmina felt her heart bursting with pride. Cookie reminded her so much of Sorab as a boy—generous, sensitive, quick to spot the pain in others. She put her arm around the boy and gave his head a silent kiss.

"We're not buying gifts for Joshy, son," Sorab said in a flat voice. "We don't exchange gifts with our neighbors."

"But he said he was only going to get a lump of coal for Christmas," the boy whined. "You heard him."

"Oh great," Susan muttered under her breath.

"That's just a figure of speech, hon," Sorab said. "His mom was just kidding him. Nobody really gets a lump of coal for Christmas."

"Yes they do." Cavas was triumphant. "The little boy in *A Tale of Two Christmases.* He was mean to the family dog and he got a lump of coal in his stocking."

Sorab pulled into the crowded parking lot of the mall and began searching for a space. "That's just a story," he said. "Anyway, we're not buying a gift for Joshy." He pulled into a space far from the Sears entrance.

"But he's my friend," Cavas blubbered as they walked toward the mall. "And I have fifteen dollars saved up."

Tehmina could see Sorab getting exasperated. She grabbed the boy's hand and held him back. "You two walk ahead," she said. "Cookie and I will follow. Go on, go ahead."

Susan shot her a grateful glance as she took her husband's hand. As the couple walked ahead, Tehmina bent toward her grandson. She knew what she was about to do was wrong, but she couldn't help herself. Before Cookie had spoken up, she herself had decided to buy the two neighbor boys a small gift each. Despite Sorab's reassurances, she was not at all convinced that that Tara was above giving her sons a lump of coal for Christmas. Any woman who could leave her children with that monster of a man was capable of anything. It was one of nature's tricks that a woman like that could give birth to two innocent, beautiful children. There was no way she was leaving the mall tonight without buying something for them. Susan and Sorab could shop on their own for a while. She would take Cavas with her and then meet up with the other two in an hour or so. Besides, she needed to find a gift for Susan's dad, anyway.

They stepped out of the cold and into the heated comfort of the building and immediately heard the familiar tinny music of the carousel that competed with the piped Christmas music playing throughout the mall. "Listen," Tehmina said to Susan and Sorab. "How about I take Cookie shopping with me for a while? That way, you two don't get dragged down by me. I'm moving slow, today."

Susan jumped at the offer. "You sure, Mom? All right, how about we meet here in the food court in about an hour? Does that give you enough time?"

She reached for Sorab's hand, but he hesitated. "Call us on the cell if you get lost or anything," he said, and Tehmina laughed.

"Don't worry. We'll be fine. I know my way around this mall. You children go enjoy yourselves."

She watched as Sorab and Susan walked away. Then she turned to face her grandson. "Cookie," she said, bending toward the boy and lowering her voice. "Are you good at keeping a secret?"

CHAPTER NINE

For God's sake, man, you're turning into a fucking woman, Sorab chided himself. Get a grip on your bloody emotions.

Ever since his father's death, Sorab had noticed this disconcerting trend—he could cry at the drop of a hat. Now, surrounded by thousands of strangers busy pursuing their own private happiness in the shape of DVD players and iPods, he was even more conscious of his runaway emotions and his growing inability to control them.

The object of Sorab's latest emotional upheaval: the sight of his son and mother sitting in the food court of the mall, sharing an order of french fries as they waited for Susan and him. Something about the angle of both their heads leaning in toward each other—one gray with the weight of the years, the other head brown and shining with the tinsel of endless opportunity—something about this sight brought the all-too-familiar sting of tears to his eyes. Susan was by his side, as laden with last-minute gifts as he was, and he wondered if she had noticed anything different about him, this worrying softness that grew within him, like a loaf of moist white bread that rose alarmingly each day. They had a name for men like that in Bombay. Milquetoast. Yah, he was turning into a bloody milquetoast.

"You okay, hon?" Susan asked, and as always he was irritated and thankful for her amazing ability to read him, to know every eyelash-thin shift within him.

"Yup, fine," he responded gruffly, but then, just like a friggin' woman, as if he had no control over his mouth, he heard himself say, "Look at them sitting there. As if they were the only two people on earth. Don't they look beautiful?"

Beautiful? No red-blooded American man would ever be caught saying "beautiful." That's how Parsi men—and that, too, Parsi men of his father's generation—talked. What the fuck was happening to him?

"They do," Susan said, and try as he did, he couldn't hear anything ironic or mocking in her tone. She sighed heavily. "Having Mom here has been so good for Cookie and," she added softly, "for you."

He tensed. "How do you mean? For me?"

Susan shrugged. "I don't know. I can't explain. It's just that—I think you need your family around you. And—you just seem—I don't know, not as much in a hurry as before, maybe? Just softer."

There you go, Sorab thought. Softer. That dreaded word. Even his wife would soon be calling him Doughboy. No wonder Grace had all but said she was going to bypass him for the next promotion. He was probably leaking his emotions all over the fucking place like some incontinent old woman, and all of them were too bloody polite to point it out to him.

Suddenly Susan was laughing. "What's so funny?" he started to ask, and she shook her head, still spluttering with laughter. "You. You're what's so funny. Good God, darling, you should see your face. Listen, I have news for you. When women say a man is softer, they mean it as a compliment. Though I've yet to meet a man who thinks of it that way."

"Well," he whispered, his voice husky. "As long as you're not referring to my you-know-what as being soft."

Susan laughed again. "No, I'm not, you idiot. I'm referring to here," and she tapped his heart with her index finger, "though I should probably also refer to up here," as she tapped his head. "But you men—you hear the word *soft* and that's all you can think of."

He shifted the bags he was carrying into his right hand and linked his free hand with hers. "When I first came to this country," he said, "I used to have these dreams. I would dream that the doorbell in my apartment would ring and I'd answer the door and my parents would be there. And I'd think to myself, 'You bloody idiot, see how easy it is for you to see them, all you have to do is answer the door.' But then I'd wake up and realize it was only a dream, that they were actually thousands of miles away, and I'd feel this awful, oppressive feeling. All the lightness of the dream, the ease of possibility, would get wiped out the minute I woke up. Know what I mean? I used to dread those dreams, and God, there were a million variations of them. Like someone would be calling my name from below the window and I'd go to answer and it would be my dad, asking to be let in." He stopped abruptly. "Why am I telling you all this right now?"

"Because it's important to you. Go on." Although they were just a few yards away from where Tehmina and Cavas sat with their backs to them, they had stopped walking. Susan motioned to an empty table at the edge of the food court and sat down. For a second, Sorab hesitated, caught between not wanting to leave his mother alone much longer but also enjoying this rare opportunity to talk to Susan alone. He sat down.

"So, anyway. For years and years I felt like a man divided. And try as I might, I couldn't bridge the damn distance. And it wasn't all bad, I'm not saying that. In fact, you know, I think this hunger that I had earlier on, this drive to succeed, maybe it was part of that same hunger. I mean, I'd paid such a high price to come here—I'd left behind a comfortable home, a familiar city, friends and parents who adored me—that I had to make it all worth it, had to justify that sacrifice. So I was a young man in a hurry, I guess."

"Boy, were you ever." Susan smiled and the look in her eyes told Sorab that she was remembering his determined, relentless courtship of her. Although Susan had been in some of his classes, he had not really noticed her until the night of a party at the home of another graduate student. They had both been a little drunk that night, and when the conversation turned to politics they had locked horns in a fiery, impassioned exchange—Susan had been a Republican in those days, a fact that Sorab could not square with the intelligent, sensitive woman in front of him—that ultimately cleared the room as the others left out of boredom or exhaustion. So it was only the two of them left standing, and still they argued at two A.M. on the streets of a frigid Ohio as Sorab walked Susan home and up the two flights to her apartment. Then they called a truce long enough to make passionate love, which somehow seemed an extension of their violent arguing. When they woke up the next morning, Sorab was smitten by this exasperatingly intelligent and beautiful girl, but Susan declared that she was bewildered by her behavior, and while the sex was lovely, thank you very much, there was no way she could date a die-hard liberal. It had taken him four long months to change her mind.

Susan squeezed his hand. "Those were good days, huh, babe? But you know what, hon? I'm glad you're no longer in such an awful hurry. I like to think I'll have you around in my old age."

He squeezed back. "It's thanks to you, really. If you hadn't married me and given me Cookie, I don't know what would have happened to me. Honest." He paused for a second. "Do you know the first time in my whole life that I truly felt at peace? I'm talking about contentment now, not passion or joy. I mean, I was thrilled when you finally married me. As for the day Cookie was born and I held him for the first time—that was like tasting heaven. But just good, old-fashioned peace? It was during Dad and Mom's visit after Cookie was born. Having my new son and my old parents in the same house, under the same roof—I can't describe that feeling to you. It was like they represented the past and you and Cookie the future, you know? I felt whole, like someone had stitched me back up. I used to think, anything could happen now—a tornado, a war, a bomb could go off. But we would all be together." He grimaced. "Sorry. You know I always get corny this time of the year."

Susan gave him that shy, rueful look that could still make his heart do a backflip. "It's what I love about you. All you Parsi men with your sentimental streak. I just wish some of your ways would rub off on Bobby. He's a grown man and still believes in all that macho American-male bullshit." Bobby was Susan's older brother and the most taciturn of men. In all the years that Sorab had known Susan's family, Bobby had probably said twenty words to him. Bobby's silent persona was a running joke in the family, what Susan called Bobby's lifelong Clint Eastwood impersonation.

"Well, at least I come by it honestly. I remember, as a kid I used to be so shocked—here was my dad, you know, this big, muscular guy, and we'd be watching some god-awful Bollywood melodrama on television and he'd be openly sobbing. Even Mummy—and you know what a softy she is—even she would look scandalized at how unself-consciously he would cry during a movie. I was always so embarrassed I never dared have a friend over when we were watching TV."

"That's because he was truly a man," Susan said fiercely, and Sorab realized with wonder that she was defending Rustom against what she thought was Sorab's criticism of him. "He was a real man—so comfortable within his skin."

He opened his mouth to protest, to explain that he agreed with her, that he was only being half-serious in describing his embarrassment at his father's easy tears, when he realized that he was not sure. Some part of him was still uneasy at the thought of his tall, powerful father dissolving into tears at the cheap histrionics of a Hindi film. Some part of him admired Bobby for his strong-and-silent persona because it conformed to his adolescent beliefs of how a real man should conduct himself. Some part of him despised his soft, middle-class Indian upbringing, where aunts and uncles were always hugging and kissing him or pulling his cheeks and telling him what a good boy he was. Perhaps it was one of the reasons he had fled India for America, so that he could leave behind the doughy softness of childhood and harden into a man. And America had been good for him—it had toughened him up, made him competitive, independent, eager to get ahead, single-minded in his pursuit of success. It had unleashed something in him. Whereas in India people were always telling him not to appear to be too ambitious, too hungry, here in America that ambition and hunger were revered, encouraged, and rewarded. When he had first arrived in graduate school he felt as if someone had let him out of a cardboard box so large that he had never even known that all his life he had been curled up inside this box, biding his time. Here he could be as competitive, as aggressive, as loud, as greedy, as expansive as he wanted. Here he could reach for the stars and nobody told him to be careful, that pride always comes before a fall, no old grandparent told him the cautionary tale of Icarus flying too close to the sun and getting burned. Here was a sky-is-the-limit country of towering ambition and large dreams, a fabled country that believed in dreams, that was itself a kind of dream. And it fit Sorab like a glove. Like a friggin' glove. It was as if the country had been designed with him in mind, him and the millions of other restless souls who were misfits in the land of their birth and who arrived at America's shores brimming with energy, bursting at the seams with pent-up ambition so combustible it felt like violence. And for him (unlike many others), for him, it all worked out. It was all going well, all following a plan—a smart, beautiful wife, a gorgeous, intelligent son, a big house in the suburbs, two imported cars in the garage, a series of jobs where he had always outperformed everyone else. But then his father had to die and that milky, sappy streak of sentimentality that had always flowed within Rustom had leaked its way into his son.

"Earth to Sorab," Susan was saying, and he jumped guiltily. "Sorry. Just lost in my thoughts."

"No kidding." Susan grinned. "Well, hon? Shall we go join the others? I can't wait to see how much money Mom has spent buying yet more gifts for her precious grandson."

"Yeah, sure. I'm just surprised Cookie hasn't spotted us yet." Still, he lingered. "Hey, Suse. I just wanna say, y'know, thank you for loving me so much. Honest. Without you, I don't know what—"

"You're welcome," Susan said softly. "And by the way, you're pretty easy to love." She rose from her chair and Sorab could hear the grin in her voice. "Also, I gotta keep my man happy, you know? Otherwise, you'll be like Percy, on your fourth American wife."

He groaned. "I just hope the poor bastard stays married this time. What an optimist Percy is, bless him. I can't imagine getting married twice, let alone four times."

"You said he's coming to Perin's party tomorrow night, right?" Susan asked.

"Are you kidding? If there's free homemade Parsi food you think any force on earth could keep Percy away?"

"Really. What was I thinking?" She strode a few paces ahead of Sorab. "Hi, Cookie," she called. "Yoo-hoo. Over here, darling."

CHAPTER TEN

Homi and Perin Jasawala lived out in the country, although it was different from any countryside that Tehmina was familiar with. Unlike India, where the countryside was made up of a few emaciated cows in dry brown fields and clusters of impoverished villages, the drive to the Jasawalas' home took them past shopping plazas, a Wal-Mart, a Best Buy, and then a series of open fields punctuated with the occasional red barn and silo. Every so often they came across a large, well-tended house sitting on acres of land, many with garages or work sheds so large that Tehmina couldn't help but think that in India a family of twenty could've lived inside one of them. As they approached the Jasawalas' home, Tehmina noticed that the houses got larger and wood and aluminum-sided homes gave way to stone-and-brick mansions.

Still, the Jasawalas' house surpassed all the others in its opulence. Other than the fact that Sorab had told Tehmina earlier that the couple had only recently moved into the home that they had had built, Tehmina would have easily believed that the Jasawalas had paid to move an old mansion from England or Wales to some farmland in Ohio. As Sorab pulled up in the circular driveway, Tehmina noticed an enormous Christmas tree that spanned the height of the tall windows on the first and second floors.

"Holy shit," Sorab breathed. "Homi's practice must be doing well."

"Well, to hear Perin tell it, it's she who brings in the serious bucks," Susan said.

"I believe that," Sorab said. "Have you seen that huge billboard as you go down Richfield Road? I think her firm probably handles ninety percent of all the immigration cases in northeast Ohio. Percy says he ran into his former boss the other day and the guy was moaning about how Perin was going to put them all out of business."

"It's the smartest thing Percy ever did, going to work for Perin."

"Yup. Though to be honest, I wasn't sure at first. I just thought—I dunno—better not to mix business with friendship."

"Well, working with Perin, he'll never starve, that's a fact. That woman is such a dynamo."

The human dynamo was waiting for them at the front door. Perin was resplendent in a red sari and gold jewelry, looking for all the world as if she was dressed for a Parsi wedding in Bombay.

"Aavo, aavo." She beamed. "Welcome to our humble home."

Sorab whistled. "Wow, Perin. Nothing humble about this house."

Perin looked away, as if embarrassed. "Oh, it's nothing, nothing," she said. "The upstairs is a little bit cramped, actually."

"Listen to her." The cathedral ceilings in the foyer made Homi's voice boom even louder as he approached them. "Imagine the gall of this woman—over nine thousand square feet and she's still complaining about the size of the house. And the funny part is, both of us grew up in tiny little apartments on Grant Road, where there was barely room for the mosquitoes, let alone human beings."

Tehmina remembered the story from her earlier visits to America. Homi and Perin had been childhood sweethearts, growing up in adjacent apartments in a building on Grant Road. Tehmina couldn't remember what Perin had told her was the reason for the long-standing enmity between the two families, but she remembered being amazed at the fact that the two of them, who had fallen in love when they were twelve, had kept their love a secret for at least the next ten years. In fact, they had secretly gotten married in a civil marriage about a month before Homi left for America, with a promise to call for his new bride as soon as he got settled. Nobody knew except Perin's best friend, who had also been a witness at their clandestine wedding. Over a year later, Perin had left behind a note for her family and boarded a plane with the money she and Homi had saved. She arrived in Ohio during the worst snowstorm in a decade and moved into Homi's tiny one-bedroom apartment. Never having seen snow before, she had showed up at the airport dressed in a long-sleeved cotton shirt and a skirt. Homi had had to give his shivering bride his coat while he went to retrieve the car he had borrowed from a friend.

And after all that—after they had struggled while Homi went to medical school and Perin got a job as a cashier at Kmart, after they began a tepid reconciliation with their respective families, after they bought their first car and later, their first home, after Homi got his first job as a psychiatrist at a state hospital, after the disappointments of trying and failing to have children, after their first, emotional trip back to India to see their families for the first time in years, after Perin's decision to go to law school and Homi's ready support—after having cobbled a life together from nothing but the strength of their devotion to each other, after all this, Homi had had an affair. And threatened to destroy everything that they had built.

Tehmina only knew about this because she had heard Homi talk about it. On television. On one of those chatty local morning shows that usually gave her a headache simply from the wattage of the television host's bright, fake smile. But here was Homi looking serious and sincere as he promoted the self-help book he had written. Using words that no self-respecting Indian would ever use—words like *manipulative* and *codependent* and *controlling.* Heck, in India we have one word for all these things, Tehmina had thought: We call it love. But what really shocked her was how casually Homi was talking about the most intimate, private aspects of his life. How freely he was discussing, with a perfect stranger, before an audience of thousands of strangers, his emotional life, his innermost thoughts and feelings. Despite Homi's apparent sincerity, Tehmina found herself stiffening with shame and embarrassment. For the umpteenth time she marveled at this strange country that her son now called home—how the lines between public and private blurred altogether. Are there no thoughts or emotions that are so sacred, so private that they feel compelled to guard them from the intrusion of the world? she marveled. Is there no behavior that one is too embarrassed to speak about? And here was Homi talking about how the sex had stopped being fun, how he and Perin had had to rebuild their sex lives after she had discovered the affair. It was all supposed to be positive and life-affirming—in fact, Homi now conducted weekend seminars to help other couples whose marriages were in trouble—but Tehmina was mortified. She couldn't help but think of Perin's embarrassed reaction to her husband's spilling of the beans.

But now, looking at the Jasawalas standing with their arms around each other, she could tell that she had misread the situation. Homi had obviously promoted the book and embarked on this new career path as marriage counselor with Perin's full blessings. And why would that be so surprising? she now asked herself. Clearly, Perin was not immune to America's unspoken insistence on self-disclosure. In India, it was just movie stars who were expected to make perfect fools of themselves by revealing the secrets of their (mostly shallow and boring) personal lives. Here, it was expected of everyone. The movie stars and rock singers were not enough to sustain the unceasing appetite for gossip and salacious details. So even ordinary people like Homi and Perin had to do their bit to feed the monster.

They had embarked on another uniquely American custom—the showing off of the new house. Labeling it the twenty-five-cent tour, Homi was escorting them from room to room of the new house. Apparently, all the other guests who were in the living room and the kitchen—which Tehmina thought was bigger than the kitchen of most restaurants—had already had the tour because they made no move to join them.

"This desk we bought in Kenya," Homi was saying. "Perin just fell in love with it. Had it shipped home." Already he had told them the story behind the Italian marble in the kitchen, the Oriental rug in the dining room, and the Japanese print that hung over the fireplace. Tehmina felt like a member of a Greek chorus—all she was expected to contribute was an occasional "oooh" and "arre wah."

"It's beautiful, yaar. You guys did a great job," Sorab said, and hearing the sincerity in her son's voice, with no hint of envy or irony, Tehmina felt her heart swell with love. She also felt a new appreciation for Sorab's expensive but more modest house. Its scale felt more manageable, more human, somehow, compared with this house, which still had the faint smell of new paint. Tehmina thought with pleasure at how Cookie kicked off his dirty shoes as soon as he walked in the door, how she sometimes found his clothes lying in a heap in the bathroom. This house was too clean, too antiseptic for her taste. Why, the Jasawalas even had white carpeting in the living room. And she realized what was missing—there was no Cookie to spill a drink on the kitchen floor, no Cookie to leave his school projects all over the dining-room table. No Cookie to humanize this house, to occupy it, to make it real with his carelessness, his childlike clumsiness, his clutter. This house needed a child to make it a home.

As if on cue, Cookie shifted by her side. "Granna, I'm bored," he announced. "Can I go downstairs to play with Shirin and all?"

Homi let out his booming laugh. "Yah, I guess this is all pretty boring," he said. Suddenly he crinkled his eyes and fell down to his knees so that he was eye level with the boy. "Hey, Cookie. So tell me. Any new adventures at school?"

"School's out."

"Oh yes, of course. That's right." Homi looked disappointed. And then, as if he couldn't help himself, "Are you doing your homework now? Or is it still against your religious principles?"

"Homi," Sorab and Susan groaned in unison.

Homi's eyes were shining. "Oops, sorry. But I can't help myself. It's such a great story."

Earlier in the year, Cookie had accidentally discovered Sorab's old collection of Calvin and Hobbes, devoured them, and decided that Calvin was his alter ego. Sorab and Susan had to endure weeks where every question that they asked him was met with a smart-aleck answer that came right out of the books. Cookie had even gone around the house doing daily polls rating Sorab's performance as a dad, much as the fictitious Calvin did. They had thought it funny until the day Cookie refused to take a test at school, scrawling on the page, "I cannot take this test as it is against my religious principles." Then they had to confiscate the incendiary comic books.

A wicked smile came over Cookie's face. But before he could respond to Homi in his best Calvinesque voice, Susan hastily grabbed the boy by the shoulders and led him toward the door of the bedroom. "Okay, hon," she said, "why don't you go downstairs and play with the other kids? We'll be down in a minute or so."

After Cookie had left, Susan turned toward Homi. "Calvin and Hobbes is a taboo subject in our house," she said. "You have to promise not to bring that up in front of Cookie."

Homi folded his hands in mock apology. "Sorry, sorry. I just can't help it. It's just so funny. He's just . . . he's such a creative kid." His face was shiny, eager. "So. Are there other stories? How has he driven the teacher mad recently?"

Sorab burst out laughing. "Saala, I'm glad we don't live too close to you. You'd be a horrible influence on my son."

"He's always been like that," Perin said. "He was just like your Cavas when he was a boy. Brimming with mischief and fun."

"Okay, I'll tell you his latest escapade," Sorab said. "But don't remind him of it, okay? You promise?"

"Promise."

"Okay, so he had this older teacher this year. Mrs. Marriott. Acts like she's eighty though she's probably only in her fifties. So Cookie's in her class and he's chewing on his pencil, right? And Mrs. Marriott tells him to remove the pencil from his mouth because it's got lead in it and can cause lead poisoning. Well, as luck would have it, Cookie's been reading this book about the history of the pencil. So he stands up and in front of the whole class tells her she's misinformed, that pencils don't contain lead but are made from graphite. Can you imagine? This poor woman being lectured by a self-righteous seven-year-old? And when Cookie adopts that professorial tone of voice, I tell you, he's insufferable."

Homi and Perin roared with laughter. "Oh my God, that's so cute," Perin wept. "Oh, I would've paid money to see the look on the teacher's face."

"Well, we did," Susan said. "Saw the look on her face, I mean. She complained to us at the next teacher's conference. And I tell you, it wasn't a look I care to see again. She looked like she wanted to skin him alive."

"And if we'd done something like this in India, they would've skinned us alive," Homi said promptly. "There, you know, the whole thing is teachers are like gods. You can have the most incompetent buffoons and still you have to respect them, just because they're teachers."

Tehmina heard the bitterness in his voice and marveled at it. All of Sorab's friends seemed so bitter when they talked about India. The education system, the corruption, the postal service, the slow-moving traffic, the bureaucracy—they seemed to criticize everything. Is that why they left in the first place—because they were so angry about everything? And had Sorab—her sunny boy with his sweet disposition—had he felt the same way? Or did he see the things to cherish—the strong family bonds, the way neighbors looked out for one another, the busy, warm aliveness of the streets, such a contrast to the sad, bleak solitariness of life here?

The doorbell rang again and they heard the door open and Percy's familiar voice saying, "Helloooo? Anybody home?"

"We're up here with Sorab and Susan," Perin yelled. "Be down in a sec. Please make yourself comfy."

But the next second they heard the sound of Percy bounding up the stairs. As usual, Tehmina's heart gave a lift when she saw Percy's cheerful face. "Hey there," he said to the group. And then, spotting Tehmina, he went up to her and kissed her on the cheek. "Hello, Mamma." He grinned. "How are you? Hope that ugly son of yours is taking good care of you. If not, just move in with us, okay? Room and board free, all for the price of your fabulous dhansak."

"I tell you a million times to stop by for dinner whenever you want, deekra," Tehmina replied. But even as she extended the invitation, she wondered if Susan was offended by her presumptuousness. "You don't need an invitation," she finished lamely.

"Arre, Mamma, be careful what riffraff you invite to the house," Sorab said, slapping his best friend on the back. "With this bugger, if you promise him food he'll move in with us permanently."

"Not a chance," Percy said promptly. "At some point I'll have to go home. Unless you can imitate my lovely Julie's talents in bed." He cast an apologetic look at Tehmina. "Pardon my French, Mamma," he added vaguely.

"Speaking of food, the party's been catered by Yasmin Shroff," Perin said. "We had her food at another party recently and thought she was quite good." She poked Percy in the ribs. "Hope her pallov-daar meets your approval."

"Oh, I'm sure it will be great. But I tell you, nobody can make daar like this lady here," Percy said, putting an arm around Tehmina. "Her chicken dhansak kept me alive when I was a young boy." And despite the lightness of his tone, a look passed between Percy and Tehmina that captured the closeness that they had shared over the years. Percy's mother had been Tehmina's best friend, and when she died of breast cancer, Tehmina was as devastated as the twelve-year-old Percy. She would have taken Percy in anyway, would have insisted that the boy stop by for tea and a light dinner after school, even if his father, Bomi, had not been the drunken wastrel that he was. But as it was, she and Rustom had decided that the young boy should be protected from his father's drunken rages and bouts of self-pity. If Tehmina had had her way, Percy would've moved in with them permanently. Instead, she tried to keep the boy over at their house as much as possible, including on weekends. Every trip or outing that the Sethnas took included a fourth member, every play or concert that they attended they bought a fourth ticket for. Lost in the fumes of alcohol, Bomi was only too happy to give up responsibility for his son. A few times they even paid the boy's school tuition when Bomi was delinquent with the fees, and soon it made sense for them to also check on Percy's progress report when they went to Cathedral for parent-teacher conferences for Sorab. They were happy to do all this in a silent, unassuming way, though each time they ran into Bomi in the street, he went into one of his loud, bombastic raves and promised to repay them for every paisa they spent on his son. The man was completely oblivious to the embarrassment he caused them, and worse, to the mortification he aroused in his only child. Still, for the most part, the Sethnas' caring for Percy went unspoken and unacknowledged, which is how they liked it. Only once did they have to intervene directly: after a sobbing Percy had shown up on their doorstep one Friday evening with red welts on his thin brown body where Bomi had hit him with his belt. Then Rustom had gone pale in the face, thrown on a shirt over his sadra, and headed for the door. A frightened Tehmina had tried to stop him, had asked him what he intended to do, but he had shaken her off, a tight, closed expression on his face she'd never seen before. He had returned an hour later and gone up directly to Percy. "He'll never touch you again, sonny," he had said quietly. "That much I promise you." When Tehmina asked him that night what had transpired between Bomi and him, he said only that they'd had a little talk. But it was true—Bomi continued to drink and the verbal abuse was undiminished, but he never struck his son again.

Now, looking at Percy's pudgy but handsome face, Tehmina marveled again at his resilience. Two years after Sorab had left for graduate school in America, Percy had followed him. Going to law school had transformed his life. Despite paying alimony to three wives, Percy still made enough money to send a check each month to Bomi for his living expenses. The poor boy who for all practical purposes was an orphan at twelve now had the largest laugh in any room, was the life of every party, and had a zest for life that Tehmina wanted for her own son. Seeing Percy now with his thick shiny hair, his Ralph Lauren shirt, his designer jeans, no one would guess at the daily abuse his father had heaped upon him, the ugly names he had been called, the grief and anger he had felt when his beloved mother had been snatched away from him. And for the first time, Tehmina felt grateful to America. She and Rustom had given Percy a shot at life, but America had given him his life. It was amazing the transformation that happened to all these young people when they came here—most of them gained weight, most of them talked louder and laughed louder, some of them even grew an inch or so in height, improbable as that seemed. But the most amazing thing was, they became happy in America. Kids who had been pencil thin, melancholy, depressed, quiet, and shy became confident, strong, talkative, happy. How could a country change someone's basic personality? Tehmina wondered. This thing in their Constitution which we used to mock in India—the pursuit of happiness or some such thing—maybe it really did something for people to have such a preposterous idea embedded in the Constitution. Maybe it gave them the freedom to feel they were worthy of happiness, that being happy was something they didn't have to apologize for or feel guilty about. Tehmina remembered all of her mother's strictures—how you should not look at yourself in the mirror lest people think you are vain; how you should never complain about anything in your life because there are millions of people worse off than you; how you should cover your mouth when you laugh because otherwise men will think you are promiscuous; how you should be satisfied with whatever God has given you because it's your destiny; how you should never eat on the streets because you attract the attention and envy of the starving people around you; how you should never boast about having money to avoid arousing the envy of your neighbors. Because of Rustom's broad-minded, large attitude, she herself had moved away from many of these beliefs. But still, it was true—she had never felt free in Bombay the way she did here. The simple act of eating an ice-cream cone on the streets and not being followed by the hungry eyes of a hundred children was a freedom, a luxury she had never experienced on the streets of Bombay. In America, she didn't feel leered at by young, sex-starved men, was not self-conscious about her breasts, was not miserably aware of her female body, didn't carry herself in that tense, guarded way that she did back home. And although it was difficult, she was forcing herself to look in the mirror as she ran her fingers through her hair when she was in a public restroom. She marveled at how American women stood for long minutes staring at themselves in the mirror, adjusting their hair, putting on makeup. Once, in the public restroom at Hunan Village, she had even seen a young woman blow herself a kiss in the mirror. *Her* mother had obviously not warned her against the sins of vanity and pride.

She felt Percy shift beside her. The others were moving into the next bedroom, with Homi holding forth on the technique the painters had used for texturing the walls. "Penny for your thoughts?" Percy whispered, and she smiled and shook her head. "Just thinking . . . about the years gone by," she answered.

"Don't. Don't think of the past, Mamma. You should be thinking about the future."

She wondered when he had started calling her Mamma. Best she remembered, he had called her Tehmina auntie all the years he'd been in India. She liked the new name, liked the closeness and intimacy it conveyed, but wondered briefly if Sorab minded. When they had taken Percy in, she had been very careful to watch Sorab's behavior for any signs of resentment or jealousy. But Sorab seemed to accept Percy's presence in their lives as calmly as he accepted the presence of the moon in the night sky. In fact, after years of being an only child, it was probably good for Sorab to have had his parents focus their energies on someone other than him.

"You're not hearing a word I'm saying, are you?" she heard Percy say, and she started. "Sorry, deekra, sorry. I wasn't trying to ignore you."

Percy rolled his eyes. "Arre, Mamma, all the women in my life ignore me. Why should you be an exception to that rule?" He took her hand and tugged her toward the edge of the bed. "Sit down for a minute. I need to talk to you."

She felt a sudden apprehension at the abrupt seriousness of his tone. She knew exactly what Percy wanted to talk about—the immigration stuff—and she felt a dread at having to think about the matter tonight.

"Good God, Mamma." Percy laughed. "You look like this bed is a guillotine."

She smiled weakly. "I know you need to know," she said. "But it's just that—"

"Mamma," Percy interrupted. "What is the problem, may I ask? Your only son is here in America, your grandson is here. And now, with Rustom uncle . . . I mean, with all that has happened last year, you have no one in Bombay. Your whole family is here. Doesn't it make sense for you to be where you have people who love you?"

Put that way, she saw the logic of what he was saying. But she also knew that her reality was more complicated than that. Deekra, a life is made up of more than your immediate family, she wanted to say to him. It is made up of all the people around you—your neighbors, even the ones you can't stand; your friends, whom you've known longer than you had known your husband; Sunil, the milkman who cheats by adding water to the milk he delivers to your doorstep; Krishna and Parvati, the homeless couple across the street; Shiva, the legless beggar who frantically wheels the skateboard he sits upon toward you to greet you with a smile; Rohit, the bhaiya who sells the freshest bhelpuri in town; Hansu, the servant who has worked in your home for the last seventeen years. It is made up of all your routines—getting up each morning at five to answer the door for the butcher, the baker, the milkman, the newspaper boy; opening the door at seven for Krishna to come fill his bucket with warm water so his family can bathe on the street; meeting with Sheroo and the other girls for lunch every few weeks; watching the Hindi version of *Who Wants to Be a Millionaire?* every Thursday evening; volunteering at the Shanti Center every Thursday. And yes, with Rustom gone, her routine had been greatly impacted—she no longer had a companion to go to the fire temple with every day, or to offer their prayers at the Bhika Behram well in Flora Fountain every Friday. Nor did she go to Paradise for dinner every Sunday. But still, Bombay was her home, the city she had come to as a young bride. She had ridden in a thousand of its cabs, she had lived through riots and holiday celebrations, she had witnessed hundreds of its thunderstorms. She gazed at Percy, the boy she had helped raise into a man, a boy who had once shared his innermost secrets and fears with her, and she wondered how to reach him, how to make him understand the simple complexity of her life.

"It's not that easy," she tried, and he interrupted her with a shake of his head. "Mamma. Of course. Of course. I know that. You don't have to tell me that. God, I still remember my first year in this country. If Sorab had not been here, I don't know what I would've done. But God, that's the whole point—you have your whole family here. Whereas I—"

She stared at him, unsure of what to say. Percy spoke into the silence. "Look, Mamma, here's the thing. What with the holidays and all, nothing would've been done by the bloody folks at the INS anyway. But after the first of the year we need to act on this jaldi-jaldi. Because you're going to have what—two, three months left on your tourist visa? And since 9/11 even the most routine thing seems to take twice as long. Not that the INS was a paragon of punctuality even before that, mind you. But I need a decision from you soon, okay? This is not something I want to leave until the last minute."

Tehmina swallowed hard and nodded. Suddenly Percy laughed. "Arre, Mamma, I'm asking you to consider living in the greatest country on earth, yaar. And you look as if I've asked you to spend the rest of your days in bloody Ethiopia or something." His face softened. "Chalo ne, Mamma. Why are you playing so hard to get? Making me chase after you just like every other woman ever has.

We need you here, yaar, Sorab and me. Heck, if for no other reason you should stay so I can eat your cooking at least once a week. You should see the anemic shrimp curry my beloved Julie makes. I tell you, any self-respecting Indian would file for divorce immediately. But what to do? The poor dear is so proud of herself for learning Indian cooking that I don't have the heart to tell her the truth. But that's why I need you here, Mamma—so that I don't waste away to nothing from Julie's so-called Indian cooking." He patted his ample belly and they both laughed. Percy put his arm around Tehmina. "But jokes aside, we do need you here. You are—I dunno—a reminder to us of something that we shouldn't forget. I can't explain it. All I know is, it's so easy here in America to get swept up with jobs and cars and houses and money. And every time I see you, I'm reminded that life is more than that. Remember how you and Rustom uncle took me in after my mother died? As long as I live I won't forget what you said to me at Mummy's funeral. I was crying so hard—not just because I was missing her but because I dreaded the thought of living alone with my daddy. I had never known such a feeling before, like I was alone in a city and all the streets were deserted. And out of all the people gathered there, all the wailing old women who were beating their breasts and shedding their crocodile tears, you were the only one who understood what I was feeling. Remember? 'You will never be alone, Percy,' you said to me. 'From today, we are your family.' You have no idea what those words did for me. It was like someone had shone a flashlight in a coal mine—I now had a path to follow to get out of the coal mine."

"Deekra, that is all ancient history," an embarrassed Tehmina murmured. "You should forget all that now."

"But that's just it," Percy replied fiercely. "You see, I don't want to forget that. In fact, remembering it is the most important thing. And that's why it will be so good for all of us to have you here permanently."

Tehmina smiled. "Now I see why you're such a good lawyer. What a golden tongue you have."

To her surprise and dismay, Percy's face flushed and his nose turned red. How well she knew that look, knew that it meant that his feelings were hurt and he was trying hard to keep his tears at bay. "I wasn't trying to trick you, Mamma," she heard him say. "I meant what I said."

Hastily, she took his hand in hers. "Of course, of course, deekra. I didn't mean to suggest—" She paused. "Okay, give me a few more days to decide. I'll let you know soon, I promise. I know this hasn't been easy for all you children. I'm sorry, I'm doing my best, but this is not an easy decision for me, you know?" To her embarrassment, she could hear the tears in her own voice. Still, she forced herself to continue. "To give up the city of one's birth, old friends whom you grew up with, an apartment that you've decorated and cleaned and furnished, all this is very hard, beta. I'm not so stupid that I don't realize what a strain this has put on Sorab and Susan, believe me. Quite the contrary. But I also—I need time. Or maybe I need a sign."

"I understand. I really do. And I wish ... But Sorab and Susan have some decisions to make, also. If they're going to move into a bigger house, they need to start planning for that, you know?"

She stared at him. "Move into a bigger house?"

Percy looked startled. "Didn't they talk to you about it? If you decide to stay, they're going to buy a bigger house. So that you can have your own bathroom and so that—so that they can have more, y'know, privacy and stuff. Preferably a house with a bedroom and bath on the first floor."

Although she knew this was not what he'd intended, she felt a chill in her heart. So the children felt the need for a bigger house. What that meant was that her presence was an imposition, an inconvenience to them. Whose idea was it to move? Susan's probably. She remembered now her daughter-in-law's pencil-thin lips and tight voice the day she had told her to please remember to take the hair out of the bathtub when she got done with her shower. At that time she hadn't thought much about it. Now she wondered which other of her thoughtless habits and behaviors affected Susan and possibly created friction between her and Sorab. She had tried to live unobtrusively in their house, tiptoeing around when she had to use the bathroom at night so as not to wake them, staying in bed later than usual so as to give them some time with each other every morning, not volunteering to do anything for Cookie unless Susan asked her to. She had tried to live in their home like a friendly spirit, eager to help in any way she could but also ready to disappear in the shadows when necessary. And all of it had been for nothing. Hadn't Percy told her as much? That the children still felt they needed distance and privacy? She imagined them talking in whispers, Susan voicing her frustrations, Sorab trying to appease his wife without insulting his mother. The thought of her son being placed in such an awkward situation made Tehmina feel nauseous.

"Mamma. What's wrong?" Percy was saying. "What did I say that's making you look like this?"

She looked at him, not bothering to keep the tears out of her eyes. "I didn't know the children felt the need for a bigger house. I have tried so hard these past few months to give them their privacy."

Percy took in a sharp intake of breath. "Oh God, Mamma. Don't take this the wrong way. Please. Look, it's different in this country. People aren't used to living with their parents and so—so they need more space and privacy, okay? It's nothing against you, honest. God, I've heard Susan say that she'd rather live with you than any of her own relatives. And anyway, Sorab was planning on buying a bigger house regardless of whether you moved here or not." She heard the wobble in his voice at this obvious untruth. Percy doesn't know how to lie, she thought. Not a good quality in a lawyer.

Tehmina rose from the bed. "Let's join the party, shall we?" she said. She tried to make her voice sound light. But her heart was cold.

"How'd it go?" Sorab whispered to Percy. The two of them were at the bar fixing drinks for themselves and their wives.

Percy shook his head. "I don't know. I made a faux pas, I think." He turned toward his friend angrily. "Saala, why didn't you tell me that you hadn't mentioned your plans to buy a new home to her?"

Sorab stared at him. "You told her that?"

"Well, yes. How the fuck was I to know you'd kept it a goddamn secret? I just thought it would help her realize that time was running short."

"Great. From the frying pan into the fire. Nice going, Percy. I know what she's going to think—that we are tired of her presence or something."

"That's exactly what she thinks. I mean, I think so, anyway. Who the fuck knows what goes through the minds of women? If they're twelve or eighty, it's the same thing."

"Oh, spare me your usual rant about the wily ways of women. Can we come back to the topic of my mother, please?"

"Yeah. Sure. Except I don't know what to tell you." Percy sighed. "Any red-blooded American woman would jump at the chance to move into a new home. But not our Indian women, oh no. They have to bring enough melodrama and psychological intrigue into the situation to make bloody Freud and Jung both spin in their graves."

Despite himself, Sorab laughed. "Fuck you, Percy. First you spill the beans to my mom and now you're trying to cover up your damn mistake with a broadsided attack on all Indian women."

"Guilty as charged. Listen, let's just get through the next few weeks, achcha? I'll talk to her again after the first of the year."

They walked back to where Susan and Julie were standing. Sorab glanced around the room to search for his mother and found her sitting on the couch next to another elderly woman from India who was visiting her daughter. "Here you go, hon," he said, handing Susan a glass of red wine.

Julie and Percy sipped their drinks. "Aha." Julie sighed. "Nobody makes a more perfect gin and tonic than my husband." Like Percy's three previous wives, Julie was also blond and petite. She reminded Sorab of Patti Boyd, the model who had married George Harrison. He idly wondered where Percy found all these wives—they looked as if they came out of a factory that produced blond and petite women. But Julie had a tough streak that belied her tiny presence. And for the first time Percy had indicated that he was open to the possibility of having children. With his first three wives, Percy had been firm about the fact that he had no desire to be a father. Sorab had often thought that it was the only area in which he could observe the scars his abusive childhood had left on Percy. In every other way, Percy truly seemed to have left his past behind him, going so far as to visit his father once a year in the small flat that he had purchased for him a few years ago. But his adamant refusal to father a child had always struck Sorab as telling, especially given the fact that Percy doted on Cookie and lavished gifts on him. It had always filled Sorab with sadness, knowing that his best friend had shut the door on the possibility of his greatest happiness.

Now, feeling happily drunk on his second beer, he turned toward Julie. "You've been such a civilizing influence on this barbarian." He grinned. "For this, we are all grateful to you."

"Oh, give me a few more years," Julie said. "You'll think he went to finishing school or something." She was smiling, but something in her voice made Sorab believe her and he felt a twinge of panic. He didn't really want Percy to *change* or anything. His friend was pretty damn perfect the way he was.

"Thanks a bloody lot, yaar," Percy said. "Even my best friend turns out to be a traitor."

"And here's another thing," Julie said, and from her tone Sorab realized that she was a bit tipsy also. "One thing I've made clear to Percy—no more divorce. I'm not the divorce type, you know? I play for keeps. So I'm here to stay, baby."

Sorab suddenly realized that he didn't like Julie very much and his heart sank with that knowledge. There was something a little brittle and hard about her, like the cashew chikki they used to eat as schoolboys. To console himself, he reached for Susan's hand and squeezed it. She squeezed back, and in an electrifying instant, he knew that she had just read his mind and told him that she agreed with his assessment. After all these years of marriage, he was still stunned by Susan's perceptiveness and the shorthand that worked between them. It made all the less savory aspects of their marriage so much easier to take, this connection that they shared. No one on earth could read him the way Susan did. At times he hated this about her because it made him feel as naked as an X-ray. But right now his heart filled with love for the smart, perceptive woman standing next to him.

He so badly wished for Percy the same kind of companionship and support that he had in his own marriage. But he had a sudden insight that Percy would never enjoy what he had—the quiet steadiness of love, the comfort of family. That his childhood had created a hole in Percy that nothing would ever fill. Maybe if he had found a woman as steadfast and intelligent as Susan, he would have stood a chance. But that was the catch—Percy would never seek out someone like Susan, someone who would knock down his defenses, threaten his glib posturing, someone who would demand to be taken seriously as a human being. Instead, he would spend his life chasing after something he could barely define or describe, trying to feed a hunger that was insatiable, and then, in sheer frustration, settle for someone like Julie or Karen or—what was his second wife's name?—Veronica. Women with thin waistlines and painted toenails who were no threat to him, who were clearly not his intellectual equals, who felt more comfortable in beauty parlors than in libraries.

Sorab had never thought about all this before and he took another swig of his beer to chase away the sad, heavy feeling that was descending on him. What would it be like to have a baby with a woman like Julie? he wondered. What kind of a life would such a child have, with parents who were children themselves, who went out to nightclubs every weekend? Would Percy change, grow up? Or would he be a pale copy of his own father—kinder certainly, nonabusive for sure—but nevertheless a father whose own greedy desires would always come before the needs of a mere child? As for Julie—he just didn't know what kind of a mother she would be. Until tonight, he had liked Julie, thought she was good for Percy, had been touched by her attempts to learn Indian cooking. Now, suddenly, he felt dyspeptic, had a bitter taste in his mouth that he knew was not from the beer. Maybe he was just massively projecting his own discontent, his own nagging sense of failure, onto Percy.

But what the fuck was he so miserable about? Hadn't he just favorably compared his own wife to a woman who was at least eight years younger? Wasn't that his own mother on the couch there, looking for all the world as if she belonged in this living room with all his other friends? Wasn't it just yesterday that he had felt weepy at the sight of his mother and son at the mall together?

"Hon," Susan was whispering. "You've had enough to drink. Why don't you switch to a Coke or something?"

Percy laughed out loud. "Henpecked, that's what all we Parsi men are." He turned toward Susan. "My dear, there was a time when your husband could drink more beers than anybody else in college."

He poked Sorab in the stomach. "Of course, that was almost twenty years ago and this belly of his wasn't nearly as—er, prosperous then."

Perin Jasawala came up to them. "Well, Percy, you've just set a world record," she said with a grin. "After all, the dinner buffet has been set out in the dining room for two full minutes. And you're still in this room."

"Well, since I've married Julie, I'm a satisfied man," Percy declared. He winked at all of them. "I'm talking about the fact that she is learning to cook Parsi dishes, of course—though I might add that I'm satisfied in—er—other rooms of our house also, if you know what I mean. And so I can resist the aromas coming from your kitchen, Perin. At least for a minute or two, that is."

Perin laughed as she moved away. "Well, dinner is served. It's an authentic Parsi wedding menu. Although the patra-ni-macchi is wrapped in parchment paper, I'm afraid. The caterer couldn't find banana leaves."

"Leaves or paper, who cares?" Percy muttered. "It's the fish I'm after, not the bloody wrapper." He looked around. "Where's Mamma? Arre, Sorab, go fetch her, yaar. If she sits on that couch listening to that old lady's boring stories any longer, she might turn into a fossil or something."

Parsis, Tehmina thought. They could come to America, attend top schools, get high degrees, marry American women, talk with American accents, own fancy cars and houses. But nothing could change a Parsi's eating habits or diminish his love for rich food. When it came to food they were still khadras, as greedy as ever. Look at this crowd of rich, sophisticated people, she marveled with amusement. They still acted the same way Parsis did at weddings in Bombay—single-minded in their pursuit of food. This was a big party—at least fifty guests, Tehmina estimated—but Bomi and Perin had provided enough food to feed twice as many people. Still, the abundance of food only made the guests even more delirious as the aromas of food that they loved and missed—the chicken farchas, the steamed fish coated with green chutney, the lamb pallov—assailed their nostrils. They weren't exactly jostling for position at the long dining table—they were much too sophisticated for that—but the air was charged with their urgency and impatience.

Susan came up to where Tehmina was leaning against the wall. "Quite a spectacle, huh, Mom?" She smiled. "Think the men will remember to fix plates for us also once they get anywhere near the food?"

Tehmina smiled back. "Yeah, this is the Parsi community at its finest. Guess they don't act all that different in America than in India."

"Well, thank God this is a buffet. If this was a sit-down dinner, they'd be standing behind the chairs of the diners, waiting for them to get done."

"You remember that?" Tehmina asked.

"God, Mom, how could I forget? Remember the reception that you and Rustom pappa threw for us in Bombay after we were married? Jeez, I thought I'd never get to sit down to eat that night, the way those people were waiting to grab the tables."

"It's a strange custom, this eating in shifts," Tehmina mused.

As superfluous as it was, Perin was circulating in the large dining room urging her guests to fill up their plates, to not be shy. Tehmina knew this was the remnant of an Indian custom and she was glad that Perin was doing it even as she realized how unnecessary it was. Still, it was better than what she had observed in the homes of Susan and Sorab's American friends. After all her visits to America, she was still appalled at the practice of not urging—even forcing—guests to help themselves to seconds. One time, when they had visited the home of Sorab's colleague Bob Carol for a buffet dinner, their hosts had actually packed the food away while they were still there. "Oh good," Bob's wife had said. "More leftovers for us." And even while Tehmina heard the good-natured joking in her voice, she was appalled. The thought of not pressing guests to help themselves to more food was as alien to her as eating with their hands was to most Americans. The only exception to this occurred when they had dined at Eva's home during their last visit. Even Solomon had fussed around them just as if they were in Bombay, filling their glasses with wine each time they took a sip, while Eva heaped food onto their plates without asking for permission. Susan had hated it, had declared that it was the height of rudeness, but Tehmina had basked in the warmth behind the gesture.

As she looked at all the food, Tehmina's thoughts flew to Josh and Jerome. What were they doing tonight? she wondered. Had they had their dinner yet? Did they have a shiny Christmas tree in their living room like the Jasawala's did? Did that mother of theirs actually buy them anything? And when would she be able to give them the gifts that she and Cookie had picked out for them?

Perin, who had worked her way up to them, interrupted her thoughts. "Susan. Tehmi. Why are you not eating?" she cried.

"Sorab and Percy are fixing us plates," Susan said.

"Oh, okay. Good, good. Listen, as always, we've ordered so much food. My Homi has this phobia about running out of food. So as usual we've overdone it. So remember to pack yourselves doggy bags, okay? Please?"

"We'll see, we'll see," Tehmina murmured. As much as she loved giving, she hated receiving gifts from people.

But Susan spoke up. "Why, Perin, that would be lovely. Thank you. That way, I won't have to worry about what to pack for lunch for Sorab and myself for tomorrow. Though watching how these

Parsis are attacking the food, we may be being unduly optimistic," she added with a laugh.

"Oh dear, no. You should see how much food there is in the kitchen." She looked around. "Is Cookie eating in the other room with the kids? Good. We ordered pizza and milk shakes for the kids. Hope he likes both."

"You really thought of everything, Perin," Tehmina said. "Thank you."

Perin grinned a wide, open grin that transformed her face. "Oh, don't mention it. We like having a good time with our friends." She suddenly leaned forward and hugged Tehmina. "It's so good to have you here, Tehmi," she said. "You are such a wonderful addition to our group. Now when are you going to make your decision and put all of us out of our misery?"

It was Perin's firm that would be handling her immigration papers, Tehmina realized. She wondered if Percy kept her abreast of all the developments. "Soon, I hope," she said weakly. "Just waiting for the holidays to be over."

"Ah, the holidays." Perin sighed. "So much pressure it puts on everybody. Still, it's hard to believe that Christmas is just three days away."

CHAPTER ELEVEN

The growling in the bathroom began again and Sorab tensed. What the hell was Mamma doing up so early? He turned his head away from the sounds coming from the bathroom and felt a stabbing pain between his eyes. Gotta stop drinking so much, he thought groggily. Both he and Susan had drunk too much at Homi's house last night. And now the last thing they needed was to be awoken by Mamma's antics. He opened a cautious eye and glanced at Susan, expecting to hear her muttering under her breath. But luckily, Susan was giggling.

Mamma was in the bathroom, sounding for all the world like a caged lion. She had always made these fierce, loud sounds while brushing her teeth and tongue. As a young boy, he had found it hilarious, the thought that his meek, mild, even-tempered mother had a ferocious animal lurking within her. "Garrrrrrrrrr. Gaaaarrrrrrrrrrrr," he would growl at the top of his lungs as he ran around the apartment, imitating her, teasing her, until his father, himself shaking with laughter, would ask him to stop. "But, Daddy, why does she make those stupid noises?" he once asked, and Rustom shrugged.

"Just one of her idiosyncrasies," he said.

"What's that mean?"

"Idiosyncrasies? It means . . . it's what makes people who they are."

He was so used to his mother unleashing her inner lion in the bathroom that he had barely noticed her furious gargling the first time his parents had visited him after his marriage. But Susan had sat up in bed, rubbing the sleep from her eyes. "What the—what on earth is that noise?"

He blushed. "That's just—I forgot to tell you. That's my mother gargling. She always makes these funny noises in the back of her throat."

Susan looked at him incredulously. "You've gotta be kidding. Jesus, it sounds like a freight train running through the house."

As if to prove her right, Tehmina emitted a particularly loud gurgle, followed by the unmistakable sound of her spitting phlegm into the sink. Susan flinched visibly. "What the hell is she *doing*?"

Sorab pulled his wife down toward him. "Aw, come on now, honey. She's old and set in her ways. Just ignore her. Just . . . chalk it up to a cultural difference, would you?" He prayed fervently that his mother would clean up the sink before she left the bathroom. Susan was a stickler for cleanliness, he knew. She had once made him rinse and wipe down the sink because he had left a fleck of hand soap in the bowl.

Susan raised her eyebrows. "Cultural difference, my foot. If I ever hear you make that awful ruckus in the bathroom, my darling Sorab, I'm filing for divorce the next day." But she was smiling.

Two years after that first visit, they had visited his parents in Bombay and Rustom had had the bright idea of taking his son and daughter-in-law to Goa, by train. It's a good way to see the country-side, he'd told Susan. That's where India lives, you know, in her villages.

It was on that train ride that Sorab realized that he was now an official member of the American middle class. Athough his father had spent a lot of money getting them reserved, first-class seats in an air-conditioned car, everything about the train repulsed Sorab. He noticed the worn-out blankets they were given to lay over the hard, drop-down wooden bunk beds, the shabby, thin, dirty-looking sheets, the paan stains in the corner of the bogey. Above all, he noticed the unspeakably filthy conditions of the bathrooms. He prayed fervently that the ladies' room was in better condition than the men's—he could, after all, hop off the train at one of its many stops and relieve himself in the bushes behind the desolate train station—but one look at Susan's pale, shocked face told him that his prayers wouldn't be answered. "How long is this train journey?" she whispered to him, making sure his parents wouldn't overhear her.

"I dunno. At least twelve, thirteen hours."

"I'm going to have to hold it. There's no way on earth I'm going in there again."

At six in the morning, the train stopped for a half hour at a rural station and they jumped off to get some fresh air. "You want—you want to walk around and see if there's a place where you can go?" an embarrassed Sorab asked his wife. "I'll keep watch."

She grimaced. "No. It's just a few more hours, anyway. I'm okay as long as I don't think about it."

Just then they heard it. And saw it. Several of their fellow passengers had also disembarked from the train and stood along the edge of the platform, carrying little plastic containers of water. They were brushing their teeth and spitting and hawking on the railroad tracks. Everybody, it seemed, gargled furiously and hawked ferociously. It was as if Tehmina had spawned a score of disciples. "Shit," Susan said, with something like awe in her voice. "It's not just your mother. It's all of India."

He bristled as he did whenever she made a generalized statement about all things Indian. "Susan, please. Don't exaggerate. It's not *all* of India. It's just some—uncouth people."

She moved away from him, her eyes dancing with glee. "Fuck. This is a genuine, bona fide, national trait. Don't deny it, honey. I'll be damned. A whole country where people make love as quietly as mice but gargle and clear their throats like wild tigers. A country where you can't hold hands in public with your own husband without getting stared at but you can perform the most private rituals in public."

Despite himself, he laughed. "You're onto something here," he said. "That's a good observation."

"What're you children giggling about?" Rustom had come up behind them.

"Oh, nothing, Dad. I'm just showing Susan the sights and sounds of our Mother India." Sorab grinned, sweeping his hand against the landscape of the row of people in front of him.

"Ah, yes. Our beloved Manibens and Pandovjis in action." Just then, a man in a white dhoti let out a particularly loud hawk and Rustom flinched. But he recovered almost immediately. "Look at that chappie over there. Thinks he's a virile, healthy male with his vigorous gargling and whatnot. Saala, my Tehmi could turn him into a mouse with one hearty gargle of her own. Just the force of one of her offerings could blast him all the way to Goa and back."

Sorab had believed that Susan had long made her peace with his mother's unfortunate habit. But this visit was so different from any of the others. For one thing, his father was not here this time—his father, who had always known how to make Susan laugh, who had teased his wife, cajoled his daughter-in-law, and forged with his son a mock, world-weary solidarity based on their malehood. And on this visit Mamma was staying so much longer than the usual four-week visits of the past. This was on his insistence, of course, which made him feel even guiltier for the fact that he had yelled at her after Persis's late-night phone call, had blamed her for a situation she was not responsible for. He remembered what Percy had said to him last night. "Saala, are you sure this is what you want? For your mother to live here permanently? It's not easy, you know. And once you make her sell the Bombay flat and everything, there's no going back. Wouldn't be fair to her, you know that."

"It's tough at times but we'll manage," he had said with a heartiness he didn't feel. "Susan, too, is convinced it's the right thing to do."

And right now, watching his wife's forgiving, indulgent countenance, Sorab was sure they were doing the best thing. "She better stop her freight-train impersonation soon," he muttered. "I have to pee badly."

"So get your lazy ass out of bed and go use the downstairs bathroom."

He yawned. "I don't want to. Besides, I gotta jump in the shower as soon as she's out. Grace has called for an eight o'clock meeting. She wants to go over everybody's vacation schedules, among other things."

Susan groaned. "That woman is an ogre. God. Why did Malcolm have to retire?"

He opened his mouth to answer but just then Tehmina emitted a particularly aggressive growl and Sorab instinctively drew the comforter over their heads. Under the covers, they both giggled like children. "I think that was the grand finale," he whispered, putting his arm around Susan's waist and finding that she was shaking with suppressed laughter.

"It's like fireworks on July Fourth," Susan whispered back. "She builds up to the climax, each morning."

Sorab thought to many a morning on this visit when neither he nor his wife had been so indulgent about his mother's morning ablutions, when, at the first sound of Tehmina's bathroom roaring, Susan would groan and roll over to her side, holding a pillow over her head. He had been slashed with so many contradictory feelings then—mortification at his mother's uncharacteristically uncouth idiosyncrasy; irritation at his wife's uncharitable response to it. Filled with gratitude for their closeness on this morning, he squeezed her hand. "Did I ever tell you I love you?"

She rolled over to face him and he noticed the crust around her still-sleepy eyes. "I feel happy this morning."

He laughed for the sheer joy of it and then, to cover it up, "Amazing what a couple of glasses of good wine do for my girl."

"Hey. I never claimed to be anything but easy. I'm a cheap date, you know that."

"Yeah, right. In that case, can I return the subwoofer that I just got installed in your car?"

Susan smiled gently. "Sure you can, hon. And then you live without sex the rest of your life."

"Speaking of which . . ." He made a quick calculation even as he was pulling Susan's body toward his. There was time to make love and still be at work by eight. His hands felt for the hem of her nightie and he cupped her buttocks after rolling it past her waist.

"Whoa, easy, cowboy," Susan said, but she was straining against him, too.

He undid the drawstrings of his pajamas hastily as he kissed her fervently, his tongue nestling deep in her mouth, which tasted of sleep and salt. Yet even as he climbed on top of her, even as he lost himself in the welcome of her body, one part of Sorab was alert, distracted. He was acutely aware of the fact that his mother was a mere few feet away from him while he was fucking his wife. He smothered Susan's mouth with kisses knowing that he was doing this in part to suppress her low but unmistakable moaning; even as Susan's frantic, incomprehensible whispers flooded his ears, even as a cruel, inexorable power flooded his body, he was listening for the sounds of his mother's footsteps as she left the bathroom. He heard her enter her room, place her brush and powder box on the dresser that was against the wall between their two bedrooms. He paced the rhythm of his thrusting so that the bed didn't squeak and sing out its painful, unmistakable beat. There was a hot, confusing pleasure in being this silent and it turned him on even while he resented the hell out of having to be this furtive. He heard the crash of something fall in the other room, but then it didn't matter because he was crashing himself, his whole body felt like a powerful wave crashing against the rocky shore. He bit down on his lip to prevent the groans that wanted to leak out of his mouth and at the same time he was excruciatingly aware of the fact that Susan had not exercised the same self-discipline, that she was moaning under him. He forced the side of his hand into her mouth and she bit down on it hard, the pain making him wince.

"Well," Susan said a few minutes later. She was leaning on her elbow, her hand under her golden hair. "That was some good-morning greeting."

He kissed the inside of her elbow. "I'd like to exchange good-morning greetings every morning," he said.

Her eyes were the color of amber. "I bet you would." She slapped him lightly on his arm. "If you're not up in thirty seconds, I'm going to beat you to the bathroom."

"I'm going, I'm going," he grumbled. He threw the covers off and leaped out of bed. Standing up over the bed, he glanced back at his sleepy wife. "Just wham, bam, thank you, man," he sniffed. "That's how all you women are—only after our bodies. I feel so—used."

Susan's soft laughter followed him out of the room.

They had had the upstairs bathroom remodeled earlier this year, and standing under the hot, rushing water, Sorab experienced that deep feeling of satisfaction that he felt each morning as his eyes wandered over the rich marble wall tile, the expensive pewter fixtures, the Jacuzzi tub. It had taken him many years to accept the fact that he enjoyed the good things in life. During his early days in America, he had been haunted by the sudden wealth that engulfed him. Even when he was a poor graduate student, he was aware of the fact that he enjoyed a standard of living that in some ways was higher than that of his parents. This despite the fact that Rustom had always earned a good living and Sorab had never known a day of hardship or destitution. But the simple act of turning on a faucet and having hot water flow from it—so much more convenient than having to fill a plastic bucket with hot water from the electric geyser and then pour that over himself with a large metal can—was something he could never take for granted. In the early days, he used to walk the streets around campus, marveling at the fact that he could drink three Pepsis a day and not think about the cost; amazed at the fact that he could buy a used Chevy eight months after arriving in America; guilt-ridden by the fact that filling the tank cost him a fraction of what it cost his father in India.

For years, visiting India had been hard on him. The beggars on the streets, the servants in the house, the unpainted, neglected walls of his parents' apartment, the persistent dust that sat on all their possessions despite daily cleanings, all mortified him. He felt guilty about everything—the fact that his father still drove his old car that didn't even have power steering; the fact that his mother sat in terrible traffic jams when she went out grocery shopping; the fact that his old servant looked older and thinner each time; the fact that men three times his age called him "sir" as they begged for money. He wanted to apologize for the relentless pounding of the monsoons, the cruel fury of the sun, the garbage on the streets, the emaciated stray dogs outside their apartment building, the blaring of the traffic horns, the murky grayness of the polluted sea. After all, he had escaped it all—and they hadn't. While he lived in an apartment building where the electricity never failed, and took showers under reliably hot water and breathed air that was crystal clear and sweet, while he drank Pepsi whenever the urge hit him and withdrew money from an ATM machine whenever he needed to, millions of people—including his own mother and father—lived trapped in a hot, polluted, overcrowded, poverty-stricken, crumbling city where the only reliable thing was chaos and unpredictability. And the worst part was, as a grad student, he didn't really have enough extra money to help any of them.

He had changed, Sorab now reflected. The sting of newness, the delight of exploration, had worn off now. Every car that he had bought since the Chevy had been more expensive, more loaded with gadgets. And now he allowed himself to enjoy things that wealth bought. He had Susan to thank for that. Her American sense of entitlement—but maybe that was too uncharitable, maybe it was her American sense of optimism, of ease with the finer things in life—had finally rubbed off on him. He now enjoyed what he had. He told himself repeatedly that he worked bloody hard for what was his—nothing had been given to him. He reminded himself that he had come to this country with $600 in his pocket. Everything that he owned, everything—car, stereo, couch, dishes, house—he had had to earn.

Sorab ran his fingers gently over the marble tile. He loved its damp coolness, the sensual smoothness, so much like touching the white softness of the inside of Susan's thigh. You'll have to take a cold shower if this line of thought continues, he grinned to himself. Instead, he turned the water to a higher temperature until it was scalding hot and adjusted the shower massager until it was pulsating on that sore spot on his upper back. Soaping himself, he eyed the extra flab on his belly distastefully. Saala, I need to get back to the gym, he told himself. For a moment he thought with nostalgia of the lean, trim lad he had been when he came to America at twenty-one. For years—despite a diet of Pepsi and Big Macs during his first two years as a graduate student—he had fought off the American curse of obesity. In the early days of his relationship with Susan, she would often comment on the prominence of his cheekbones and how his sunken cheeks drew attention to his dark, fiery eyes. During their lovemaking, she would trace the hollow of his chest bones, run her hands down his tight, firm belly. I'm going to have to fatten you up, she'd whisper, but her admiring glance belied her words.

Sorab pinched the extra flab on his belly, holding it between his thumb and index finger. Twenty pounds, he said to himself, though I'd settle for losing even fifteen. And no more overeating during this holiday season. All these parties and the cookies and stuff everybody's bringing to the office are killing me. And I'm joining the gym first thing in January. But even while he made his resolution he thought of how difficult it would be to stick to it. Having Mamma here was like suddenly having a second child that he was responsible for. Each evening he came home and felt compelled to spend time with her, knowing that she'd been alone at home all day, knowing how pale and dull and lonely his suburban life must feel to her, compared to the colorful, busy, active, people-filled life she led in Bombay. Here, with the windows shut for the winter, the house felt as sealed and silent as a tomb. There, the open balcony allowed the sounds of the bustling city—the sounds of *life,* it suddenly seemed to Sorab—the piercing, nasal cries of the fruit vendors, the wailing of children, the dry wheezing of the BEST buses, the incessant blaring of horns—to penetrate into the apartment. There, the doorbell rang at least fifty times a day as the newspaper boy and the butcher and the doodhwalla and the servants and the neighbors and the friends who happened to be in the neighborhood stopped by. Here, she could go an entire week without answering the door. Thank God for Eva Metzembaum, Sorab thought. At least she gets Mamma out of the house a couple of times a week.

He thought with sudden dread of the long, cold, hard winter months that awaited her. For now, there was the excitement of the holidays, the constant trips to the mall, the planning of menus, the whirl of parties. Even the weather had been unusually warm for December. Why, they had actually had a couple of days where the sky was blue instead of the pewter noncolor that Sorab always described as Ohio gray. But what would Mamma do all alone during the winter months? He could encourage her to take some classes at the Community Center, maybe, but then there was the question of transportation. Fucking Rosemont Heights, Sorab thought. All these taxes and not even a decent public transportation system.

He stepped out of the tub and found that he was shaking despite the steamy hotness of the room. He reached hastily for the towel, thinking he was cold, when he suddenly recognized the source of his trembling. He was scared. Scared of the future that awaited him—that awaited all of them. This situation with Mamma is an awful gamble, he thought. What if she hates it here? What if she can't stand the coldness of this place—not just the winter cold but the coldness of a life not filled with noise and color and crowds and bustle? His life here was like a pastoral painting compared to the tumultuous cityscape of her life. He himself had come to appreciate—to even love—the solitude, the bleakness of the winter landscape. But would she?

He was asking her for so much. To give up her hometown, her friends, an apartment filled with a thousand happy memories, a city whose very existence throbbed in her blood, whose mad, manic rhythm was the beat of her heart. And in exchange for what? In exchange for—himself. And to some extent, her grandson. Sorab suddenly saw the pomposity of his offer. What did he really have to offer her except the harbor of family? Of being close to the one person whom she loved more than life itself? Was that plenty? Was that enough? He felt small, inadequate to the task. The magnitude of what he was doing, what he was asking her for, hit him hard. He stood in the middle of the bathroom rubbing the towel vigorously across his back and chest, trying to rub something warm and life-affirming into his suddenly cold muscles. But nothing was erasing the icy pit that was forming in the middle of his stomach.

It had seemed so clear in the days after his father had died. He had stayed in Bombay for six weeks (thank God good old Malcolm was still at the company then; Grace would've demanded that he return superditiously fast immediately after the funeral), meeting with the lawyers and accountants, taking care of all of his father's papers. Mamma was like a zombie during those days, taking her orders from him, deferring to him on every major financial decision, walking around in a haze of shock and grief. This is impossible, she kept repeating. Rustom can't be dead. There has been a mistake.

The first time he'd suggested that she move permanently to America, it was simply a gesture of kindness, his words building a rope to pull her out of the swampy waters of grief that she was drowning in. You're not going to live here by yourself, Mamma, he had said firmly, playing the role of the responsible son, the new head of the household. You're going to move in with us. Just settle all of Daddy's affairs and then come live with us in Ohio. But instead of his words rescuing her from her sorrow, they became the rope that rescued him from his bewilderment and helplessness and guilt. The offer became his way out, the way he could escape the oppressiveness of his mother's bereavement, the enormity of the tragedy that had befallen her. It helped him leave that apartment that loomed so large in his memory, helped him reduce to a manageable size his own choking grief over the death of a father he had adored, and find the courage to board the plane that took him back to his real life. Be brave. I'll see you in America in just a few months, he'd said to his mother at the airport, and was rewarded by the hopeful light that flared briefly in her dull eyes.

He remembered something else now: the note he had given her on the way to the airport. The previous night, his last night in Bombay, he had been sitting on the balcony listening to the Beatles' "Across the Universe" on his iPod and on an impulse had scribbled down one of the verses on a piece of paper. He had always loved that song, had even sung it at his high school talent show, and now he found himself sitting on the rocking chair on the balcony, tears streaming down his cheeks. *Limitless, undying love,* he whispered to himself, holding on to the line as if it were a rosary, and then he was thinking of his father and leaving home when he was twenty-one for reasons that were unclear to him even now, and the years he'd spent away, the years he could've spent instead enjoying his father's company, going for walks with him, laughing at his jokes, watching the same sunsets, a million ordinary moments in Rustom's company that he had forfeited in order to have America. And it was all gone now, the opportunity, the dream, the possibility, the restoration. It was over. His father was dead and a door had shut. But then he thought: But that's the magic of John Lennon's words, their sheer generosity. This is a limitless, undying love that does not confine, that does not imprison or hold back, but that dances ahead of you like a shimmering sprite, that entices, that beckons you until you follow, all the way across the universe. This was a different kind of love from Parsi love, from Indian love, which believed in hoarding, in gathering close, in not letting go. Though truth to tell, his parents had been grand, hadn't they? It was only now, now that he had Cookie, now that he knew the possessiveness of fatherly love, that he could appreciate the enormity of their sacrifice, how his ambition must have felt like a knife in their hearts. And still they had smiled and still they had said yes. Yes to him, to his dreams, to his future, even if it meant destroying their own dreams of their future.

Sorab wiped the tears from his face. He looked at the words he'd written, and they so perfectly reflected what he was thinking and feeling that for a moment he felt as though he'd composed those lines himself. This is what Mamma needed to do. Only he was capable of giving her this, now that her husband was gone, this limitless love. It was up to him to make her hear the siren call of these lyrics, to convince her that she needed to follow him across the universe.

He gave the handwritten lyrics to his mother the next day, without a word of explanation. "Come see us soon," he whispered to her at the airport before walking away to where the plane waited. He spent the long ride back home plotting how to break the news of his preposterous offer to Susan. He expected her to resist, braced himself for being chastised for his arrogance, his selfishness, to have undertaken such a huge step without consulting with his wife. But when, two days after his return, he had stammered out what he'd told his mother, Susan had looked at him with bemusement. "I know," she said.

"Know what?"

"That you offered for her to come live with us."

He was stunned. "How could you know? I barely knew what I was saying until the words were out of my mouth. And once I'd said them, it seemed like it was the logical—no, the only—thing to do."

Susan smiled. "My dear Sorab. I know you better than you know yourself."

"What the hell does that mean?" He paused. "So, are you really mad?"

"Mad? No, not at all. It's the right thing to do. She's what? Sixty-five? Sixty-six? There's no way she can live in that apartment by herself. She probably doesn't even know how to pay the electric bill.

You know how Dad did everything. And you will go out of your mind with worry every time she has a cold or a stomachache. No, of course she has to move here."

He stared at her with tears in his eyes. He felt suddenly humbled. "I . . . I was so sure . . ."

"Sorab," Susan said softly. "It's okay, hon. I love Mom, too, you know. And she's so easy to be around, thank heavens. It'll be okay. Besides, it's what your father would've wanted."

God, we were both so bloody pious then, Sorab now thought. But then what did we know? No way to have known how much easier it was to have them here when Dad was around. How much he did to lighten the mood at home, how much easier it was to manage Mamma with him in the picture. And what a difference between having them visit for a few weeks in the summer as opposed to having Mamma here for six months during the winter months, when the dark and cold conspired to keep them at home. He had heard Susan snap at Mamma a few times in the past month alone, and had to bite down on his tongue, remind himself of the pressures on his wife. Maybe Susan was right about her insistence about moving into a bigger home if Mamma agreed to stay. But the truth of the matter was, the thought of a bigger mortgage made him nervous. The skirmish with Grace over his vacation schedule, her numerous insinuations about his work performance, were making him feel vulnerable about his job. The woman was so unpredictable, so irrational, that he wouldn't put it past her to fire him. And despite Susan's unflagging confidence in him, he was not sure that he could land another job quickly enough. The economy was pretty lousy and the newspapers were filled with stories of former vice presidents and managers accepting jobs at half of their former salaries. And truth to tell, he felt sluggish and flabby these days. He didn't have the snap and the zip that had made him a marketing legend at twenty-six. Grace's caustic comments, her disparaging looks, had destroyed something in him, and the situation at home was not helping either.

Sorab zipped his pants with such venom that for a minute he thought he'd broken the zipper. As he reached for his crisp white shirt he realized that he was dragging his feet, that he was putting off going to work. He thought of all the years when he had been the first one in the office, bursting with ideas and ambition. From the time he got out of grad school, armed with letters of recommendation that were almost embarrassing in their effusiveness, his climb had been steady and effortless. And the beauty of it was, he had done it in his own way, had disarmed his rivals, had earned the undying affection of his employees and his bosses. So that at the age of thirty-eight, Sorab Sethna could hold his head high and make the remarkable claim that he had not a single enemy in the world, that he knew of no man or woman or child who wished him ill. That had been his father's gift to him, this ability to walk through the world as if it was a perfumed garden. And it had worked, it had all worked, until a silly, inconsequential woman named Grace Butler had walked into his life.

Sorab's eyes filled with the tears that came so easily these days. Fuck, he thought. You just got out of the shower, you idiot. What're you going to do, show up for your meeting with tear marks on your face? And what do you think Mamma's reaction is going to be if you go downstairs for breakfast looking like that Edvard Munch painting?

The thought of breakfast made him groan even as his stomach growled. Mamma was such a fabulous cook, it was almost illegal. And a month ago she'd gotten it into her head that the cold cereal that he ate for breakfast was simply not enough. So she'd taken to getting up in the morning to fix him a hot breakfast. Each morning as he gobbled down the egg akuri or the omelet that she prepared for him, he felt caught between Susan's watchful, cautionary glare and his mother's indulgent, pleased gaze.

Maybe she'll decide to go back, after all. Sorab was running a hasty hand through his hair when the treacherous thought hit him. He stared at himself in the mirror, appalled. Is that what you want, you bastard? he asked himself. If that's the case, why are you putting Mamma and Susan and everybody else through all this drama? He looked with distaste at a face that suddenly seemed weak and shifty to him. Who are you? he said to his reflection. What do you want? Who have you become? When there was no answer, he forced himself to imagine the house without his mother in it and was gratified at the pang of loss and loneliness that accompanied that image. But the next second he imagined the relief—the relief of not having to be quiet when he made love to his wife, the relief of not having to entertain his mother when he returned home after a long day at work, the relief of not having to move into a bigger house, of not having to get entangled into more debt, a larger mortgage. But then he thought of his mother alone in that apartment in Bombay, of her sleeping alone in the bed she had shared with her husband for decades, thought of those walls with the peeling paint, imagined her sick and unable to take care of herself, imagined her growing old alone in a distant city, away from her son and grandson, alone, solitary, paying the price for her only son's youthful ambition, for his having abandoned the city of his birth for greener pastures. And now he was in a position to share those pastures with her and why shouldn't he? He thought of the poisonous, polluted air in Bombay that assaulted the eyes and the throat, thought of the bronchitis that she developed with alarming regularity from breathing that air, thought of the cruel, muggy heat of the unforgiving sun, and knew that he could rescue his mother from all that if he kept her here. And yet he knew that this was not a game, that this was deadly serious, and that if he was asking his mother to change the course of her destiny and move to a strange land, he had better be damn sure of his own motives.

What do you want? he asked himself again. And what are you willing to sacrifice to get what you want?

His only answer was a face in the mirror that looked back at him silently. He noticed that it was the face of a frightened man.

CHAPTER TWELVE

Christmas Eve, Tehmina sighed, and she had still not dropped the gifts off for the two boys next door. Each time she passed by the living room, with its pile of gifts so high that it looked like a small store, she felt a twinge of guilt at the sight of so much affluence. And then she felt a twinge of guilt about feeling guilty because after all, most of the gifts were for her darling Cookie and what kind of a grandmother resented the fact that her only grandson was getting showered with toys and books and clothes? In India, she and Rustom had bought Sorab one gift for Christmas—usually a new pair of shoes or a pants-and-shirt set. This was her first Christmas in America, and despite her having seen a hundred movies and picture postcards depicting a white Christmas, nothing had prepared her for this roaring frenzy of consumption that had everyone walking around in a kind of delirium. She had foolishly imagined just the opposite—that a country with such year-round material wealth would shrug its collective shoulders at the thought of buying one more thing.

And that was the other discordant thing—where was the white Christmas Sorab had all but promised her when he'd enticed her to visit in the fall? That Bing Crosby had made her fantasize about most of her life? Here in Rosemont Heights, the grass was still visible, and although a cold, sharp wind blew today, it didn't carry snow with it. The only sign of snow was in the black, slushy mounds that had been shoveled to the side of the driveway a few days ago.

Looking out of her window, she saw the blur of a small animal whiz past at the far end of the backyard. Probably a neighbor's cat. Or maybe some poor stray animal foraging for food. She sighed. Until a few months ago, the squirrels had been out, stealing the seeds that Susan replaced daily in the bird feeder. Susan used to get indignant about the squirrels eating up the birdseed until one day Tehmina had said to her gently, "Beta, what's the use of getting upset about things in the natural world? We may as well be upset that the lion eats the deer. And who's to say the squirrel doesn't need the food more than the birds? At least they can fly from one place to another."

Susan had chuckled and shaken her head ruefully. "True enough. Sorry. I just so love seeing those beautiful birds in our yard."

Now Tehmina eyed the empty bird feeder that they'd still not taken down. It was hanging by a tree deep into the backyard and close to the fence that they shared with Antonio's house. Should she brave this wind to go out to put some seeds in it, in case there were poor creatures out there starving to death? She decided she would. And while she was at it, may as well put a saucer of milk out for that cat or whatever animal she had spotted. She'd put it far away from the house and clean it up before the children came home from work.

Imagine working on Christmas Eve, Tehmina thought while she went looking for the birdseed. And then she paused, struck by a sour, suspicious thought: What if the children had lied to her about being at work and were instead spending the day together, just to get some privacy? Before the sour feeling could settle in her stomach, before she could remember Sorab's plan to move into a bigger house that Percy had blurted out at Homi's party, she forced herself to be indignant at her own pettiness. And so what if they are? she chided herself. Weren't you young once? Or are you so old that you've forgotten what young people need? And anyway, you know how hard both children work. Probably working their hearts out right now while you sit around thinking evil thoughts about them. When has Sorab ever lied to you, you stupid woman? Good thing Rustom isn't here to read your suspicious mind—a good one-two-three dressing-down he'd give you. And despite herself, she smiled at how single-mindedly Rustom used to side with their daughter-in-law. Even though such blind loyalty irritated her at times, she had understood what he was doing—trying to squelch any possible discord in the family before it ever raised its ugly head. And implicit in this was the fact of Rustom and Tehmina's love for each other and the rock-solid sturdiness of their marriage. Rustom was tough on her because he took for granted that she knew of his unquestioned devotion to her. Some women might have resented being taken for granted. But Tehmina saw it for what it was—a declaration of love. And she liked the fact that her husband saw her as this tough old dame, his comrade-in-arms, even if she didn't feel so strong herself. Somehow, Rustom's thinking so made it true.

Grabbing the jar of birdseed, she slid open the patio door to let herself out into the backyard. As soon as she stepped onto the deck, the wind bit into her with such venom, she gasped for breath. Did people ever get used to this cold? she wondered. Would she be able to live here year after year, in this land of pewter skies and naked trees? She made her way down the deck and toward the frozen ground of the yard to where the bird feeder stood. The cold was making her hip ache and her fingers were already icicles. She wished she had thought of wearing gloves before coming out here, but it was so difficult to do anything with gloves on. Oh, why couldn't Sorab have emigrated to Australia or something? She and Rustom had been so proud when Sorab had gained admission to all three of the American universities he had applied to. But of course, at that time they had fully expected their only son to return home to them after getting his degree. There was little evidence to support that optimistic belief—most of the Parsi children they knew who had left India had never returned. But much as a smoker believes that cancer is something that happens to other people, they had been confident that their family would be the exception to that rule. After all, with Rustom's business contacts, Sorab would have never lacked job opportunities in Bombay.

But then Sorab had met Susan and the course of all their lives altered. Tehmina still remembered the day when Sorab had phoned her to say that he had met the woman he wanted to marry and could she and Daddy please start applying for visas so that they could be with him and his bride on his wedding day? She had gotten off the phone stunned, with tears in her eyes. She had so hoped that Sorab would have settled down with a nice Parsi girl, someone that Tehmina could love unreservedly as her daughter. And what now of her dreams of throwing a lavish Bombay wedding for her only child? For the last several years, every time she attended a Parsi wedding, Tehmina had made a mental note of who the good caterers and florists were, which band she liked, which reception hall she preferred. For years she had thought about which of her grandmother's jewelry she would present to her future daughter-in-law on the engagement day, on the wedding day, on her first wedding anniversary. And now Sorab was getting married to a girl they had never met in a place they had never been. A white American girl named Susan. They knew nothing about her parents, her family, her upbringing, whether her accent was so thick they'd have a hard time understanding her, whether she would be respectful of them and their traditions, whether she would turn her nose up at visiting Bombay or whether she would love it, whether she would like the gold and diamond jewelry that had been in the family for at least three generations. On the day of Sorab's unexpected phone call, she had waited for Rustom to get home from work so that she could break the calamitous news to him in person. "Why such a long face, darling?" Rustom had asked as he walked in the door.

"Sorab phoned today," she had replied. "He—he's getting married. In America. To a white American. Susan is the name. Said he wants us to attend the wedding." The tears rolled down her cheeks and she had made no attempt to brush them away.

There was a short pause. Then, "Well, we better apply for the visa right away. You know how long that can take." Taking in her thunderstruck face, Rustom frowned. "I'm assuming that your tears are tears of joy, Tehmi. Because this is a happy occasion. Our Sorab is getting married."

She looked at him uncomprehendingly. "Did you hear what I said? He's getting married in America. He's going to settle in America."

"I heard what you said. I am also hearing something that you apparently are not—the trumpet calls of Sorab's destiny." His face softened and he crossed the room to sit beside her. "Tehmina," he said. "Don't fight destiny, darling. Our son is in love. He is happy. He has found someone to make him happy. That's good news, not bad."

She was sobbing openly now, her head buried in his chest. "But—he'll be so far away," she blubbered. "When I agreed to his going to America, I didn't think—didn't think he wouldn't be coming back. At all. Ever."

Rustom sighed. "Ever is a long time, jannu. Life takes so many turns and detours. One never knows. And anyway, the point is, our son needs us now. Needs our blessings, our approval, our happiness.

And I'll be damned if anybody gets in the way of that—even my own silly wisp of a wife." He smiled and stroked her hair.

Several months later, after they had seen their son married in a beautiful outdoor ceremony on the banks of Lake Erie, Rustom made a confession: knowing that his mother would react badly to the news, Sorab had phoned his father at his office and broken the news to him first. Learning of her husband's treachery, Tehmina had turned to him in mock anger. "You luchcha. You mean you knew the news when you came home that evening? And still you let me go through that whole scene?"

Rustom grinned. "Oh, a few tears never hurt anyone. It was good for you to shed your crocodile tears. And besides, don't you love our Susan now? Aren't you glad our Sorab found such a beautiful, smart wife, instead of some illiterate Parsi girl from the village that you would've undoubtedly found for our son?"

"Arre wah. How dare you say that? As if I would've let my son marry someone like that. I would've found a doctor or a lawyer girl for my Sorab. So many girls would've stood in line for a chance to marry him."

Rustom turned a lazy, teasing eye on his wife. "Only a mother would think that. Whereas truth be told, Sorab got the better end of the bargain. That Susan is quite a catch."

She was about to protest when she caught the gleam in his eye. "Bas, this is what you live for," she complained. "To tease me every chance you get."

"My dear, a man must still have a few things to look forward to in his old age."

Now, as she poured the seeds into the feeder with hands that shook from the cold and from emotion, Tehmina thought that that was what she missed the most—with Rustom gone, there was no one in her life to tease her the way he used to.

Her thoughts were interrupted by the loud slam of a door. The next second she heard the familiar voices of the boys next door. "Oh man, I wish there was snow so we could build a snowman," she heard one of them say.

"I don't care," the other voice said. "I don't even care how cold it is. I just wanna stay out of the house as long as I can."

"I know," said the voice she now recognized as Joshua's. "Boy, Mom's in a baaaad mood today."

"Today?" The boys were walking toward the fence and now Tehmina could hear the bitterness in Jerome's voice. "Mom's always in a nasty mood."

Tehmina's heart sank. She longed to reach out to the boys to say something that would calm them down, but she was paralyzed by two forces—Susan's clear wish that she didn't want to associate with Tara's family and her own fear at being caught talking to the boys by Tara. She really didn't like that woman. And if Tara ever said anything mean about her Sorab again, Tehmina didn't know how she would react.

Before she could move, Tehmina heard the kitchen door open again. "Josh. Jerome. You two get in the house right this minute," she heard Tara yell. "I swear, if I have to stare at those dirty dishes one more second, I'm gonna give you two a whipping you'll never forget."

On her side of the fence, Tehmina froze. Surely Tara was joking. Go in, she silently willed the boys. Go in and finish your chores, boys, and get your banshee of a mother off your backs.

And so her heart sank when she heard Jerome whisper to his brother, "Get back behind the bushes. She'll never find us there."

She could hear the rustle of the bushes and was sure Tara had heard it, too. What were they doing? Was this some kind of an elaborate game that they played with their mother? But surely the anger she had heard in Tara's voice was real.

They were so close to her now that if she'd stuck her finger out from between the boards of the fence that separated the two yards, she could've almost touched them. She heard them shuffling; heard one of them let out a nervous giggle. And unconsciously, she found herself imitating their furtive behavior so that she was half crouching near the fence, afraid that Tara would spot her and realize that she had witnessed the ugly scene. She felt a quick flash of anger but was unsure if she was angry at herself for acting like a fugitive in her own yard or at the woman next door for having put her in this position.

"Listen, you little fuckers," she heard Tara say, "I'm late already and you're just making me later. You get in the house right now if you know what's good for you."

"She's real mad, Jerome," she heard Josh say. "We better go in."

"Stay right here," Jerome whispered fiercely. "She'll kill you if she sees you right now. Anyway, she'll be gone in a few minutes."

What kind of a mother threatened her children like this? What kind of a mother made her children so afraid of her that they hid in the bushes on a cold Christmas Eve? Tehmina's eyes stung with tears which she no longer attributed to the cold. She debated whether to get up from her half crouch and pull herself up to her full height. Surely Tara would stop her yelling if she saw that someone was witnessing her behavior. She had always heard stories about how, in America, people were afraid to discipline their own children for fear that someone might report them to the police. Surely seeing Tehmina standing there would be enough for Tara to come to her senses.

But before she could move, she heard Tara making her way swiftly through the yard. "Oh, shit," she heard Jerome breathe, and then the woman was upon the two young boys. Tehmina heard the rustle of the bush as Tara parted it and then sounds that made the hair on her hands stand up—the mad thuds as Tara brought some mysterious object crashing down on her children's small bodies, a boy's bloodcurdling screams, Tara's heavy, erratic breathing—even her breathing sounds angry and mad, Tehmina thought frantically—and Jerome's urgent, hot pleas for her to stop, she was really hurting Joshy. Tehmina looked around, waited for the neighbors to come running from all directions as they would in Bombay, waited for herself to draw herself to her full height and roar out a warning to Tara to stop her madness at once. But nothing happened. There were no urgent footsteps; no tall, strong man came and pulled the object of her violence out of Tara's hands; no neighborhood woman came and held the sobbing boys to her breast; no neighborhood child looked at Tara with big, accusing, shaming eyes. And even more inexplicably, she, Tehmina herself, did nothing, kept hiding behind the fence as if she was the one who had committed a shameful deed, as if she was the sinner.

"Now get in the house," she heard Tara say to the blubbering boys. "And stay in there until I get back. I'll be back in two hours, tops. And if those dishes aren't done by the time I return, you better not even be alive."

"Mom," Jerome said urgently. "Josh's lip is bleeding."

"Serves him right for hiding in the bushes. Probably cut himself on something. Now git, both of you, before I lose my temper again."

Through the crack in the fence, Tehmina saw Tara stand in the driveway with her hand on her hips while the boys flew into the house and shut the door behind them. She heard Tara muttering under her breath as she went to her car and got in. She heard her gun the car and then peel out of the driveway and down the street. Incredulous, she stayed in her hidden position for a full minute. Surely Tara was bluffing. Surely she wouldn't leave two injured boys at home all alone.

When Tehmina finally allowed herself to stand up, her legs were shaking. At first she thought it was from the cold and the uncomfortable half crouch she had held herself in in order to avoid being seen by her neighbors. But then she noticed that her whole body was trembling and she realized, with a kind of amazement, that she was angry. Coldly, murderously angry. Angry enough to spit in Tara's hideous face if she saw her again.

She paced in the yard, unsure of what to do, of how to get rid of this anger that was making her body rattle like the leaves on the ground. The thought of entering her comfortable, quiet home while there were two sobbing, hurting young children next door was out of the question. But if she went to the front of their house and rang their doorbell, Susan would find out. Surely some nosy neighbor—probably that old man Henderson who lived across the street from them and who was out in his yard day and night regardless of the weather—surely he'd mention something to Susan the next time he saw her.

Think, she yelled silently to herself. Do something. While you're pacing around here like an old cow, those two boys could be bleeding to death. And that wicked woman will be back home in no time—you heard her say that yourself. In desperation, she eyed the fence. It was about six feet high, she judged. But the wooden deck would help. If she stood on one of the lawn chairs that were on the deck, surely she could climb over the fence and into Antonio's backyard. She could knock on the kitchen door, undetected by the prying eyes of Mr. Henderson or any other neighbor, and just make sure that the children were all right. Even before the thought had fully formed in her head, an agitated Tehmina pulled the chair close to the fence. Climbing gingerly on it, she stood still for a moment, finding her balance. Then, she cautiously reached out and slipped her left leg over the fence, shifting her weight until her other leg was dangling above the chair and she found herself in the improbable position of sitting with her buttocks hanging in the space between the two stakes of the fence. The rounded top of the fence poked uncomfortably into the small of her back, so she knew that she couldn't stay in this position for long. She was also afraid that the fence would give way under her weight. For the first time in her life, Tehmina wished she was even thinner than she was. This was all she needed—for a section of the fence to come crashing down and having to explain the cause of its collapse to an accusing, indignant Tara and a tight-lipped Susan. She wished Cookie was home so she could have used his swift, lithe, athletic body to jump over the fence and act as her messenger of comfort and hope to the other two boys. Instead, here she was, with her stupid, lumpen, middle-aged body, stuck on a fence with a leg dangling on either side of it.

The wind kicked in and got under the khameez she was wearing, making it billow like a sail on a boat. She shifted a fraction of an inch on the fence and the next second she heard—or perhaps felt—a tear in her loose, baggy pants. She was mortified. How was she going to go over to her neighbor's home now, with a tear right near her bottom? Of course, the khameez was probably long enough to cover the ungainly sight of her underwear sticking out from under the torn shalwar. Still, she eyed the recently vacated chair longingly, contemplating the urge to abandon this crazy mission and go back into the warm comfort and safety of her home. What if someone caught her now, a sixty-six-year-old woman perched atop a fence that might give way at any minute? Surely they would lock her up in some American asylum where grim-faced doctors would eye her as if she was a species from some other planet. The boys were probably okay, were probably used to occasional whackings from their mother. And really, she had done nothing yet that was irreversible—she had not called out to Tara to stop her mad beating, had not consoled the sobbing boys, had not yet knocked on their door like she intended to. No, all she had done was impulsively put herself in a situation where she was sitting atop a fence like a flag planted on a mountain.

The memory of Jerome's tearful voice drove her on. She forced herself to shift her body as she brought her other leg slowly around the fence. Despite the bitter cold, her face was sweaty from the physical and mental effort this took. What had happened to her? she wondered. In high school she had run track and had been a hurdler. Was no part of that athletic, strong schoolgirl still alive in her? Was that girl totally buried under the mounds of time, under the shrill complaints of arthritis and muscle pain? Had she been rubbed out completely by the pungent layers of Tiger Balm and Iodex?

Because she needed the help of that girl now. Tehmina knew this as she eyed the six-foot drop from where she sat on the fence to the bottom of Antonio's yard. She had forgotten that there was no deck on his side of the fence, no built-up area that would soften her fall as she dropped onto the other side. A bitter gust of wind blew and froze the sweat on her face. Her eyes watered because of the cold and because she was afraid. What if she twisted her ankle? She, who was here on a rescue mission, would have to be rescued herself. She would go from being savior to victim in a moment's time. Instead of her checking in on them, poor Josh and Jerome would have to take care of their ungainly visitor who would have dropped into their yard much like a heavy, clumsy bird with a broken wing.

Tehmina, Rustom called out to her. For heaven's sake, jannu. Just bloody *jump*. She startled at the sound of his voice, so clear it might have come from someone standing behind her. And for the rest of her life she believed that Rustom had actually stood behind her on the deck and that her beloved had not so gently given her rumpus a helpful push. Because the next thing she knew, she had loosened her tight grip on the tip of the fence, and even as she let go her feet were struggling to position themselves correctly for the landing. She half landed on her feet and half on her knees. The ground was so cold that she immediately used the heels of her hands to push herself off the ground, thereby leaving thin scratches on them. She stood still and upright for a moment, willing her body to not betray her now, to not surprise her with any new, sharp pain. But she was fine.

Quickly, she made her way toward the back of the house. Climbing the two wooden steps that led to the kitchen door, she knocked on it. There was no response. Cupping her eyes in order to keep the sunlight out, she rested her face against the glass door and peered inside. There was no sign of the boys. If she didn't know better, she would've thought nobody was home. Her eyes took in the large brown stain on the light ceramic floor, the dirty dishes in the sink. But no sign of the boys.

She knocked louder this time. "Josh. Jerome. Open the door. It's Tehmi—it's Cookie's granna. From next door."

No answer. She felt panic rise and tried her best to squelch it. She tried the doorknob. It turned easily under her hand. Feeling like an intruder, she entered the disheveled kitchen. The voice in her head was clanging like a fire alarm. You shouldn't be here, she said to herself. You can go to jail for this, breaking into someone's house. Maybe you should turn back right now and no one will know that you were here.

Her feet followed their own dictates. They led her into the living room. Tehmina noticed two things simultaneously: one, the living room looked like someone had fought a war in it. There were papers and pizza boxes everywhere. All four of the couch cushions were on the floor. Two overflowing ashtrays spilled their contents onto a filthy coffee table.

Two, she noticed a movement in the corner between the wall and the TV cabinet. Josh and Jerome were crouched in that corner, huddled close to each other and as quiet as mice. They are the only beautiful things in this catastrophic room, Tehmina thought.

Tehmina was watching the boys sipping hot chocolate in her kitchen, a worried expression on her face. The enormity of what she had done was beginning to dawn on her. She had talked the two frightened boys into leaving their house. On their way out she had grabbed a bar stool and they had each stood on it to leap over the fence and onto the chair on the deck that waited for them on the other side. In other words, she had snuck two children out of their own home. Their mother would be home any minute and how long before she discovered the bar stool near the fence and figured things out? And now she was sitting with two boys whom she had kidnapped, in a house that didn't belong to her, a house that belonged to a woman who had expressly told her that she wanted nothing to do with her troublesome neighbors next door.

"What time will your mom be home?" she asked, and noticed how Jerome's face darkened.

"I dunno." He shrugged. "She's gone over to Ernie's house. Could be two, three hours."

She saw the boys looking at her expectantly, waiting for her to do something. But she felt heavy, sluggish, unable to think, as if she had used up all her energy in her earlier, manic adventure. "How is your lip?" she asked Josh. She had already cleaned it, and had noticed how Josh's eyes had glistened with tears when she had put some antiseptic on it. The boy also had a nasty bruise above his left eye, which Tehmina had bathed with a washcloth and warm water. Gazing at it now, she longed for the iodine that occupied a permanent place in her medicine cabinet at home. As far as she knew, nobody in America kept iodine at home.

"It's okay," Josh mumbled. "It just hurts when I smile." He looked so subdued that Tehmina's heart broke. That wicked woman has damaged the spirit of this beautiful boy, she thought. Like trampling on a flower.

"Well, if it hurts to smile, then don't smile, dummy," Jerome said, and there was something malicious and cruel in his voice. It's already happening, Tehmina thought. The mother's meanness is trickling into the veins of another generation, drip, drip, drip, like the fresh coffee that drips into the pot every morning.

"Don't talk to your brother like that, sonny," she said automatically, and was unprepared for the angry look that she saw on Jerome's face.

"I want to go home," he declared. "My mom will be home soon."

Tehmina panicked. There was no way she was letting these boys back into that house, she thought. The knowledge of this propelled her into action. "How about something to eat?" she asked. "Would you like some fruit? No? Some spinach pies?" She peered into the fridge and silently cursed her rotten luck. They had been eating out so much because of the holidays that the fridge, which was always overflowing with her cooking, was virtually bare. No mutton cutlets, no chops, no curry rice. Not that these boys would've liked any of these things, anyway. She had a sudden inspiration. "I know," she said. "How about a grilled cheese sandwich? With chips on the side?"

She left the boys munching on their sandwiches while she went into the living room to use the phone. She hesitated for a moment but then dialed the number for Sorab's secretary. "Janet?" she said, "Is Sorab there? This is his mother."

"Oh, hi, Tammy," Janet replied. "He's in meetings all afternoon, I'm afraid. But I can interrupt him, if it's an emergency."

Did the fact that she had two young boys sitting in her kitchen without the permission or knowledge of their mother constitute an emergency? Tehmina imagined the look of horror on her son's face when she broke the news to him. In this country, did they send people to jail for what she had done—entering someone's home and whisking two young children away? And how could she possibly tell her son how she'd done it—how she'd jumped over a fence like a jewel thief? She might as well confess that she'd walked over the rooftops of all the homes in the neighborhood and slid down the chimney. Suddenly, inexplicably, she felt the urge to giggle. I'm going mad, she thought. "No," she told Janet on the phone. "Don't disturb him.

It's nothing much, really. Just had a question for him. Well, Merry Christmas to you, dear."

The doorbell rang just as she hung up and for a second she froze in horror. Surely that was Tara. She must have returned home while Tehmina was on the phone, and figured out that her sons were being held hostage at the house next door. Tehmina felt sick to her stomach. She knew she had no right to hold on to those boys. But she also knew, as sure as she knew anything, that Tara had no right to those boys either, that she had forfeited the exquisite privilege of motherhood with her cruelty and brutality. And that there was no way she, Tehmina, was giving up those boys to Tara without a fight.

"Granna," she heard the beloved voice yell, "hurry up and open the door. It's cold out here."

She felt as if she could pass out in relief. Of course. It was Cookie, returning home from his playdate at Bill Steinberg's house. But on her way to the door, she stopped, struck by another thought: under no circumstances could she let Mary Steinberg, who was undoubtedly dropping Cookie off, into the house. "Coming," she yelled, but crept back into the kitchen.

"You know how to play police-police?" she asked the startled boys, and when they shook their heads no, "When I say 'freeze,' you just stop whatever you're doing and freeze in that position. You can't move or talk or anything. Okay, let's play a practice round. You can't move until I say 'unfreeze,' okay?"

She saw Jerome eye the last of his sandwich with regret, but both boys sat as still as statues while she pulled the kitchen door shut and headed to the foyer. She opened the door on Cookie and Mary, their faces red with waiting in the cold. "Sorry, sorry," she said. "I was in the middle of something. So much work to do, getting ready for Christmas and all. I'm sure you understand."

Mary laughed lightly. "Well, we don't exactly celebrate Christmas. But I do know what you mean." She made a slight movement as if to follow Cookie into the house. "Do you need help with anything?"

Tehmina didn't loosen her grip on the front door. Nor did she concede an inch of ground. "Oh, God, no. Just stuff I have to do myself." She held Cookie by the shoulder and moved him toward her so that he was blocking Mary's path also. "And now that Cookie's home I have one less thing to worry about. Thanks so much for dropping him off, Mary."

"Oh, yeah. No problem." Mary was looking at her strangely. "Well, okay. I guess I should get back home, anyway." She bent toward Cookie. "Bye, little guy. You come over for a playdate soon, you understand?"

Cookie nodded. "Oh. I forgot to tell Billy. Can you tell him I'm going to get a Pneumatic Power Destroyer for Christmas?" He glanced at his grandmother. "At least, I hope so."

They stood in the doorway until Mary Steinberg got into her car and drove away. Then Tehmina turned toward her grandson. "Ae, Cookie," she said. "We have some company."

"Company?" Cookie asked. "Who? Who is it?"

"All right, calm down, calm down. They're in the kitchen. It's Jerome and Josh from next door."

"Jerome and Joshy? Yeeeeaaaaaaah." Cookie went tearing into the kitchen.

"Unfreeze," Tehmina said, and Jerome immediately put the last of his sandwich into this mouth.

"Hey. Did you come over for a playdate?" Cookie asked. Then, noticing Joshua's bruised and swollen face, "Hey, what happened to you, Joshy?"

"My mommy whupped me."

Cookie stared at him without comprehension. "You mean, you fell?" he asked at last.

Jerome banged his hand on the kitchen table. "No, he means our mamma whupped him. She beat us for being bad." His face was red and ugly with rage. He also looked as if he was about to burst into tears.

"Boys," Tehmina said. "No shouting, please. We must all be quiet. And think. Think." She looked around the room and saw three young faces staring back at her, looking to her for guidance, looking to her to make sense out of their lives. She did not feel up to the task. I'm as confused as you are, she wanted to say to them. I don't know what to do any more than you do. Instead, noticing the teary look on her grandson's face, she barked, "Cookie. I want you to go up to your room and wash your face. All dirty you are."

"But, Granna, I took a bath this morning," the boy protested.

"I don't care—" she began when she was interrupted by a giggle. It was Josh.

"All dirty you are," he repeated, wriggling up his nose.

Cookie flashed his grandmother a now-look-what-you've-done glare. But he headed toward his room, stomping all the way up the stairs to make his displeasure known.

Tehmina sat down abruptly. This whole thing was getting away from her, like a ball of yarn that rolled and unraveled on the floor. How foolish she had been in thinking she could do something to help these poor boys. Apart from feeding them a grilled cheese sandwich and giving them a few gifts at Christmastime, there was little she could do for them. She could not protect them from their mother's wrath and ignorance. She could not save them from their destiny. She thought of all the years she had volunteered at the orphanage in Bombay, how she and the other Parsi ladies had held fund-raisers and bake sales to raise money. She remembered the abandoned infants she had cradled in her arms, the toddlers she had bathed and dressed during her weekly visits to the center. Had she altered or saved a single life because of her efforts? Probably not. Sure, she had brought a little comfort, a little cheer to some of the children there. But that was the extent of it. It was she who had gained the most, she who had left there each week feeling richer, wiser. And that was the point of it—she had left at the end of each visit. Gone back to her home, reentered the life that she had with her husband and her son. And so it would be with these two boys sitting in front of her, looking as sad as a lost wallet. The wallet didn't belong to her; she would have to return it to its unworthy but rightful owner.

She was debating how to frame her words, what to say to the boys, when Cookie sauntered back into the room. One look at his dirt-streaked face told her that he had not done her bidding. "Did you wash your face like I asked you to?" she said.

"No, I didn't, Granna. I was busy," Cookie said importantly.

"Busy? Busy doing what?"

Cookie glanced at Jerome and Josh and then lowered his voice. "I just called 911."

CHAPTER THIRTEEN

You did, what?" Tehmina cried in disbelief.

"I just called 911," Cookie repeated. Then, looking at her aghast face, "That's what we are taught to do in school, if a grown-up hits a kid."

Jerome jumped up off the chair. "You crazy fool," he yelled. "What you go do that for? Now my mommy is going to be real mad. She's gonna kick my ass for sure." He turned and grabbed his younger brother's arm. "Come on, Joshy. We're going home."

Joshy began to cry. "I don't wanna go home," he sobbed. "I wanna stay here with this lady. She's nice." He looked at Tehmina with his big, wet eyes. "Can I have some more potato chips?"

Tehmina looked at the three upturned faces looking to her to make the next move. "Okay," she said more loudly than she'd intended. "Calm down. Everybody just calm down. We need to think." She turned to Jerome. "Nobody's leaving this house until I say so. Understand? Now I want you children to sit quietly while I . . . I . . . make a phone call."

Throwing her grandson a helpless glance, Tehmina walked back into the living room. She really had to get hold of Sorab now, now that Cookie had done such a foolish thing. She had picked up the receiver when she heard the front doorbell ring. Oh my God, surely they couldn't be here already. She stood still for a second, the phone receiver still in her hand, when she caught a movement out of the corner of her eye. It was Cookie darting from the kitchen toward the front door. Before she could stop him, he had opened the door and three policemen, two in uniform and one in regular clothes, were walking in.

She hung up. "I'm afraid there's been a mistake," she said, forcing her face into a smile. "My grandson misunderstood the situation and—"

The tall officer with the red hair stopped looking around the room and focused on her. "Good afternoon," he said evenly. "I'm Officer Bruce and this here is my partner, Officer Curtis. And this is Luke Johnson, from the *Daily Mirror*. He's trailing us for the day. And you are the owner of this house?"

"Yes. No. I mean, I'm visiting my son. From India." Tehmina knew she was sounding flustered and tried to control her emotions.

"I see. And you name is, ma'am?"

"Tehmina Sethna. Though I also go by Tammy."

After he had made her spell out her name, Bruce looked up from his notebook and frowned at her. "Okay, Mrs. Sethna. What have we got here? Seems like we got a call that there was some trouble with a neighbor, ma'am? You heard the mother beating up on her kids?"

Tehmina desperately wished that Sorab and Susan were home right now. How did one talk to police officers in America? she wondered. "Well, she wasn't exactly . . . that is, I mean, you know, I didn't really see anything—"

"They're here," Cookie yelled. "In the kitchen. And Joshy has a big, fat bruise from where his mommy beat him."

The two officers exchanged glances and Tehmina saw the third man flip open a notebook and take one step toward her. "They're here?" Officer Curtis said. "How'd they get to your house? Did they run away or something?"

Tehmina gulped hard. She could feel her face redden. What did an American jail look like? she wondered. Surely it didn't have rats in it, like Indian jails did. She was deathly afraid of rats. "I went and got them," she stammered. "After their mother left in her car. I—I was worried. Just wanted to make sure they were okay. And when I saw the little one bleeding, I just, I just wanted to bring them here and cheer them up. You know, give them some food and hot cocoa."

Officer Curtis smiled slightly and the mood in the room visibly changed. But he immediately grew serious again. "Is the mother back home? Does she know her kids are here?"

"I haven't heard the car return yet. It's loud—a loose muffler maybe?—and I've been listening for it."

"I bet you have," Officer Bruce muttered under his breath, but Tehmina heard him and wondered what he meant. Would they charge her with kidnapping? If so, how would Susan and Sorab ever live it down? Had she jeopardized her children's future by her rash act? And how would Persis and all the rest of them in India react to the news?

"Well, let's go see the kids, shall we?" Curtis said, and they all headed for the kitchen, an excited Cookie leading the way.

Tehmina saw Jerome flinch when the policemen entered the kitchen. She noticed that Josh had helped himself to more potato chips.

"Howdy, boys," Curtis said, his voice low and calm. He ruffled Joshua's hair. "Seems like quite a shiner you have here, kiddo. What happened?"

"My mommy hit us. For staying out in the cold instead of coming in and washing the dishes like we was s'pposed to. Oww," he yelled as Jerome pinched his arm. "What you do that for?"

Jerome glared at him and then turned to the officers. "He's lying," he said. "He just fell down and hurt himself."

"I see." Curtis chewed on his lower lip. "And where's your mom now, kiddo? She at home?"

"Naw," Jerome replied. "She's with her boyfriend."

Tehmina saw Curtis shoot a warning look at his partner. "Uh-huh." His voice was friendly, noncommittal. "She do that often? Leave you alone at home?"

"Not often. Just sometimes, when she needs something."

"When she needs to get away from us," Josh said guilelessly, and the innocence in his voice tore at Tehmina's heart. She sensed rather than saw that the boy's words had affected the other adults the same way.

Officer Curtis smiled gently and put his arm around Josh. "Why would she need to get away from you, big guy?" he asked.

"Because I'm trouble. I drive her crazy." In amazement, Tehmina noticed that Josh was bragging, that there was some kind of misguided pride in his words.

"So what does she do when you're driving her crazy?" Curtis's voice was soft, low, like a well-oiled motor.

"She whups—" Josh bit down on his tongue and glanced anxiously at his older brother for guidance. "I fell down and hurt my lip," he said.

Officer Curtis straightened and Tehmina noticed the glint in his gray eyes. "Well, let's walk over to your house and have a look around, shall we?" he said. He stopped, as if struck by a thought. "How'd you get in the front door, ma'am?" he asked. "Did the mother leave it unlocked? Or did the kids let you in?"

Tehmina stared at him. She moved her mouth but no words came. She caught the narrowing of the officer's eyes as he waited for an answer. Oh my God, he thinks I'm lying or hiding something, she thought.

"I jumped," she blurted out. "Over the fence. That is, in the backyard. I—I didn't want to go up the front driveway. Too many prying eyes, you see."

Now it was the officers' turn to stare at her. "You jumped over a fence? In this weather?" Officer Bruce asked. His glance said what he was too polite to say—*with this middle-aged, unathletic body?*

The third man, who had been writing furiously in his notebook, spoke for the first time. "I say, I'd like to see the fence."

Officer Bruce chuckled. "I bet you would." He turned to Tehmina. "Do you mind showing us how you did it, ma'am?"

Tehmina felt her face burning with shame as she opened the glass sliding doors and stood on the deck. The chair was still where she had left it. She pointed to it, a pleading look in her eyes. "I stood on that," she said. "And then, you know, jumped over."

The officer with the notebook—who Tehmina now noticed was merely a young man, barely in his twenties—burst out laughing. "But that's fantastic," he said. "Wish I'd had a picture of that."

Tehmina blushed. Was this youngster laughing at her? But the boy, who Tehmina assumed was a plainsclothes officer, had a face that was open, guileless, and Tehmina noticed that his eyes shone when he looked at her.

Curtis cleared his throat. "Well, I won't ask you for a reenactment, ma'am," he said, and this time she heard the smile in his voice. "But that's quite a feat you accomplished." He was peering over the fence. "How old did you say you were, again?"

"Sixty-six," Tehmina said, and from the expression on their faces, she might as well have told them she was two hundred.

The December wind bit at them again and Tehmina shivered. Noticing this, the young man looked away from his notebook and said, "Damn cold day, even with no snow. We'd better go inside."

This time, there was no mistaking the friendliness he threw her way. She was glad. Officers Bruce and Curtis were polite and courteous, but there was something distant and wooden about them. Maybe it was their close-cropped hair. Maybe it was their rock-hard bodies and erect postures that made them look robotlike. In contrast, the young man, dressed in jeans and a woolen pullover, looked small, human-scaled, approachable. She smiled back at him.

Once inside, she ordered Cookie up to her room. The little one had already seen enough. She braced herself for an argument, but Officer Curtis turned to the boy and told him he was deputizing him to go up to his room and keep guard. To her amazement, Cookie turned around and left the kitchen without saying another word.

The young man with the notebook sat at the kitchen bar with Josh and Jerome and spoke to them in his low, pleasant voice. Even though he wrote nonstop in his notebook, he kept his eyes focused on the two boys. Tehmina wanted to join them but she was aware of the other two officers huddled together near the glass doors. Whatever they were discussing, she wanted to make sure she heard. She hovered at their periphery for a few moments, and then Officer Bruce turned toward her. "Right," he said, as if continuing a conversation. "So here's what we're gonna do, ma'am. Curtis here will take the boys to the Children's Services home while I wait for the mother to return."

Tehmina felt her stomach drop. "What do you mean? Take the boys to Children's Services?" she whispered. "What exactly is that?"

Officer Bruce raised an eyebrow, as if surprised by her question. "Well, ma'am, we're going to have to place the mother under arrest. And obviously those boys can't stay by themselves. So we need to get the ball rolling—you know, see if there's a relative that we can place them with temporarily. That's the way things are done in this country," he added.

Tehmina looked around for a chair, not sure that she could trust her legs to support her any longer. She shut her eyes. Please let them be gone when I open my eyes, she prayed. Please let this all be a bad dream.

"Would you like a drink of water, ma'am?" Officer Curtis was saying when she opened her eyes.

She struggled to find her composure. "No, no thanks," she replied. "It's just that—you see, I never intended to get Tara in trouble. And those boys love their mother, you see, and if you take them away, I don't know what . . . I just feel so terrible with all this."

"Miss Tammy." It was the young man with the notebook, who had left the kids and was now standing behind her. "You really shouldn't feel bad about any of this, ma'am. You're—why, you're a hero. Not too many Americans would've done what you just did, ma'am, I can tell you that."

But that's just the trouble, Tehmina thought, seeing Susan's disapproving face before her eyes. I've acted like a typical Indian—interfering and poking my nose in things that are not my business.

She turned to the other two senior officers in desperation. "Can we—can we just forget about this whole thing? I mean, I didn't even call you, you know. That was my grandson and he—he made a mistake."

Curtis smiled sadly. "On the contrary, ma'am. He did exactly the right thing."

"Just as you did," the young man added fiercely. Despite her confusion, Tehmina heard the fierceness in his voice, his fervent need to believe, and was flattered and irritated all at once.

"Okay," Officer Curtis said in his take-charge voice. "I'm afraid we're wasting time here. We want to get the boys removed before Mom gets home. And with it being Christmas Eve and all, all the paperwork's gonna take twice as long as usual." He walked to where Josh and Jerome sat across from Cookie.

"Okay, boys." He smiled. "We're going for a ride. Ever ridden in a police cruiser before?"

"Whee!" Josh said, but Jerome stared at the officer, a sullen expression on his face.

"Where're we going?" he said.

Officer Curtis was sweating ever so slightly. "We're going for a car ride, son," he said. "And then you're going to spend the night with some nice people, okay? You got any relatives around here?"

Suddenly Tehmina found her voice. "They can stay here," she said. She would deal with Susan's anger, she told herself.

Officer Curtis appeared irritated. "No can do, lady," he said shortly. "There's procedure that I have to follow." He turned back to the boys. "Maybe there's a favorite relative you'd like to spend Christmas with?"

"They have an uncle," Tehmina said. "He's—that is, that's his house, next door. He and his wife now live in—" She couldn't remember the name of the place Antonio had moved to. "Wait. We have his phone number in our book." She rushed out of the room, unable to look either boy in the eye.

When she returned, Curtis was standing near the front door with the two boys. Whatever he had said to them while she was away had obviously broken down the last of Jerome's resistance. "Here it is," she said, handing over the slip of paper she'd written Antonio's information on.

Jerome scowled. "Stupid bitch," he said, looking her straight in the eye, and Tehmina flinched as if he had landed a well-placed blow on her jaw. Her eyes immediately filled with tears of guilt and hurt and something else—some sense of sympathy and pity for Jerome. For having caused his current situation. For not having been there for him early enough to prevent him from turning into the kind of boy who would talk like this to his elders.

"Whoa, kiddo," Officer Curtis said, tapping Jerome lightly on his shoulder. "Watch that mouth."

"Wait," Tehmina said as she remembered the Christmas gifts she had bought for the boys. She turned to Curtis. "Please. If you don't mind. I bought—that is, I have a little something for the boys. For Christmas. It's up in my room. If you would just—"

Curtis smiled. "Go ahead, ma'am. Take your time."

Joshy's eyes grew wide when he saw the colorfully wrapped gift. Jerome pretended to be uninterested for a moment, but then his curiosity got the better of him and he grabbed the gift she was holding out to him. "Thanks," he mumbled, not looking at her.

"Boy, oh boy," Josh breathed, making as if to tear open the wrapping paper.

"Not here, buddy," Curtis said, putting his hand on the boy's thin wrist. "You can open it in the cruiser."

When Tehmina opened the front door to let them out, she was surprised to see a second police car in the driveway. When had the two of them radioed for a second cruiser? She stood at the door and waited until both boys had climbed into the car. Inexplicably, Joshy turned around to wave to her just before he ducked into the vehicle. She waved back, although her mouth felt as if it was padded with cotton balls. What have I done? she thought. Oh, Rustom, what have I done?

When she went back inside, Officer Bruce was out on the deck, keeping a lookout for Tara's car to pull into her driveway. The other man was sitting at the bar, furiously scribbling something into his notebook. He looked up as she entered the kitchen and smiled at her. She smiled back, thankful for his warm presence.

"So how do you feel?" he said quietly.

She shook her head, not allowing herself to speak. He clucked his tongue in sympathy and the kind look on his face made the tears come unbidden to her eyes. "Those poor children," she began.

"They're lucky," he said, and again, there was that fierceness in his voice. "At least they had someone stick up for them. Maybe they'll have a chance in life now. And no matter what happens, they'll always remember this day."

Tehmina's laugh was the flavor of sour apples. "Yah, remember the day they were taken away from their mother."

"No. The day someone stood up for them. The day someone said what was happening to them was wrong."

Suddenly Tara's tired, dirty face rose before Tehmina's eyes and she felt a pang of pity. All of her murderous rage against the woman had vanished now, leaving a melancholy weariness in its place. "She's so young—the mother. And poor. And not so educated, you know?" She wanted this young man, so clean and clear in his judgments, in his righteousness, she wanted him to understand something about life—about its grayness, its murkiness.

"I see," he said. "So you feel sorry for her?"

He was writing everything down, and suddenly she was cautious. Hadn't she heard about the good-cop, bad-cop routine? Maybe this was a trap and his sympathy, his flattery, an act. Maybe he was trying to make her say that she felt sorry for Tara so that they could charge her with a crime, also. Tehmina felt old and confused and disoriented. "I don't know," she mumbled.

She glanced out into the yard, where Bruce was pacing the deck, rubbing his hands against the chill. "Your partner will catch a cold. He can come in and wait," she said.

The young man stared at her. "My partner? He's not my partner, Miss Tammy. That is, I'm not a cop. I'm a reporter, with the *Daily Mirror.* I'm just following the guys around for the day, you know, doing a day-in-the-life piece. Sorry. I—I thought Bruce had introduced me when we came in." He stuck his hand out. "I'm Luke Johnson."

"Oh." Tehmina was flustered. Why had she assumed that the boy was a policeman? Up close, she could see how young he was. And what was day-in-the-life-peace? Must be some Christmas thing, she decided. "We get both newspapers," she said vaguely. "My son . . . he likes to read. Also, the *New York Times*, on Sunday."

Luke grimaced. "Glad to know *someone* still reads," he said. He was quiet for a moment and then resumed the conversation as if they were at a cocktail party. "Yeah, we're the smaller of the two dailies. I'm surprised the big, bad Goliath hasn't swallowed us up completely. So few towns even have two newspapers, you know? But we still beat their ass on stories every day."

"I see," Tehmina said, trying to stifle a yawn. She still didn't understand what this young man was doing in her kitchen. Then, to be polite, "In Bombay we have hundreds of newspapers. Seems like someone starts a new one every day."

"Sounds like paradise." The young man sighed. "Bombay." He played with the word in his mouth, rolling it around like a piece of rich dark chocolate. "They call it Mumbai now, right? That's my goal, you know—to be a foreign correspondent. I mean, the *Mirror* is a feisty little paper, but I want to travel the world."

Tehmina smiled. "So why are you wasting your time talking to a silly old lady, dearie?" she said. Reared on the serious, dignified *Times of India*, Tehmina thought of news as important stories that dealt with politics, inflation, government corruption, foreign policy. Talking to a mad Indian woman who had jumped over a fence to rescue two boys and instead gambled with their futures would never make her definition of news.

Luke set his pen down for emphasis. "Are you kidding? This is—"

The rest of his sentence was cut off by the familiar sound of Tara's muffler. They both heard it despite the closed glass door and they both tensed and looked at Officer Bruce. The man was now sitting on the chair that Tehmina had propped against the fence so that he could look down on Tara pulling into her driveway, but she couldn't see him. He signaled to Tehmina and Luke to stay in the house. A few seconds went by and then they heard the slamming of the car door. Another few seconds and then Bruce stood up and came into the house. "Right," he said. "The mother's home. From what you told us"—he consulted his watch—"she's been gone for over two hours." He turned to face Tehmina. "Time to go have a chat with Mom," he said lightly, but Tehmina could hear the iron in his voice. "And, ma'am, I just wanted to thank you for doing your duty. I just wish we had more good citizens like you." He glanced at Luke. "This enough excitement for you? You coming next door?"

"Of course," Luke said, shutting his notebook. "But if you'd just give me a moment." He pulled a small digital camera out of his pants pocket and took a picture of Tehmina, who was too stunned and blinded by the camera's flash to protest. Luke flashed her a grin as bright as the camera's light. "It was a pleasure meeting you, Miss Tammy. Merry Christmas."

"Merry Christmas," she repeated by rote. The irony stuck in her throat like a pit from a bitter fruit.

Fifteen minutes later she watched from the picture window in the living room as Officer Bruce led Tara into the police cruiser. In the weak midafternoon sun Tara looked small, diminished. Tehmina tried to muster up the rage she'd felt at the woman only a few hours ago and found that the effort already felt like a memory or a dream. Now all she felt was a deep, suffocating pity for Tara, for Josh, for Jerome, for all of them. So much for my good intentions, she thought. Unbidden, an Omar Khayyám poem came to her:

The moving finger writes and having writ
Moves on: nor all thy Piety nor Wit

Shall lure it back to cancel half a line,
Nor all thy Tears wash out a Word of it.

She went upstairs to find Cookie, unsure of what kind of mood he would be in. She realized that she was going to have to tell her grandson that this afternoon's incident had to remain yet another secret between him and her. There was no reason why she should upset Sorab and Susan with this, and that, too, on Christmas Eve. Like a wet rag stuffed down her throat, this secret would be her punishment for poking her nose where it didn't belong.

But then she caught herself. There was no possible way that she could keep the events of this afternoon a secret from Sorab and Susan. After all, two police cars had been parked in front of her house. Two uniformed police officers had entered her house. Surely some of their neighbors had noted all the commotion. If this had been Bombay, of course, at least twenty neighbors would have alerted Sorab by now. Despite her grim mood, Tehmina smiled at the memory of the time when their neighbor Mani Poonawalla had squealed on an indignant Rustom. Her husband had been home from work for a few days after having suffered from chest pains. Although the doctor had ultimately decided it was merely indigestion, blood tests had revealed that Rustom had high cholesterol levels, a fact that Tehmina had unwittingly shared with their sixth-floor neighbor, Mani, who immediately appointed herself the custodian of Rustom's health. On the fourth day of Rustom's confinement, Tehmina finally left him home alone for a few hours to go shopping with one of her friends. Three hours after she had left home, her cell phone rang. It was a breathless Mani calling to inform Tehmina that in her absence, Rustom had ordered two malai na khajas from Parsi Dairy Farm to be delivered to their apartment. As luck would have it, the delivery boy had accidentally rung Mani's doorbell instead of Rustom's. The woman had promptly confiscated the sweetmeat and then phoned Rustom to chastise him for his sneaky ways. And despite his pleadings, she was now calling Tehmina to tell her what her husband—who, according to Mani, obviously had a death wish—had done. At the time, Tehmina had not known how to respond to the tattletale Mani—she was at once grateful and appalled by the woman's nosiness. But Rustom had not been so conflicted. For days, he railed and ranted about the shocking manners of their neighbors, of how nobody in Bombay ever minded their own business, of what he would do to that damn busybody Mani once he was well enough. And what the hell had the blasted woman done with his khajas, anyway? he wanted to know. Most likely stuffed her own loud mouth with them.

Smiling at the memory, Tehmina made her way up the stairs to Cookie's room when a thought stopped her. Old man Henderson. Their neighbor across the street. Rosemont Heights' own version of Mani Poonawalla. Rain or shine, Henderson, who appeared to be in his late seventies, was out in his front yard, raking leaves, blowing snow, washing his driveway. During a visit a few summers ago, Tehmina had seen the old man climb on a tall metal ladder and scrub and rinse the roof of his house. She had assumed this was just another strange American custom, but Susan had assured her that nobody but nobody washed his or her roof and you'd have to have a really strong obsessive-compulsive gene to do *that*. Even in the winter months, the old man was always outdoors, even if he did nothing but walk up and down his driveway. In the Sethna household, Henderson had become a kind of shorthand. "Hey, hon, would you like to do a Henderson?" Susan would ask Sorab if she wanted him to do something outrageous, such as rearranging the spices in the kitchen cabinet in alphabetical order. Or, Sorab would say, in response to a request by his wife, "Who do you think I am? Old man Henderson?"

Now Tehmina tried to remember if she'd seen Henderson lurking around this morning. Had his car been in the driveway today? Or, was it possible that the old man had actually left his house and gone somewhere? But she knew with a sinking heart that Henderson had probably witnessed the excitement across the street. What would he do? Would he phone Sorab or Susan, à la Mani? Or would he wait until he encountered one of them on the street a few days later; would he flag Sorab's car down on his way home from work?

Tehmina felt a faint glimmer of hope at the last thought. It was inevitable, she knew, that the children be told about the events of this afternoon, inevitable that she would have to face Susan's thin-lipped displeasure when her daughter-in-law found out how flagrantly Tehmina had violated her wishes. But . . . maybe she could delay the inevitable, postpone the excruciating moment when she would see the children's appalled reactions reflected in their eyes. If only she could put off their knowing until after Christmas, she thought, and allowed her heart to lift a tad bit at the possibility.

But this meant asking Cookie to keep another secret from his parents. Yet another secret, along with the gift they'd bought for the boys next door. Not fair to burden a poor child in this way. So much for trying to help others, she scolded herself as she reached Cookie's room. You better start by making sure your own grandson doesn't become a liar and a thief because of your bad influence.

CHAPTER FOURTEEN

Christmas morn. How little those words had meant to him as a child in hot, steamy Bombay, Sorab thought. But now, with a son of his own who he knew would be awake any minute now and running down the stairs as light as rainfall, Sorab had come to cherish this morning more than any other of the year. It was hard not to be a romantic when one was a father, he mused. Children had a way of making you see past the groaning dullness of daily living to the red, beating heart of the universe.

With one ear cocked for the sound of Cookie's footsteps, Sorab put on the kettle to boil water for three cups of tea. He would surprise the two women sleeping upstairs by taking them tea in bed. He tore some mint leaves from the plant in the dining room, crushed them in his hand, and threw them into the water. Next, he added sugar to the three yellow pottery mugs sitting in a row on the kitchen counter. He knew the routine—one teaspoon for Mamma, two for himself, and a half for Susan. He was tempted to add more sugar to his wife's cup, it being Christmas morning and all, but he resisted the urge. For a woman who drank her coffee black, it was amazing that Susan could even tolerate the milky, sweet tea that his mother made for both of them when they came home from work every evening.

The water was close to a boil—Sorab was watching it intently so that he could add the black tea leaves as soon as it came to an aggressive boil—when the phone rang. Damn, he whispered to himself. The ring was sure to disturb Susan and Mamma. What idiot was calling this early in the morning? He eyed the boiling water, unsure of what to do, and then, with an angry sigh, he turned the stove down to low. Thank God he hadn't added the tea yet. "Hello?" he spoke into the phone, sure it was a wrong number.

He heard a sharp gasp at the other end. "Well, I'm glad you're up," said a male voice he didn't recognize. "Probably plotting how to ruin someone else's Christmas, too. Shit, after everything I've done for you and your missus . . ." So it was a wrong number.

"I'm sorry," Sorab said calmly. "I'm afraid you have a wrong number." He hung up.

He had barely crossed the kitchen when the phone rang again. This time, he didn't try to keep the annoyance out of his voice. "Listen here," he said, but his words were drowned by the torrent of words that came down the phone line. "Don't you listen-here me, Sorab," the voice said. "I know you too damn well for this display of innocence. I can't believe . . ."

The man had said his name. And the voice, the slight trace of an accent was familiar, too. "Antonio?" he said cautiously.

"Ah, good, so you're not such a hotshot that you've forgotten your old neighbor. I was thinking your backstabbing mother had fucked you up, too."

His *mother*? What the hell was Antonio talking about? Sorab tried to recall the last time he had seen his former neighbor. Antonio was getting up in the years, he knew. But could he be suffering from dementia or something? But even so, why would he choose to call Sorab and that, too, on Christmas morning, for Pete's sake? And where was his wife? Why was he unsupervised? "Antonio, can I speak to Marita, please?" he said.

The voice at the other end roared. "Speak to Marita? Why, you son of a gun, my missus is so distraught, I can't get her to stop crying. Her half sister sitting in jail and her nephews miserable being with us. We don't even have a lousy gift in the house for them. And all because your goddamn mother doesn't know how to mind her own beeswax. And here I am, blasphamizing the Lord on Christmas Day. Heaven help me—and God help you when—" Antonio's voice suddenly cracked. "Ah, Sorab, how could you? I was the one who told you about your house, remember? And this is how you repay me?"

A long string of panic, like the thin note of a flute, began to wind its way in Sorab's gut. He fought to keep himself from getting entangled into it. "Antonio, please. Calm down, man. What are you saying? Is Tara really in jail? Why? What happened?"

The hysterical voice was quieted at last. "You tellin' me you don't know?" Then, with high-pitched fury, "Or are you lying like a rug? 'Cause if you are, Sorab, I swear I'll choke you with my—"

"Antonio. What are you saying? Know what? I was at work all day yesterday and by the time I got home, I only had time to change and then we met our friends for dinner. We were all gone until at least eleven o'clock—"

"Yeah, I know. I tried calling you last night but—"

"So how could we know what was going on next door?" Sorab continued. He didn't try to keep the indignation out of his voice. "And besides, we've been neighbors for how many years? You know my family doesn't believe in being nosy or interfering in other people's business. We're not gossipy folks, Antonio. You know that."

His caller laughed, a dry, metallic sound. "Not nosy . . . don't believe in . . . why, that's rich, Sorab. That's priceless. Maybe you should give your mother some lessons in good manners."

Okay, you bastard, Sorab thought. One more dig about Mamma and you're history. "Please leave my mother out of whatever this is," he said coldly. "You've got no right to talk about her in this manner."

He heard a choking sound. "No right . . . You know, you thank your lucky stars I don't live next door to you anymore. If I did, there's no telling what I'd do to you. Though of course, if I did live next door, none of yesterday's fracas would've happened, right?"

Sorab eyed the simmering water across the kitchen. He's an old man, he told himself. Don't lose your temper with him. "I'm telling you for the last time, Antonio. I don't have a clue what—"

"Go get your hands on today's *Daily Mirror*," Antonio yelled. "Then we'll talk." And Sorab was left holding a dead receiver in his hand.

So much for surprising the two women with tea in bed. It was a miracle the phone and his yelling had not woken anyone up, not even Cookie. He listened for the sound of footsteps in the rooms above him but heard nothing. With a sigh, he turned off the stove and headed for the front door. Better to see what was in the paper that had Antonio so riled up before the others woke up. Though he didn't see why, even if that horrible woman next door had been arrested, that should ruin his family's Christmas. He grabbed a Christmas cookie from the counter on his way out of the kitchen.

He picked up the paper from the front step, brushing off the dew from the plastic wrap. Unfolding it, he scanned it quickly. The top story of the day was about how the troops were celebrating Christmas in hostile Iraq. Nothing new there. Next, his eyes scanned the bottom half of the paper below the fold and he froze. There was a large color picture of Mamma. His mother. A picture of her in his hometown paper. Was it a case of mistaken identity? A bold black headline read A CHRISTMAS MIRACLE.

He walked backward in his living room, running into the coffee table and then collapsing on the couch. He read the article fast, scanning it quickly to understand the gist of the story, to understand what rational reason there could be for his mother to have her picture in the newspaper. His eyes narrowed when he saw his own name in print. His jaw dropped when he came to the bit about her leaping over the fence, like she was some goddamn comic-book hero. Now he was sure the reporter had her mixed up with someone else. Mamma, who refused to even go to the gym in the housing complex, Mamma, who had to rest if they walked too fast in the park, yeah, he could just see his mother jumping over the fence. She might as well jump over the moon. But then he read the bit about how she did it and his heart began to thud. The crazy woman. And to think she brought—kidnapped—the children into this house. What if one of them had fallen and broken his nose? Had she ever heard about liability insurance? About being sued? What did she think this was, India, where interfering in other people's business was a national pastime? And where had Cookie been when all this tamasha was unfolding? Why had she phoned the cops? Was she nuts? And why hadn't she said a word about it last night, when they were having dinner with the Vakils at Tanjore Palace? And what on earth possessed her to talk to the newspaper reporter? He flipped back to the front page and stared at her picture, took in the disheveled hair, the uneasy smile. It was a terrible picture of her, he decided. Nothing like the dignified, sober woman he knew and loved.

Women, Sorab thought with a shake of his head. What treacherous creatures they could be. Unbidden, a picture of Grace Butler's well-coiffed face rose before him. She would probably see or hear about this story. He felt sick at the thought. He knew what she would think. Who except a third-world ignoramus would do something as uncouth as jump over a fence to go spy on a neighbor? Mamma had just guaranteed Gerry Frazier's promotion. Sorab knew *Gerry's* mother would never do such an impulsive, thoughtless thing.

He turned back to the page where the story continued. Why is this news at all? he thought. Here the country is at war, the economy is in the toilet, the Israeli-Palestinian situation is as wretched as ever, the whole world hates us, and this is what these idiots decide to publish in their paper? A silly old woman jumping over a fence is so important it makes front-page news? What a trivial, dummied-down country this has become, he thought. He remembered that he had read somewhere that America's two top exports were arms and entertainment and how that sounded like an epitaph, the symptoms of a dying civilization. Bombs and Michael Jackson, that's what we import, he'd thought.

But he had more important things to focus on than the slow demise of America. He looked at the small, black-and-white picture of Tara being escorted from her home and the scowl on her face made him shudder. What would happen to this woman? Would they send her home in a few days? If so, what would she and her dreadful boyfriend do to them? After this unpleasantness, living next door to Tara would be torture. Now the woman would have righteousness on her side because Mamma had clearly overstepped her boundaries, crossed the line. And the result had been a mother who had had her children taken away from her. Looking at Tara's hard, unforgiving face, Sorab knew that she was not the kind of woman who would let them forget that fact anytime soon.

He had to tell Susan. Sorab's stomach heaved when he thought of how Susan would react. He remembered that his wife had expressly asked his mother to not associate with the people next door. And Mamma had blithely ignored her request. What in the world had possessed her? For a weak moment, an image rose before Sorab's eyes—a picture of his parents welcoming a lost, forlorn Percy into their home. How proud he had been then. But this is different, he told himself fiercely. Here, she is a stranger in this country, doesn't even have her immigration papers straightened out. And let's face it—she's a guest in this home. I mean, thank God Susan is the kind of wife who agreed to let Mamma live here. Don't know too many American women who would be happy with their mother-in-law living with them. And Susan's been such a trouper about it all. The way Mamma has been moping around the house . . .

He was afraid of Susan, he realized. He was afraid of her reaction, her outrage, her anger when she found out how his mother had violated her request. And then to blather in the newspaper about it. Maybe this would be the last straw. Maybe they would have to reconsider their invitation to ask Mamma to live here permanently. Sorab found he was shaking with indignation and anger. The earlier mood of mellow good cheer had vanished like a boat in a storm. The twinkling lights of the huge Christmas tree suddenly seemed as if they were mocking his earlier good spirits. He now dreaded the sound of Cookie's impatient footsteps down the stairs. So much for a Merry Christmas, he thought gloomily as he trudged up the stairs toward his bedroom.

Despite his bad temper, the sight of Susan sleeping stirred him as it always did. He saw the faint beginnings of a worry line on her forehead and his heart softened at the sight. Susan had always had the kind of simple, midwestern beauty that moved him, but as she grew older, he found that she grew even more attractive in his eyes. Time, age, experience were leaving their mark on that smooth face and he found that irresistible. There are women who age badly, he thought. Thank God Susan is not one of them.

He sat on the edge of the bed. "Darling," he whispered. "It's Christmas. Time to wake up. Come on now, I have something to tell you."

Tehmina felt the frost in the room as soon as she walked in. Susan and Sorab were sitting at the dining table, sipping their cups of tea. They both looked up as she walked in in her nightgown, and exchanged a quick glance. Cookie was nowhere in sight. Her heart constricted. They know, she thought. Henderson has blabbered the news to them.

"Good morning," she said. "Merry Christmas."

"Merry Christmas," Susan replied automatically. To Tehmina's great dismay, Sorab said nothing, just chewed on his upper lip.

"Good morning, beta," she said again, and this time he shook himself from his chair and went into the kitchen, returning with a cup of tea for her.

"Good tea," she said. "Is Cookie not up yet?" So far, she was the only one carrying on a conversation.

"I'll wake him up in a minute. But first, Mamma, we need to talk." Sorab lifted the newspaper from the chair, ran his fingers over the middle fold, and placed it in front of his mother. "Mamma, what on earth is this?"

Tehmina's hands shook so badly upon seeing her face in the newspaper, she spilled some of the tea on the red-and-gold tablecloth. She heard Susan suppress a sigh before she got up to get some wet paper towels. Her face turned pale as her eyes took in the headline and the first few lines of the story. *She is a visitor to America*, the story began. *She is a stranger to this country. But to two frightened young Rosemont Heights boys, Bombay native Tehmina Sethna, 66, turned out to be a Christmastime angel.*

How in the world had the newspaper gotten the story? she wondered. And how did they get that picture of her? And then she remembered: Of course, it was that young boy who had come with the police yesterday. Hadn't he said something about following them around to write a story about peace? Hadn't he told her he worked for a newspaper? At that time she had not understood that he would actually write about her. She had thought—what *had* she thought? Actually, she had not thought much about anything yesterday, had she? Wasn't that the whole problem—her thoughtless behavior—which had resulted in two boys being taken away from their mother? And once the police arrived, it was as though her mind had scattered, like birds after a gunshot. She had been flustered, scared, panicked at the thought of Sorab and Susan finding out. And while she was extracting promises from little Cookie to not say anything, while she was getting the kitchen back in order after everyone had left yesterday, while she was going through the motions of enjoying dinner with the Vakils yesterday evening while her mind kept wondering how Josh and Jerome were doing—while she was pretending that everything was normal, that newspaper boy had been writing a story that all the world could read. A story that advertised her stupidity, her carelessness.

"Mamma, look at me," Sorab was saying, but Tehmina could not look up from the newspaper. She kept her eyes focused on the face in the paper, a face that was horribly familiar but nevertheless looked like the face of a stranger. Did she really look so old and ugly? Did her eyes really look so wild and confused? She saw a damp spot on the photograph grow and realized that she was crying.

At last, she found the courage to look up. "I'm sorry. I'm so sorry. I didn't think. I just heard those boys in pain and I don't know what happened. I went mad, I think."

"I just wish I hadn't had to find out from Antonio and the newspaper," Sorab murmured. "I would've hoped you would've had—"

"I know. I know, my darling. I was going to tell you, I swear. But we were out so late last night and I—I just wanted to get through today before spoiling your mood. I'm really sorry."

"What I don't get is, we'd told you," Susan said. "We'd asked you not to have anything to do with that family. And it really bothers me that you had our Cookie witness this scene. I don't even know what all this means—whether you—we—whether we have put ourselves at risk. What happens when they let that woman out?"

Tehmina stared at her in horror. She had not even thought of that. "I'll go," she said wildly. "I'll go back to India as soon as I can get a ticket. That way, I won't be here when Tara gets home. I'm so ashamed, my dears, I can't even—"

"Okay. That's enough. It's Christmas morning, for crying out loud." Sorab spoke with more vigor than she had heard in his voice in a long time. "What's happened has happened. No point in spoiling the whole day." He turned toward his mother. "And no talk of returning to Bombay, understand, Mamma? Whatever it is, we'll face it." He flung a warning glance Susan's way and forced his face into a weak smile. "Besides, you don't know this crazy country. Tomorrow it will be another scandal about Michael Jackson or Tom Cruise or somebody, and everybody's attention will turn to that. I'm in advertising—believe me, I know. And for the first time I say, thank God for short attention spans."

But Susan still looked unhappy. "I've tried to live my life so quietly," she began when they were all distracted by a loud, thundering noise that sounded like an army on the move. It was Cookie racing down the stairs and bursting into the room.

"It's Christmas, it's Christmas," he yelled, hopping from foot to foot. "Let's see what Santa brought me."

"Cookie," Susan chided. "How about a good morning for everybody?"

But the boy was too excited to be reasoned with. "Come on, come on, let's open presents," he yelled, pulling on his father's hand.

All three of the adults laughed. This boy is like a flower, Tehmina thought. His beauty and scent fill the room.

"We'll talk later," Sorab said as he let himself be pulled into the next room. "But first, come on, let's go open our presents."

Cookie demanded that he open all his gifts first. The gift paper flew around him like a mad wind as he tore into it. Tehmina felt sick at the waste. If this was Bombay, she would've made sure Cookie opened each gift carefully so that the paper could be reused. But here, his parents seemed to encourage the frantic plundering. "Ooh boy, wait'll Brian sees this," Cookie said about a gift. A few seconds later, "Thanks, Granna," and a quick peck on Tehmina's cheek before he went back to his spot on the floor, where the mounds of open boxes and paper grew around him.

"You're welcome," she gasped, knowing that Susan had put Tehmina's name on a gift that she had purchased for her son. "Thank you," she mouthed to Susan, and was rewarded with a tight smile and a quick nod.

The phone rang just as Cookie was opening his ninth gift. "Want to stop for a second, buddy?" Sorab asked, but seeing his son's crestfallen face, he laughed. "What the hell am I saying? Keep going, I'll be right back."

Tehmina watched Sorab answer the phone at the other end of the living room. "Yes? Oh, hello, Joe," she heard him say. "What a lovely surprise. Yes, merry Christmas to you, too. How is Heather?" Something in her son's voice, a certain formality made Tehmina listen closely.

"Granna, Mom, look at this. A gift certificate for a new bike from Uncle Bobby. And I get to pick it out," Cookie screamed, drowning out some of Sorab's conversation. "Hooray."

Tehmina's ears picked up when she heard Sorab refer to her. "Yup, that's my mom, all right," he was saying. "A bona fide hero. Oh, sure. Sure. I'll pass on your good wishes to her."

Who was Sorab talking to? He sounded so stiff. But if not a

friend, who could be calling so early on Christmas morning? It was not even eight o'clock. She glanced at Susan, but she was squatting on the floor, seemingly lost in putting in batteries in one of Cookie's new toys.

"What's that?" she heard Sorab say. "Oh, Grace? She's okay, I guess. There's always an adjustment period, you know." So he was talking to someone from work. Did these Americans never stop working? Did they not even take Christmas Day off? There was a pause. And then Sorab said, "Oh, Joe, I'd love to. Dinner sounds great. You just let me know the day, okay? If you want to wait till after the holidays, I understand. Just let me know."

After he hung up, Sorab stood by the phone for a second, staring at the receiver. Then he walked back toward them, a funny expression on his face. "That was Joe Canfield," he said. "The big boss. He's the one who founded the agency and he's now chairman of the board of directors. Seems like he saw the story about Mamma's exploits in the paper this morning. Says he wants to have dinner with a genuine American hero." Sorab's eyes were shining. "Hon, I guess we're gonna have dinner at Joe's home."

Tehmina looked anxiously at Susan, hoping that the phone call would redeem her a bit. Susan looked bemused. "I didn't think Joe Canfield even knew our phone number. Hey, maybe we can make some money shamelessly exploiting our Christmastime Miracle here," she added lightly. Tehmina noticed that for the first time this morning, her daughter-in-law actually looked directly at her.

Cookie made a hissing sound and pulled impatiently at his dad's pajama sleeve. "Dad, did you see what Uncle Bob sent me? A gift certificate for a new bike," Cookie said.

Sorab patted his son's head. "Yes, my darling," he said. He turned to his wife but before he could say anything, the phone rang again. This time, Susan jumped up from the floor. "I'll get it," she said.

A moment later she handed the phone to Tehmina, her right eyebrow raised. "It's Eva Metzembaum. Says she wants to talk to the American hero." She turned to Sorab as Tehmina got on the phone. "Maybe we should start charging admission," Tehmina heard her say. She was unsure of whether she heard irritation or amusement in her daughter-in-law's voice.

"Hello?" Tehmina whispered, conscious of the fact that Sorab and Susan were staring at her. "What are you doing up this early, Eva?" Tehmina knew that Eva was a self-proclaimed night owl who slept in each morning.

"My Solomon woke me up after he saw the newspaper. I nearly fell off my bed when I saw your mug in the newspaper." Eva's voice sounded breathless, as if she had been vacuuming the house all morning. "Oh, Tehmina, I'm so proud of you, I could burst. Doesn't surprise me at all, what you did. Those poor children. Though why'd you have to go leaping over fences, honey? Could've fallen and broken your neck, you could. But let me tell you, I could've dropped dead myself when I saw your puss staring back at me from the paper."

Tehmina felt such a strong longing to see her friend that her eyes filled with tears. She suddenly felt very tired, as if she'd already been up for twenty-four hours. She had barely slept last night, debating when to break the news of yesterday's events to the children. And the day was just beginning. Susan and Sorab hadn't even opened their gifts yet. "How are you, Eva?" she asked.

"Me? Sassy as ever. Who cares? The main question is, how are you, darlin'?"

"I'm okay. Just tired." Tehmina could feel three pairs of eyes following her conversation. "Listen, Eva. Can I call you back later today?"

She heard Eva take a quick breath. "Trouble at home, darlin'? Yes, I guess your daughter-in-law wouldn't be too pleased with all this commotion. Listen, you just call me when you can, okay? And remember—no matter what anyone says, you did the right thing. You keep your chin up, honey. We'll talk soon."

Tehmina held on to the phone until she heard the dial tone. Then she went back to her seat on the couch. Cookie, who had been absorbed in spilling and assembling all the contents of his LEGO set, looked up. "I'm glad you're here with us, Granna," he declared. And scampering off the floor, he jumped in her lap and flung his arms around her neck. She hugged him back, squeezing him so tightly, the boy squealed. "Granna. You're hurting me. I'm gonna be as flat as a pancake."

Susan rose. "Speaking of pancakes . . . how about some blueberry pancakes for breakfast?"

"Yay," Cookie yelled. "And some French toast."

"And some rava." Sorab joined in with enthusiasm. He looked at his mother and his eyes said what he could not, asked for her forgiveness and told her that she was forgiven. "Please, Mamma? Will you make some of your saffron rava?"

Tehmina's heart sang. For the first time today she felt some hope stir within her. Maybe things would turn out okay after all. "My first Christmas in America with my son and he has to ask me whether I'll make him rava?" She smiled. "Of course I will."

"Okay, it's a plan," Susan said. "We'll open all the adult presents after breakfast, okay, honey?" she said to Cookie.

The boy gave an exaggerated shrug. "Okay. If you can wait that long," he drawled. There was something so grown-up and world-weary in his tone that they all laughed.

They had all finished breakfast and Tehmina and Susan were cleaning up in the kitchen when the doorbell rang. They heard Sorab, who was helping Cookie assemble some of his new toys, mutter under his breath and then call out, "I'll get it."

"Holy shit," he yelled the next second. "Er, ladies, you better get into the living room as fast as you can."

The two women looked at each other for a brief second. Now what? Susan's look seemed to say. Then they wiped their hands and hurried into the living room. Sorab was standing at the picture window and they joined him there. They gasped. It was a scene from a movie. All three local television channels had their vans parked on the street. Men with cameras mounted on their shoulders were filming their house. A female reporter was standing in front of the Channel 3 truck and speaking into a microphone. There were two other people in sneakers, notebooks in their hands and cameras dangling around their necks, who were walking up and down the street. "What the heck?" Susan breathed.

Sorab expelled his breath. "Mamma," he said. "What the hell have you unleashed?" There was bemused shock in his tone.

The doorbell rang again, more persistently this time. Swearing under his breath, Sorab went to the front door and opened it. "Yes?" he said.

The young man in blue jeans was stomping his feet lightly to ward off the cold. "Hi, sir," he said. "I'm Luke Johnson with the *Daily Mirror*. I met your mom yester—"

"Ah, so you're the guy who's turned our lives upside down," Sorab said, but there was no real anger in his voice. "Thanks to you, we now have to deal with all this." He pointed to the astonishing landscape in front of him.

Luke grimaced. "Sorry. It's probably a slow news day, it being Christmas and all. In any case, I was wondering . . ."

There was sudden yelling and turmoil on the street as the other reporters caught Luke talking to someone inside the house. The long-haired female reporter trotted up the brickway toward the house, followed closely by her photographer. "Excuse me," she called. "Can we ask you a few questions?"

Sorab decided he liked the look of the young man before him. The others he wasn't too sure of. There were too many of them anyway.

"You better get in," he said, stepping aside for Luke to enter. By the time the female reporter was climbing up the three stone steps, he had shut the door. She rang the doorbell angrily, but he ignored it.

"Hey," he heard her yell through the door. "That's not fair."

Luke Johnson grinned. "Thanks," he said. And then, spotting Tehmina, "Hi, Miss Tammy. Merry Christmas."

"You naughty boy," Tehmina scolded. "You didn't tell me you were going to put me in the paper."

Luke looked confused. And appalled. "I'm sorry, ma'am. I thought I did, honest. That is, I told you I was a newspaper reporter. See, the way it works is, I never know if something's going to be a story until I run it past my editor."

Her face softened as Tehmina saw that she had upset him. "Well, what's done is done."

Susan stepped up. "Hello, I'm Susan Sethna, Tehmina's daughter-in-law," she said coolly. "What can we do for you today?"

Luke straightened, as if he had heard the glass in Susan's voice. He assumed a formal, professional voice, different from the easy manner he had around Tehmina. "I'm here to do a follow-up piece on Miss Tammy, ma'am. Something along the lines of, y'know, a personality profile."

"No more interviews," Sorab interjected. "Listen, we're just regular people, you know? We don't like to be in the limelight. And this is such an unfortunate story anyway. We don't want it to seem like we're exploiting someone else's tragedy. Right, Mom?"

Tehmina nodded, though she wished Sorab had let her speak for herself. After all, Luke was here to interview her, not them. "Yes, I don't want any more publicity, please."

The doorbell rang again, more persistent this time. "Listen," Luke said urgently. "They're not going to go away. You may as well give them some reaction." Seeing their stubborn expressions, he tried again. "This is a feel-good, human-interest story," he said. "My editor even put it on the national wire last night—that's when . . . that's so that any other newspaper in the country can pick it up. You have to understand—people need something to feel good about. Look at the rest of today's paper—it's all about the war and bombs going off and all that crap. And here's a woman who is not even an American who does what most of us wouldn't do. You know what I mean? Look," he continued desperately, "a lot of good may come out of this story. You may convince someone else to do the right thing. It could inspire someone else—"

"Okay," Sorab interrupted. "Let me do this. I need to call my best friend who's a lawyer and get his advice, okay?" He turned to face Luke. "You don't understand—this is not how we were planning on spending Christmas Day. I have to be back at work tomorrow, thanks to the whims of my lovely boss. So this is my only day off, okay? And I didn't plan on spending it talking to the media." For a moment, Sorab looked teary, as if he was trying to fight off the self-pity that threatened to engulf him. Then he turned around abruptly to call Percy.

Tehmina was left alone facing Luke. She noticed the flecks of snow on his brown hair and her fingers itched to dust them off. She remembered how sweet the boy had been to her yesterday, how his warmth and kindness had balanced the stiff politeness of the two officers. Now she looked deeply into Luke Johnson's face and decided she liked him. There was something open and sincere and trustworthy about the boy's face. Also, he had known pain. She didn't know how she knew that, but she was sure of it. It was in his eyes. "Why did you come back today in such cold weather, sonny?" she said to him. "What more do you need to know about an old lady like myself?"

"Apparently, our newsroom phones have been ringing off the hook this morning, ma'am," Luke said. "My editor called me at home this morning and told me to get the heck out here and talk to you some more. Turns out our readers really want to help those two kids—and know more about you."

"Now the two boys, I can understand. But why—"

"Mamma," Sorab interjected. "Let me call Percy before you say anything else."

Something about Sorab's tone—the way he insinuated Luke was not to be trusted and that she had to get permission from Percy before trusting her own instincts—infuriated her. Keep your chin up, Eva had said to her, and Tehmina found herself tilting her head back as she looked at her son. Her eyes were steady and unwavering as she took in his anxious face, the way in which his hands were gripping the phone. For the first time in a year she felt as if the natural order of things had been restored: she was the parent again and Sorab was the child. "Go ahead and call Percy. He can advise us about what to do about the rest of them out there. But this young man here, I'm going to talk to him."

Ignoring the startled, hurt looks Sorab and Susan gave her, she led Luke Johnson into the kitchen.

CHAPTER FIFTEEN

Tehmina decided to wear her blue sari with the embroidered border to Joe Canfield's home. After all, from everything Sorab had said, Joe was an important man. She had not seen Sorab this excited about a dinner invitation ever—his behavior reminded Tehmina of Cookie's excitement on Christmas Day.

Christmas. Only four days had passed since then, but it was as if a lifetime had gone by. What a crazy country this was. Instead of fretting about the two boys living with their aunt and uncle, instead of worrying about Tara, who, despite all her sins, was a mother and was undoubtedly missing her children—instead of those appropriate responses, it was as if all of Rosemont Heights was busy singing her praises. And not just Rosemont Heights. She had received letters from as far away as Oregon and Florida. God knows how someone in Oregon had heard of her, much less secured her address. And the mayor of Rosemont Heights had herself phoned Tehmina to offer her congratulations. Congratulations for what? Tehmina had almost said. But she was beginning to suspect the answer—in America, being a celebrity was a celebration in itself; something to be congratulated for.

"Oh, Mamma, relax." Sorab had laughed when she told him about the mayor's phone call. Sorab had been in an unusually good mood in the days since Christmas. "Enjoy your fifteen minutes of fame." Tehmina had stared at him quizzically and Sorab had to explain what the American expression meant and who Andy Warhol was.

But even Sorab had been shaken by what had happened yesterday. She and Susan had gone to Kmart to return some gifts. Susan was at the returns counter while Tehmina wandered aimlessly through the store. As she ran her hands through the coats on the rack, a strange man who wore horn-rimmed glasses under his bald, egglike head had approached her. "You the lady in the papers, right?" he said. "The Christmas Angel?"

Tehmina had blushed, unsure of what to say. But the man helped her out. "God bless you, lady."

"Thank you," Tehmina said, ready to continue on her way. But the man blocked her path. "It's folks like you fulfilling the prophecy."

Tehmina stared at him. "Excuse me?" she said.

"Yes, ma'am, the end of the world is coming for sure," the man said. "You a Christian?" he asked suddenly.

"No, I'm a Parsi. A Zoroastrian? Originally from Persia?"

"Never heard of it," the man said. "But no matter. Jesus Christ can save your soul from eternal damnation, if you'll let Him. Will you pray with me?" And to Tehmina's utter mortification, the stranger took her hand and bowed his head in prayer.

"I'm not . . . that is, excuse me," she said, trying to pull her hand from his and frantically looking around for Susan. And as if Susan had heard her silent cry for help, her daughter-in-law materialized behind her.

"What the hell?"

"Susan. I'm glad you're here," a flustered Tehmina said. But the praying man drowned out her voice. "If you don't mind, ma'am," he hissed at Susan. "Can't you see we're engaged in the business of the Lord? And no cussing before the holy circle."

"Listen, mister, I don't know who you are, but if you don't let go of my mother right this minute, I'm going to call the store security." Even as she said those words, Susan was looking around.

Despite her fear and embarrassment, Susan's words penetrated Tehmina's heart. Susan had called her her mother. Not her mother-in-law. Her mother. The joy that she felt at that realization gave her courage to pull her hand out of the man's manic grip. "Come on, let's go," she muttered to Susan, but the man followed them, brushing past the winter coats and the sweaters.

"It's the Lord you're running away from, not me," he said. "Your souls will fry like bacon in an eternal hell if you don't embrace Christ as your personal savior."

"Is this man bothering you, ladies?" It was a tall, slender African-American man with short dark hair in the men's sweaters section. And then, without waiting for an answer, "Listen, buster. I'm the manager of the store. If you don't leave in five seconds, I'm calling the police."

The man looked as if he was going to argue, but he suddenly fell silent, reminding Tehmina of how a balloon deflated when someone let the air out of it. Without another word, he left, all the time muttering to himself.

"Thank you so much, Mr.—?" Susan looked for his name tag.

The man laughed. "Actually, the name's Peter. But I'm not the manager, just a customer. Sometimes you have to lie to God's messengers." He winked at them and both women laughed.

"Well, thank you so much, anyway," Susan said, and Tehmina nodded.

"Hey, no problem, no problem." He turned toward Tehmina and

his look was serious. "I just want you to know, ma'am, that we're not all nuts in this country. Like, I'm a Christian myself, but I don't believe in converting people in the middle of Kmart." They all laughed again. "Though if I may say this—that was a pretty neat thing you did, rescuing those two boys. I—I just want you to know that. I have two young boys myself and I can't imagine—" He shuddered.

Tehmina liked this chocolate-colored man so much she wanted to invite him for dinner. "Thank you very much," she said. She knew her words were inadequate, but she hoped he knew that his words meant more to her than the call from the mayor.

"You're welcome," he said lightly, and then, with a nod of his head, he walked away.

"There are so many good people in the world." Tehmina sighed, watching his retreating form.

"Yeah, and there are so many nut jobs, too," Susan replied. "You have to be really careful, Mom, especially now that you're famous." Susan chuckled at the last word.

How did Susan do this, she wondered, making her feel guilty about something she had nothing to do with? Was it her fault that a crazy man had approached her at Kmart and decided to score extra points in heaven by converting her? But then she remembered her picture in the paper and how she'd broken her promise to Susan. Also, the memory of Susan referring to her as her mother was still fresh and perfumed in Tehmina's mind. "Sorry," she said, taking Susan's hand. "All my life I've been like this—attracting all the loonies to me. God knows why."

Susan squeezed her hand. "Because they all know a soft touch when they spot one." She smiled. And as if that wasn't enough to make Tehmina choke, "Your goodness just radiates out of you, Mamma. Everybody sees it."

Now Tehmina was really embarrassed. "What nonsense you speak."

"Nonsense? Heck, you think I don't notice? If I go to the store by myself or even with Sorab, nobody gives me a second look. But if I'm in line with you, even the surliest of cashiers are suddenly laughing and chatting with me. Same thing when we used to go for walks at Greendale Park last fall, remember? Perfect strangers would be beaming at us."

"It's because they see the way you and Sorab take care of me," Tehmina said. "People like to see that—like to see love in a family."

"I know. And our family has plenty of that, thank God."

Tehmina was suddenly struck by a thought: Susan was becoming more like all of them, she realized. More emotional, more sentimental, more—well, more Parsi. Less American. Less white. It was as if Sorab's influence on her was finally showing. She suppressed a boastful thought: that it was her influence, her devotion to her son, her open displays of affection toward Cookie, that were changing Susan, were making her less brittle, more pliable.

When did this start happening? she asked herself. Just a week or so ago she was complaining to Eva about Susan, was acutely aware of the thinness of her smile, the brittleness in her voice and laughter. And then she realized—it was the article. The article and her ensuing celebrity had eased the tension at home.

Now, getting ready for Joe Canfield's party, Tehmina wondered whether to put on the diamond earrings that Rustom had gotten made for her fortieth birthday. She didn't want to look too ostentatious. She knew that here in America, even rich women wore costume jewelry—and didn't even try to hide the fact. Whereas in India, even the poorest of slum women would own at least some gold and that, too, twenty-four-karat. In America, you couldn't even buy twenty-four-karat gold. She remembered the time Sorab had informed her of this. Her immediate thought had been, then how can they claim to be the richest country in the world? She picked up the diamond earrings and held them to her ear. They twinkled like the lights on the Christmas tree in the living room. Tehmina decided she would wear them. After all, Joe Canfield had made it clear that the party was in her honor. And all the man knew of her was that horrible picture in the paper—although Luke had redeemed himself with a nicer picture in the follow-up story he wrote the next day. Still, Tehmina knew how much first impressions counted and she wanted to make sure that she impressed Sorab's boss. Anything she could do to further her son's career, she would do. Already, Joe Canfield had invited Sorab to play racquetball with him earlier in the week—something he had done only once before, soon after he'd hired Sorab.

She put on the diamond earrings. "Good decision, Tehmina," she heard Rustom say. She spun around. There he was leaning against the wall, one hand in his right pocket. Looking more at home in his son's house than she had ever felt.

"Darling. How . . . how long have you been standing here?"

"Arre wah. My wife is all dolled up like a film actress and you think I'd miss a chance to admire her beauty?"

"Remember when you got me these earrings?" Tehmina's eyes filled with tears.

"I remember," he said softly. "I remember everything."

"I've missed you so much these past few days, janu. So much has happened since we last spoke."

"I know," he said. "I've been watching you."

"But I need to—"

"Mamma," Sorab said as he entered the room. "Are you almost ready?" Then, taking in the earrings and the sari, "Wow. You look like a queen."

"Sorab . . ." Tehmina spun around, but Rustom was gone, the corner wall he had been leaning against looking bewilderingly empty.

"God, Mamma, what's wrong? You look like you've seen a ghost."

Tehmina jumped guiltily. "Nothing. You just startled me, that's all."

"Sorry. Just wanted to bring up more of your fan mail. Some of these are from Hawaii and Arizona, even. Probably more people sending checks for the two boys. All made out to you, of course. I can't believe how trusting people are—what if you decided to cash these checks and keep the money for yourself?"

"Sorab." Tehmina was shocked. "I would never do that."

"Oh, relax, Mamma. I never said you would. I just said, how do these strangers know that you won't?"

"Beta, there has to be some trust in the world," she said. "Otherwise, where would we all be?"

Sorab took a few steps and leaned over and kissed the top of her head. "I know. Right you are, O famous one. Now, are you ready?"

Joe and Heather Canfield lived in a big old house on Lake Erie. Faded Oriental rugs covered the rich hardwood floors, while dark abstract paintings hung from the walls. Tehmina took in the weathered leather furniture, the built-in bookcases, the old fireplace, the crown molding, and felt her body relax. This old house felt so much more—more *real*—than Sorab's carpeted, modern house and the Jasawala's freshly built palace. Why did Sorab and all his friends live in these new, soulless houses when there were houses like this available? she wondered. Joe Canfield's house felt broken-in, worn, and comfortable as an old shoe. There was something distinctive about it, something that bore the imprint of the owner and the weight of family history. Whereas, even though the Jasawalas had designed their home, it felt anonymous, interchangeable, like any person could come along and occupy that house. Was it a question of old money versus new money? Tehmina asked herself. Maybe because Joe Canfield was a rich man, he could afford to not replace a carpet that was fraying or a couch that had a tear in it. What was that old Gujarati saying? Something to the effect of: If a poor man is caught eating peanuts, the world will say it's because he can't afford almonds. Whereas if a rich man is eating peanuts, people would say it's because he needs a break from eating almonds every day. So maybe immigrants such as the Jasawalas had to constantly prove their success to the world. That's what she liked about Joe's house, she realized—it had nothing to prove to anyone. It just stood in the same space it had occupied for God knows how many years, and if it was a little bent and if it was a little shabby, well, so be it.

Even though it was too dark to see the lake, and although the windows were shut, Tehmina could hear the distant waves pound against the rocks as they sat sipping wine in Joe and Heather's living room. The sound of the waves reminded her of the Arabian Sea and that in turn reminded her of her beloved Bombay. She felt an acute homesickness. Something about this house, with its high ceilings and crown molding was reminding her of her own Colaba apartment.

"So, Tammy, what news of the two boys?" Joe was saying to her.

She jumped and forced herself to stop listening to the waves and focus on the man before her. "They're with their aunt and uncle," she said. "Actually, I got a card from them yesterday." She glanced at Sorab and Susan in apology. "I . . . I forgot to tell you . . . I had bought them some Christmas gifts and they wrote to thank me for those." She didn't tell them what Jerome had added at the bottom of the card. *I am sorry for calling you a bad name. Thank you for helping us.*

All four of them burst out laughing. "And when did you give them their gifts, Tammy?" She could tell that Joe was enjoying himself, delighting in her quaintness, wanting some inside information that was not in the newspaper stories.

"Just when—when the police were taking them away. I remembered. And I wanted to give them something because they looked so scared." Tehmina felt all eyes upon her and squirmed inwardly. She wished someone would change the topic and take the focus off of her.

As if she had detected her discomfort, Heather said, "Okay, Joe, call off the third degree." She turned to Tehmina with a smile. "I apologize for my husband's bad manners. His curiosity is worse than a two-year-old's."

"Yes, but that's what's made Joe such a success," Sorab said. And even to Tehmina's biased, affectionate ear, her son's words sounded a little too fawning and obvious.

But Joe didn't seem to have noticed. "Well, Tammy, you've sure seen all sides of our beautiful country—the good and the bad. So, can I ask? What's your favorite thing about America?"

"Making rainbows," she said immediately.

Joe raised his left eyebrow. "Making rainbows? What's that?"

"You know how, in the summer when you're watering the outdoor plants with the water hose, you can sometimes create rainbows? I love that. You see, in Bombay we all live in apartment buildings and none of us have lawns and water hoses or anything like that. So we never get to make our own rainbows. We just have to wait until Mother Nature decides to bless us with one."

Joe Canfield let out his breath. "Boy, what a powerful metaphor that is. Sort of sums up America, doesn't it?" He turned to Sorab and spoke in the tone of a little schoolboy. "Can I borrow your mother for a few years? Please?"

"Take a number." Sorab grinned happily. "There's a long list of people ahead of you."

Tehmina blushed, and as if they were all aware of her embarrassment, everybody laughed. Then the doorbell rang and they looked at Joe, curious. Joe rose from the couch. "Oh, Sorab, I forgot to mention it," he said casually as he went to answer the door. "I invited Grace and her boyfriend Bryan, also."

Sorab's face turned white. The smile faded from his lips and he struggled to find it again. "Oh, sure," he murmured. Tehmina felt her insides drop and her earlier good feeling about Joe suddenly turned sour. Why had Joe not mentioned that he had invited Sorab's boss to the party? Dirty pool, she said to herself.

There was a flurry of activity at the front door and then they were in the living room, Joe carrying an enormous bouquet of flowers which Grace had obviously presented him with. Thinking about the bottle of wine and the embroidered tablecloth from India that they had presented to their host earlier this evening, Tehmina felt small and cheap. They should've brought flowers also.

Heather gave her guests a quick peck on the cheek and then hurried in to find a vase for the flowers.

Grace Butler was tall, slim, blond, and Tehmina disliked her immediately. Her boyfriend was also tall, slim, and blond, but he had a nice face and Tehmina felt a twinge of sympathy for him. Still, she forced her face into a smile as Grace came up to her and kissed her on the cheek. "Oh my, it's the heroine of Rosemont Heights," the younger woman said. "Wow, you look quite different than the picture in the paper," her sharp eyes taking in the sari and the glittering diamonds. "Why, that's quite an adventure you had, eh? Isn't it supersize depressing, though, about those poor boys? What awfulistic luck, having a mom like that."

Was this woman speaking another language, some hybrid form of English she wasn't familiar with? "Nice to meet you, Grace," Tehmina said quietly.

"Oh, the pleasure is all mine. Absolutely fantabulous to meet a genuine hero."

"Hello, Grace." Even across the room Tehmina heard the starch in her son's voice. "I thought you were out skiing this week." Sorab was standing up looking as stiff as Al Gore. Relax, beta, she said to herself. You are worth ten times this shallow woman. Don't let her scare you.

"Oh, hi, Sorab. And hey, Susan. Good to see you again. How's your son? Custard, is it?"

"Cookie," Susan said quietly. "But that's just his nickname. His real name is Cavas."

"That's right," Grace said gaily. "I knew it was some kind of dessert." She turned around and took her boyfriend's hand. "Oh, and this is Bryan. Bryan, this is Sorab and his wife, Susan. Sorab works for me."

"Works *with* me," Joe said lightly, wagging his finger at Grace. "At Canfield, we all work together."

"Whatever," Grace said. She rolled her eyes. "Joe's a millionaire, but I swear he's a socialist or something," she said to Bryan.

"Not a socialist. Just a democrat."

Was it her imagination or did Joe have a bite in his voice? Tehmina wondered. She had a quick insight: Joe didn't like Grace Butler very much.

"Would you like some wine, Grace? Bryan? Red or white?"

"What kind of reds do you have?" Grace asked.

"Oh, God, I don't know. Probably some Merlot and some Cabernet. A Pinot Noir, maybe."

"Merlot?" Grace screeched. "Good God, Joe. Didn't you see *Sideways*? Nobody drinks Merlot anymore. It's so . . . so . . ."

"I do," said Heather, entering the room. "I like it." She shrugged. "Sorry. Guess I'm just a country bumpkin."

There was a second's pause and then Grace recovered her stride. "Well. I tell you what, Joe. How about some of that Pinot Noir for me? And Bryan'll take that, too, won't you, darling? What vintage is it?"

"Vintage?" Now Joe was openly laughing. "I haven't the foggiest idea. We buy our wines at Trader Joe's."

Grace seemed nonplussed. But only for a moment. "Oh, Joe, you have to let me introduce you to this stupendous wineshop in our neighborhood. They have wine tastings the first Friday of each month." She turned to Bryan. "Darling, let's invite Joe and Heather to the next one, shall we? And then we can go to that new sushi place for dinner."

"I hate sushi," Heather said. And this time, Tehmina definitely heard something in her voice. She doesn't like Grace, she realized. She caught Joe throw his wife a warning glance.

Before Grace could respond, Sorab sailed to her rescue. "So how was the ski trip?"

"The ski trip? Oh, God, what a depressoid bust. It turned out we didn't have reservations at the place we thought we did. Bryan fucked up royally, didn't you, darling? And I refused to go to any other place. I mean, this place we were gonna go to was extraordinarily brilliant—a hot tub in the room, in-room massages. Just fantabulous. So, anyway, we've just been hanging out at home, you know, taking day trips, that kind of thing."

Before she could help herself, the words were out of Tehmina's mouth. "Oh, so then Sorab could've had the week off. He couldn't take it because you were out of town, I thought." Out of the corner of her eye, she saw her son casting an appalled look her way.

"That was no big deal," Sorab began, but Heather interrupted him.

"What isn't a big deal?"

Grace's lips tightened. "Oh, just some internal office stuff," she said sharply.

"Well, if it's office stuff, then I guess it's my business." Joe's tone was light, but there was no mistaking the seriousness with which he spoke. "What happened?"

Grace sighed. "Well, Sorab and I had a misunderstanding. He

thought he was taking the week after Christmas off, but Bryan and I had already planned the ski trip. So I . . . we agreed that I would take some time off for some much-needed R and R."

Joe frowned. "You hadn't put in for the week off?" he said to Sorab.

Sorab blushed. He stared at the tips of his shoes. He looks like a schoolboy unwilling to tell on his friend, Tehmina thought, her heart warming at the sight of her son. "I did," he said finally. "I had."

"At the beginning of the year, like we always do?" Joe was dogged. Tehmina suddenly saw why he had been so successful in his business. Even though Joe was no longer involved in the day-to-day running of the company, his attachment to the agency he had founded over twenty-five years ago was obvious.

"Yup," Sorab said.

Joe turned to Grace. "But that's our company policy. People put in for their vacations at the start of the year."

"Well, Joe, that may be a model that's worked in the past, but the business world is changing so fast. We all have to change with the times, ready to be flexible and ready to—"

"Grace," Joe interrupted softly. "In case you haven't noticed—that old model has worked quite well for me."

Grace's jaw went slack. "I wasn't trying to . . ." She fell silent.

The room fell so quiet Tehmina could hear the pounding of the waves again. Susan spoke up to fill the void. "So, Bryan," she said brightly. "What do you do for a living?"

Bryan jumped at the mention of his name. Tehmina had a feeling that when he was with Grace Butler, Bryan was not used to people paying him any attention. "Ah, I'm a massage therapist?" he said, as if he was asking permission rather than stating a fact. "And I'm also a personal trainer, on the side?"

"Oh, that's good to know," Sorab said, patting his belly. "I'm so bloody out of shape, I got to do something about this body."

"Bullshit," Joe said immediately. "You beat the crap out of me at racquetball the other day. Of course, you're a great deal younger than I am, but still . . ."

"You played racquetball together?" Grace asked, looking from one man to the other. "When was this? I guess—I didn't realize you were friends."

Joe looked directly into Grace's green eyes. "Oh, Sorab and I go back a ways," he said. Tehmina saw her son's head jerk up at the obvious lie. But looking around the room, she noticed that both Susan and Heather had the same expressions on their faces—they were smiling small, secretive smiles, as if they were enjoying Grace's discomfort.

Bryan cleared his throat. "Er—just give me a call if you ever need a trainer," he said, as if the last exchange had not occurred. He fished into his pocket for his wallet. "Here's my card," he said, leaning forward to hand it to Sorab.

Sorab glanced at it and then pocketed it. "Thanks. I may call you sooner than you think."

"Well, is everybody hungry?" Heather said, rising to her feet. "Why don't you all give me a few minutes to put the food out and then come into the dining room?"

Tehmina rose automatically. "May I help you?" she said.

Heather looked as if she was about to refuse, but then she smiled. "Sure," she said, putting her arm around Tehmina as if they'd been friends for years. "The kitchen is this way."

"No couples sitting next to each other," Heather said as they trooped into the dining room a few minutes later. "That's the only rule. Other than that, grab a seat wherever you like." She pulled Tehmina into the seat beside her.

The menu was coriander-crusted grilled salmon, baked chicken with pecan crust, couscous with dried apricots and parsley, a pasta dish with basil and fresh mozzarella cheese, and homemade bread.

"Heather," Susan gasped. "You must've spent the last two days locked in the kitchen."

"Oh God, no. All these are easy dishes, believe me."

"Well, I *must* have the recipes for the salmon and the chicken. Are you someone who is okay with sharing recipes?"

"Of course. I've never understood women who guard their recipes as if they are state secrets. And these days, with the Internet and everything, it seems even more ridiculous."

"Do you like Indian food?" Tehmina asked.

"We *love* Indian food," Heather said. "Joe, tell them your story about your year in England."

"Well, this was after I got done with grad school. I decided to spend a year abroad. So I spend about four months in England, Scotland, and Wales—you know, tracing my family's heritage, that sort of thing. Just hitchhiking to different places. And I loved every minute of it except for the god-awful food. If I'd had to eat their goddamn black pudding or bangers and mash one more time, I swear I would've died. So anyway, I finally get to London. And I stumble upon this tiny curry joint. And with each bite I feel some part of my soul being restored. I ate at the same goddamn place for the rest of my time in London. The owner—his name was Gautam Patel, I still remember—would save me a spot every single evening. By the end of my time there, I had curry seeping out of my pores instead of sweat."

"Well, our Parsi food is a little different than what you get at Indian restaurants here, but if you like—I would love to cook for you sometime before I go back."

"Go back?" Heather leaned over and put her arm around Tehmina and gave her a tight squeeze. "You're not going anywhere, I hope?"

Tehmina felt Susan's and Sorab's eyes on her. What on earth had made her say she was going back? She herself didn't know whether she was or wasn't. Did she? "I . . . I just meant . . . in any case, we would love to have you over for a home-cooked Parsi meal. And you, too," she said to Grace, although her stomach dropped at the thought of having this woman and her handsome-but-dumb-as-a-cardboard-box boyfriend in their home.

"Oh, thanks, but I can't do any kind of ethnic food. I have such a dread-appalling stomach, it's loathsomely wicked."

"Dread-appalling?" Joe laughed. "Grace, where did you learn to speak English?"

Grace laughed back. "Oh, I just get so tired with our language. Imagine, using the same words they used in Shakespeare's time. That's so ... so ..."

"Sixteenth century?" Sorab said.

"Exactly." Grace had completely missed the irony in Sorab's voice.

The others, all except for Bryan, smiled to themselves. "Well, it seems to have worked for Shakespeare," Tehmina heard Joe say almost to himself.

"Oh, Mrs. Sethna," Grace said, turning her green eyes toward her. "I meant to ask. How are those two little boys doing?"

Tehmina was touched. Maybe Grace was not as shallow as she seemed. "They're fine," she said warmly. "They're staying with their aunt for now."

"Reason I was asking ... I had a superscintillating idea during the drive here. Bryan always says that's the way my brain works, never shuts off, even at night, don't you, baby? Drives the poor boy crazy at times. But anyway, I was thinking we should run a full-page ad in both local papers featuring you and maybe the two boys. And there'd be no copy, just 'Canfield and Associates salutes Tehmina Sethna, mother of one of our employees.' Just a lot of white space, real tasteful." She turned to Joe and Sorab. "What do you think?"

"Well, there would be legal issues surrounding the use of photos of the two kids." Tehmina could tell Sorab was choosing his words with great care. "They are minors, after all. And with the mother in jail—"

"I think it's a terrible idea," Joe said forcefully. "It's exploitative, it's *not* tasteful, it's downright tacky."

"Joe," Heather whispered, her face white. "Please."

He ignored her. "In fact, I have to be honest with you, Grace. This really makes me doubt your judgment. It makes me wonder whether you understand the culture of our firm at all."

Grace couldn't look more thunderstruck if Joe had punched her in the stomach, Tehmina thought, and felt a twinge of pity for the woman. But the next moment, she bounced back. "Okay," she said lightly. "So you don't like the idea."

But Joe was not done. "It's not just that the idea is bad. It's the thought process behind it that—"

"Joe." Heather's voice was as sharp as a spear. "This is a dinner party. You can't talk shop to our guests all evening."

With obvious effort, Joe stopped himself. There was a moment of awful, tense silence while they watched Joe wrestling for calm. "Okay, no more work talk," he said, and turned to Tehmina. "Oh, by the way, I went online yesterday, researching the Parsis." And, reading the startled expression on Tehmina's face, he continued, "Hey, I had to know everything about our celebrity guest. Anyway, I came across this beautiful story about when the Zoroastrians first came to India from Iran? How their chief matched his wits with the Hindu king? Do you know the story?"

Did she know the story? Every Parsi child who had ever drunk at her mother's breast knew the legend of how the small, tired group of Persians fleeing Islamic persecution in Iran had arrived in the small Indian town of Sanjan, seeking political refuge. The Hindu ruler, unable to make this group of Farsi-speaking foreigners understand that he couldn't possibly accommodate any newcomers, had greeted them on the beach with a glass of milk filled to the brim. No vacancy, the full glass was supposed to symbolize. But the Zoroastrian head priest was a brilliant man. Removing a small quantity of sugar from their supplies, he dissolved the sugar in the glass, careful not to spill a drop of milk. This was his famous answer—the answer that became a source of pride and a blueprint for future generations: Like sugar in milk, our presence will sweeten the flavor of your life, without displacing you or causing you any trouble. And so they were allowed to stay and became the Parsis of India.

Without bothering to relate the story to Bryan or Grace, Joe continued to face Tehmina. "I thought of you when I read that story," he said quietly. "That's what you've done, you know. Sweetened our lives with your presence. Just like your ancestors did in India."

Tehmina blushed. "Thank you," she said quietly, aware, without having to look up, that across the room her son was bursting with pride.

Grace looked from one to the other. "Hey, someone fill me in. What's the story?"

Joe looked bemused. "Oh, you don't need to know everything, Grace," he said lightly. Eyeing her empty glass, he stood up. "I'm afraid I'm not being a very good host. Would you care for some more of my Trader Joe's special, my dear?"

"Sure."

The rest of the evening passed pleasantly enough. Once, the conversation veered dangerously toward work, but Heather expertly steered it back to talk of movies and restaurants and books. Sorab told the story about Cookie giving his teacher grief over her misstatement about the lead pencils and they all laughed. "Well, I could've sworn they were made of lead, myself," Bryan said, and Tehmina found herself liking this man, as robust and dumb as a piece of steak.

For dessert, Heather served cappuccino and fruit tarts that she had baked herself. Joe controlled himself for a few minutes and then broke down. "Ah, to hell with this. What's dessert without some chocolate?" He came back with a big bar of Lindt hazelnut chocolate. Heather rolled her eyes.

When it was time to leave, Joe signaled to Sorab to accompany him to the next room. "Come help me with the coats, would you?" They were gone for almost ten minutes. Tehmina could hear an occasional murmur from the library, but both men were speaking too softly for her to catch anything they were saying. She thought that Grace was straining to hear what they were saying, but Heather and Susan kept a constant stream of conversation going.

After they walked out of the big front door, the Sethnas stood in the Canfields' driveway talking to Grace and Bryan for a minute. Then, Susan shivered. "Time to take this one home," Sorab said, putting his arm around his wife.

Sorab waited until Byran had pulled out of the driveway and then slowly backed out himself. He let out a huge laugh, one that was equal parts relief and joy. "Well, that was some evening, wasn't it?" he said, and when they agreed, he laughed some more. "Well, ladies, this may be awfully premature of me—excuse me, awfulfantastically premature of me—but there may be a promotion in my future." Hearing their sharp intake of breath, he continued, "That's right. Seems like business is not doing as well as it ought to be. And Joe seems ready to set adrift the amazing, unsinkable Grace Butler."

Sorab whistled all the way home.

CHAPTER SIXTEEN

Still in bed and glancing at the alarm clock, Tehmina was shocked to see that it was nine o'clock. Thank God Susan had dropped Cookie off on a playdate earlier this morning. She would hate to have her grandson see his slovenly grandmother still in bed, unable to command her eyes open this morning. She had woken up briefly a few hours ago to use the bathroom and had yawned her good-byes to the children at that time. Sorab had looked at her curiously, but if he was surprised or hurt by the fact that she padded her way back to her bedroom instead of into the kitchen as she normally did, he didn't comment on it.

She was tired, Tehmina realized. Too much was happening too fast. The fan letters, the call from the mayor, the knowing smiles from perfect strangers, the good-natured ribbing from the women in Eva's card club, the solicitous attention paid to her by Joe and Heather Canfield, even the cautious, attentive way in which Sorab was treating her, it was all overwhelming. And instead of feeling pride or joy, Tehmina wanted to cry. All this attention was making her feel terribly alone, was making her miss her Rustom more than ever. Now more than ever she needed Rustom's solid, no-nonsense, affable presence. With just the right sharp, insightful, dartlike words, Rustom would puncture this recent bubble of celebrity and admiration that had engulfed her.

And she was worried about the boys. Other than the card from Jerome, she had not heard from them. She wanted to know how Joshy was, whether the bruises on his face were healing. She wanted to know how Jerome was, whether the bruises on his heart were healing. Were the boys missing their mother? How could they not? She still remembered the look on Percy's young face when his mother had passed away. But of course, that was different. Shirin had been a wonderful, loving mother and wife. But surely children missed their mothers regardless of what sins they committed against them? Was being with Antonio any kind of consolation? Other than an occasional hello and wave, she remembered very little about Antonio's wife from when they had lived next door to the Sethnas. For all of Antonio's joviality and friendliness, he and his wife had pretty much kept to themselves. Now Tehmina wondered: What if Tara's half sister was like Tara—cruel, abusive, violent? What if, God forbid, she smelled of alcohol in the morning, like Tara did? What if—thanks to her interference—the boys had descended from the frying pan into the fire? Was someone supervising Antonio's wife, making sure the boys were not being ill treated? Would the police be checking on them? She decided to call Percy and find out about this. Percy was a lawyer, surely he would know. Also, she realized with a start, Percy was one person whose behavior around her had not changed since the newspaper article ran. Percy's gaze when he looked at her was not starstruck or awed or amused or admiring. Rather, Percy's steady look said that what she had done for the two boys was exactly what he would've expected her to do. That he was not surprised by what she had done. In some ways, Percy knew her better than Sorab did, she thought.

Yes, she would call Percy and see if he could check on the two boys. But not yet, she thought with a yawn. First, she was going to sleep a little longer. Tomorrow, Sorab and Susan were throwing their annual New Year's Eve party and she knew she'd be spending the day in the kitchen. She needed to rest today, to let sleep iron the fatigue out of her bones. She'd call Percy after she got up.

When the doorbell rang, the sound of it got mangled in the dream she was having about hacking her way through a green forest where large plantain leaves were blocking her path. At first she thought the doorbell was the screeching of the forest birds overhead and then slowly the sound disentangled itself from her dream and with a groan of recognition she turned onto her side and rolled out of bed. It's the UPS man, she thought. For the past few weeks, Christmas gifts from out-of-town relatives and friends had been delivered to the door. Tehmina had gotten used to signing for the boxes.

Smoothening her hair with her right hand, blinking the sleep out of her eyes, miserably aware of her musty-smelling body and her sour, unwashed mouth, Tehmina opened the front door. And blinked. Instead of a young man in a brown UPS uniform, there stood Tara. A very angry-looking Tara.

"Listen," she said before Tehmina could say a word. "I just want to tell you, you-all got me all wrong. And you had no business interfering in my business. Them—those are my babies, not yours. I carried them in my belly for nine months, not you. And you think you can just come by and, and—" Tehmina noticed that Tara was so angry she was shaking, her knees knocking against each other. A slight spittle formed on the right side of her mouth.

Tehmina was wide-awake now and fearful. But the fear was affecting her much as sleep had a minute ago, grabbing her limbs, making her movements dull and slow. "I—I don't know what to say," she began.

Tara's eyes were spiteful. "No, you say nothin' and just listen to me, you old bitch," she said. "I'm telling you, you just stay out of my business. I'm going to get my babies back, no matter what I got to do. If you-all think I'm going to leave them with my holier-than-thou sister, you-all got another thought coming. And next time you interfere with me, I won't be standing here talkin' calmly. The next time—"

"The next time you will do *what*?" The roar that came from inside of Tehmina was so loud she had to fight a moment's urge to see if someone—someone much bigger and braver than her—was standing right behind her. Her mouth felt hot, as if she had a fever. The gall of this acne-faced woman. She was threatening her, treating her like she had treated her poor sons. She, Tehmina Sethna, who had graduated with the highest marks from Calcutta University's best college. She, the daughter of a cultured, dignified father who had been the personal physician of Calcutta's mayor. She, the daughter of a mother who had been one of the finest cellists in the city. She, the wife of a man who had never so much as raised his eyebrow at her, let alone his voice. And here she was, being threatened by this ugly girl with the face of a hen. Anger made her voice even louder. "What will you do next time, Tara? Beat me? Hurt me, like you did those two innocent boys? Make my lip swell up and bleed, like you did Joshy's?"

Tara looked as surprised as Tehmina felt. "You, you . . . listen, you keep your voice down, y'hear?" she spluttered.

"For what? To protect you from your shame? A grown woman hitting a little boy? And that, too, a mother?" Tehmina groped for the right words, her mind racing to express the disgust and outrage that she felt for the woman in front of her. She was no longer frightened of Tara. Her anger had liberated her, so that she was now frightened *for* Tara, frightened of what she would do to this stupid, lazy, unkempt woman standing before her. She stared at Tara, wanting to find the right words, wanting to fire them like bullets into Tara's empty heart. But no words came close to expressing the revulsion she was feeling. "Shame on you," she cried at last. And then, "Thuu, thuu," she dry-spat on the ground in front of her, her face screwed up in disgust.

Tara's eyes widened. "What the hell are you doing, you crazy bitch?"

Tehmina looked straight into Tara's eyes. "I am saying that you are not worthy of the title of mother. I am saying you—"

Suddenly Tara was crying, her thin white face pinched as a raisin. "You don't know what I've been through. You—it's easy for people like you, with your fuckin' fancy cars and everything. I've seen how you dote on that grandson of yours. Well, my own mother was hardly there for me, you understand? I've been on my own since I was sixteen years old. And my dad, that old drunken geezer, he, he would've whored me to the highest bidder. You don't know what I've seen, lady, so you shut your—"

"Enough." Tehmina held her hands to her ears. She felt as if she was watching one of those horrible American television shows that came on in the afternoon on which people aired all their dirty linen in public. "This is none of my business, Tara, what you do."

"Is this girl here bothering you, miss?" An old man with a stoop was making his way up the brick walkway in front of their house. In his hand, he held a long-handled snow shovel. "Because if she is, I can take care of her for you," he added as he tapped the shovel lightly against the brick. With a start, Tehmina realized it was old man Henderson from across the street. Her heart sank. Another neighborhood scene involving her. That's all that she needed.

Tara whirled around to face Henderson. "Go away," she said. "Shoo, you old codger. Jeez, what a fucked-up neighborhood this is. A bunch of geriatric busybodies spying on each other."

Henderson stood his ground. "She bothering you?" he asked again, ignoring Tara.

Tehmina noticed that the man's eyes were tearing, probably from the cold. She drew herself to her full height and threw Tara a contemptuous look. "Nothing that I can't handle. Thank you for your help, just the same, Mr. Henderson."

Without another word, the old man nodded and walked away. Watching his retreating back, Tehmina was almost sorry to see him go and have to face the thin, tear-streaked face in front of her. "Tara," she said quietly, "I think you should leave now before someone calls the police." And then, because she could not help herself, "You're still young, my dear. Try to get your life in order. God has blessed you with two beautiful children. Don't turn your back on that gift."

Tara raised her voice in a wail. "I've been tryin'. It's just so hard being a single parent. And them boys can be such devils, you have no idea. You just see them—"

Tehmina gripped the doorknob. "I will not listen to you speak poorly of your children. If they're bad, you're the one who has made them such. Good-bye, Tara. Please do not come here again." Firmly, resolutely, she closed the door. And then latched it from the inside.

"Hey, lady, don't you slam the door in my face, goddammit," she heard Tara yell from the other side. Then the sound of the doorbell ringing insistently. "Tara," Tehmina said quietly from the other side. "If you're not gone in five seconds, I'm phoning the police."

There was a final fuck-you. Then, as if a curtain had dropped, silence fell on the house. Tehmina waited, scarcely believing that Tara had left. But as the silence extended, Tehmina became aware of the thudding of her heart and the weakness in her legs. Her stomach felt as if it had sour, months-old milk in it.

She went into the kitchen to make herself a cup of tea to calm her nerves. Engrossed in clipping the mint leaves and opening the fridge to get out the milk, she was surprised to hear the sound of pots and spoons banging on the kitchen counter. She was even more surprised to realize that she was the one doing the banging and that she was quietly, murderously angry. Furious. A body-trembling, mind-pulsating furious. Her blood boiling like the water she was now pouring into the mug.

Damn that Tara. Damn her. How dare she show up at the front door like that, spewing her poison, bad-mouthing her children, insulting poor Mr. Henderson, and threatening her. The gall of the woman. Tehmina remembered now that Percy had suggested that they get a restraining order against Tara. But Sorab had balked. "Let's just wait and see what happens, bossie," he'd demurred. "Chances are a few days in the lockup will set the woman straight."

But her time in jail had made Tara even more spiteful. Tehmina forced herself to not remember what Tara had said about her mother and her drunken father. She did not want a thin thread of pity to fray from this tapestry of anger and outrage that she was weaving. She did not want to feel sorry for Tara; she would not allow herself to. A woman should not beat her children. Even in this jumble-tumble world, that much was an absolute. No exceptions. No exceptions. Still, an image arose in Tehmina's mind, that of Krishna and Parvati, the homeless couple who lived on the street across from her apartment building in Bombay. Krishna made his living washing cars and running errands for the middle-class residents of the building while Parvati worked odd jobs in their homes. But every night Krishna's patrons would hear the sounds of him beating his wife after he'd return from the bootlegger's joint. And every morning, they would hear the sound of the children wailing as Parvati slapped them and cursed at her misfortune in begetting them. Rustom and Tehmina had intervened a few times, chastised both husband and wife for their respective violence, threatened not to use their services anymore if they continued in their ways, but to no avail. Krishna would cry and blame the alcohol for turning him into a demon; Parvati would beat her forehead with her open palm and blame her demonic husband for making her unleash her frustrations on her children. And yet, despite the daily violence, Tehmina had marveled at the intimate way in which this tiny family huddled together around a small stove for their evening meals, had witnessed Parvati laughing as she lovingly combed her daughter's long hair, had registered the panicked look in Krishna's eyes when Parvati had taken ill with typhoid fever. Reality was complicated; Tehmina knew that. India had taught her that lesson, over and over again.

So why this reluctance to see Tara in her whole, complicated self? Why this hardening of the heart, this self-righteous desire to not acknowledge the roots of Tara's poor behavior toward her children? Hadn't Tehmina seen it often in her volunteer work, how abuse stalked the generations, how it dripped its black poison from one empty vessel into another?

She did not know the answer to that first question. Perhaps it was because she had seen Joshy's swollen lip up close; seen how the little boy had winced when she had dabbed it with rubbing alcohol; seen how Jerome's eyes had become guarded and shuttered when he had lied about how his brother had sustained his bruises. Or, perhaps it was because this was America and Tara was an American and Tehmina simply expected more from the most powerful country in the world. Krishna and Parvati were poor, impoverished, illiterate, half starving. How could she blame Krishna for looking to the bottle as an antidote to his misery? How could she not understand why Parvati hit her children when the woman often pummeled her own chest out of remorse and frustration? But Tara. Born white in America.

Living in a good, middle-class home, even if it didn't belong to her. Able to afford a car, even if the muffler didn't work. Able to send her children to school for free. Able to go into a grocery store and spend less of her income on food than people in any other country. All this and it wasn't enough? If someone like Tara couldn't be happy, what chance did people in the rest of the world have?

Having drunk her tea, Tehmina walked to the sink. She began to rinse out the cup before she remembered. Susan was always asking her to please use the dishwasher and not wash things by hand. Such a crass idiot you are, Tehmina scolded herself. Still can't get used to the dishwasher, can you? And here you are, passing judgment on other people.

But then, remembering how dismissively Tara had spoken to Henderson—shoo, she'd said to the old man, as if he was a crow at a picnic—Tehmina felt her temper spike again. She would not have Tara stop by this house and dirty it with her spewings. What if Cookie had been home and witnessed this ugliness? Already the boy asked daily about how and where Josh and Jerome were. And Tehmina had to swallow the lump in her throat and lie that the boys were doing fine.

She felt a strong urge to find out how the brothers were faring. Also, a desire to get Tara's half sister to intervene, to make clear to Tara that she could not disrupt Tehmina's life each time her anger got the better of her.

Walking into the living room she flipped open Sorab's phone book to the *A*s. Surely Antonio was not as angry with her as he was the day he called Sorab? In any case, her own indignation at Tara's recent behavior could match the man's temper. Still, her fingers hesitated over the phone for a split second before she forced them to dial Antonio's number. Please let the wife answer the phone, she prayed.

The phone had rung only once before she heard a gruff male voice. "'Yallo?" Antonio said.

Tehmina gulped. "Antonio?" she said. "This is Tehmi—Tammy. Sorab's mother. Is . . . is Mrs. Antonio there?" Too late she realized she didn't remember his wife's name.

She heard a sharp intake of breath and then a long silence. Had the man hung up on her? "Antonio?" she said again.

"Jussa minute," she heard him say. He sat the phone down with a clank. "Marita," she heard him yell. "Phone for you. It's Sorab's mother."

"Helloo?" The voice over the phone was buttery and smooth. It reminded Tehmina of the white, sugared cream she used to eat over the hard, crusty bread at the old Irani restaurants. "Can I help you?"

Tehmina realized she had been holding her breath. Now she spoke on the exhale. "Hello, Mrs. Antonio?" What was Antonio's surname? Why hadn't Sorab written it in the book? "I was—this is Tehmina Sethna. I don't know if you remember me? Anyway, I was just calling to find out how Josh and Jerome were doing."

"Oh, hello, darling. Of course I remember you. And I'm so ashamed. I've been meaning to call you for days. But you know how it is with the holidays and all. And having two little boys at home—I tell you, I've never felt my age as much as this past week. But did you get the card from Jerome, darling?"

Marita's voice was so silken, so honeylike, that Tehmina thought she was mocking her. What is wrong with this family? First, Marita's sister screams at me from my doorstep, then her husband is barely civil. And now she talks to me as if I'm a six-year-old child. Just say it, she wanted to say to her. If you're angry at me, too, just let me know.

"Anyways, darling, you should've heard the dressing-down I gave my husband soon as I learned that he'd called your poor son," Marita continued. "On Christmas Day, too, God help him. You mark my words, I'm gonna drag Antonio to your home to apologize to your son soon as the holidays are over. See if I don't. In the meantime, darling, you tell your son how very sorry I am, won't you?"

Despite herself, Tehmina could feel her body uncurl. It was beginning to dawn on her that Marita was apologizing to her. "That's okay," she said weakly. "Antonio was right. I had no right to interfere—"

"No right!" The silken voice had a thread of denim in it now. "Oh, honey, don't say that. Don't you ever say that. Oh, darling, I just wish someone had interfered a long time ago. Could've saved those poor boys so much grief. And who knows, maybe helped that troubled sister of mine along the ways. That woman needs help so bad, honey. Always was a little disturbed, even as a child. We were born to the same mother, you know. But different fathers. My mamma and pappa and I came to the States from Sicily when I was a child of seven. But I still remember the home country, Tammy. One never forgets one's home, right? Oh, such a land, it is. Sicily. Full of music and sunshine and passion. And that's how my father was also, God bless his soul. A peasant by trade but a gentleman by character. Full of laughter and music. So unlike the American devil that my poor mamma married years after my pappa died. By then I was out of the house and happily married, thank God. So I hardly knew my half sister, see? And poor Mama, she bore what that animal did to her so silently. But that Tara was a wild urchin, even as a child. More like her father than like my gentle mother. I didn't know what was happening in that house, I swear to you, Tammy. If I'd have known—"

"Mrs. Antonio," Tehmina interrupted. She was learning far more about this family than she wished to. "I only called to say—"

"Oh call me Marita, honey. Everybody calls—"

"Marita. Tara was over at my house today." She heard a gasp at the other end of the phone line. "She was in a very angry mood, I can tell you. In fact—"

"Why, that dirty liar," Marita said. "We were the ones who went to bail her out. And the first words I said to her were, You better not go bothering those nice people in the house next door. Because I knew she'd try some trick, see? And we warned her to leave you be. And she looks me dead in the eye and promises. Lying like a rug to my face. Oh, my dear, I am so—what's the word—mortified. I'm so sorry. Oh, wait'll I tell Antonio. He'll drag her out of our house by her nose, for sure."

"Listen, " Tehmina said desperately. "I'm not trying to cause any more friction in your family. After all—" with a bitter laugh— "I think I've caused enough problems. But I tell you, I can't have Tara threatening my family. I have a little grandson. I'm afraid of what . . ." She shuddered, unable to finish her thoughts.

Marita clicked her tongue. "You got nothing to be afraid of, Tammy. I promise you that. It was my stupid mistake to have Tara move into our house. Badgered my husband until he gave in. He told me that that no-good sister of mine was nothing but trouble, but did I listen? No, I was thinking of those poor boys living in a shelter or with that monster boyfriend of hers. But after this, I wash my hands of her. S'long as we have the boys, I don't care where she goes or what she does."

"But do you have the boys? Won't Tara get them back soon?"

The silken voice now had a coil of steel running through it. "We're gonna have to convince that old judge, won't we, honey? I'm not giving up those boys without a fight, I'll tell you that. I told Tara that she's got to go into rehab, get a job and an apartment, get her life in order before she can think of getting those boys back. And upon my word, my tightwad husband will hire the best lawyer if we have to. But I'm keeping those boys, honey, until all this hardness melts out of their hearts."

Tehmina felt something melt in her own heart at those words. So

Marita had noticed it, too, the toughness that the boys wore like skin. Thank God. She suddenly felt much lighter, almost buoyant.

"I'd love to see Joshy and Jerome one of these days," she said. "That is, if they're not too angry with me."

She heard the concern and puzzlement in Marita's voice. "Angry? For what? Listen, honey, if it weren't for you, they'd still be living with that crazy mother of theirs, getting beat up and yelled at and being half starved. You should see them at my house, darling. Not that I'm bragging on myself, but in just a few days, I swear both children have gained weight. We've been stuffing them with good, homemade food. None of that junk food they were raised on. And just this morning, Jerome put his arms around me after breakfast and said, 'I love you.' In all the years I've known these boys, I've barely seen the older one smile, let alone say anything like that." She paused. "Tell you what, Tammy. Why don't you come out to see us for lunch sometime next week? On Wednesday, maybe?"

"I can't," Tehmina said miserably. "That is, I don't drive."

"Oh. Well, no reason we can't come see you. I know the boys would like that. Except, wait. If Tara is still next door—let me talk to Antonio, honey, about how soon he wants her out of there. And anyway, better for the boys not to see their old neighborhood, don't you think?"

"What if I got a friend to drive me to Richwood mall? Do you ever go there?"

"Richwood? Oh, sure. That was my old stomping ground, when we lived in Rosemont Heights. The boys'll like that also. Maybe we could eat at the food court. That old Italian joint still there? Mamma Santa's?"

"I'm not sure. But let me ask my friend if she can take me there on Tuesday. Will it be okay if I phone you on Sunday, Mrs. Antonio?"

"Marita. Of course it's okay. Will be nice to see you again, sweetheart. The boys have been talking about you nonstop since they got here."

"About me?"

"Yeah. About how nice you are and stuff. And Joshy in particular goes on and on about some cheese sandwich you made him. I've tried five different ways but guess it doesn't come close. That's another thing you're gonna have to do when we meet, darling. Give me your cheese sandwich recipe."

Tehmina laughed. "I'll phone you on Sunday."

"Good. We'll meet Tuesday, God willing and the creek don't rise. Happy New Year to you and yours, my dear."

Tehmina got off the phone and walked across the living room to sit in the recliner. She looked around the room. A patch of sunlight fell in a square on the gray carpet. But she was distracted, lost in her thoughts. The boys were talking about her. About her cheese sandwich, God bless them. She would ask Eva to take her to the mall next week. There, she would see Joshy and Jerome again. The boys she would meet at the mall would be plump as kittens, would no longer have that hunted expression they usually wore. Hopefully, Joshy's bruises would have healed by then. Hopefully, Jerome would smile at her. Maybe he'd even whisper an *I love you* to her.

You're being silly, she scolded herself. But she couldn't keep the smile from her lips. Happy New Year, Marita had said. And now, for the first time, Tehmina allowed herself the possibility that it might be a happy new year, after all.

CHAPTER SEVENTEEN

Oi, deekra, I hope it's okay but I've invited a few of my friends to tonight's party," Tehmina said.

Sorab looked startled. But then he flung his arms around his mother and grinned. "Your *friends*? Who is it, a new boyfriend?"

Susan smacked Sorab lightly on his arm. "Hush, baby. Who have you invited, Mamma?" Her face was curious but open, with none of the guardedness from just a few days ago.

"Just Eva and her husband. Though God knows if Solomon will come. I told Eva we'll leave the garage door open for him, in case he has an urge to tinker with some cars." Tehmina grinned at her own wickedness. "And oh—I know it's short notice, but I'm thinking of also inviting Luke."

"The newspaper guy?" Sorab groaned. "Gosh, Mamma. Has this celebrity stuff gone to your head or what? You think every party should now have a newspaper reporter present?"

"I just feel sorry for him, deekra. He has no family in the area.

His parents live in North Carolina and he's only been in Ohio for six months."

Sorab laughed. "Trust my mother to know the guy's whole biography," he said to Susan. "He interviewed you for what, twenty minutes? Sounds like you ended up interviewing him."

"And why would he be alone on New Year's Eve?" Susan added. "Doesn't he have a girlfriend or something?"

"That I don't know." Then, seeing both their faces, "Well, if you think it's a bad idea, I don't have to invite him. Anyway, I'm sure he has other plans. Maybe I can ask him over for tea sometime next week."

Sorab turned to Susan. "Do you remember the time Mamma invited the cashier at Giant Eagle for dinner? All because the woman eyed the coconut milk cans she'd bought and asked her how to make curry?"

They all laughed. "But this is what we love about you, our darling Christmas miracle," Sorab continued in an exaggerated tone. "So, invite your lost-puppy-dog reporter if you have to. As long as you make it clear to him that he's not here as a snoop."

"He's not a snoop," Tehmina began indignantly, and Sorab burst out laughing. "Mamma. Dear God, Mamma. You should see the expression on your face. Do you always have to be the guardian of the underdogs?"

Before Tehmina could reply, they heard Cookie at the top of the stairs. "Dad, I'm not late, just slow today, okay?" the boy yelled. "Wait for me."

"You better get down here if you don't want to be late for your playdate, little fella," Sorab yelled. "And you can't go until you get some breakfast in you."

Cookie came grumbling down the stairs. He held his shoes in one hand and his sock in the other. The other sock was on his foot. "I don't want any stupid breakfast," he said. "And stop calling me little fella. I'm not little anymore."

"So what should I call you? Big fella?"

"Just call me Cookie, the way Mom does."

"Okay, little fella. Cookie, it is."

Cookie rushed to his father with an indignant squeal and pretended to beat him on his chest. "Okay, okay, that's enough." Sorab laughed, grabbing the boy's thin wrists. "Now sit down and eat your breakfast."

"Tim's mom is taking us to the science museum today," Cookie said with his mouth full.

"Cookie! Swallow before you talk, please," Susan said.

The boy swallowed. "It's the dinosaur exhibit. Tim's already seen it once. And his mom said we could have lunch at the museum. I loooove the hot chocolate there," he added, smacking his lips. "Yum, yum, yum."

Tehmina smiled. Cookie reminded her of a blade of grass blowing in the wind—slender, active, stretching toward the sun. This is peace, she thought, this sharing of a meal with my family. Even though she knew she would be alone the rest of the day—both children were working on New Year's Eve, although Susan had promised to come home early to help her prepare for the party tonight—for once, the thought didn't depress her. She felt as if she was recovering from the flu—the sluggish, tired feeling that she had felt in the months after Rustom's death was finally leaving her bones. She had been feeling better ever since the conversation with Marita yesterday. This morning, she felt alive, strong, hopeful. Yes, that was it—that was the new feeling that was making her skin tingle, making her blood rush faster, making her muscles feel smooth and strong. It was hope. She had lost that feeling for so long that she had been convinced that some part of her was as dead as Rustom was dead and would never come back to life again.

"Who are you calling dead, woman?" she heard Rustom say, and she jumped. He had never before spoken to her when there were other people around them. She looked around the dining room furtively, but luckily, Rustom was nowhere to be seen. She glanced at Sorab to see if he'd heard anything, but he was reading the paper as he ate his cereal.

Still, the promise of another conversation with her husband, the sense that he was waiting for the others to leave the house, made her impatient. She busied herself loading the dishwasher while Sorab and Susan gathered their work things and got ready. As always, she stood outside the door and waved them good-bye.

"Bye, Granna," Cookie yelled. "Love you lots."

"Mamma, go in the house," Sorab said. "You'll catch a cold."

"I'll try to be home as soon as I can, okay, Mom?" Susan called. "Don't tire yourself out. Leave some of the work for me."

Then they were gone, Susan in her blue Corolla and Sorab and Cookie in Sorab's black Saab.

Tehmina went inside the house. "Rustom?" she said softly. "Janu?"

No reply. Feeling a little foolish, she went into the dining room looking for Rustom. If only the mayor of Rosemont Heights knew that her hero was a woman who talked to her husband's ghost, she thought with a giggle.

There was no sign of him. Maybe she had imagined his voice earlier. She fought the feeling of disappointment, told herself it was time to get busy. There was so much to do to prepare for tonight. Just frying the lamb kebabs alone would take hours. Not to mention making the chutneys for the bhelpuri and samosas they were going to serve as appetizers. Also, she had promised Susan that she would pick up Cookie's books and toys from the living-room floor and put them back into his room. In fact, maybe she'd tidy up the house first and then start with the cooking.

She went into the living room and the first thing she noticed was the open book on the coffee table. She didn't remember seeing that book last night. As she drew closer and read the title, her heart started beating fast and the tears came involuntarily to her eyes. It was Rustom's old, dog-eared copy of *The Rubáiyát of Omar Khayyám*, which now belonged to Sorab. She had felt as if she was parting with her right arm when she presented the book to her son last fall. A lifetime of memories, a million images of Rustom thumbing through the slim volume, lay within the yellowing pages of the book. But she knew that it was proper that Sorab inherit his father's book. It was his legacy, his right to own the book whose lyrical poetry and generous philosophy had meant so much to his father. Still, her hands had shaken when she had removed the book from her suitcase and given it to her son.

Now, eyeing the book on the coffee table, her hands shook again. The book had not been here last night when they'd finished watching the DVD and gone to bed. She was sure of that. And the chances of Sorab having brought it down to read this morning were slim. The boy was lucky if he got to read the newspaper before he left for work, let alone a book. Which meant that it was Rustom who had . . . now she was sure that she'd heard his voice earlier this morning at breakfast.

Steadying her hands, she picked up the Khayyám. Was it her imagination or did the book really feel warm, as if someone had touched it recently? Her eyes fell on the open page. It was one of Rustom's favorite verses:

Ah, fill the Cup:—what boots it to repeat
How Time is slipping underneath our Feet:
Unborn TOMORROW, and dead YESTERDAY,
Why fret about them if TODAY be sweet!

"Rustom. Janu," she whispered. "I know you are here. Please, darling. There's no one else at home right now. Come talk to me."

"What do you think I've been doing, woman?" Rustom replied. He was seated on the love seat near the window.

"Oh, Rustom," she said. "I'm so glad you're here. There's so much I want to tell you—so much has happened this past week, you won't believe."

"How are the two boys?"

She stared at him openmouthed. "You know?"

"What, you think I don't read the papers?" He grinned. "Seriously, though, don't you remember me pushing you off the bloody fence, Tehmi? Saala, if it wasn't for me, you'd still be dithering on that fence, frozen into a Popsicle by now."

She laughed. "What do you do, spy on me?"

"Yes. No."

"Well, I'm glad you do. Makes me feel less lonely, knowing you're watching me."

"Yes, well, that's what I'm wanting to talk to you about. Listen, Tehmi. After today, I won't be able to . . . that is, we won't be able to meet like this. You know, I sometimes regret that I didn't force you to make more decisions when I was—around. Always, I was doing the thinking for us. And then, the damn heart attack was so sudden—I tried fighting, believe me, I knew what a shock it would be to you, but it was too late to change things. Anyway, all that's water under the bridge. What's important is where you go from now on."

"But, Rustom, I'm not going anywhere."

"But you are. You must. Life is nothing if not movement. Tehmina, listen to me: get off the fence. Once and for all, get off the bloody fence. Whether you live here or in Bombay, I don't care. But wherever you decide to live, be happy. Darling, this indecisive dithering and wavering has gone on for too long. It's time to choose. So choose."

She was silent, clouds of feeling—shame, hope, confusion, hurt—floating across her face.

"My love," Rustom said, and his voice had an urgency she'd never heard before. "Why fret about the future if today be sweet? It's all you have, darling, is today. Shit, now I'm talking in clichés, too." His voice cracked. "But seriously. You don't know how lucky you are, Tehmi. I didn't know it either, until I stopped having my todays. You think I don't wish I could be with my wife, my family, my grandson, anytime I bloody feel like it?" He suddenly sounded angry. "Tehmi. Don't try and factor in every possible what-if. The future is none of your damn business. You decide based on what you know today. You. Choose. *Today*."

"Rustom," she cried. "I'm upsetting you. Please, darling, don't be angry at me. I swear I'll—"

He laughed and there was raw glass in laughter. "Angry at you? Woman, I'd forgotten how silly you sometimes are. Darling, I'm angry at myself. Don't you see? I hate seeing you struggle like this. I hate thinking that it was the giving out of my weak heart that has created this dilemma for you. Even this, even these visits to you, are a sign of my weakness, don't you see? I have no business being here. And once you make up your mind, I will leave and return to where I belong."

"Leave? Rustom, you've left me once. If you ever leave me again, I don't know if—"

Rustom smiled sadly. "Look at us. Two old, pathetic people. Ah, Tehmi, what is this pale, bloodless meeting, compared to the passion and delight we've enjoyed? Why should we settle for these clandestine meetings? You are worthy of so much more, dear. You are alive—take your place among the living."

How well she knew that tone. Once Rustom made up his mind, nothing could change it. Tehmina closed her eyes and pushed her tears back. She could feel Rustom's eyes on her. Then she heard him say, "Do you know what my favorite Khayyám verse is?"

She shook her head, her eyes still closed. "Imagine, all these years and I never asked you."

"It's the most predictable one, I'm afraid." He smiled. "But that's the amazing thing about love, isn't it? It reduces everything to a cliché." Rustom's voice was a feather barely touching her face:

Here with a Loaf of Bread beneath the Bough,
A Flask of Wine, a Book of Verse—and Thou
Beside me singing in the Wilderness—
And Wilderness is Paradise now.

I don't know how I'm going to get through the rest of my life without this man, she thought.

"Yah, yah, you said that at the funeral, also," Rustom replied. "And look at you—you're fine. I always told you—you're as tough as an ox."

"Did you just read my mind?" Her voice was equal parts astonishment and indignation.

Rustom crossed the room in the time it took her to blink and kissed her lightly on her forehead. "Darling, I've always read your mind. I don't have to be dead in order to do that."

Despite the wet puddle of grief inside her, she smiled. She knew he was right. She reached out to take his hand. The doorbell rang. She looked around frantically. "I don't know who that is. Will you wait for me until—" She realized she was talking to an empty room. And the room wasn't talking back. Rustom had vanished. "Rustom, listen," she whispered urgently. "I don't have to answer the door." But the room remained still and silent.

She had never hated anyone as much as she hated the caller as she moved heavily to answer the door. If it is Tara at the door, I swear she will leave here holding her head in her hands, she vowed. And if it is the UPS man, well, he better be delivering the Hope Diamond.

Her anger vanished as soon as she opened the door. Eva was leaning against the house, shivering lightly. Tehmina took in the red nose and the teary eyes. Must be the cold, Tehmina thought. But then she was struck by another, scarier thought. Eva had never shown up at her house without calling before. "Eva," she gasped as she made way for her friend to enter. "Is everything okay? Is Solomon—"

"Fine," Eva said. "Solomon is fine."

Eva turned to face Tehmina. "Sorry for barging in like this," she mumbled. "You know I never show up without calling. But what to do"—her face crumbled—"I just needed the comfort of a friend today."

Eva crying? Her big, cheerful, brazen friend crying like other lesser mortals? Sure, Tehmina knew Eva was softhearted. But still, she had never seen her friend like this. She was used to Eva's bawdy jokes, the wattage from her ever-present grin making up for the weak Ohio sunlight. Cancer, Tehmina thought. It had to be cancer. Why hadn't Eva told her she was going for tests?

"You will be all right, my friend," she said, trying to embrace Eva and coming up awkwardly against her bulk. She settled for putting her hand on her shoulder. "I will be here, I will help you through it all."

Eva removed a large, red scarf from her dress pocket and mopped her face. She eyed Tehmina quizzically. "Help me through what, honey?"

Tehmina stared at her openmouthed, unable to say the dreaded word. The two women looked at each other and then Eva said, "I know it's early in the day, but how about a little wine? You got anything?"

Should she be drinking alcohol if she was sick? Tehmina bit down on her tongue. "Sure. As long as you can open it. I can never get that corkscrew to work."

Eva followed her into the kitchen. "What're you reading?" she asked, and Tehmina realized that she was still carrying the Khayyám book with her.

"A book of poems by Omar Khayyám. You know him? My Rustom loved his work," she said, and it felt strange to talk about Rustom in the past tense when she could still feel his lips on her forehead.

Eva looked sheepish. "I've heard of him, I think. Can I borrow it?"

Tehmina's heart sank. The thought of the book leaving this house, leaving her protective gaze, made her sick. "It was my husband's book, but it now belongs to Sorab," she said. "I—I could ask him."

She felt Eva's intense blue eyes, at once so innocent and shrewd, on her. "I understand," she said softly. "In any case, I'm sure the library has a copy."

Eva poured a generous amount of wine into the two water glasses Tehmina had set before her, ignoring Tehmina's protestations of "enough, enough."

"Well," Eva said after taking a deep sip, "here's to family."

"To family," Tehmina echoed.

Eva's face crumbled again, like a sandy cliff washed by a wave. "Yah, here's to family. Even when they treat you like shit." This time, she didn't even try to hide her tears, letting them stream down her face and into her glass.

So maybe Eva wasn't sick after all. "What happened, Eva? Did you have a fight with Solomon?"

"Solomon? Heck, he's the only steady thing in my life, Tehmina. No, it's my son, David. He and his goy wife called from Florida today. Remember we were to go down to see them on the tenth, like we do every year? Well, turns out they don't want us to come this year. We were dis-invited, you could say." Eva's voice sounded hoarse, as if hurt was stuck like sand in her throat.

"But, Eva, why? What happened?"

"Nothing. Nothing happened. They're just tired, that's all. Seems like the holiday season has worn them out and they need time to recover." Eva rolled her eyes. "Can you imagine, a Jewish boy needing to recover from Christmas? What business did he have getting so exhausted, anyway? That's what comes from marrying a Christian. Runs my David ragged, from stringing lights on a Christmas tree and drinking eggnog and singing carols and God knows what else."

Despite herself, Tehmina smiled. "We do all those things, also, Eva," she said cautiously.

Eva let out a gust of air. "Granted. But you have a son who loves his mother, hon. Who's not ashamed of her. Who—" Eva choked on her words, her eyes red and bulging. "Who does not see his parents as a burden. Who does not have to *recover* before he can see his mom and dad."

"So—does he not want you to visit at all this year?"

"Who knows? Just said they couldn't do it this month. Said he needed some breathing space. So breathe! As if me and Solomon would be sitting on their windpipe. As it is, we live like thieves in my own son's house, tiptoeing around the place. Well. Maybe it's good riddance. Maybe we'll go to the Caribbean instead, like we've always wanted to." Her eyes glistened. "If only my poor Solomon had not been so hurt by the phone call. He's so upset, the poor man. Just shook his head when he hung up the phone and went into the bedroom without saying a word. As for me"—she tried to smile, but her chin trembled—"I'm a wreck, as you can see. All I could think to do was get in the car and come to your place."

"I'm glad you did," Tehmina said. She wanted to say more, something smooth and consoling, but she was aware of an uncharacteristic embarrassment. It was the embarrassment that the rich and the comfortable feel in the presence of the have-nots. Eva was right. She could never imagine Sorab and Susan treating her in the manner David had treated his parents. Here she was, being wooed and cajoled by her son to stay with him permanently. And she was the one playing hard to get, she was the one keeping them all on edge while she tried to make up her mind. She wished she could tell Eva about Rustom's lecture of a few minutes ago, urging her to rejoin the living. But that would mean explaining his presence in her living room, and as much as she trusted Eva, she didn't know if she could trust her to understand that. Her closest friend in America didn't need to know that her neighbor and card partner was also a loon.

Still, the need to comfort the obviously hurting woman in front of her was great. "Eva," she said. "Have you had anything to eat today? Are you hungry, dear?"

Eva perked up. "What have you got? Have you started cooking for tonight?"

"Not yet. But there's plenty of food in the fridge. What would you like?"

In the end, she fixed Eva a masala omelet, with some daal on the side. Tehmina protested this odd mishmash of breakfast and lunch, but Eva was insistent. Watching Eva smack her lips as she ate with obvious relish, Tehmina felt that old, deep satisfaction she did every time she fed somebody. She remembered the first meal that Percy had had at her home after dear Shirin's death. She had made him his favorite doodhi murumba as a special treat, to whet his appetite. How skinny the boy had been until she got hold of him. Percy the Pencil, the boys in the neighborhood used to tease him. But a year of her cooking had taken care of that. She thought of Josh and Jerome munching on their grilled cheese sandwiches in the same kitchen where Eva now sat, pouring out her hurt and grief in between mouthfuls of food. How ravenous Josh and Jerome had been. Which reminded her, she had to ask Eva about a ride to the mall on Tuesday.

Maybe she could take along some Bombay-style chicken sandwiches for the boys. No spices in those, so they should like that.

"Eva, something to ask. Are you free on Tuesday?"

Eva chewed on her food as she thought. "Think so. Whassup?"

"Nothing; that is, I need a ride to the mall. I think I'm going to meet Josh and Jerome there. Antonio's wife is bringing them there."

Eva laughed appreciatively. "How'd you pull that off? You're unstoppable, Tammy, you know that?" She grew serious. "Your son and daughter-in-law know about this? They won't have a problem?"

"I haven't told them, yet. I mean, if I'm to consider living here permanently, Eva, I have to make my own decisions, no? After all, they already have a child. They don't have to treat me like one."

There was something in Eva's eyes Tehmina hadn't seen before. It was respect. "Attagirl, Tammy," she said softly.

Eva got up and swept the crumbs into her empty plate. She walked in her stockinged feet up to the dishwasher. "That was delish," she said. "Thank you, sweetheart. Never knew red wine and omelets were so good for a broken heart."

"Oh, Eva. I think it will be okay with David. Just . . . when you call him tomorrow, just tell him how disappointed you are. He probably doesn't even realize."

"Who said anything about calling him tomorrow?"

Tehmina stared at her. "It will be New Year's Day. Won't you call to wish him?"

"Guess he knows our phone number as well as we know his," Eva mumbled.

"Oh, Eva, this is not like you, at all. David doesn't stop being your son just because he's hurt you. Come on, don't be like this."

"I don't know what you mean." She could tell from the strain in Eva's voice that it was taking all of her manners to resist the urge to tell her to mind her own business. But then Eva, of all people, should know how bad I am at minding my own business, Tehmina smiled to herself.

"I'll tell you what I mean," Tehmina persisted. "What I mean is, Eva, none of us are getting any younger. There's no time to waste, dear, don't you see? So who cares whose turn or duty it is to call? I mean, if we were all going to live to be four hundred, then maybe we could afford all this formality. But as it is . . ." She ran out of words as abruptly as the taps used to run out of water when she was a young girl in Calcutta. "Eva," she finished. "Call David tomorrow. You must. You're the mother. You must bear it."

"Ai, ai, ai. First you are a Christmas angel, now you wanna be a Jewish yenta? Stop with your lectures, already. If I wake up tomorrow and feel like calling the boy, I will. Who knows?" Eva reached out to take Tehmina's slender hand in her beefy one. "Now, let me help you in the kitchen. What needs done?"

"Oh, you don't need to help. I can manage, really. Susan is planning on coming home early from work."

"What, now you're a Christian martyr? Come on, put me to work. God knows a little bit of exercise won't hurt me," Eva said, patting her ample hips.

Glancing at the kitchen clock, Tehmina was surprised at how late in the day it was. "Is this possible that it's already noon?" she cried. "My God, Eva, now I really do need your help. I swear, this wine made me lose all track of time. Will you help me peel some onions and chop some cilantro?" She rose, but Eva gripped her wrist and forced her to sit back down. As always, Tehmina was surprised by how strong Eva was.

"Wait. We've forgotten the most important part."

"What?"

"Dessert." Eva grinned. "Whacha gonna feed me for dessert?"

She had made three hundred cocktail-size kebabs and they were almost all gone. Percy was popping one in his mouth right now. "Ah, Mamma," he said to her. "What good memories these kebabs bring back. You remember the Sunday lunch you used to make? God, I can still recite the menu by heart—chicken dhansak, kebabs, kachuber. And of course—Rustom uncle used to always pick up two bags of potato wafers from Royal Café."

Tehmina smiled. "Rustom always wanted something crunchy with his food."

"I remember the first time I ate at your house on a Sunday. There was Rustom uncle—this important, successful businessman who I was always a little afraid of, you know? And there he is, munching wafers like a schoolboy. I liked him from that moment."

"He was very fond of you, too. I think the day you graduated from law school was one of the proudest days of his life."

"God bless him." Percy sighed. "Everything that I am and have today, I owe to him—to both of you." Knowing that the loans and scholarships that he had were not enough, Rustom had given Percy $3,000 to help with his first year in America and Percy always claimed that the money was the difference between being able to afford going to law school in America and staying in India. "If not for your generosity, I'd still be in India, killing flies for a living."

"Everything you've achieved you've achieved on your own, beta," Tehmina said. "We were just glad to be able to help you fulfill your destiny, that's all."

"And now it's my turn to help you fulfill yours," Percy said immediately.

Tehmina laughed. "Such a lawyer you've become. How do you manage to turn every conversation around like this?"

Before Percy could reply, Tehmina found herself engulfed in a warm, tight hug by a pair of arms that held her from behind. "Hello, friend," Eva's voice boomed in her ear. "Long time no see. Hope some of those lamb kebabs are still left. I've been singing their praises to Sol ever since I left your home earlier today."

"How is Solomon?" She looked around the room. "Where is Solomon?"

"Solomon is Solomon," Eva said dismissively. "He's talking to your Sorab. And then he'll find a nice, quiet corner somewhere. You know how shy he is. But if your cooking doesn't draw him out from wherever he's hiding, then he's a lost cause for sure."

Tehmina lowered her voice. "How are you feeling, Eva?"

"Fine. Much better. Been thinking about what you said earlier. About us mothers having to take the high road and all. And I couldn't stand to not talk to my David in the new year, anyways."

Tehmina smiled. "Good. I'm glad."

Out of the corner of her eye, Tehmina saw Joe and Heather Canfield entering the room looking around for their host. Where was Sorab? she wondered. "Excuse me, Eva," she said. "Sorab's boss is here."

"Go, go," Eva said, giving her a little push. "Go say hello to the big man."

Joe kissed her on both cheeks. Heather simply flung her arm around her, as if they were old friends.

"Welcome to our home," Tehmina said. "I don't know where Sorab is. But I'll tell him you are here."

"Sorab? Ah, who cares where he is?" Joe said breezily. "It's his beautiful mother we've come to see. In any case," he continued casually, "I'll be seeing plenty of your son. I have a little meeting set up for the third with Grace Butler. And after that meeting, your son and I will be seeing much more of each other."

Tehmina stared at him, afraid to believe what she thought she was hearing. Sorab will be so good running your company for you, she wanted to say. Maybe I'm a little biased being his mother and all, but my boy will really be a good boss—honest, fair, smart. But then her happiness was pricked by another thought. Why did someone's good fortune have to always come at another's expense? "What will happen to Grace?" she asked.

Joe burst out laughing. "Tammy, Tammy," he cried. "Are you for real? Are you sure you're not computer-generated?" His mouth twisted. "Grace is a survivor. People like her always land on their feet. And she makes a great first impression—believe me, I know, to my eternal mortification."

Cookie bounded over to her. "Granna," he said, tugging her sleeve. "I want some ice cream."

"And who is this?" Joe said, getting down on his haunches to face the boy. "Wait, don't tell me, I know your name. It's . . . Chocolate, right? No? Oh, I know. It's Cocoa. *No?* Okay, let me think. Ah yes, it's Custard. No? Is it Cake? Candy? What's that? Oh, that's right—Candy's a girl's name."

Cookie was giggling and hopping from foot to foot. "No, no, no. It's Cookie," he yelled. "And that's just a nickname. My real name is Cavas." He looked up at Heather. "Who're you?" he asked. "You're pretty."

Joe stood up. "Maybe I should ditch the father and have the son come to work for us," he told Tehmina. "He'll know how to charm the customers."

Tehmina fairly burst with pride. "I'm so glad both of you are here," she said to them. "Now, please, come get something to eat." She glanced at Joe shyly. "I even made some shrimp curry for you."

Joe groaned. He put his head on Tehmina's shoulder. "Won't you please adopt me?" he said in that little-boy voice that made her laugh.

"Hey, I'm in line way ahead of you," a voice said. It was Percy. He stuck his hand out. "I'm Percy Soonawalla. An old family friend."

"Good to meet you. I'm Joe Canfield and this is my wife, Heather. What do you do, Percy?"

Leaving Percy with her guests, Tehmina excused herself. The party was going well, all the guests seemed to be enjoying themselves, and Susan and some of her friends had taken charge of heating the food and bringing it out. This was a good time to escape for a few minutes and rest. She had been like this her whole life. At every party she had ever attended or hosted, there came a moment when a melancholy feeling came over her, making her feel isolated and alone even in the midst of the swirling merriment around her. She decided to go up to her room and lie down for a few minutes. She had worked all day and she knew that she had to be up at least until midnight to usher in the new year. Besides, she was hoping that Rustom would come to her tonight, to at least see her one last time. The thought of facing a new year without him accentuated that lonely, melancholy feeling.

She fell asleep almost as soon as she laid her head on the bed. But her sleep was restless, punctured by the voices and laughter that drifted like smoke into her bedroom from the party below. When she awoke from her nap, it was dark and her heart was thudding, as if she had spotted an intruder in her room. This is the trouble with napping before bedtime, she chided herself. It makes me feel awful when I wake up.

She decided to splash some water on her face and use the bathroom before rejoining the party. She turned on the light of the bathroom and her eyes fell on the open book that sat on the toilet tank. It was the Omar Khayyám. How had it gotten up here? She was sure she had left it downstairs after Eva came over this afternoon. She tried to remember if she'd put it back in its place on the bookcase in the living room, but couldn't. Maybe Susan had brought it up here?

But why would she do that? She flipped the book over, curious to see what page Rustom had left open for her.

Ah! my Beloved, fill the Cup that clears
To-day of past Regrets and future Fears
To-morrow?—Why, To-morrow I may be
Myself with Yesterday's Sev'n Thousand Years

Tehmina laughed. Rustom had never been a subtle man. Nor was he the most patient of men. She was afraid that if she didn't make a decision soon, she would wake up one morning to find her bedroom wallpapered with verses from the *Rubáiyát*. And the floor and ceiling, too. Rustom obviously thought an ancient Persian poet had something to teach an elderly Persian woman.

Darling, she whispered. Are you here? But there was no answer. And the texture of this silence was different. Tehmina knew that immediately. This was not a breathing, listening silence. This silence had a void in it, a hollow in its center. Rustom was gone. He had been true to his word. He had really left her this time. Left her to wherever her own decisions would take her. From here on out, she was on her own.

Past regrets and future fears, she thought. That pretty much summed up how she had lived this past year. She took a few steps across the tiled floor to get a new bar of soap out of the bathroom closet and then froze. One floor below her were gathered all the people she loved, and the realization made her shiver. Sorab, Cookie, Susan, Percy, Eva, Solomon, even Joe and Heather—it seemed as if her family kept growing. What was the term she had heard on *Oprah* a few weeks ago? *Family of choice.*

Choice. Making a decision. Getting off the fence. In a few hours, it would be a new year. Whatever decision she made now—and Tehmina knew that she would make the decision now, before she went back downstairs to join the party—whatever she decided now, she would carry the consequences of that decision into the new year. Home, she thought. Where is my home? Where do I belong? She thought of her apartment in Bombay, the chipping walls that needed a coat of paint, the precious Hussein painting that hung above the sofa, the teakwood closet where Rustom's suits still hung, the new Bajaj stove that he had bought her just two years ago. The thought of leaving that apartment, of selling the home she had spent most of her married life in, made her eyeballs hurt. Bombay suddenly loomed large in her imagination. She forgot the squalor, the slums, the black cloud of pollution, the unbearable heat, the dizzying crowds. Instead, she saw the golden sky at twilight, the vast sea beyond the Art Deco buildings of Marine Drive, the beauty of the old colonial buildings of South Bombay, the dark, cool quiet of a fire temple. Instead of the wretched humidity and sweat-inducing heat, she remembered the warmth of a Bombay morning; instead of the overcrowded, dangerous buses, she remembered streets festive with people, with life-affirming humanity, such a contrast to the dead, empty streets that greeted her in Rosemont Heights each evening. But then she thought: And who among those millions of people out on the streets of Bombay cares if I live or die? Her best friend, Zinobia, would care, some of the neighbors like Persis would care, the heads of the institutions where she volunteered would care. But who else? Whereas here, despite the barrenness of civic life, despite the cold winters and the deserted streets, despite the fact that there were housing complexes built without sidewalks, there were people who cared very much about her well-being. Who worried, who fretted, who had their own lives and destinies tied up in hers. And—and now she forced herself to swallow her natural modesty—here there were people who, despite what she had earlier believed, needed her. She could see that now. Cookie needed her, needed what only a grandmother could give him. Susan's mother lived too far away to give him the gift of her consistent presence. Susan needed her, to polish some of her rough edges, to coax out of her the softness that a hectic schedule and too many responsibilities had buried. As for the boys—Percy, Sorab, and now maybe even Joe—Tehmina knew she had enough love for all of them.

She knew another thing also. She would stay. Here in America. It wasn't so much a decision as an acknowledgment of something she already knew, a logical culmination of her thought process. Unlike the movies, no drums thundered in the background, no trumpets heralded her arriving at her decision. Because, in fact, the decision had been made a few days ago. When she had loosened her grip on that fence, when she had found the courage to jump, she had landed in more than Antonio's yard. She had landed in America. The fence had been the dividing line between the past and the future, between India and America. Tehmina marveled at the fact that she hadn't known this until a second ago, that her body, her mind, were only now catching up with her destiny. The moving finger writes, she thought. The room was quiet as Tehmina splashed water on her face. For the first time in months that nervous, agitated feeling that was lodged in her stomach left her.

She would stay. But on her own terms. And the main thing was that she had to have her own apartment. There was no reason for the children to sell this house in order to buy a bigger one. Yes, she would insist on that—that she have her own place. That way, she could have her independence and the children could have their privacy. She had never lived alone for a day in her whole life—she had left her father's house to move into the apartment with Rustom—but somehow, the thought didn't faze her. In fact, she felt daring, excited at the prospect.

Sorab would fight her on this, for sure. He and Susan would not understand, might even be hurt. But she would hold firm. She would combat their passionate arguments with cold reason. And she would not back down. After all, she was a woman who had leaped over a fence. Who had temporarily kidnapped two boys. Who had prayed with a nutcase in the middle of Kmart. Who had received a phone call from the mayor. Who had perfect strangers come up to shake her hand. She was a celebrity, a star. She was an American hero enjoying her fifteen minutes of fame. She was unbeatable, invincible.

Tehmina giggled. What a crackpot you've become, she chided herself. What landlord is going to rent a place to a crazy woman? But already she was thinking of how she would decorate her apartment. The Hussein she would definitely bring back from Bombay. Also, some of the smaller pieces of furniture. And in the summer, she would go shopping for plants with Susan. Maybe the apartment would have a little balcony where she could grow flowers. And make rainbows.

She hurried down the stairs and Sorab was by her side. "Mamma, where were you?" he said. "I was getting worried—didn't see you anywhere."

"I was in my room. Just freshening up."

He peered at her. "Are you okay, Mamma? You look—I don't know—a little flushed."

"I'm fine," she said. She opened her mouth to tell him and then stopped herself. No, she would wait. She would wait until they had ushered in the new year. She would wait until the countdown had ended, until they had counted backward from ten, nine, eight . . . until they had reached zero and the room had dissolved into whoops of celebration and silent prayers of hope. She would wait until she had hugged and held her son and told him how much she loved him, until she had whispered to Susan how grateful she was to have such a wonderful daughter-in-law, until she had squeezed Cookie and told him he was part of her liver, and until the boy screwed up his nose and said "Yuck." She would wait until she wandered around this room filled with people she knew and loved, until she had wished every last one of them a new year filled with hope and dreams and yearning. She would not wish any of them success or prosperity or wealth because the magic was in the dreaming. She knew that now. America had taught her that. How wise, to talk about the *pursuit* of happiness and not of happiness itself.

She would wait till a few minutes after midnight and then she would pull Susan and Sorab away for a moment. Maybe she'd take them into the kitchen or into the small sitting room adjacent to the living room. And then, alone with her children, she would tell them her decision. How long have you known? they would ask her in wonder, and she would say, "Just this evening." How did you decide? they would ask, and she would shake her head and say, "I don't know. It wasn't a decision exactly. Just a knowledge." And then, if she was in a mischievous mood, she would quote some Omar Khayyám, just to watch her son groan and say, "Oh no. You, too, Mamma?"

"Oh, how well I know this look." Sorab was laughing. "What are you up to now, Mamma?"

She gave her son a wide-eyed look. "What do you mean, beta?"

"Nothing." Sorab lowered his voice. "Mamma," he whispered. "Keep this to yourself for now, achcha? But Joe just told me that he was letting Grace go. He wants me to take over."

"I just hope Joe knows how lucky he is," she said, her eyes shining with tears. "He will thank his lucky stars for the day he made this decision."

Sorab laughed. "Good old Mamma. But this is all thanks to you, anyway. It was you who brought me to Joe's attention."

"Darling, gold can lie below the surface for a hundred years. But sooner or later, its luster attracts someone's attention. This is the result of your own hard work."

"Sorab, honey, do me a favor and run to the basement and bring out a few more bottles of red wine?" Susan said, coming up to them. Turning to Tehmina, "Did he tell you the good news?"

"Yes. I'm so proud of him."

"So am I." Susan grinned. "You having a good time, Mom? You're not too tired? I'm so sorry you had to do so much of the cooking yourself."

"It was nothing. Besides, I had Eva helping me."

"Say, speaking of Eva, her husband seems to have hit it off quite well with Tanya Davar." Susan raised her eyebrows as she walked away. "Maybe Eva should keep an eye on her husband," she said in a singsong voice that made Tehmina laugh.

Eva. She needed to find Eva to ask her a question. She walked into the living room and looked around until she found her standing in a small group. She waited politely until Eva finished telling the joke about Jewish people and Chinese food, and then tugged at her elbow. "Can I speak to you for a moment? Alone?" she murmured.

Eva turned and took her arm as they walked away. "Is everything okay?" she asked, and Tehmina noticed with gratitude the worry and concern in her voice.

"Everything's fine," she replied.

When they got to a spot where no one was around, Tehmina turned to face Eva.

"Eva," she said, her eyes and voice steady, "this may seem like the wrong time, but I have a big favor to ask."

"Are you kidding me? For you, anything. Even if you tell me you want to run away to Vegas with my Solomon, I'll agree." Eva's grin got wider. "In fact, I may even pay you to run off with him."

Tehmina laughed. "Stop being so silly. But seriously, listen. Here's what I want to ask." She took in a deep breath and then exhaled, knowing that the question would seal her decision to stay. "Eva," she said. "Will you teach me how to drive?"

Her answer was a whoop. Eva hugged her until Tehmina thought her bones would melt from the pressure of joy.